WEBS
OF
FATE

WEBS
OF
FATE

A NOVEL

DARLENE QUINN

GREENLEAF
BOOK GROUP PRESS

Published by Greenleaf Book Group Press
Austin, TX
www.gbgpress.com

Distributed by Greenleaf Book Group

For ordering information or special discounts for bulk purchases, please contact Greenleaf Book Group at PO Box 91869, Austin, TX 78709, 512.891.6100.

Design and composition by Greenleaf Book Group LLC and Alex Head
Cover design by Greenleaf Book Group LLC

Publisher's Cataloging-In-Publication Data
(Prepared by The Donohue Group, Inc.)
Quinn, Darlene.
  Webs of fate : a novel / Darlene Quinn. -- 1st ed.
    p. ; cm.
  Published in 2011 as a hardcover and an e-book.
  Prequel to: Webs of Power.
  ISBN: 978-1-60832-389-0 (paperback)
  1. Upper class women--United States--Fiction. 2. Retail trade--United States--Fiction. 3. Kidnapping--Fiction. 4. Conspiracy--Fiction. 5. Man-woman relationships--Fiction. I. Title. II. Title: Webs of power.
PS3617.U562 W44 2012
813/.6   2012937958

Part of the Tree Neutral® program, which offsets the number of trees consumed in the production and printing of this book by taking proactive steps, such as planting trees in direct proportion to the number of trees used: www.treeneutral.com

TreeNeutral

Printed in the United States of America on acid-free paper

12 13 14 15 16   10 9 8 7 6 5 4 3 2 1

First Edition

To my husband, Jack—the most incredible partner and support system any author could ask for

And in memory of my parents, Charles and Evelyn Stafford—their unwavering belief in me was a true blessing

ACKNOWLEDGMENTS

While much of an author's work is done alone, the final version of any work of fiction is touched by many. This story could not have been conveyed without the generosity, wisdom, and guidance of the following individuals.

As always, I owe my firsthand retail education and the ring of authenticity throughout this work of fiction to the former executives and the sales and sales-support associates of Bullock's/Bullocks Wilshire: Allen Questrom, master of merchandising, retail, and company turnarounds, who led Federated Department Stores out of bankruptcy and on to the acquisition of R. H. Macy & Company, Inc., and The Broadway/Emporium Stores, Terry Lundgren, chairman, president, and CEO of Macy's, Inc. (formerly known as Federated Department Stores); Rosemary Troy of Troy's in Palm Desert; Glenn Ellison, currently with Tommy Bahama in Palm Desert; and Loretta Cahill, sales associate extraordinaire at Bloomingdale's Newport Beach.

In matters outside the world of retail, I would like to thank Gary Olson (first vice president of wealth management with Morgan Stanley/

Smith Barney) and Bob Hughes (MDRT with American General), who assisted in regard to financial ramification; Lieutenant Ann Clark (officer in charge, West Los Angeles Police Department, Detective Section); and Raymond P. Lombardo, Private Investigator (former lieutenant with the Los Angeles Police Department). My good friends Beverly and Ed Cruchley for their inspiration for easy dialogue. For my transition from memo writing to fiction, I'd like to thank Margaret Thompson Davis, best-selling Scottish author and mentor; Frank Gaspar, author of *Stealing Fatima* and endowed chair and distinguished professor at the University of Massachusetts; Elizabeth George, *New York Times* bestselling author of *This Body of Death*; Maralys Wills, author of *Higher than Eagles*; and my former critique group members and first readers, Roy King, Barbara McClousky, Susan Posner, Wesla Kerr (*Matty McGuire series*), Tom Kirkbride (*Gamadin Series*), Robert S. Telford (*Charlie Tanner Could Walk on Air*), and Evelyn Marshall (*The Provider*) who gave encouragement and guidance through the many drafts of my first novel. Also, I would like to thank my ARC review committee: Nanci Gee, Shirley Williams, Barbee Heiny, Fran Romero, Marge England, Carol Hess, Lisa DeVincent, Kristee Bedgood, Wesla Kerr, Barbara Casey, Sue Short, Kim Anderson, Paula Harris, Nancy Raynesford, Kami Weeks, Margie Brown, and Ginny Wilcox.

I couldn't do without the folks at EMSI: Marsha Friedman, Steve Friedman, award-winning journalist Tony Panaccio, Rich Ghazarian, Russ Handle, Lisa Hess, Rachel Friedman, Russ Hadler, Suzanne Best, and Ginny Grimsley (who keeps us all sane and on the same page). It's a joy to work with this savvy group of publicists, all of whom are dedicated professionals with great senses of humor.

Thank you to Barbara McClousky, my first draft reader. I must also thank Greenleaf Book Group, and in particular Justin Branch, senior consultant; Bryan Carroll, production manager; Lisa Woods, book designer; Neil Gonzalez, master of cover design; Caryn Lusinchi, marketing manager; Andrea Newsome, marketing associate; Kristen Sears, distribution manager; Jenn McMurray, senior distribution associate; Emily Laskowski, distribution associate; Linda O'Doughda, editor, whose incredible sense of pacing and eye for story I could not do without; freelance copy editor Amy D. McIlwaine, for ensuring accuracy and order with her fabulous sense of time and place; and Jan McInroy for her meticulous line edit. Your collective enthusiasm and dedication have not only enhanced this work of fiction but also made the journey to publication an exciting and enjoyable adventure.

Thanks also to Brennan Harvey, Writers of the Future Award winner, who attempts to keep my website as current as possible.

And finally, a special thanks to my administrative assistant, Kathy Porter, who is an invaluable part of my team, an international award-winning science fiction writer in her own right and author of Earth's Ultimate Conflict.

PROLOGUE

Chilled to the bone, Danielle Norman slid back on the mahogany folding chair. The president's steel-gray eyes seemed to be boring into hers.

"The future of Bentleys Royale is in your hands," he said.

This closing remark hit her with the force of a tsunami. Danielle had taken a seat in the back row in the hope of slipping out ahead of the other buyers and executives at the conclusion of David Jerome's annual State of the Business address. Now, dropping her gaze from Mr. Jerome's, she studied the paisley pattern of the burgundy carpet, picturing his shock and sense of betrayal once he found out what she'd done.

I can't go through with it, she said to herself. And with sudden clarity, she knew what she must do.

To avoid notice, Danielle silently pushed herself to her feet and crept from the tearoom. She tiptoed across the marble tiles, stopped in front of the third elevator, and ventured a quick glance over her shoulder. If some people noticed her early departure, she hoped they would assume she was leaving for her red-eye flight. And she was—but first she would put an end to the plan that was already in motion.

She pushed the UP button. Her nails bit into her palms as she prayed harder than she'd ever prayed before.

Don't let it be too late.

The muscular young man, his blond hair pulled back in a ponytail, looked at his watch for the umpteenth time. "What's keeping her?" he said to a tall, lanky man in a charcoal-gray pin-striped suit, who was in the process of wedging a piece of wood under the door that led from the display storage room to the rooftop.

The lanky man rose to his full six-foot-two height. "Take it easy," he said, his voice breaking as he suppressed a cough. "Danielle knows this is the only chance she has to save her job. Besides, she and I have a midnight flight to New York. The annual meeting can go on forever. She'll be here any minute."

As he spoke, they heard the elevator grind to a stop. The door slid open. Danielle stood stock-still inside the lift. Even in the dim light, the tall man saw that her face appeared drained of color, and yet there was a strong set to her jaw. He reached out, taking her by the elbow to guide her across the three-inch gap between the lift and the less-than-pristine floor of the storage room. He felt her resistance and paused.

Holy mother of God, he thought. *This is no time for her to be having second thoughts.*

But that was exactly what appeared to be happening. Danielle refused to take another step forward. Her gaze flashed from the tall man to his unfamiliar ponytailed friend, then back to him. She did not meet his eyes.

"This is all wrong. I can't go through with it," she said, her voice a fraction of a decibel above a whisper. Tears filled her eyes as she gripped his arms. "I'll make it up to you somehow. I swear I will, but you have to help—"

In two long strides, the ponytailed man grabbed Danielle's arm and yanked her toward the door to the rooftop. Her head collided with the sharp corner of a metal cabinet, and she dropped to the floor like a sack of stones.

The tall man froze, his eyes riveted on the lifeless body of the young buyer, the blood instantly pooling around her head. "Oh my God! You've killed her!" he shouted.

The other man knelt down beside her, then shook his head and pulled off his sweatshirt. He quickly wound it around Danielle's head and wrapped his fingers around her thin wrist. "She's not dead."

Sucking in his breath, the tall man did his best to keep the panic out of his voice. "She's not moving. And . . . the blood . . ." It was already soaking through the yellow sweatshirt.

"She's not dead," the ponytailed man repeated. "She's still breathing. It looks a lot worse than it is. She just hit her head, and head wounds bleed like there's no tomorrow. But you'd better find a way to bring her back to her senses. She could seriously screw up our plan." He paused before continuing, his voice low with dread. "Hell, she could screw up our whole future."

CHAPTER

1

At the buzz of the intercom, Ashleigh McDowell's gaze shot to the clock. It was nearly six. She dropped her pen into its marble holder, pushed her yellow pad aside, then wavered for a split second before tapping the telephone speaker button.

"Betty, I'm running late, would—"

"It's Mr. Jerome," her secretary cut in.

Sliding her stockinged feet back into her pumps, Ashleigh hastily gathered the loose pages of last year's human resources plan and shoved them back into the manila folder while Betty put the president's call through.

"When did you last see Danielle Norman?" The president's slow, measured speech pattern funneled through the static of his speakerphone.

Ashleigh's blood turned icy cold. Why was he asking about Danielle? "Friday afternoon."

"Did she say anything about canceling her New York trip?"

"No." *Of course not, Mr. Jerome,* she wanted to shout. *You know how critical this buying trip is for Danielle.*

In the space of a few months Danielle's world had been torn apart. Along with the plummeting profits in her department, her marriage had crumbled. She was no longer considered Bentleys Royale's most promising young buyer. In fact, her position was now in jeopardy, and with a categorically unsupportive merchandise manager, she was fighting an uphill battle. Without her career, Ashleigh knew, Danielle had nothing—and this buying trip was virtually her last chance to salvage it.

"Come up to my office right away," came the president's deliberate voice again.

The line went dead.

Puzzled by David Jerome's tone as much as by the nature of his question, Ashleigh felt her mouth go dry, and she dropped the receiver back in the cradle.

A vivid picture of Danielle Norman, the vivacious, curly-haired blonde with expressive gray eyes, whom she loved like a sister, flashed through Ashleigh's mind. Taking a deep breath, she grabbed her Chanel handbag and ubiquitous leather organizer, brushed a loose strand of hair from her cheek, tucking it neatly into her French braid, and headed for the door. Mitchell's words echoed in her head: *Is it too much to ask that you leave your office on time?* But she had no choice. Mr. Jerome had been quite clear—and this sounded important.

Getting away from the store before the six forty-five PM security lockup was always difficult. And now, with the future of Bentleys Royale hanging by a thread, there was never enough time. If Mitchell didn't understand that now, he never would.

As she hurried to the elevators, Ashleigh's gaze fell to the large diamond on her left hand. *Has Mitchell actually changed that much in the few short weeks since he slipped this ring on my finger? Or has the man I've grown to trust and thought I could love simply been a figment of my imagination?*

But she closed off that chamber of her mind, like a room of an overly large house in the dead of winter. Her thoughts turned back to Danielle Norman. What had happened to her? Had she missed her flight? She would never have just decided not to make the trip, especially without a word. Whatever had happened, it had to be something beyond her control. For Danielle not to have shown up in New York, it had to be something catastrophic.

CHAPTER

2

Ashleigh strode purposefully through the gourmet cookware department. She was about to press the elevator button when she heard someone calling her name.

"Miss McDowell . . . Miss McDowell," the voice rang out.

Ashleigh hit the button, then looked over her shoulder to see Dorothea Sable racing toward her. The sound of Dorothea's brisk footsteps echoed across the square tiles. By the time she reached Ashleigh, she was short of breath.

"Glad I caught you," wheezed Dorothea, a smile brightening her oval face. She carried an emerald-green knit dress, held just high enough to clear the floor. Though the passage of years had dimmed the buyer's beauty, she was still arresting. Her hair, as dark as Ashleigh's was blond, was meticulously coiffed. She wore a royal blue suit from this season's Blackwell collection, its long jacket concealing those extra ten pounds she continually stewed over. "The new St. Johns just arrived for the trunk show on Monday. Just look at this one—it's to die for!" From Dorothea the words sounded neither phony nor trite. Each garment she selected was like one of her own children. The children she'd never had.

She held the dress up to Ashleigh. "It was made for you. With your coloring and that willowy body—ah, to be young again!" she sighed.

"You know my weakness for St. John." Ashleigh smiled. Glancing up at the indicators, she noted that all six elevators were above the third level. She pushed the glowing button repeatedly and looked back at Dorothea. "If you'll leave the dress in my office, I promise I'll try it on tomorrow morning before the trunk show."

Dorothea's eyes did not waver, but she hesitated slightly before saying what was really on her mind. Shifting her weight, she finally pulled in her breath and proceeded in her usual style—direct, with no nonsense. "Have you heard from Danielle Norman?"

How quickly word travels! Stunned, Ashleigh moved the burgundy organizer to her other arm and attempted to veil her mounting unease. "She was flying to New York last night."

Dorothea shook her head, and her mouth wore a puzzled frown. "The phone lines from New York have been buzzing since early this morning. Danielle had an eight o'clock appointment at Anne Klein, but she didn't show up."

Ashleigh's breath caught in her throat as the significance of missing that particular appointment registered.

"Nobody knows what to think. Danielle didn't check into the Ambassador, and she"—Dorothea's voice faltered—"she didn't cancel her guaranteed reservation."

Ashleigh shivered. Ever since Adele Watson's appointment as divisional merchandise manager of Moderate and Fine Apparel, it seemed that Danielle was in a no-win situation. Adele was sure to make the most out of this.

"I've left messages at Danielle's house," Dorothea continued. She raised her troubled eyes to meet Ashleigh's. "No answer." Carefully folding the St. John garment over her arm, she smoothed the nonexistent wrinkles. "Danielle was so excited. Getting that first appointment at Anne Klein was a real coup. And God knows she needs a break." She hesitated, and appeared to be checking that Ashleigh understood. "She's been picking my brain for weeks. We went over ways to approach the vendor for a markdown allowance and ad money. Danielle even came to my house Sunday night to go over her spiel for that eight o'clock appointment." She nodded with pride. "It was pretty darn good."

Shaking her head ruefully again, Dorothea said, "That was only two days ago."

Ashleigh reached out and placed a hand gently on the distraught woman's arm. "Danielle is lucky to have a friend like you," she said.

"I don't know what's happened, but let's try not to jump to conclusions until we know more. There's probably a simple explanation, and as you've said, there are already enough rumors floating around."

Oh, how Ashleigh hoped this was true, how she wished that she could think of an explanation. But it was no use—not a single logical or plausible one surfaced. The doors to one of the elevators opened. "Try not to worry" was all she could muster. The words fell flat, and Ashleigh knew it. She inclined her head toward the St. John draped over the buyer's arm. "Thanks for thinking of me."

Dorothea turned and darted in the direction of the Personnel offices, and Ashleigh stepped into the elevator, her mind troubled.

To avoid stopping on every level, Ashleigh placed one finger on the 5 button and another on the one marked CLOSE DOOR. She kept both depressed—a trick she'd learned from one of the maintenance engineers. She adjusted her skirt and flipped a strand of hair off her forehead, wondering what to expect when she arrived on the fifth level. The words *Benevolent Dictator* sprang to mind. That's what her colleagues called the president—out of earshot, of course. While there was little conversation about the benevolence, tales of his notorious commands of "Report to my office immediately" were always a source of amusement and one-upmanship. Regarding Ashleigh he was usually more considerate of her time. But there was never any doubt that Mr. Jerome expected her to be available when he needed her. And for reasons she did not understand, since she had become engaged to Mitchell Wainwright, Jerome's relationship with her had seemed strained.

Her eyes wandered around the elegant lift, and she realized her irritation had little to do with Mr. Jerome's call. If Danielle was in trouble, Ashleigh would do anything in her power to help her. Instead, Ashleigh's anger turned inward. *Why have I given Mitchell the power to make me feel guilty? I have nothing to feel guilty about. So what is this uneasy feeling deep in the pit of my stomach?*

When the doors slid open, she saw that the fifth level was nearly deserted. Across from the elevators, a sales associate in a crisp pink smock assisted a last-minute patron with his purchase of Godiva chocolates. To her left, the celebrated tearoom was dim and silent. Down from the elevators, the double mahogany doors with D.M.J. embossed in gold were slightly ajar.

With her thoughts still focused on Danielle, Ashleigh reached for the brass handle of one of the doors leading to Mr. Jerome's inner office. Before her fingers could curl around it, the handle was yanked from her grasp, and the door flew open. The six-foot-three frame of Conrad Taylor, the recently appointed vice president of finance and operations, dominated the narrow corridor.

Ashleigh struggled to regain her composure.

He smiled. "Sorry. Didn't mean to startle you."

Gossip in the retail grapevine had it that Conrad Taylor would be the next president of Bentley's. Although he'd joined the organization less than six months before, this was a rumor Ashleigh was inclined to believe. While the vice president had spent little time with the specialty store division until quite recently, this was the second time she'd seen him in their headquarters store in less than a week.

She had noticed the way he'd handled himself at the monthly management meetings at the Bentley's corporate offices. In that arena, she had viewed him as bright, perceptive, and quick to respond. Rational as well. But in Friday's meeting at Bentleys Royale, his suggestions had been jarring. He had revealed a department store mentality—a lack of understanding for the unique talents and taste level that set the specialty store buyers apart from those of the department stores.

Conrad Taylor was a recurring topic of conversation among the female executives, and Ashleigh was amused by the number of otherwise intelligent women who acted like schoolgirls in his presence. An abundance of handsome, flawlessly groomed males were drawn to careers in retailing—many of whom had little, if any, romantic interest in women. But for reasons she could not clearly explain, she had no doubt as to this man's sexual orientation.

Perhaps it's something to do with his eyes . . .

His deep-set blue eyes held hers for a few awkward seconds before Ashleigh broke the silence to tell him that she must be on her way. He held the door open and stepped back, allowing her to pass, then headed toward the elevators.

Thoughts of Conrad Taylor vanished as she hurried along the fourteen-foot-long corridor to Mr. Jerome's office. Concern for Danielle Norman dominated her mind. Now she searched her memory to recall every detail of their last conversation.

Approaching the president's door, she saw that Méchie, Mr. Jerome's secretary, was not in her office. *Strange.* Just inside the door, she noticed Mr. Jerome's Oxxford suit jacket on a sculptured hanger on the coat tree, but he was not there either. It was after six. His call had seemed urgent—he had demanded that she come to his office. Besides, she knew Mr. Jerome would not leave his office without his jacket. Not under any circumstances.

Where is he?

Stepping from the elevator onto the polished tiles of the first level, Conrad Taylor remembered his first trip to Bentleys Royale, when he'd viewed it through Danielle's eyes. The grandeur of the headquarters store now hit him anew. Becoming a buyer at Bentleys Royale had been, for Danielle, a dream come true. "It's a cathedral of merchandising," Danielle had exclaimed before giving him the grand tour of the landmark building.

They had met during Danielle's short tenure at Buffum's Department Stores. Conrad cared about Danielle—he always would. But never in the way he once did. Six years her senior, he blamed only himself for their madcap affair. Since he'd joined the management team at Bentley's they had kept their past relationship concealed from the corporate world of retailing—from anyone even remotely connected to it.

Passing under the high ceiling in the central hall, a basilica glowing with warmth and color, he thought of Danielle's phone call early Monday morning. *If only I hadn't been in such a rush,* he berated himself. Shaking his head as if that could change the course of his thoughts, Conrad cut across the marble floor in front of the men's fragrance bar, with its faint aroma of Polo, and made a sharp left turn toward Better Sportswear.

He stopped momentarily in Danielle's department, giving a cursory glance at the newer merchandise. The selection of fresh transitional fashions—the fabric weights and colors that bridged the seasons—was meager. Danielle hadn't understated that fact, and he found he had to agree. No unauthorized merchandise had been delivered to the headquarters store. So where was all the merchandise that accounted for her overbought status?

Danielle's parting words had been churning through his mind ever since he had found out she didn't show up in New York. "Never mind," she'd said. "I'll handle it myself," and she'd hung up the phone, leaving the hum of GTE ringing in his ear and the sound of her unsteady voice in his memory.

Later that evening he'd decided to wait before returning Danielle's call; first he would investigate the discrepancies surfacing in her department. *How could I have dismissed her cry for help?* he thought now as he looked at her merchandise selection. The truth of his thoughtlessness pained him.

His mind spun back to the last time Danielle had reached out for him. The image of that night was forever emblazoned in his memory.

As he turned the key in the lock of his Long Beach condo, he heard the jangle of the phone. Aware of the late hour, he quickly unlocked the door and covered the distance to the phone in an instant.

"Conrad Taylor." There was no answer at first. But the line was not dead. "Hello," he repeated more loudly into the phone.

"Conrad, it's Danielle."

He strained to hear her.

"I'm sorry," she began. Conrad thought he heard her swallow hard. "I'm scared. Please . . . Can you come?" Her voice was barely audible, and he had difficulty hearing her between the gulping sobs.

"Are you alright?" He paused. *Of course she's not.* "What's happened?"

"It's Ted. He's been drinking and . . . He just left but . . . I'm afraid he's coming back."

That bastard. Conrad gripped the phone, dumping his jacket to the floor. It was all he could do to think logically. "Are you hurt?"

Their brief fling had ended long before she'd married Ted Norman. More than their age difference, they'd found that their wants and needs were worlds apart. Yet Conrad and Danielle had remained close friends, and he felt a need to protect her as if she were a younger and very dear sister. She had triumphed over horrifying nightmares, but she remained vulnerable—and so very proud.

He heard what sounded like a stifled sob as she stuttered, "I . . . I . . ."

"Danielle," he interrupted. "Call 911 now. I'll meet you at the hospital."

"No. I can't. Please . . . come to the house?"

With one eye on the rearview mirror, and driving well beyond the speed limit, it took Conrad less than a half hour to get from Long Beach to West L.A. As he pulled up in front of Danielle's, he saw that the garage door stood wide open with only her yellow Volkswagen inside. He leaped from his car and sprinted across the uncut lawn to the dimly illuminated front porch. Banging on the door, he called Danielle's name. He was prepared to give another series of knocks when the door eased open a fraction. Danielle peered out.

Unfastening the door chain, she stepped back as the door swung open. The living room was veiled in darkness. Only the light from the porch permitted faint visibility. But when Conrad reached for the light switch, she took hold of his wrist.

"No, please don't," she pleaded.

He gently removed her hand and flipped the switch. In the brief glimpse of her face before her hands shot up to cover it, he saw a nasty gash above her lip. She'd already begun to bruise. Blood splotches stained the front of her torn blouse and skirt. He wrapped his arms around her protectively and led her to the living room couch.

"Is Ted here?" he asked as his eyes scanned the room, his fists clenching into tight balls.

She shook her head, her hands still covering her face.

Conrad leaned across her to turn on the end-table lamp and then sat down beside her. "Where is he?" When she didn't answer, he said, a little more gently, "Danielle. Look at me. Please."

Reluctantly, she lowered her hands.

Jesus, he thought, tilting her face toward the light. "What in the hell happened?" he asked. "Is this . . . Has he ever hit you before?"

She had to force the words out. "Not like this. Please don't tell anyone." Her voice shook.

Conrad's body tensed, but he bit back words of contempt. "First I'm taking you to the hospital. That gash above your lip needs stitches. Then we'll talk."

Although Danielle's physical wounds had healed quickly, Conrad sensed that Ted had broken her spirit that night. Still, he could not wrap his mind around her disappearance now. It just wasn't like her—not the fiercely loyal young woman he knew her to be.

Forcing his thoughts to the speech he was to deliver to the city planning commission in less than an hour, he headed for the Men's Clothing department, passing the glass cases of the Lalique collection and the Steuben room. His staccato footsteps died abruptly when he reached the plush paisley carpeting of Men's Clothing.

"Goot eef-ning, Mr. Taylor," the stocky sales associate greeted him in his broad German accent, reaching up and slipping the suit from the brass hook above his head.

"Hope I didn't keep you."

"No problem, Mr. Taylor." The associate smiled. "Just finishing up my paperwork." He began to remove the jacket from the hanger.

"Sorry," Conrad said. "Don't have time to try it on. I have absolute faith in Andre. He's one of the finest tailors this side of Savile Row."

Moments later, carrying his suit in the fabric garment bag with the embroidered Bentleys Royale logo, Conrad climbed the wide staircase of the associates' exit. He was struck by a familiar scent as a slim, curly-headed blonde dashed past in the opposite direction. *Charlie.* It had been Danielle's favorite fragrance—perhaps it still was.

As his thoughts cut back to Danielle once more, he tried to make sense out of what he knew. Recently, nearly paranoid over the possibility of losing her job, she'd adopted a habit of being early for all her business appointments—usually no less than ten minutes early. This was quite an accomplishment for the freewheeling Danielle he had known. Her fear of her divisional merchandise manager, Adele Watson, was so acute that she did everything in her power to avoid giving the woman the slightest reason to find fault. She would never have just abandoned her responsibilities like this. *So where in the hell can she be?*

The sun was low on the horizon when Conrad flung open the door and stepped out onto the walkway to the motor court. In 1929 Bentleys Royale had been the city's first department store built in the suburbs, so its most appealing entrance was placed in the rear, where valets in livery welcomed patrons and parked their cars. The last rays of lingering sunlight danced through the porte cochere, illuminating the vibrant colors of the ceiling fresco. As he passed the window, his attention was drawn to the Chanel display. The mannequin looked enough like Ashleigh McDowell to be her sister.

Danielle had placed Ashleigh on a pedestal, Conrad knew, and trusted her completely. She relied on her counsel. And yet he felt sure that Danielle had not told Ashleigh of her involvement with him. He was also certain that Ashleigh had never made the connection, had never associated him with the man Danielle had dated at Buffum's.

Bounding up the stairs from the underground parking area two steps at a time and barging into Conrad's thoughts came an unkempt man more than six feet tall, with a tanklike body that made one think *big*, not *tall*. His tousled hair, thinning at the crown, and wrinkled clothing gave the appearance of a man who had left his bed with no time for basic grooming. His tie was slightly askew, and his Bentley's badge hung loosely through a buttonhole on his lapel.

"Got here quick as I could," panted Ross Pocino, the corporate security director, his voice husky.

"Mr. Jerome would like you to come straight up to his office."

"Sure enough, boss."

"And, Pocino, please remove your Bentley's badge and pick up one with the Bentleys Royale logo at the security desk."

Pocino rolled his eyes as he ran his pudgy fingers through his hair. "Right, must have that Bentleys Royale image," he said with a smirk.

Conrad nodded.

"Got it, boss. No Bentley's badge, and no apostrophe in Bentleys Royale." His gaze shot skyward.

Conrad knew there was no point in explaining the rationale behind Mr. Jerome's obsessive and costly removal of the apostrophe. Committed to creating a separate and distinctive image for the specialty stores, Jerome and his management team had diligently seen to it that every apostrophe was removed from their stores and had insisted that anything bearing the old logo be disposed of. This included business cards, matchbook covers, merchandise labels, and a multitude of other items.

"And, Ross, before you go through the store, please straighten your tie and run a comb through your hair." As Pocino's brows tightened, Conrad added, "To be treated as a professional—"

He stopped abruptly. They'd had this discussion before. *Not again. I sound like a pompous ass.* Conrad himself was more comfortable in a worn pair of Levi's and a sports shirt, but he realized the importance of forgoing some of those basic creature comforts when necessary. While Pocino possessed the kind of expertise that would be hard to replace, deep down Conrad knew that the corporate world was not Pocino's forte and never would be. It was just a matter of time.

Conrad took a deep breath. "Enough said." He scribbled his home number on the back of his business card and handed it to the former LAPD detective. "Please keep me up to date. Give me a call at this number anytime. If I'm not home, leave a message on my machine. I'd like to know if you surface any new information."

If Pocino wondered why this information couldn't wait until morning, it wasn't evident. He merely crammed the card into his breast pocket and bolted off.

Willing himself to concentrate on his presentation for the city planning commission, Conrad continued down the stairs to the underground parking. Like it or not, there was nothing more he could do about Danielle. Not right now, at any rate.

David Jerome tightened his grip on the telephone receiver. "I don't care if it takes all night, Chris. I want a complete rundown, by vendor and retail dollars, no later than nine o'clock tomorrow morning. Is that clear?" His voice bounced off the walls of the narrow file room beyond his secretary's office.

The racket from the dot matrix printer halted, and Jerome made eye contact with his secretary. Inclining his head toward the computer print-outs, now scrolled to the floor, he placed a hand over the mouthpiece and said, "Please see if Ashleigh's here yet."

Méchie nodded. Tearing the last sheet from the printer, she scooped the pile into her arms and, pushing open the door with a toe of her sensible pumps, hurried through her office toward her boss's.

As Méchie disappeared from view, Jerome returned his full attention to Chris Ferrari. "Damn it, Chris. Don't tell me what Bentley's is doing. You are director of operations for Bentleys Royale. Must I remind you that the Royale division is not Central's number one priority? It's *yours*. At least, it better be."

Holding the receiver away from his ear, Jerome removed his rimless glasses, set them on the unpretentious metal desk, and rubbed his pulsating temples. Heat rose from his collar to his cheeks, and before Ferrari could spit out a single sentence of his infuriating brand of rationalization, he shouted, "No excuses! I want action!" Lowering his voice, he went on, in precise, measured syllables. "It's a pox on your house and mine as well when Taylor—any corporate executive, for that matter—is the first to uncover problems in your bailiwick."

Pulling the folding chair away from the desk in the back room, Jerome raised his foot and planted a custom-made shoe firmly on the seat. His voice rose again, and he made no attempt to control it. "I don't like surprises. Won't tolerate them! If you can't handle the job, I'll hire someone who can." He slammed the phone down, severing the connection, and shook his head gravely. Before the end of his first week on board, he'd known that Ferrari was a misfit. There was no getting around it; the specialty store division was just not Ferrari's cup of tea.

The president pushed back his chair. Every time he thought about how Central Personnel discounted his forty years of experience, it made his blood boil. In a multimillion-dollar corporation where success and even survival are measured by this year's bottom line, you'd think that Personnel could help cut company losses. But instead of leaping into action, they continued to stifle progress with a bunch of red tape, plodding along as if they reported to a court of law.

As Jerome headed for his office, his thoughts lingered on Chris Ferrari. The man was smart as hell and had a good track record with the Bentley's Department Stores group, or so he'd been told. But somehow Ferrari lacked that entrepreneurial sense of pride—a quality that Jerome demanded at every level, from housekeeping on down to himself.

Generally not one to be swayed by new management fads or lingo, he'd related to the idea behind the current organizational buzzword—the inverted pyramid. It fit his way of thinking. In his world, no one was more important than the sales associates—the top of the pyramid was exactly where they belonged. Yet he could not transmit those standards of excellence to Ferrari. Either you had it or you didn't.

Ferrari didn't.

In the president's vacant office, Ashleigh felt a distinct chill in the air. From where she stood, she glanced through the window nearest the entry. Very little daylight remained, and dark tones dominated the room, imposing what she could only describe as an aura of foreboding.

The armchairs, ordinarily in front of the Mr. Jerome's massive desk, were at the far end of room, beside the oval table. Compulsively, she crossed the room to straighten the high-backed chairs around the table where the president reigned over small group meetings. Mr. Jerome might not verbally agree, but Ashleigh did not doubt that he was well aware of Adele Watson's impact in the downward spiral of Danielle's career. Adele liked to play it safe and shied away from major investments in the risky couture lines. Danielle wasn't the first of Adele's buyers to fall victim to cuts in funding for top-of-the-line merchandise. Under Adele's supervision, Bentleys Royale had lost its fur buyer and its designer dress buyer—neither of whom had been in trouble before she came on the scene.

Ashleigh knew that Danielle possessed the desire and the discrimination to be the best Better Sportswear buyer in the country. In the past she had backed that up with solid sales performance and bottom-line profit. Danielle had once had it all, and everyone had adored her.

Of course, Adele Watson was not solely responsible for Danielle's downfall. To be fair, even if Danielle had not lost her mentor and former divisional merchandise manager, one who truly appreciated Danielle's unique talent, her personal situation was bound to affect her performance. The problem was that when Danielle needed support and guidance, it was not there. Instead, Adele had put her on probation. Worse yet, after Ted Norman came into Danielle's life, Ashleigh and Danielle had drifted apart.

That was all my fault, Ashleigh thought. *Why did I have to be so outspoken about the men in Danielle's life?* The fact that she had been right about Ted Norman brought no comfort. She should have done a better job of concealing her distaste for him.

For a brief moment David Jerome paused at the threshold of his office. Ashleigh's back was to him, and she began to pull an armchair away from the management table across the floor so that it faced his desk. *Now that's Bentleys Royale,* he thought. It wasn't the Chanel suit or Bruno Magli shoes that made the difference. It was Ashleigh herself.

Ashleigh not only had an eye for excellence but also was the heartbeat of morale at all levels. On the whole, she had made his tedious dealings with Personnel somewhat tolerable. Her engagement to Mitchell Wainwright had been unexpected and jarring. Wainwright was a key player in the dangerous phenomenon of hostile takeovers that was sweeping the nation. Acquisitions were one thing, hostile takeovers quite another. Somehow, Jerome could not imagine Mitchell's father, his old friend Mitchell Wainwright II, sanctioning this new business with leveraged buyouts, and he wondered if young Wainwright was now calling the shots. Either way, Ashleigh's unfortunate relationship with Wainwright was bound to play havoc with her dedication to Bentleys Royale.

Lowering himself into the leather chair behind his desk, Jerome shifted his mind back to the problem at hand. "Can you shed some light on Danielle Norman's disappearance?" he asked without preamble.

Ashleigh sat at the edge of the armchair. Her eyes met his in her usual direct manner. "On Friday, Danielle told me that she was elated over her early appointment at Anne Klein."

Jerome interlaced his fingers and leaned toward Ashleigh, both elbows planted on the desktop. "She never showed up—didn't even have the decency to call," he responded. The raw sense of betrayal caught in his throat. His thoughts momentarily shifted to Adele Watson. Adele had inherited a talented group of buyers in the Fine Apparel division, and her bottom-line profits were substantial. But could he actually attribute those results to Adele? Jerome wondered. Did her buyers achieve those impressive figures in spite of her, as he suspected, rather than because of her?

But that wasn't the question at hand. "I've given Danielle Norman every benefit of the doubt. But now . . . she has not only embarrassed me," he said. "She has put the reputation of Bentleys Royale on the line."

"I can't believe Danielle would intentionally fail to show up," Ashleigh said. "That appointment was too important to her."

"What did Danielle have to say when she came in to see you?"

Ashleigh knew Mr. Jerome asked no idle questions. She saw his knuckles whiten as his thin fingers gripped the arms of his chair. She spoke rapidly, not taking time to pull her thoughts together. "Danielle said that she couldn't seem to do anything right in Adele's eyes. She feels—"

"I don't care how she feels." He gave a dismissive gesture with the back of his hand. "What did she *say*?"

"Danielle said Adele cut her open-to-buy again." Ashleigh wasn't familiar with all the subtle nuances of preparing an open-to-buy, but she understood all she needed to know. It was just like a checkbook: the amount of money a buyer could spend each month within a season. "She said that without fresh merchandise, she couldn't meet her sales objective. She feels—she *said* Adele was setting her up to fail."

Jerome stared down at the white dots on his navy silk tie and adjusted the precisely tied knot.

Taking a deep breath, Ashleigh slid back in her chair and waited. Unfortunately, she knew that Danielle's fears were well grounded. Adele was ruthless toward buyers she could not control, and Danielle refused to be manipulated. Ashleigh recalled sitting in on Danielle's probationary review, listening to Adele's claim that Danielle lacked flexibility.

Thank God, Mr. Jerome had challenged this, saying, "Danielle Norman is a buyer with a strong point of view—a keystone for success in merchandising."

Adele had countered, "She's just plain stubborn. She's not a team player."

In either case, Danielle's career was her life. Ashleigh knew she put her heart and soul into it and was determined to succeed. It seemed Adele was equally determined that she should fail.

Ashleigh shifted in her seat, an uneasy feeling rising in her chest.

Finally, Jerome looked up from his tie and said, "You . . . can think . . . of no . . . reason . . . why Danielle—?"

"No," Ashleigh replied, impatient with his deliberate cadence. "Just the opposite." She paused momentarily, realizing that she had interrupted, then forged ahead. "Adele told Danielle that she wasn't to go to New York without a revised open-to-buy plan. And since numbers are still Danielle's greatest . . . challenge, she said it would take her most of the weekend to revise the plan. A friend was coming over on Saturday to help her."

Ashleigh looked down, studying the pattern of the Oriental rug. She forced herself to continue. "She also said she had to go to the La Jolla and Palm Springs stores on Monday."

"Why in the h—?" Jerome raised the flat of his hand from the arm of the chair and, lowering his voice, began again. "Why would she choose Monday to journey out to the stores?"

"She didn't say. I assumed the store visits must be necessary. Last night, after the State of the Business meeting, she planned to take the red-eye to New York."

It was a full five seconds before Mr. Jerome said through clenched teeth, "She didn't show up in New York. She—"

The intercom buzzed sharply.

Picking up the phone, Jerome listened for a moment and then said, "Tell him to look over those printouts. I'll be right with him." Then he hung up. "Excuse me," he said to Ashleigh as he rose to his feet. "This won't take long."

Ashleigh nodded. She didn't bother glancing at the clock on Mr. Jerome's desk; she knew it was getting late. She would never make it on time. She didn't like breaking promises to Mitchell, but she wasn't in charge here. Although the freeways would probably be bottlenecked by now, she still might be able to make the cocktail party that seemed so important to her fiancé—if Mr. Jerome returned quickly. But as each moment passed, that was appearing less and less likely.

CHAPTER
6

Where could Danielle possibly be? Ashleigh asked herself, and her mind flitted back to Friday morning.

Ashleigh unlocked the door to her office. It was seven forty-five. Hearing a muffled ringing from her secretary's office, she looked down at the flashing light on her private line—the bell to her phone was, as usual, switched off. Dropping her handbag on the table, she reached for the phone.

It was Danielle, calling from home. "Can you see me this morning?" After a split-second pause, she added, "Please."

Ashleigh's calendar was full—one appointment colliding with the next—yet Danielle's voice conveyed a sense of urgency that she could not dismiss. "Of course," she said. "Could you come before nine? About eight or eight thirty?"

Danielle quickly agreed. But the time came and went, and she failed to show up.

At the first opportunity, Ashleigh popped her head out of her office and peered into the reception area, asking her secretary, "Has Danielle called?"

"Yes, she called about nine fifteen. She had car trouble."

Danielle's concerned voice echoed in Ashleigh's head, and she blamed herself for not asking Betty to interrupt if Danielle called. "This is Danielle's last day in the store," she said, doing her best to control her frustration. "She's going to New York on Monday. I must see her today." Checking the clock above the coffeemaker, she said, "Please arrange for her to come down to my office at twelve thirty." She hesitated and glanced up to the ceiling as if looking for insight. "If that's a problem, let me know while she's still on the line."

Danielle arrived promptly at twelve thirty, wearing a navy Donna Karan dress from a collection that had not yet been received in the store. As she walked in, she held her chin high. Yet Ashleigh was alarmed. The dark color accented Danielle's pale, translucent skin, and her arms were so thin that they appeared skeletal.

Is she healthy? Ashleigh wondered. How could Danielle manage to maintain a wardrobe of perfectly fitting designer clothes of the current season when she continued to lose weight at such an alarming rate? She was even more curious about that unwavering air of self-confidence that Danielle continued to project, a confidence that Ashleigh knew the young woman no longer possessed.

The moment the door closed behind her, Danielle dropped the pretense and moved as if in slow motion. Her eyes did not meet Ashleigh's until after she absently lowered herself into one of the straight-backed chairs, and arranged and rearranged her notebook and Louis Vuitton bag on the table beside her. When she finally looked up, Ashleigh noticed that her eyes looked dull; the spark she'd once seen there was gone.

Though only three years Danielle's senior, Ashleigh felt maternal toward the troubled young buyer, whom she'd known since she was a knobby-kneed teenager. It hurt to realize that she could no longer protect Danielle as she once had. She longed for the closeness they had shared before their careers and Danielle's marriage had come between them. Danielle's self-confidence had plummeted with the decline of her sales figures. What she needed more than anything was reassurance that her job performance would be evaluated fairly. Something Ashleigh could not give her. *If only I had the power.*

Danielle began to ramble incoherently, her hands muffling the words on her lips. Ashleigh leaned forward, trying to make sense out of the phrases Danielle mumbled into her palm.

Danielle drew her hands away from her face. She quickly dried her eyes and lifted her chin. "I'm not a feather duster," she said, "and, damn it, Adele Watson isn't going to turn me into one!" She was no longer mumbling—now her voice was clear and full of conviction.

Ashleigh realized at once that Danielle had picked up on the challenge that the Bentley's CEO, Mark Toddman, had given the troops at the recent State of the Business meeting, using the phrase "peacock to feather duster." Ashleigh realized that it had become more than a cliché for Danielle.

"I wish we had more time," Danielle said, looking across to the glass-domed clock on the credenza.

Ashleigh did not turn. Instead she glanced down at the tiny rectangular clock she had glued to the back of her marble notepaper box, which sat near the center of the circular table. Though she had a need to manage time, it was in her desire to avoid the appearance of looking at the clock. "We have another ten minutes before I'm due in the training room for the assistant buyers' workshop," she said.

"It's okay. I need to bounce some things off you, but it can wait," Danielle said, and she abruptly pushed her chair back.

Gesturing that she should remain seated, Ashleigh picked up a pencil and ran her finger down the calendar page. "I should be through at five thirty—five forty-five at the latest."

"I have to get to the DC before four," Danielle said, shaking her head from side to side, "to check on a shipment we should have received last week."

Ashleigh nodded, recalling that the Distribution Center's office hours were from seven to four. "How about this weekend? We could have dinner at the yacht club, and if you have time we could stop in and see Charles for a few minutes. I know he'd love to see you."

Danielle shook her head. Her eyes filled with sadness as she pulled herself to her feet. "Oh, how I'd love to see Charles," she said wistfully. Then with a determined set to her jaw, she continued, "But I must work on my open-to-buy, and I'm afraid there are too few hours as it is. Besides, I've already taken enough of your time."

Ashleigh wanted to protest, but Danielle quickly added, "I'd like to see you when I get back from New York. How about a week from Tuesday, first thing in the morning?"

Ashleigh flipped her calendar, and they scheduled a seven thirty appointment. Whatever it was that Danielle wanted to share with her, it would have to wait.

As the minutes ticked away and there was no sign of Mr. Jerome, Ashleigh thought about that meeting. *Danielle had no intention of giving up. Her trip to New York was critical.*

The president finally strode back into the office. "When Danielle didn't show up at Anne Klein," he continued, as if there had been no break in their conversation, "Adele called the Consolidated buying offices. Danielle hadn't signed in. Then she called the Ambassador Hotel. Hadn't checked in there, either."

Ashleigh recrossed her legs and smoothed her skirt. "Mr. Jerome, I know for a fact that Danielle is banking her career on this buy."

Mr. Jerome leaned forward and slammed his palm down on the edge of the desktop. "Danielle is considerably overbought," his voice thundered.

Ashleigh sat in stunned silence. She looked beyond his words, knowing that she was not the target of his anger. *Danielle's concern over stock levels was real.* "If she was overbought, why did Adele send her to New York?"

"Obviously because we didn't know." Mr. Jerome's face was now beet red. He sat rigid, pushing down on the chair arms. Several moments passed. Ashleigh wished he would say something, anything. The silence was deafening. She had to break it.

"Maybe Danielle was in an accident."

At last he spoke, totally ignoring her concern. "Conrad Taylor was here this afternoon." The words came in slow, measured syllables, and his voice was flat. "He pulled up Danielle's departments on the computer—it appears that she is overbought by thousands of dollars."

Before Ashleigh could formulate a single question, Jerome continued. "This doesn't sound like the buyer we believed in, does it? Of course, there's a chance that some of the purchases were credited to her department in error. But the entire discrepancy cannot be due to an input error." The harsh tone returned to his voice. "The amount is far too large."

Incredulous, Ashleigh shot forward in her chair, but Jerome held out his hand as if to restrain her from speaking. "Even if the future of Bentleys Royale were not in jeopardy," he said, "I wouldn't tolerate Danielle Norman, or any buyer, breaking the rules. It's unfair. It's disloyal. How could she be so damned stupid, so self-centered as to put us at this kind of risk?"

Ashleigh winced as if she'd received a physical blow.

At the sound of voices in the hallway, Mr. Jerome leaned forward and pressed a concealed button. The massive door slammed shut. Pushing his chair back, he laced his fingers behind his head and switched focus. "I've asked for the help of the corporate Security office. Ross Pocino is in the outer office. He's agreed to go check out Danielle's house. However, in case she is there, I'm not comfortable with him going there alone." He fell silent.

His unspoken request came as no surprise. Though Pocino's title—corporate director of asset protection—sounded official, his image left much to be desired. Ashleigh knew that Conrad Taylor had inherited this particular employee when he came on board at Bentley's. There hadn't been sufficient time to make a change, even if that was Taylor's intention. But they sure presented a picture in contrasts if there ever was one—Conrad, immaculately tailored, and Pocino, an unmade bed with the tact of a toddler. *He must really know the security part of his job.* She knew of his reputation for playing supercop, and was as reluctant as Jerome was to have Pocino confront Danielle.

Plus, Ashleigh had to find out for herself if Danielle was there—no matter how unlikely it now seemed. She spoke up. "Mr. Jerome, I'd like to go."

"That would be a great relief." Jerome's eyes held hers. "Ashleigh, I don't have to tell you that this is a time to be particularly circumspect. I will not tolerate this situation being turned into a whirlwind of rumors. I expect you to be sure that doesn't happen."

Ashleigh nodded. *If only I possessed that kind of power.*

"Under the present circumstances, your personal relationship with Danielle is awkward. It must remain low-key and between the two of us."

She did not respond to this last comment, only nodding slightly as she excused herself to call Mitchell. But it chilled her and made her uneasy.

Outside Jerome's office, Pocino's substantial bulk filled the narrow corridor.

"I'll meet you at the security counter," Ashleigh said as she edged past him and headed for the elevators.

"Sure thing. Be right there," he said, disappearing into Méchie's office.

Ashleigh's heels clicked a rapid cadence on the tiled floors of the deserted lower level as she hurried toward her office. Not bothering to unlock her own door, she picked up the phone on Betty's desk and dialed Mitchell's number. She quickly filled him in on the emergency and braced herself as her fiancé exploded into a nonstop tirade.

She held the phone a few inches from her ear and let him rant, wondering when he had actually changed from the man she thought she knew. Or had she simply been blind to his true nature?

"You're director of human resources, not super sleuth!" he exclaimed. "I had plans for tonight—you know that! You've no damned business making house calls, and Jerome is out of line asking you to go out there with that half-witted baboon." He paused, but not long enough for Ashleigh to collect her thoughts and respond. "Where are your priorities?"

"Mitchell . . ." She was about to tell him that Jerome had not actually asked her to go, but she didn't get the chance. The phone went dead.

Shocked and angry, Ashleigh dropped it back into the cradle.

Tension between them had been building steadily in the few weeks since their engagement. Until now, it had remained an unspoken undercurrent, more unsettling than overt. But she almost welcomed the sting of words he'd just hurled at her. She was not sorry that it was out in the open now. This was something she could deal with As she headed to meet Pocino, a realization came over her: When Mitchell had hung up on her, more than the phone connection had been severed.

The moment the door banged behind Pocino, Jerome experienced an unsettling tightness in the pit of his stomach. He should have insisted that Ashleigh remain in his office while he laid out the ground rules to Pocino. *Well, too late now.* He shrugged. *Somehow she'll handle it.*

Ashleigh had not questioned the unorthodox trip. Had he taken unnecessary advantage of her keen sense of responsibility? Jerome's phone rang—loud and unmuffled. He picked it up before the second ring.

James O'Brien's voice boomed above the static of the tie-line. The corporate VP of Personnel had an annoying habit of giving advice when none was asked for or wanted. Still, Jerome respected the man and his intelligence. He also relied on his counsel when Ashleigh was unavailable or when a situation demanded O'Brien's years of experience.

"It's less than eight hours since Danielle Norman came up missing," O'Brien said. "You know as well as I do that the police won't touch anything like this in less than forty-eight without probable cause. And yet you jump right on in. On top of that, you involve a Personnel executive."

"Wait a second, Jim. Get off your high horse and let me put you in the picture." *How has O'Brien gotten wind of Ashleigh's role?* Then his mind turned to his recent conversation with Conrad Taylor. He hadn't told Taylor about Ashleigh's trip to Danielle's. Then it dawned on him. Pocino reported to Taylor and he must have checked in when he left the office.

Silence filled the room. Jerome leaned back in his chair and swung his feet squarely on top of his open desk drawer, pausing long enough to restore the calm to his tone. With no further challenge, he proceeded to bring O'Brien up to date, finishing with, "If Adele Watson hadn't picked up the ball in New York, we'd have missed out on fifteen thousand dollars in co-op advertising from Anne Klein for *Vogue* and *Harper's*."

"Another nail in Danielle Norman's coffin, hammered home by her adoring boss," O'Brien remarked.

Ignoring the sarcasm, Jerome went on. "By the way, Adele Watson delivered quite a scathing attack on Ashleigh McDowell. She said that she should have put Danielle on a six-month probation rather than a full year, and if it hadn't been for Ashleigh, that's what she would have done."

"Now, that's not fair, and you know it."

Cutting in, Jerome said, "Look, you and I know that it's not true. Adele Watson has her own truths and sense of fairness." The moment the words slipped out, he regretted them. He certainly didn't want to sound off to O'Brien about his divisional merchandise manager. Not now. Not until he got his own house in order and knew exactly how he wanted to handle Adele. "But let's not digress."

"Right. I haven't shared the faith you and Ashleigh place in Danielle Norman, and her recent performance does not validate her ability. Even if I did, Ashleigh has no damned business going out to her house."

"Look, Jim. Let's agree to disagree, and move on." Jerome looked through the open French doors, which led to his adjoining rooftop patio, the backdrop for small parties such as the recent reception for Princess Margaret. He listened to the hum of the traffic on Royale Boulevard and the occasional screech of brakes. Neither man spoke. Jerome didn't want to be the first to break the silence. *What was it that Ashleigh said during that recent session on management effectiveness?* Barely had the question crossed his mind when it came to him. *Silence—the ultimate power.*

Finally, he heard, "David?"

"Yes?"

Clearing his throat, O'Brien asked, "Are you sure that Ashleigh can be objective in regard to Danielle Norman?"

CHAPTER

8

Pocino swung the passenger door of his flashy red Mustang open wide. He stood to the inside of the opening, creating a narrow passage for Ashleigh to slip through.

An overpowering aroma of Old Spice hit her as she slid silently into her seat.

"Has anyone checked the hospitals?"

Pocino sauntered around the metallic machine, maneuvered his bulky frame beneath the steering wheel, and gave her a broad grin. "Yeah. Even checked the morgue, but as I suspected, Ms. Norman wasn't in any accident, and I'd bet my bottom dollar we're not going to find her at her pad."

"Where do you think she is?"

"Haven't a clue. But Central Purchasing has some damned interesting stats from her departments. She's definitely been on the take."

"That's ridiculous. She may be guilty of poor judgment, but she's no thief." Ashleigh had to admit to herself, though, that Danielle wouldn't be the first buyer to risk unauthorized purchases in hopes of rescuing the bottom line of her department and, in turn, her career.

"By the way," Pocino said, his grin still spreading from ear to ear, "how is it that Mitchell Wainwright *the Third* has turned his fair-haired maiden loose for an evening of detective work?"

"Knock it off, Ross. I'm concerned about Danielle. I know she had every intention of going to New York."

"Afraid you're in for a rude awakening." Pocino's grin faded, and he reached over to punch the stereo button. It boomed on, several decibels too loud. Out blared "You Picked a Fine Time to Leave Me, Lucille," and the driver of the car alongside them jerked his head in their direction.

Ashleigh couldn't remember ever being in such a disheveled automobile. Pocino's new '86 model looked as though it had already accumulated years of rubbish, and it reeked of tobacco. She glanced over her left shoulder, half expecting to find a trench coat and a bottle of bourbon in a brown paper bag in the backseat. Instead, it was strewn with newspapers, torn ticket stubs, a box of Havana cigars, a carton of unfiltered Camels, and black notebook binders crammed with papers. Ashleigh's foot touched a crushed beer can. She glanced down to see a stained carpet and miscellaneous bits of debris. All this was in contrast to the outside of Pocino's car, which was polished to a high gloss. It reminded Ashleigh of stories her fastidious grandmother told about fashionably dressed ladies who wore stained underwear.

While the glass-rattling bass vibrated through the car, Ashleigh stared out the window glimpsing the last slice of sun as it slipped from view. As if triggered by the sun's disappearance, the streetlamps flicked on, giving off a soft orange glow. She was about to ask Pocino to lower the volume, but when they turned south on Hoover, Mitchell's angry words echoed through her troubled mind, replacing the annoyance of the thunderous sounds.

The Santa Monica Freeway was like the parking lot of the Hollywood Bowl after a sellout. Pocino's heavy foot shifted awkwardly from the accelerator to the brake. Muttering under his breath, he gradually managed to maneuver the car to the right lane, scarcely in time to exit onto the Bundy turnoff.

Ashleigh braced herself against the door and said, "Would you mind slowing down a bit?"

To her surprise, he responded with no apparent agitation, slowing to the speed of the surrounding traffic.

"Well, here we are." Pocino jerked the Mustang to a stop and turned off the engine. The past half hour's country-western music faded, but the pulsating remained in her temples.

Danielle's shuttered house—her only asset at the close of a turbulent marriage—was situated in a quiet residential area. The streetlamps were set far apart, shedding almost no illumination on the walkway to Danielle's small dwelling.

"Wait here while I take a look around. If you want to listen to the radio, be my guest!" Pocino pointed to the ignition and his untidy accumulation of keys. There were well over a dozen keys on unmatched chains, held together with twists of string and thin wire. Ashleigh gave a halfhearted smile, thinking of the stories those keys might tell. But when her thoughts returned to Danielle, her smile vanished.

Pocino heaved himself out of the car. She could picture him in a Jeep or perhaps a Ford Bronco, but nothing like this small sports car. *What had possessed him to choose such an unsuitable car?*

By now it was dark, and there was no moonlight. Through the shutters that hung slightly askew on the front windows, slivers of light were visible.

Ashleigh watched Pocino as he pounded on the door and attempted to look inside, but it appeared that no one was home. She didn't think he would break in, but with Pocino she couldn't be sure. He disappeared under the bougainvillea-covered archway toward the back of the house. *What is he doing?* As Ashleigh strained to see what Pocino was up to, the headlights of a small car flicked off as it passed the Mustang and continued at a glacial pace down the street.

In the unlikely event that Danielle was in the house, Pocino's appearance would be anything but soothing. So, unable to sit still another moment, Ashleigh opened the car door and drew herself out of the bucket seat.

A gentle breeze touched her cheek, heightening her senses, as she noiselessly closed the door and headed up the walkway. Three sway-backed steps led to the front door. Even in the dim light she noticed that the paint on the wooden porch and the window trim was nearly translucent in some places, and badly blistered or chipped in others.

Ashleigh recalled Danielle's excitement upon buying the house. "We did it! We really did it!" she'd squealed, one sentence running over the next, as she fanned a fistful of photos across the desk in Ashleigh's office. "It needs a lot of work, but Ted can do a lot of the repairs. It'll be fun. It's just like a dollhouse . . . *and* it's in West L.A." That was less than two years ago, and by the looks of things, the outside of the house must have been a low priority on Ted's list of things to do.

Now that her eyes had adjusted to the dark, Ashleigh noticed the tangle of untrimmed bushes to her left and the overgrown lawn to her right, bordering the pathway where Pocino had disappeared between the house and the garage.

Ashleigh cautiously opened the screen door and rapped softly with the brass butterfly knocker. There was no answer. She tried to peer inside through the diamond-shaped glass at the top of the door. It was too thick, and the wide, beveled edges distorted the view. She saw only blurred light in what must be the living room. She knocked more boldly and called Danielle's name. Still no answer.

As she stood waiting, she heard a crackle in the shrubbery.

A cold chill swept over her. She snapped her head to look over her left shoulder, in the direction of the sound. She saw nothing, yet she knew someone was there. It couldn't be Pocino—she had just seen him take the pathway along the right side of the house toward the rear. Whirling around, she looked out into the darkness. Hardly breathing, Ashleigh braced her back against the doorjamb. She listened, her eyes searching the unlit area beyond the prickly bushes.

Once again she heard the crunch of small branches in the dense shrubbery.

She tried to call out to Pocino, but the cry froze in her throat when she heard heavy footfalls pounding toward her, down the walkway to the right, the path Pocino had taken. Ashleigh jerked her head in that direction. Was she surrounded?

She pushed herself harder against the doorjamb, as if she might be able to evaporate into it. She had nothing with which to defend herself. Her eyes darted to the left of the porch, and at last her cry tumbled out. "Ross! Ross!"

At that same moment, he leaped up on the porch beside her, not bothering to walk around to the steps. As he stood, towering over her, Ashleigh scarcely registered the difficulty of this feat for a man Pocino's size.

"I told you to wait in the car!" he barked.

Ashleigh glared up at him, half in defiance, half in fear. But the sounds from the bushes dominated her mind, and she pointed to the shrubbery. "I heard someone over there."

"What? Why didn't you say something?"

She peered into the hedges by way of response.

Pocino flicked on the flashlight, directing the beam into the bushes. "Most likely a cat or some other animal. Nothing to worry about."

"I wasn't hallucinating. I'm sure it couldn't have been a cat, unless it weighed over a hundred pounds."

"Look, if there was someone there, he's vanished without a trace." He thrust the flashlight toward Ashleigh. "Take a look for yourself."

Clenching her teeth, Ashleigh turned to close the screen. Her eyes were drawn to an envelope wedged between the door and the doorframe, well below eye level. She hadn't seen it before. Pulling the pale pink envelope from the doorjamb, she looked up at Pocino. He reached out, but she yanked her hand from his grasp. Among the shadows of Danielle's dimly illuminated porch, his expression was unreadable. He made no comment, but shone the flashlight on the envelope as she read it.

Ruthie was scrawled across the envelope in burgundy letters. Ashleigh immediately recognized the handwriting as Danielle's.

Carefully opening the envelope, she unfolded the soft pink notepaper bordered in burgundy. Three small butterflies covered the left-hand corner, further identifying the author. To Danielle the butterfly had been a symbol of freedom as well as beauty. It was her personal fingerprint. She had confided to Ashleigh that she had a tiny butterfly tattooed on her left shoulder blade.

Ashleigh blinked deliberately, attempting to shut out the visions of Danielle cascading through her mind. She forced her mind to concentrate on the note. Apparently Ruthie cleaned Danielle's house—the note listed a number of housecleaning priorities. Ashleigh read the last part of the note aloud: "'I'll be in New York until late Monday, so I won't need you until a week from Wednesday. Your check is on the dining room table.' It's signed 'Danielle.'"

When Ashleigh noticed that the last few lines of the note had been written in blue ink, she frowned and looked at Pocino.

Pocino stared down at her. "What's wrong?"

"It's probably nothing, but . . . it's just so unlike Danielle to finish a note in another color of ink."

"Is the writing different?" He reached for the note.

She held on to it. "No, it's Danielle's handwriting." And yet this note troubled her. She didn't try to explain Danielle's obsessive use of the color signature, or how she kept a full supply of burgundy felt-tip pens in her desk and her handbag. Pressed for time, most people could easily pick up the closest pen around and think little about it—but not Danielle.

"Women!" scoffed Pocino. "I can't believe it! It's just a note to her cleaning lady. What's the big deal?"

Ashleigh wondered if perhaps she was letting her imagination get away from her. After all, Danielle was on a tight schedule, was bound to be in a hurry. Ashleigh's mind raced off in a dozen different scenarios, aborting each one abruptly when it led nowhere. "Ross, I know Danielle was on her way to New York. Something had to have happened between this house and the airport . . . or maybe even in New York."

"You have your ideas . . . Mine are based on something a lot stronger than intuition."

She said nothing but stepped to the front windows. *Why is he so hostile? What makes this guy tick?* She cupped her hands around her eyes and leaned against the cool glass, straining to see inside where the drapes weren't completely closed.

"Hey." Pocino placed a heavy hand on her shoulder. "We're out of here. Nothing more we can do tonight."

Ashleigh challenged him. "We can't just walk away!"

"Short of breaking down the doors, what would you suggest?"

"Did you check to see if any of the windows were unlocked?"

His bushy eyebrows rose. "Locked up tight as a drum."

"How about the garage?"

"Locked, and there's a shade on the window. Can't see inside." He heaved an exaggerated sigh. "At this point, I'm not breaking down any darn windows or doors. She's only been missing since morning." With an exasperated shake of his head, he said, "Let's go."

"There has to be something more we can do." She touched her tongue to her top lip. "Let's go back to my office and call the airlines to see if Danielle was on that flight last night."

"Hold it!" Pocino held up his immense right hand. "It's after seven. Store's closed."

"Right." Ashleigh's voice echoed her disappointment.

"Besides, airlines don't give out information about passengers." He paused. "But I have a buddy. He's a cop at the Rampart station, and he can get all that so-called privileged information. I also have some pull at the Hamburger Hamlet not far from here. We'll get a bite to eat, then we can use their phone."

"Ross, I'm not hungry."

Pocino shrugged. "Okay, I'll just turn it over to the police."

Ashleigh watched as he aggressively pounded toward his car. She glanced down at the note in her hand, hesitated for a second, then placed the paper back in the envelope and replaced it in the doorjamb. Then her rapid footsteps crunched over the leaves strewn across the walkway, ending abruptly as she reached the spot where Pocino stood. He thrust the passenger door open and stepped back.

Surrounded by darkness, the silence thick between them, Ashleigh felt a moment of panic. Too many unanswered questions. Gathering herself together, she did her best impression of a smile and said, "Ross, I didn't mean to be abrupt. I would appreciate your help." She sighed inwardly. *It's too late to join Mitchell even I really wanted to.* "Will you help me, Ross?"

"I told you, I know a place where I can grab a bite to eat and use their phones."

"Okay. Let's go."

"Hold it! I'm not finished. Don't be gettin' any grand ideas that you're in charge."

"Fair enough." This time she didn't have to force the smile.

CHAPTER
10

"We're in luck," Pocino commented as he nosed into a parking spot in front of the Hamburger Hamlet on Wilshire Boulevard.

Ashleigh opened her own door before Pocino could reach for it and sprang out of the Mustang. She looked down and brushed a clump of long white hairs off her black skirt. It was difficult to picture this bulldog of a man caring for an animal. *But what do I really know about him? There has to be a lot more than meets the eye.*

Walking through the double doors of the Hamburger Hamlet, she saw it was standing room only. Without hesitation, Pocino grabbed two menus and mumbled, "This way." Ashleigh followed him straight through the coffee shop. As they passed down the aisle, he nodded with familiarity at several of the waiters.

When Ashleigh seemed reluctant to weave her way through the crowded restaurant, he said, "Hey, lighten up. A friend of mine manages this joint!"

As he ushered her into the sparsely furnished manager's office, she said, "Ross, I've just thought of something."

"Well, spit it out," Pocino said.

"This isn't a joke."

He held up his substantial right hand in a gesture of truce. "Meant no offense. Didn't know you were so touchy." He plopped down in one of the folding chairs beside the metal desk in the small office. "Now what was it you wanted to say? I'm all ears." He leaned back, tipping precariously on the two back legs of the armless chair, and waited.

"I came in this morning about seven thirty."

"Seven thirty? My God, Ashleigh, are you shooting for CEO?"

She frowned, then continued. "There was only one car in the associates' parking lot. It was a yellow VW like Danielle's, but I didn't think it could be hers since I knew she'd gone to New York. But around nine thirty, Betty, my secretary, said that one of our security agents asked her to have someone talk to Danielle about leaving her car in the lot overnight."

Pocino nodded.

"I thought Security was mistaken—that it couldn't be Danielle's," Ashleigh went on. "I asked Betty to go out and check, but when she did, there was no yellow VW."

Pocino plunked the front legs of his chair down with a jolt. "Why in the hell didn't you tell me this before?" He leaned toward her. "Did you tell Jerome?"

"No. I just now made the connection."

"I'll ask my buddy at Rampart to report the car as stolen and put out an APB."

Ashleigh rummaged through her handbag and pulled out her wallet. She poured the change into her open palm. "While you call your friend, I need to make a quick call."

"Be my guest." He pointed with his head toward the phone and reached for one of the menus he'd tossed on the desk. "I'll get our order in and call my buddy when I return."

"It's long distance."

"No problemo. You need some privacy while you check in with today's *numero uno* corporate raider?"

Ordinarily, Ashleigh might have defended Mitchell. She might have told Pocino that her fiancé was one of the good guys. He was not one of the raiders who drove companies into the ground strictly for his own profit. He bought companies with potential and had them run by experienced management. *I make them lean, mean, and profitable* was his mantra. But why bother explaining all this to Pocino?

She snatched the phone from its cradle. "For your information, I'm not calling Mitchell Wainwright—the First, Second, *or* Third!"

The moment Pocino disappeared from view, though she knew she was being compulsive, Ashleigh tried Danielle's number once more.

In a flash, Pocino returned, poking his head back through the office door. "Sure you don't want anything more than coffee and rice pudding?"

Ashleigh nodded. Danielle's answering machine clicked on after the first ring. This time she left no message.

When Pocino stepped back through the door, the aroma from his Caliente Burger and fries filled the air of the small office. Ashleigh did her best to ignore the churning sensation in the pit of her stomach, not knowing if it was a result of the food or of her concern for Danielle. *This is probably an exercise in futility,* she thought.

Pocino took a hearty bite from the burger while dialing the phone. Wiping his chin with the sleeve of his shirt, he asked to speak to Sergeant Flynn, his contact at LAPD. By the time the sergeant came on the line, Pocino had devoured most of his burger. He hastily dropped the remainder into Hamburger Hamlet's special woven basket as he launched into a short monologue, bringing his friend up to date. "Yeah. Continental. I need to know if Danielle Norman boarded last night's red-eye to JFK."

Ashleigh crossed and uncrossed her legs, doing her best to come up with a plausible reason for Danielle's failure to show up in New York. She felt so darn helpless just sitting here watching the cocky head honcho of Security gobble down the rest of his French fries while gripping the receiver in his other pudgy hand.

After what seemed like a very long time, Pocino said, "No surprise there. Once we find her, she's got plenty of explaining to do." There was an unsettling smugness in his tone. He gave a cursory glance in Ashleigh's direction before asking, "Were there any other no-shows? You don't say." He paused, strummed his fingers on the desk for a few seconds, and then stopped abruptly. "How about checking on the seat allocation?" After a few more breathless seconds, Pocino slammed his fist on the table, and a broad grin covered his round face. "Bingo. That gives us something to go on. I owe you."

After disconnecting, he turned to Ashleigh. "Danielle was a no-show on Monday night. So was Mr. Jeff Bradley, and their seats just happened to be side by side."

"Jeff Bradley?" Ashleigh said aloud. "That name sounds familiar."

"Bradley was the Men's Furnishings buyer for Bentleys Royale. Think he was terminated before your time."

Ashleigh nodded, then repeated, "Terminated?"

"Yeah. Shady vendor dealings. Of course, you Personnel types probably have some fancier term for it."

"What is he doing now?"

"Heard he went to work for Robinson's but got canned from there, too. And now he's working for an outside resource of some sort. Not sure what he sells, but don't think it has anything to do with menswear." Pocino winked. "If you get my drift."

Ashleigh was silent. "Is he one of Danielle's vendors?"

Ross shrugged. "Probably. I'll look into it." He paused, then heaved himself to his feet. "Be back in a shake."

Alone in the small office, Ashleigh collected her thoughts. Was it a coincidence that neither Danielle nor Jeff Bradley had caught the flight? Unfortunately, Danielle's superior sense of taste in selecting upscale merchandise did not translate to her selection of men. In that arena, her track record had been dismal.

"Hey. Where are you?" Pocino waved his hairy arm in front of Ashleigh's eyes before plunking down in the chair beside her.

She blinked and gave a weak smile. Feeling tightness in the muscles of her shoulders and neck, she leaned back in her chair and stretched her arms up, then back as far as she could. Her weary eyes dropped to her watch. It wasn't quite nine, but it seemed a lot later.

She yawned. "Ross, I'm beat. Let's call it a day."

"Yeah. Done all we can for now." Pocino began gathering his notes, which were scribbled on the back of two Hamburger Hamlet place mats. "How about meeting at nine tomorrow morning in your office?"

Ashleigh nodded.

He gave her a broad grin. "By the way, Flynn is checking all the other airlines to see if Danielle Norman or Jeff Bradley was scheduled on any other flights. Like, maybe out of the country. That is, if the little bimbo and her *friend* used their own names."

Ashleigh stiffened. She had let far too many of Pocino's innuendos about Danielle slide by. "Danielle Norman is no bimbo. She is a talented young buyer. I don't know what has happened recently, but I intend to find out." Confronting his mocking eyes dead on, she said, "I understand you have other thoughts, but until we have a lot more information, let's stop the speculation and stick to the facts."

"Yes, ma'am," Pocino said with another unsettling grin.

"Enough!" Ashleigh bolted to her feet. "Have I done something to offend you?"

"Like what?"

"I have no idea, Ross. But from the time we left the store, I've been barraged by your snide remarks and sarcasm. What is it that set you off?"

"Well, I'll be damned!" Pocino exclaimed as he rose slowly. "Didn't realize there was so much fire behind those classy doe eyes."

Ashleigh said nothing, allowing an uncomfortable silence to settle between them.

Pocino held her gaze but raised his arms in a gesture of surrender. "Sorry. Didn't realize I'd been out of line."

Ashleigh's eyes did not waver. "Hostile is more like it."

"Okay. Let's just say I didn't appreciate being talked to like a schoolboy by your boss."

"What does that have to do with me?"

Pocino took a step back and leaned against the metal desk, uncharacteristically taking a moment to assemble his thoughts rather than blurting out the first thing that came into his head. "Sorry," he said again. "Meant no offense. It's not you. It's the whole Bentleys Royale attitude that's getting to me."

"Meaning . . . ?"

"Like I said, it's not you. But it seems to me that most everyone in that goddamned store, clear on down to the housekeeping staff, thinks they're better than the rest of us peons."

Pocino went on. "And I'm afraid your highfalutin fiancé, Mr. Mitchell Wainwright *the Third*, gets to me like fingernails on a chalkboard."

What does he know about Mitchell? "Why is that?"

"I've just got a bad feeling about him and that Australian fellow."

"Philip Sloane?"

"Yeah, that's the guy. I've heard about their takeovers of businesses they know little or nothing about—heard just enough to turn my blood cold."

Ashleigh didn't want to talk about Mitchell or his business. Maybe her preconceived assessment of Pocino was as inaccurate as his was of her, but she could not see herself talking about Mitchell with him—not now, not ever. She sighed. "Ross, let's begin again. I came with you tonight to find out what happened to Danielle Norman. That's all. And I appreciate your help."

Pocino smiled warmly for the first time that night. "Got it. I'll take you to your car. We can meet again tomorrow morning."

When Pocino pulled up beside Ashleigh's white Thunderbird in the underground parking lot of Bentleys Royale, he said, "Now just hold it a sec, and I'll open your door."

Ashleigh forced herself to stay seated as Pocino plodded around the car. This time when he pulled the door open, he gave her sufficient room to slip out.

"Thank you. See you in the morning."

He gave a departing "Ciao."

Sliding into her own car, Ashleigh felt a splinter of sadness for the large man. But as the fresh scent of the Thunderbird's clean leather surrounded her, all of her thoughts turned from Pocino. She wondered if Mitchell would be at her condo when she returned. She wasn't up to a confrontation—not right now. Her head pounded with the force of the surf at high tide. All she wanted was to be alone and to go straight to bed. Even though she suspected that sleep would evade her.

CHAPTER
11

At the sound of a faint tap, Ashleigh slammed on the brakes. Shaken, and realizing that her mind had drifted, she slowly backed up a few feet from the familiar wooden arm of the parking lot barrier. The associates' lot, set back from the underground patron parking, was dark except for the low beam of her headlights. She sat for a moment in silence, then took a deep breath and pulled herself together. The arm of the barrier, clearly illuminated by her car lights, appeared unharmed.

Absently, she rummaged through the pocket on the inside of the door until her fingers came across the plastic card. She quickly inserted it. Waiting for the sluggish arm to rise, she flipped on the stereo, turned the volume down low, and exchanged the time-management tape in the cassette player for the one with the old Sinatra ballads.

As she pulled out of the lot onto Royale Place, Ashleigh glanced up at the store's landmark silhouetted against the sky. The tower's three broken windowpanes, an ongoing topic within the management team, were concealed in darkness but still visible in her mind. Unarguably, they must be repaired. However, reinforcing the impressive tower from the ever-present threat of earthquake was a higher priority, and this work came with a staggering six-hundred-thousand-dollar price tag. Since the building had been named a historical landmark, Chris Ferrari was seeking financial assistance from the California Heritage Society, so for now, more-pressing budget needs dictated that the eyesore must remain.

Side one of the cassette tape ended. Ashleigh tapped the EJECT button and glanced in her rearview mirror. A dark blue Karmann Ghia, a few car lengths behind her, had run the stop sign. About the same vintage, she guessed, as the one her best friend, Beverly, drove in their college days, only Bev's was red.

Almost at once, the scream of a motorcycle policeman's siren broke the silence, and the small car pulled to the curb. Ashleigh turned the tape over, popped it back in. Her thoughts returned to Pocino, and she wondered if he might have a point. *Have I allowed emotions to cloud my judgment?* If so, sticking her head in the sand wasn't going to do Danielle one bit of good.

Her mind raced through the possibilities, each more unsettling than the last, yet nothing could convince her that Danielle had intentionally failed to show up in New York. That left some pretty frightening alternatives. She ticked them off with the fingers of her left hand. Number one—she pressed her index finger on the steering wheel—Danielle had been in an accident and was unconscious somewhere. Pocino had said the local hospitals had been checked, but had anyone else seen her or talked to her since her trip to Palm Springs and La Jolla on Monday? There must be scores of hospitals between Danielle's house and those two stores.

If Danielle hasn't been in an accident, then could she have been kidnapped? Ashleigh didn't know much about kidnapping, but she did know there had to be a motive. What possible motive could there be? The idea instantly died.

As she pressed her third finger on the wheel, a chill shot through her. Could Danielle be dead? But that led back to some sort of accident . . . or did it? The media were filled with reports of rape and murder. She tried to dispel the thought of someone doing intentional harm to Danielle.

Turning off the Harbor Freeway onto the 405, with her ring finger pressing hard into the wheel as she waited for a fourth possibility to arise, her thoughts shifted to her fiancé. She didn't want to think about him, but if it was all a mistake, better to face up to it now and deal with it.

She had to be honest with herself: Mitchell was not the man whom she could see herself spending her life with. Their engagement had not been impulsive—she had thought about it long and hard for more than a year. Her career was a major part of her life, but she wanted more, and in the past year Mitchell had made her feel so alive. He had been so charming, so attentive. He'd brought out the best in her. And yet almost from the day that he placed the pretentious ring on her finger—one that she would never have chosen for herself—she knew she'd made a terrible mistake. The ring was not the problem. She had missed loving and being loved, and now she realized that she had simply willed herself to love Mitchell. The feelings she had for him were nothing like those she had felt for Dan. *But that was so long ago . . .*

The nightly fireworks on the *Queen Mary* were over by the time Ashleigh turned off the Long Beach Freeway and headed down Shoreline Drive. The brilliance of the grand old ship dominated the skyline. A string of bright white lights, strung from bow to stern, silhouetted the three smokestacks below.

Belmont Shore would still be humming with young people looking for action, so Ashleigh continued down Ocean Boulevard, avoiding the congestion she was sure to find on Second Street. She enjoyed the still, cool evening and the throbbing pulse of the waves, unmuffled in this small area where the breakwater terminated.

Turning up Bay Shore, Ashleigh noticed an elderly couple, hand in hand, walking along the edge of the still waters of the bay, and smiled. But her smile faded the moment she spotted Mitchell's silver El Dorado parked in front of her condo.

Stepping out of the elevator on the third floor, with her key in hand, she saw that her door stood wide open. She paused before walking in and closing the door behind her. It was cold inside, as cold as the eyes that stared back at her from across the room.

Mitchell's scowl caused rugged lines to spread across his forehead and around his eyes. He rose from the armchair beside the fireplace and raised his wrist, looking pointedly at his Rolex.

"Do you realize what time it is?" he said quietly.

Ashleigh's eyes met the frigid stare of Mitchell's as she tossed her handbag on the coffee table. She made no attempt to soften the edge in her staccato answer. "Yes, I do. When I saw your car, I looked at the clock on my dashboard." She sank onto the edge of her over-stuffed couch.

Mitchell stood there, staring at her. Although the tension between them had been growing, until tonight there had been no angry words.

"Where have you been?" He crossed the room in three long strides and towered over her.

Ashleigh kicked off her shoes and drew her feet up beneath her. "Mitchell, I don't react well to intimidation. Please sit down." She pointed to the armchair across from the sofa. Deep within, Ashleigh heard a door slam shut.

Mitchell seated himself on the arm of the chair. "First of all, I think you owe me an explanation. I called the Kramers and told them you'd been detained, and we'd meet them at the club after the symphony. Of course, I had no idea you'd be so late—still can't imagine what kept you." He did not raise his voice, but the tone was commanding.

"If you hadn't hung up, you might be better informed."

"There was nothing left to say. You had your own priorities, so I put down the phone. I saw no point in taking more of the time you so willingly give to Bentleys Royale." His eyes held hers without a hint of warmth.

"I'm sorry about the cocktail party and the symphony. I know it was important to you, but it couldn't be helped. I'm afraid that something terrible has happened to Danielle. She's been in an accident . . . or maybe worse."

"That may be. But how does sending you out to play detective help her?" Mitchell's eyes bored into her, then fell to her ring. She was twisting it. He leaned forward. Ashleigh quickly slipped the ring off her finger.

Mitchell jumped to his feet and was again in front of her, staring at her hand. Seating himself quickly on the couch, he tried to draw her to him.

"No, Mitchell," she said as she pulled away. "This isn't about missing a cocktail party or the symphony. I care for you. I really do. But *this* . . . it's all wrong." She stared down at the ring burning between her thumb and index finger. "I can't marry you."

"Ashleigh, you're tired. Let's not blow things out of proportion."

"Mitchell, it's not just tonight." She searched for the words to make him understand.

He rose abruptly from the couch. "Look, Ashleigh, there are a lot of things we need to settle, but this isn't the time. I've got to be in Atlanta tomorrow and on my toes for this round of negotiations."

She remembered that Mitchell himself planned to handle all the details of this particular deal and that he expected to be away for an unprecedented two weeks. He'd told her that Philip Sloane was hot on his heels—vying for a leveraged buyout of the same small Atlanta-based publishing company.

"Two weeks won't change anything. Our engagement was a mistake."

He held up a hand. "That's enough for now. My flight leaves at five-twenty tomorrow morning. No point saying things we'll regret."

She looked down at the oversized diamond that sparkled in the palm of her hand. "From the day you slipped this ring on my finger, nothing has been the same."

He raised his voice at last. "I said, not tonight! You don't just throw in the towel the first time things don't go your way."

Ashleigh stood up to face him. "Mitchell, stop talking to me like I'm one of your subordinates!" Her voice was strong and clear. "We'll talk when you get back from Atlanta, but I want you to take your ring now!"

"Stop talking nonsense!" Mitchell grabbed his suit jacket and headed for the door. "It's time you stopped living in a dream world. Dan McIntyre is dead! I can't take his place. Nobody can."

Ashleigh was speechless, but Mitchell rambled on.

"I'll see you in a couple of weeks. You'll come to your senses. Then we'll talk."

The door banged shut, and Ashleigh stood in stunned silence. Shaking with blind rage, she flung the diamond ring toward the closed door. It bounced on the thick carpet, rolled to a stop, and glared up at her.

Early Wednesday morning, Ashleigh switched on the bedside lamp. The first thing she saw was the diamond ring , which now lay on the bedside table. She quickly refocused on the clock. Five minutes to four, and she was wide-awake.

She rubbed her eyes, stretched, and dialed Danielle's number. The answering machine clicked on after one ring, just as it had the night before. After the long, piercing beep, she left a message. "Danielle, this is Ashleigh. Please pick up the phone." Ashleigh squeezed her eyes shut tight. *Please, please be there.* The prayer drummed through her head, hammered in her heart.

Danielle just has to be alive, she thought. She had come such a long way from that vulnerable, bedraggled teenager who had appeared at Ashleigh's door shortly after her brother's death, with nowhere else to go. "I can't take it anymore," she'd said. The memory pained Ashleigh. She'd promised Dan five years ago that she would look after his younger sister, but somewhere along the way she had failed.

Snapping back to the present, she pleaded, "If you don't want to call the store, call me at home. I'll keep checking for messages." Her voice broke. "I . . . I have to know that you're alright. Nothing else matters." She left her home number and the number to her private line at Bentleys Royale, although she knew Danielle already had both. If Danielle was able to she would check her messages—if not at the house, then over the phone.

Throwing back the covers, Ashleigh climbed out of bed. In bare feet, she padded across the white carpet to her dressing alcove, slipped into a silk robe, and with a critical eye, inspected the heap of clothing that she'd carelessly stripped off and left on the chair before falling into bed the night before.

She wondered with vague indifference why it was that she, who managed her business life with orderliness and precision, hardly ever carried the same process through to her personal life. In her office, in a matter of seconds, she could lay her hands on whatever scrap of information she needed—no matter how obscure. But at the moment, rummaging through her crowded closet, she was unable to find a single empty hanger. Although her condo was immaculate at first glance, the closets and drawers were cluttered and unorganized.

At last she found the sculptured hanger for her suit and began straightening the closet as if her grandmother were right there beside her, speaking softly and wringing her hands, insistent yet unobtrusive.

Inevitably when Ashleigh arose extra early and imagined she had time to spare, the minutes seemed to vanish at a rapid pace. Now, as she was dashing to the door, a long, narrow white box on the entry table caught her eye. She stopped in midstride. It hadn't been there the night before. She was sure of it. She would have seen it when she had bent down to pick up the ring.

Glancing down at the ring she had reluctantly placed back on her finger, she raised the lid of the white box. The fragrance filled the entry. Ashleigh's breath caught in her throat, sticking there unpleasantly.

Why would Mitchell send white roses when he knew . . . ? A picture of Gran in her coffin flashed before her eyes. For a moment she doubted herself. *Hadn't she mentioned . . . ?* She had. Ashleigh had specifically told him that white roses reminded her of death. Gran, who had been a pillar of strength under even the most trying circumstances, had fallen apart at the sight of them—a hurtful reminder of the tragic death of her own young daughter, Ashleigh's mother.

Now, the very sight or scent of white roses always brought unbidden tears to Ashleigh's eyes—and yet, for Gran's memorial service, Mitchell had filled the chapel with dozens of white roses. And here he was, sending them once again.

Setting her handbag on the table, Ashleigh plucked the tiny white envelope from the clear plastic pitchfork and removed the card.

The symphony isn't important. You are! Let's put last night behind us. My plane isn't leaving for another two hours, but I already miss you.

Mitchell

He hadn't apologized; she hadn't expected him to and didn't want him to. But the roses telegraphed a clear message, and the note another—his insensitivity, and her failure to make him understand. The issue was not the symphony. It was love. The kind of love she had felt for Dan. The unselfish love that Gran and Grandpa Charles had shared for all those years. Now that she knew, with absolute certainty, that what she felt for Mitchell was not love, she would not—she *could* not—marry him.

Good looks, money, power . . . None of it was worth a damn without true love. She had tried to convince herself that her idea of love did not exist in the real world. But deep down, she didn't believe that. *I found it once,* she thought. *I won't settle for less.*

Yes, Dan was dead. But she had found a way to get through that. Today it was no longer the man that she missed as much as the love they once shared.

Ashleigh replaced the lid on the flowers, tucked the box under her arm, and headed for the kitchen. She wrote a note for her cleaning lady: *There is another box of roses in the refrigerator. Please take them.* She placed it under the magnetic clip on the refrigerator door, then swung open the door and set the flowers kitty-corner on an empty shelf.

As the door swished shut, she frowned, looking up pointedly at the kitchen clock. It wasn't even six thirty yet. Mitchell hadn't left much before midnight. He had the money and the power to do some amazing things, but how had he managed to get these flowers here so early?

CHAPTER
13

As Ashleigh drove down Alvorada, the answer came to her with sudden clarity, as if a glass of ice water had been pitched in her face. She saw Christine Yates, Mitchell's devoted secretary, with the key to Ashleigh's condo in her slim, smooth hand. Could it have been she who had delivered the bouquet, she who had arranged for the flowers at Gran's memorial service? Mitchell could call on Miss Yates at any time, and she prided herself on always being able to deliver. Ashleigh suspected that Miss Yates had been in love with him for years. Yes, it was obvious. Miss Yates had delivered the white roses.

When Ashleigh turned off Alvorada onto Seventh, the tower of Bentleys Royale, bathed in the brilliance of the reflected sun, came into view. She could have drawn that shape in her sleep.

As she pulled into the upper parking area, a faded-blue Ford sped across her path, scattering fallen leaves and loose gravel. It jerked to a stop several feet from Ashleigh. Leaving the motor still running, the security agent shot out of her car and ran toward the door.

"Sorry I'm late, Miss McDowell." She dug deep in her oversized handbag, producing a huge ring of keys.

Ashleigh glanced down at her watch; Terri was not late. With only a few associates cleared to enter the store before nine, the associates' entrance was seldom opened before seven forty-five.

Ashleigh smiled. "I just arrived."

"Well, I didn't want you to wait on me." She hesitated, then blurted, "Miss McDowell, I heard that Danielle Norman was missing and . . ."

It had already begun! The Bentleys Royale rumor mill was telegraphing information—though she feared it would be a scarce smattering of facts with a great deal of creative fiction to fill in the gaps.

"Missing?" Ashleigh parroted, waiting for Terri to reveal more.

The security agent confirmed Ashleigh's suspicions: The other buyers, still in New York, were heating up the wires. The gossip would soon be spreading throughout the stores, if it hadn't started already. Mr. Jerome would not be pleased.

With a wan smile Ashleigh said, "Our jungle telegraph seems to be alive and kicking . . . and very creative." Then she slipped past Terri and descended the stairs. She did not stop by her own office. While the offices were quiet, there was something far more important she needed to do.

CHAPTER
14

Ashleigh headed directly to Danielle's congested office on the mezzanine behind the sportswear deck. The buyer's desk, jammed against her assistant's, was cluttered, and her calendar was buried under a mass of computer printouts.

Ashleigh slid into the antiquated desk chair and tugged the oversized calendar free. She scanned the page and spotted *Monday, January 13*. In bold burgundy letters, she saw *LJ, PS*—the initials for the La Jolla and Palm Springs stores—and a solid mass of scribbling, followed by *11:55 Red Eye*. She squinted her eyes and turned the calendar first in one direction and then the other, slanting it at odd angles, but she could not make out the words that had been written under the heavy squiggles.

Giving up, she scanned the next large square: *Tuesday, January 14—8:00 Anne Klein* was the first entry, followed by a list of other resource appointments. Next, on Wednesday the sixteenth—today's date—*Ruthie* was written at the top of the box, followed by more appointments, scheduled one after the other at close intervals, beginning at eight AM and ending at six PM. In the adjacent squares, additional resource names had been printed, but no appointment times were assigned to them. A dark pencil line ran across the boxes, beginning Tuesday the fifteenth and ending Monday the twenty-first, which was marked *Rtn*.

Ashleigh's throat went dry. She stared at her own name written beside *7:30*—the appointment they had scheduled for the morning following Danielle's planned return.

Pushing the calendar back, she pulled Danielle's Rolodex toward her and began fingering through the cards. If Danielle had listed Ruthie's number under anything but *R*, there was little hope of finding it. She flipped through scores of cards, finally reaching the one she was after. As she suspected, it was filed under *R* with the name *Ruthie* printed in Danielle's familiar script, followed by a seven-digit number.

Ashleigh plucked the phone from the cradle and dialed the number. There was no answer, and no answering machine picked up. She stared at the phone as it continued to ring, then hung up and began to search for a scrap of paper. She pulled open the top desk drawer.

The contrast inside the desk drawer was startling. Inside, everything was sparse, neat, and orderly. Her eyes fell on a tidy bundle of burgundy felt-tip pens. Then she noticed the familiar soft-pink notepaper, bordered in burgundy, with three tiny butterflies in the upper left-hand corner.

As Ashleigh reached for a pen, a fresh, clean scent filled the small room. Turning her head, she saw Conrad Taylor in the doorway. *What is* he *doing here?*

"Good morning," he said. "I hadn't expected to find anyone in so early." His dark hair fell rakishly over equally dark brows, contrasting with the formality of his three-piece suit.

"I usually come in early," she said.

He nodded, then changed the subject. "I was surprised that David Jerome asked you to accompany Pocino last night."

Before she could respond, he murmured, "It's so out of character for her." His eyes scanned the cramped office before coming to rest on Ashleigh's.

She resisted the temptation to ask how he knew what was or was not out of character for Danielle, and why he'd come to her office. "Mr. Taylor—," she began.

A smile warmed his face. "Please, call me Conrad."

Swiveling the chair slightly to face him squarely, she nodded. Unable to take her mind off Danielle's calendar, she twisted back around and pointed across the two-inch squares. "It certainly doesn't look like Danielle planned to miss her New York appointments."

As he leaned over to get a better look, his hands firmly planted on the arms of her chair, Ashleigh felt the warmth of his breath on her neck.

His clean, masculine scent surrounded her. She felt an urgent need to move away.

"It most certainly does not," he agreed.

Knowing that she could not move without pushing the chair straight into him, she discreetly leaned farther forward. It was no good; the scent followed her. Just as she was about to excuse herself, her foot touched something beneath Danielle's desk and she let out a soft cry.

Conrad stepped away from her chair.

Ashleigh leaned back, cocked her head in an attempt to see under the desk, quickly slid the chair backward and bent down, then, lightheaded sat back and stared up at Conrad. She clutched a handbag in her fist.

It was the oversized Louis Vuitton handbag that Danielle always carried.

Setting the LV bag on top of the calendar, she slowly unbuckled the main compartment. It was stuffed to capacity. Her head buzzing with possibilities, she tugged on a burgundy eel-skin wallet with an unsteady hand. "Everything's here," she said, her voice so low that Conrad had to step closer. "Even her driver's license." There were several business cards, seventeen dollars, some loose coins, and her credit cards—an alarming number of which were for department and specialty stores.

Conrad cleared a space on the less cluttered desk of Danielle's assistant, Jan, and reached for the bag. "Would you hand me that, please?" he asked, pointing to an empty container on the bookshelf.

Ashleigh placed the shallow carton on the top of the desk.

He spread the contents of the handbag inside the confines of the cardboard container, then handed her Danielle's per diem check, her Continental Airlines ticket, and a folded piece of paper. He continued to look through the remaining pile: makeup, Kleenex, pencils, spare business cards, and other detritus.

Ashleigh stepped back from the desk. Her knees felt like they might give way.

Conrad looked at her as if the flush she felt had drained the color from her face. "Sit down," he said, pulling the chair around for her. He gestured toward the pile on the desk, then continued to pore through the accumulation.

Ashleigh unfolded the paper he had handed her. "It's Danielle's itinerary," she said. "The same as her calendar, just a little more detail."

Conrad looked up. "Such as . . . ?"

"Her last appointment is for three o'clock at Yves Saint Laurent this coming Monday."

Conrad sighed heavily. "The police will have to be called in." He picked up the phone. "But first I'd like to have Pocino on-site."

At eight-twenty Ashleigh cut through her reception area, stopping beside the coffeemaker to punch the button before unlocking her own office.

Conrad had not been able to reach Pocino. Since the security director was due in her office at nine, they had left the handbag and its contents on the assistant buyer's desk and turned the lock located in the middle of the doorknob. Ashleigh had also taped a note on Jan's desk, asking Danielle's assistant to come to her office, and Conrad had gone downtown for his touch-base meeting with Mark Toddman, the CEO.

Ashleigh entered her office, sat down automatically, reached for a yellow pad, and began writing. She had to bring some sort of order to her mind—had to prevent it from going in circles. Sick inside, she listed what she currently knew about Danielle and what was left to find out.

The list complete, she reached for the phone and dialed 233, the extension for Dorothea Sable. The busy signal vibrated in her ear. That was a good sign. Dorothea generally arrived early, preferring to make her calls to New York before the daily onslaught that meant limited access to the vital trunk lines.

Ashleigh hung up, cradled the phone, then hit the speaker button and punched redial. The buzzing began anew as she deposited her handbag in the credenza cabinet. No telling how long this might continue; Dorothea did most of her business by telephone. On the third try, though, Dorothea picked up the phone.

Ashleigh got straight to the point. "What do you know about Jeff Bradley?"

After a brief hesitation, Dorothea said, "Ashleigh, what I have to say is for your ears only. Danielle has been seeing quite a lot of him." Again she hesitated. "Nothing romantic," she added. "You know he used to be our Men's Furnishings buyer."

"Yes."

"Well, then you must know that he was fired. And why."

Ashleigh didn't know the whole story, but she did not venture to say so. Dorothea soon admitted that the buyers didn't actually know the grounds for his termination, although this had not curtailed speculation.

As soon as she got off the phone, Ashleigh intended to locate Jeff Bradley's personnel file. Hopefully it hadn't been purged.

"What else do you know about Bradley?" she asked.

"Well, I suppose you know that he's one of Danielle's resources." Dorothea spoke softly now. "Lady Adrianna is a terrific line. I just hope that . . . Oh, never mind."

"You hope that Danielle's purchases aren't too heavy with that vendor?" Ashleigh filled in.

"I've already said too much. Please don't get me wrong. I'm extremely fond of Danielle, and I think she has her head screwed on pretty straight. She knows her patron."

There was a brief silence. Ashleigh asked, "Is there anything else you can tell me?"

"Not much. Only . . . I heard that Mr. Jerome gave Bradley a good recommendation for a buying position at Robinson's." She hesitated before adding, "Bradley had a messy divorce while he was here. And I think he has a couple of kids."

When at last Ashleigh dropped the phone in the cradle, she tried to sort out what she'd learned. It was not quite twenty-four hours since Danielle had missed her appointment in New York, but Ashleigh could no longer deny that Danielle was in serious trouble.

Could Jeff Bradley be involved in Danielle's disappearance? If so, what was his motive?

If Danielle was alive . . . Ashleigh refused to think about the alternative. She shot up from the chair and hurried through the doorway to Betty's vacant desk. Pulling open the top right-hand drawer, she felt for the file cabinet key in the far corner, found it, then crossed the room and unlocked the file drawers.

She knelt down and pulled the bottom drawer open—the one that housed records of terminated executives. Fingering through the fat files under *B*, she found Bradley's folder. It was an unusually thin one, but she was in luck: There was a passport-size photo—an amenity that had gone by the wayside in recent rounds of budget cuts. Bradley's face was familiar. Fine-boned, an aristocratic nose, small eyes set close together. She'd seen him in the store frequently, often with his ubiquitous vendor sample trunk. In fact, it seemed that she had seen him quite recently, maybe even this week, but she wasn't sure.

She leafed through the file and finally spotted the phrase *Grounds for Termination*. The verbiage was vague: "questionable vendor dealings." Weren't those nearly the exact words that Pocino had used? It was the typical Personnel mumbo jumbo that drove Ashleigh wild. This type of weasel wording was a sure sign that management had a strong conviction about Bradley's wrongdoings but was not prepared to go to court.

This conjured up a multitude of possibilities. Had Jeff Bradley given too much business to a single vendor? Or could his negotiations have driven a vendor out of business? While buyers were challenged to get the best value—meaning the best price and the finest-quality goods—company policy prohibited merchants from taking unfair advantage. No, it must have been something more blatant; otherwise, the record would be specific. Perhaps vendor kickbacks?

As Ashleigh remembered Dorothea's words, her thoughts went in a different direction. *Mr. Jerome would never recommend a thief for a buying job. Not even to the competition.* She unconsciously tapped her fingers on the outside of the file folder. Scanning the sheets from top to bottom, she found no additional clues.

"You're here bright and early," came a voice from the connecting doorway as Pocino sauntered through. Unsightly water rings spotted the front of his navy blazer, and he tugged at his belt, worn just below his ample belly. "Terri said you arrived before she did."

"Barely." She slipped Bradley's folder back in the file. "Mr. Taylor tried to reach you about an hour ago."

"Just came from Ms. Norman's office. Police are on their way."

"What do you think?"

"Jury's still out. Gotta admit, most dames don't go running off without their purse."

Ashleigh felt cold. Maybe it had been better when Pocino had challenged her. She gestured to the coffee machine and the tray of empty mugs. "Help yourself," she said, slipping the file key back into Betty's desk.

Pocino strode to her office instead. She followed and almost ran into him when he stopped abruptly in the doorway.

With a puzzled frown above his heavy brows, he asked, "This your office?"

"You know it is."

"Where in the hell . . . Sorry. Where's your desk?" He nodded in the direction of the large round table.

"I prefer this," she said, slipping between the credenza and the table and into her chair.   Pocino remained standing, a scowl on his broad face. "But you've got no drawers."

"I do." Ashleigh laid her hand on the eight-foot credenza. The dark walnut veneer was identical to that of the round table in front of her. Locks with inconspicuous keyholes had been added to the file drawers on either side of the cabinet's sliding doors. This setup suited Ashleigh's work style.

"To each his own." Pocino grinned as he pulled out a chair across from Ashleigh and plopped down. "Looks like it belongs in a dining room, if you ask me."

I didn't, she thought. She had a lot more than furniture on her mind.

He smiled broadly after she filled him in on what she had learned about Bradley. "Maybe I was wrong about you. You just might be in the wrong field. The only problem is, you still seem to be hung up on Danielle Norman's innocence."

"I don't know what I believe." She shifted the focus. "Mr. Jerome has asked Chris Ferrari to pull all the vendor transactions for Danielle's departments for the past six weeks."

"So I've heard." A grimace marked Pocino's round face.

Heavy footfalls pounded down the corridor, stopping just short of the door. "Anybody here?" Ferrari shouted before pushing on the half-open door and bursting into the office. In his hand he held up a clutch of papers. "Here it is!"

Ashleigh looked from Pocino to Ferrari. The store had not yet opened, and Ferrari was without his suit jacket. In his colorful paisley-print suspenders and rolled-up shirtsleeves, and with his dark eyes and jet-black hair, he fit right in with a central casting image of a Mafia hit man. His expression made him look as if he was ready to explode. He held out an inch-high stack of vendor printouts with the computer-feed margins still attached.

"Danielle Norman put through purchases in excess of three hundred thousand dollars, the lion's share going to Lady Adrianna, Medley Originals, and a so-called La Salliano.

"I checked on La Salliano. There's no such vendor on the books. Not on I. Magnin's, Saks', or Neiman's. And they just appeared on ours this month. Somehow they have a duns number for billing."

He shot a glance at Ashleigh and explained, "A number issued by Dunn and Bradstreet is required by all creditors."

She nodded, not bothering to say that she knew what a duns number was.

"But nobody knows how this La Salliano got one. No one knows anything about them. They're phony as hell."

CHAPTER
17

Ferrari watched the color drain from Ashleigh's face. He seemed to be enjoying her discomfort.

He fanned the results of his painstaking research across the table as Pocino heaved himself out of the chair to get a good look at the paperwork.

"Well, that about wraps it up. No wonder the dame's taken a powder." Pocino looked pointedly from Ferrari to Ashleigh. "By now, it's crystal clear that Danielle Norman's no wide-eyed innocent."

Pushing a wisp of hair out of her expressive dark eyes, Ashleigh rose to her feet and slipped around one of the high-backed chairs for a better view. Ferrari stepped back as Ashleigh studied the printouts.

Their positions made them natural adversaries. While ultimately responsible for the budgets, he had damned little control. His hands were tied as long as the personnel director of the headquarters store reported to Ashleigh—and not to him, as he felt she should. With Ashleigh ultimately in control of salary increases and hiring rates, he was screwed. And he'd learned there was no point in going to the boss when she exceeded the salary guidelines, which she often did. She had Jerome's ear, and her standard justification, "We must be competitive if we want to hire and retain quality associates," invariably won the old man's support. The hell with the havoc it rained on his painstakingly planned budget—and so on his own annual performance review. His last rating was "good," which was only good enough for the company to fork out a meager three percent pay increase. With the burden of having to maintain that cursed Bentleys Royale image, he was barely making it on his pittance of a salary.

Ferrari had another card to play. Medley Originals, owned and operated by none other than Ashleigh's wealthy fiancé, was a major contributor to Danielle's overbought status.

The impact of his revelation hit the intended mark. Ashleigh had not launched into her usual battery of incisive questions. But knowing it wouldn't take her long to regroup, he said, "We don't have all the answers, but we've surfaced one hell of a lot of questions."

Finally, she spoke. "Did you check the purchase orders?"

"Of course! A sad attempt at forging Adele's signature."

Ashleigh frowned. "Even if these orders went through"—her slim finger pointed down to the printouts—"wouldn't our merchandising control systems prevent payments for merchandise before it's received?" She looked to Ferrari for confirmation. Then, as if it had just occurred to her, she asked, "Have payments been made to the phony vendor?"

"Central Purchasing is looking into it as we speak. But whether she got away with it or not isn't the point. The intention is clear."

"I know it looks bad," she replied, again indicating the damning evidence on the table, "but I just can't believe that Danielle is capable of stealing from Bentleys Royale, or anyone else."

As Ashleigh dropped back into her chair, Pocino shook his head, chuckling. "Boy, have you lost your perspective on this one."

"I don't think it's a laughing matter. But since you seem to know all the answers, where is she now? And why would she leave her handbag and all her identification behind?"

"Maybe she has a new identity." Pocino smiled cynically. "And for that kind of skullduggery, I'd say she had the perfect partner. Damned clever, if you ask me. A purse left behind—the perfect red herring for buying a chunk of time."

Ashleigh challenged him instantly, asking, "Explain to me, then—why would Danielle abandon her home? It's her only real asset, and she even arranged to have it cleaned. And why would she leave her car in the parking lot if—"

"Hold it." Pocino held up a beefy hand. "There you go again! Who said Danielle left her car? It sure as hell isn't here."

"Are you trying to tell me she was here yesterday morning?" Ferrari asked.

"Maybe—maybe not." Pocino rocked back on his heels. "The police should be here any minute, and I'm keeping in touch with Sergeant Flynn. There's already an APB out on her car. We're not letting this broad take off with all that dough."

Ashleigh glared at Pocino, and he said no more. It seemed to have quelled him—for only a moment. After an awkward silence, he pointed to the flashing light on her telephone.

"Hey. I must be going deaf."

Ashleigh heard the faint ringing from Betty's office. Her eyes riveted on Pocino, she picked up the receiver. After a brief pause, she said, "It's for you," and handed the phone to him.

"Sergeant Flynn."

Pocino spoke into the receiver. "What's up?" For a minute or two he just listened, then said, "Look, Flynn, I told you I thought the dame was on the take. Well, we've got the proof. Over three hundred thousand dollars in unauthorized orders, and we've uncovered a fictitious vendor." He paused. "Okay . . . Where do we go from here? Well, how about Bradley? . . . Yeah, got it. Keep in touch . . . Hold it! How about a credit check? . . . Great. Call me back at extension 315. I'll be here for the next hour or so. Ciao."

Pocino returned the receiver to Ashleigh, his closing *Ciao* still piercing the silence of the room.

"What did he say?" Ashleigh asked.

Pocino balanced himself on the edge of the credenza and crossed one hefty leg over the other. "Well, let me fill you in. They haven't located the car, but Flynn says homicide is now involved . . ." He turned to Ferrari. "I'll be damned if I know what's keeping those guys. How about checking at the security desk again?"

Ashleigh picked up the phone. "This is Ashleigh McDowell. Have the police arrived?" She paused to wait for the answer. "Please call when they do. Mr. Pocino and Mr. Ferrari are in my office." She replaced the receiver.

"Anyway," Pocino continued, "no problem getting a search warrant now. The car could be in the garage, but my guess is they left town by car—could be hers or maybe Bradley's."

Unable to hold back, Ashleigh said, "It makes no sense. Three hundred thousand dollars is a lot of money, but hardly enough—"

"They were probably headed for some out-of-town airport," Pocino said, ignoring her. "Flynn will get that search warrant for Norman's garage and her pad ASAP, but they've got nothing on Bradley to authorize a search." He went on, "You're probably right about the money. There's most likely more currency unaccounted for."

Then, without warning, he sprang to his feet and hit his head with the heel of his palm. "That's it! The resource Bradley represents now—it's Lady Adrianna. I'd be willing to bet that Lady Adrianna finds themselves short of merchandise, and that Bradley has also been doing a bit of creative bookkeeping." He settled himself firmly on the credenza, lifted his meaty forearms, and clasped his hands behind his head, his jowls lifting in a smirk.

"Wait a minute." Ferrari frowned. "I've been listening to the two of you banter back and forth, and I haven't the foggiest notion what you're talking about. What's this Bradley character got to do with Danielle Norman?"

Ashleigh started to fill him in, until Pocino took over. His speculation went far beyond her own, but now no longer sure of what to believe, she let him continue without interruption.

Their meeting ended when the phone's light flashed, indicating her private line, and the two men left her to answer it. As she suspected, it was Mr. Jerome. His voice sputtered in and out over the distinct blare of his cellular phone. Ashleigh pictured him maneuvering his full-sized Cadillac down the crowded streets of Los Angeles, and she tried to ignore the crackle of background static. She and the entire management team had learned to edit their communications while the boss was behind that wheel.

This morning his message was simple and direct. He was about five minutes from the store and would like to see her as soon as he arrived.

She hung up, immediately reached for her yellow pad, and began jotting down the salient points of what she needed to tell him. Though she'd spoken to him the night before from Hamburger Hamlet, now there was so much more to relay. She must organize her thoughts quickly.

Interrupted again by her private line, Ashleigh was tempted to ignore it. But her compulsive nature prevailed and she picked it up—to her immediate regret.

"I tried to reach you last night," came the voice over the line. Adele Watson cleared her throat. "I suppose you've heard about the spot Danielle Norman has left us in?"

Ashleigh leaned forward on one elbow, not bothering to answer the rhetorical question. She cradled the receiver on her shoulder and found herself drawing circles in the margins of her yellow pad.

Adele continued, "Well, my dear, just let me tell you . . . If only the *powers that be* had listened to me, we wouldn't be in this mess."

Ashleigh closed her eyes. She couldn't stomach this conversation right now. "Adele, I need to call you back. I was just on my way to Mr. Jerome's office when you called."

"No, I'll be in the market. I'll call you this afternoon to discuss candidates to replace Danielle Norman. And, my dear, since you'll be seeing the boss, you might want to run one possibility by him: Sue Barns."

It was pointless to remind Adele that Sue had been in her position for only six weeks.

"I'll be back on Saturday," Adele continued, "and I'd like to interview Sue."

"I'll talk with you this afternoon," Ashleigh replied.

The receiver was midway between her ear and the phone cradle when she heard Adele bleat, "Another thing . . ."

Always another thing. Today, Ashleigh had no time to indulge Adele's endless litany of dissatisfactions. She continued the downward motion of the receiver until it rested firmly in the cradle.

A few minutes later, as she stepped from the elevator, an earsplitting blare assaulted her ears.

Jerome was at the end of the corridor, calmly withdrawing a small leather notepad from his inside breast pocket. He glanced up and gave Ashleigh a nod, then slowly began to punch numbers into the panel to the left of the office door. In spite of the ear-piercing racket, he asked, "Did Adele finally get in touch with you?"

Finally? "Yes," she replied. If Adele had, in fact, tried to reach Ashleigh earlier, she'd left no message. But explanations invariably sounded like excuses, so she said nothing further.

The alarm continued to echo off the walls of the narrow corridor. Two security agents arrived as Jerome punched in the last number. He quickly waved them off. "Sorry to bother you."

After brief *Good mornings*, the agents were on their way—no questions asked. This was not the first time the preoccupied president had set off the alarm.

Jerome stopped to pick up a pile of papers from his inbox on Méchie's desk before heading to his own desk.

As Ashleigh took her usual place across from him, she noticed that Mr. Jerome had not removed his jacket. *He must have an appointment with someone from the outside.* She quickly reorganized her agenda.

Jerome began, "By the way, I stopped by Personnel and told Catherine to fire Walt Adams if he came in late again today."

"I'll look into it when I get back to my office." She'd learned neither to challenge nor to ask questions until she had all the facts, and she trusted that her new personnel director would not blindly follow the president's dictates.

He pressed the intercom button and began flipping through papers.

"Yes, Mr. Jerome." Méchie's voice echoed into the room.

"The moment the committee members from California Heritage arrive, please buzz me."

If only he'd put the papers down, thought Ashleigh. She needed his undivided attention.

In answer to her silent request, Jerome looked up and said, "I spoke to Ferrari briefly. He's coming up later with the details on the Better Sportswear purchases." He paused. "As much as we have so far . . . I'd like to have our own house in order before Central goes poking around."

He stopped abruptly. A familiar expression registered on his face, and Ashleigh knew even before he reached for the phone what he intended to do. He hit the speaker button and punched in Ferrari's extension.

Ferrari answered his own phone, as was his habit. He did everything in his power to avoid criticism from the boss. In Ashleigh's opinion, Ferrari had the most difficult job in the organization. His peers often joked that Ferrari met with Mr. Jerome each morning to outline ways to cut expenses and that he was called up each afternoon to add a new project. This was not entirely untrue. Ferrari's challenge was to keep the aging store in tip-top condition, staffed with quality associates—a no-win situation, since whatever size budget he submitted was cut in the annual expense wars.

"Chris, is Ross Pocino still in the store?"

"He's right here."

Jerome said, "Ashleigh is with me," and shifted in his chair while adjusting the volume. "Put on your speaker so the four of us can talk."

A low click signaled that the speaker had been switched on.

"Ross?"

"Yes, Mr. Jerome, I'm here." Pocino's voice came across loudly, but somewhat restrained and formal, over the usual background noise.

"Thank you for your help last night and for being here this morning." Jerome paused in his methodical manner. "It goes without saying that we have a sensitive situation. You're a professional, and I don't have to tell you that these recent findings are not to be grist for the rumor mill." Continuing in that plodding cadence that Ashleigh found to be so nerve-racking, he said, "This could be just the tip of the iceberg, and I want to make sure it's not discussed outside the doors of these offices." As though addressing children, he concluded, "Is that understood?"

Ashleigh nodded her head as the two men voiced their agreement.

Almost as an afterthought, Jerome added, "Ross, I realize you must discuss this with your boss, but no one other than Mr. Taylor should be privy to these preliminary findings." Pocino knew to wait out Jerome's next pause, after which the president asked, "Do you have any trouble with that?" He received the commitment he was after and disengaged the phone.

Between the interruptions of Méchie's arrival, his instructions to her, and a phone call from one of his tennis buddies, Ashleigh told Mr. Jerome about finding Danielle's handbag and shared what she'd learned about Jeff Bradley.

Adjusting his position, Jerome leaned forward, his arms folded. "O'Brien called soon after you left last night. I don't have to tell you that we don't always see eye to eye regarding the role of Personnel, your role in particular, but he was right about one thing: I was wrong in sending you to Danielle Norman's."

Ashleigh started to object, but the president's look was foreboding. "He asked if I thought you could be objective regarding Danielle." The lines on his forehead deepened. "What I want to know is, how much does O'Brien know about your relationship with Danielle Norman?"

Where to begin? O'Brien knew far more about her personal life than Mr. Jerome did. Though Ashleigh maintained a purely professional relationship with O'Brien, she had been an assistant in Bentley's corporate Personnel when Danielle had come to her. O'Brien had been her mentor, and before she'd crossed the line from the department stores division, he had taken a rather paternal interest in her.

She shifted her mind back to the present. *Just give a simple answer. Enough of the truth to satisfy Mr. Jerome,* Ashleigh said to herself as she saw the president strumming his fingers on the edge of his desk.

"Mr. O'Brien knows that Danielle lived with my grandmother when she first came to California and that she finished her last year of high school and started at Long Beach City College while she lived there. He also knows that I helped her get her first job in retail at Buffum's."

"It's too bad she didn't stay there." He stopped when she winced. "I'm sorry. That's not fair. It's not even true. I'm just so damned frustrated. I believed in that girl." He removed his glasses and rubbed the bridge of his nose. "You told me that your personal relationship with Danielle had no bearing on your professional one. You told me that you could be objective, and I believed you." His tone was sharp and his sense of betrayal undisguised. "Is this still the case?"

Ashleigh did not look away; she wanted to, but she didn't. She straightened her back and sat tall. "Yes," she responded, although she was beginning to doubt that she could maintain her professional objectivity when it came to Danielle. Especially now, when her fate was unknown.

"It slipped my mind that Danielle was almost a family member during your time in the Bentley's corporate offices. O'Brien's challenge knocked me off balance." Holding his glasses by one of the temples, Jerome swung them slowly to and fro in a hypnotic, thoughtful motion.

The word *objective* was still ringing in her ears. How could she be objective about Danielle? She'd thought that she could separate her personal relationship from her job performance. Now she wasn't sure. All she wanted was to know that Danielle was alright, that she was still alive. *To hell with the job.*

"Let's not belabor the point." The president's tone was harsh. "You must distance yourself from this current Danielle Norman situation. Do you understand?"

Ashleigh understood, but he was asking the impossible.

"It's not enough that *I* believe in you. To be any good to me and to Bentleys Royale, you must maintain the confidence and respect of Toddman and O'Brien as well as everyone else." Jerome pushed back in his chair, opened the file drawer at the bottom of his desk, and rested his legs—crossed at the ankles—on top of the open drawer. A sure sign that this lecture was not to be brief. "With performance reviews coming up, your credibility must be impeccable." His charcoal-gray eyes bored into hers, and he repeated, "Is that understood?"

Again she nodded, a lump forming in her throat.

"The only role you are to have regarding Danielle Norman is to find her replacement. Understood?"

Ashleigh's head was swimming. She didn't respond, but Mr. Jerome seemed so wrapped up in what he had to say that he didn't seem to notice.

"I don't question your objectivity." His face softened. "And I'm not trying to put the onus on you. We both believed in Danielle, and I thought she had the ability to pull it together. I appreciated you backing me on the extended probation." His eyes drifted from hers toward the patio. "It seemed the right thing to do—right for the business and the only fair decision for a dedicated young buyer with a superb taste level." He heaved a sigh. "Apparently, we were wrong."

Shifting to the next business at hand, Jerome asked about Adele Watson's call and handled as routine her request for candidates to replace Danielle.

After the initial impact of Adele's call, Ashleigh too had had to admit that it was prudent to prepare a list of potential candidates to take Danielle's place. She tried to focus objectively on the candidates, but her head was filled with pictures of Danielle's courageous battle against tremendous odds to save her job. And even this would now be taken from her.

"Ashleigh." Jerome's voice broke into her thoughts. "I have no intention of setting up interviews until we know more." He leaned back in the chair, his arms stretched back and resting behind his head. "How about Dorothea Sable's assistant?"

It took her a moment to realize that Jerome had jumped back to considering candidates. She knew he couldn't possibly keep track of all the young executives and their current performance. He often relied on gut instinct instead. But his instincts, she had to admit, were more often right than wrong. Still, Ashleigh answered, "She's not promotable. Her last performance evaluation was only *good*."

He did not challenge her, at least not for the moment. Instead he moved on to Sue Barns, the La Jolla divisional merchandise manager whom Adele had requested to interview.

Ashleigh felt her energy drain. *Maybe Ferrari's isn't the most difficult position after all.* With carefully chosen words, she reminded Mr. Jerome of his promise to the vice president of stores that a store's divisional merchandise manager would remain in position a minimum of one full year. Then she sat back and prepared herself for his predictable wrath and the rationale that she could almost recite verbatim.

"Ashleigh, I don't know if Sue is the right candidate or not, but if she is, there's no need for her to be in a suburban store for a year. If she still wants to be a general manager in the future, there's no reason why she can't become one. As long as she proves she can get results and she's the best candidate, she can learn on the job, just like the others."

And be a roaring success like some of our recent appointments. The one in the Newport Beach store was proving to be premature, Ashleigh thought sardonically, but she held her tongue. She would fight for the sake of Sue's long-range career goals and for the store, but not now. She knew of two candidates who were far more suitable for the Better Sportswear position.

"How about some of the other assistants?"

Ashleigh sighed inwardly. She had hoped she could delay presenting their names to him until the next time they met. She leaned down, picked up her organizer, and flipped to the assistant buyer section.

Just in time, the intercom blared, and Jerome punched the speaker button.

"Mr. Ferrari wants to know if he should come back later." Méchie's use of the director of operations' surname indicated there was someone besides the two of them in her office.

"No. Tell him I'll be with him in just a minute."

As Ashleigh pushed the armchair away from his desk, he reminded her, "I am quite serious about your staying clear of any involvement in the Danielle Norman affair other than what is directly related to her replacement."

She rose and gave a nod to indicate that she had heard what he said. She knew that she could not do as he asked. She must tell him so—but not now. "I will make a list of candidates for Better Sportswear with all the relevant background," she said and quickly added, "That will be on your desk by tomorrow morning."

Before Ashleigh reached the door at the opposite end of the corridor, Ferrari called out to her. He was midway between Méchie's and the president's office. When she turned, he said in his casual, by-the-way manner, "What's the best way to reach Mitchell Wainwright?"

CHAPTER
20

"Miss McDowell."

The deep, resonant tone was unmistakable. Ashleigh stopped in mid-stride, just past the double doors that led into the associates' cafeteria. Dean Delaney walked toward her, carrying a Styrofoam cup. A slim, middle-aged man, Delaney was the Men's Clothing buyer. While his manner tended to be formal, he had a wonderful sense of humor and was respected by his peers. But today, as she walked across the polished tiles to meet him, Ashleigh noticed that Dean's smile fell short of his eyes.

"I need to talk to you about Danielle Norman and Jeff Bradley."

Two men from Marking and Receiving walked in, their loud voices echoing off the walls of the small room. Almost in chorus they smiled and said, "Morning, Miss McDowell." Spotting Delaney, one said, "Glad we ran into you, Mr. Delaney. You've got some merchandise in trouble." He frowned and bit down on his lower lip in concentration. "Hickey Freeman, I think. Anyway, the truck's here from the DC, and they said they can't leave it because they don't have any paperwork."

"They still here?" Delaney's voice rose in alarm.

"Just have a few racks to unload. You might still catch 'em."

Delaney turned to Ashleigh and said, "I've got to run." He thrust the Styrofoam cup into her hands and bolted to the back door and down the broad concrete staircase.

So much for calm, cool, and collected. She took a sip of the untouched and steaming coffee, then walked over and set the cups in one of the plastic boxes on the convayer belt. Her mind turned to Delaney's unfinished message, and she was tempted to run after him.

She tried to distract herself, to avoid the issue of Danielle's disappearance as Mr. Jerome had asked her to, all the while knowing in her heart that she couldn't just leave Danielle's fate in the hands of people who didn't care personally for her. Still, by the time she reached the first level, she had her morning agenda organized. She passed the pay phones; then, impulsively resetting her priorities, she headed for Danielle's department.

There was a hum of activity in the Cosmetics department as the associates tidied their displays. It occurred to Ashleigh that it probably was not much different from the way it was in the days when young starlets like Angela Lansbury, June Lockhart, and Nancy Davis, now the wife of President Reagan, stood behind these very counters. She returned the greeting of several associates, noting their clear, glowing complexions.

She rounded the corner of the Men's Fragrance counter and headed to Better Sportswear—a showcase of Danielle's merchandise presentation skills. The shortage of new, transitional merchandise, however, was apparent even to Ashleigh's untrained eye. So where was all the unauthorized merchandise? A pleasant, rather rotund associate was assisting a petite patron in the selection of an Anne Klein blazer. Despite the associate's own proportions, which hardly resembled the patron profile for the department, Ashleigh knew she had an outstanding following. The associate gave Ashleigh a quick smile, then immediately returned her full attention to the patron.

Ashleigh fingered through the Medley Originals sweaters, which were displayed in new Lucite bins, and looked up when the associate returned from the dressing room, her dark eyes filled with enthusiasm. She pointed to her special twenty-four-karat, gold-plated associates' badge with two sparkling diamond chips, which identified Angela as a member of the honorary Hundred-Thousand-Dollar Club. Though inflation had more than doubled the average sale over the past two decades, for the sake of morale, the sales requirement for the honorary club had not been raised.

The associate's pride was telegraphed through every pore when Ashleigh congratulated her.

"We just received more Medley sweaters from La Jolla. I haven't checked them in yet, but I know Mrs. Norman would love for you to see them. They're in the stockroom."

"Thank you, Angela, but I must get to my office."

As Ashleigh hurried off down the alternate staircase located near the north entrance of the store, she wondered why Danielle had transferred merchandise from La Jolla. Although she was not familiar with the sophisticated computerized reports, Ashleigh knew that buyers planned sales and stock by store. Buyers rarely consolidated merchandise in the headquarters store except during a major sale. But Medley Originals seldom, if ever, went on sale, and the ones that she'd just seen in the bins were not reduced in price.

What had Danielle been thinking? Something was terribly wrong.

Holding the receiver to her ear, Betty looked up as Ashleigh reached for her messages. "She just walked in." Betty pointed to the receiver and whispered, "It's Mrs. Wainwright."

Ashleigh stopped in her tracks. *Mitchell's mother is the last person I want to talk to.* "I'll be right with her."

Betty placed the call on hold.

Stepping into her office, Ashleigh sighed. *If only I hadn't insisted that Betty refrain from screening my calls . . .*

She threw her organizer on the table, slid into her chair, and reached for the phone—but paused. Betty stood in the doorway with a look on her face that said, "I need to talk to you *now*." Ashleigh looked at her expectantly.

"Catherine needs to see you right away."

Ashleigh smiled. Mr. Jerome's directive to fire an associate on the spot had most likely left the personnel director reeling. "Ask her to come over in about ten minutes." Then she picked up the receiver. "Hello, Naomi. Sorry to keep you waiting." She tried to sound bright and cheerful, but knew she failed miserably.

"It's too bad you weren't able to make it to the symphony. It was marvelous." Without taking a breath, Naomi Wainwright continued, "I tried to reach you this morning. Did you know that your answering machine is not working?"

Ashleigh smiled to herself. Last night after Mitchell left, she had turned it off.

Naomi rattled on. "I spoke to Mitchell this morning . . . Is everything alright?"

Would Mitchell have told his mother anything about their confrontation last night? Somehow Ashleigh knew he would not. *If only he had. Maybe that would help put an end to this charade.* She twisted the ring on her finger. She disliked being less than honest, but she sidestepped the question. "Why do you ask?"

"Mitchell seemed so . . . well, so uptight when he called."

Ashleigh could picture the woman sitting in the spacious room that she called her "morning room." She had never been at ease with Mitchell's mother, even though the stylish older woman tried to be friendly. She often felt tongue-tied around her—as she did now.

"I think his mind is on the negotiations for the Atlanta company," Ashleigh said.

"Yes, I'm sure you're right, but I do worry about him. He's taken on so much since his father's illness. Well, never mind. I know you must be busy, so I'll get on with it. We're giving a small reception for the McNabs. The governor just appointed Ronald to the Superior Court, and we thought . . ." She took a breath. "Mitchell *has* introduced you to the McNabs, hasn't he?"

"Yes." Ashleigh glanced down at her small clock. It was nearly ten thirty. She had to think quickly. "Thank you for the invitation, but I'll be in Palm Springs this weekend." She began formulating plans as they spoke. Naomi Wainwright was not used to taking no for an answer.

"Oh, that's a shame. Will you be in the store tomorrow?"

"Yes."

"That's lovely, dear. I plan to be in L.A. What time do you have lunch?"

"I'm afraid I won't be able to break away for lunch."

"Nonsense, my dear. Surely David allows you time to eat lunch! If you'd like, I'll give him a jingle."

The tension was thick enough to scrape off the pale blue walls. Ashleigh was aware of the friendship between Mr. Jerome and Mitchell's parents, dating back a decade or so. "That won't be necessary." She couldn't quite manage to dislodge the icy note from her tone. "I'll clear my calendar. How about one o'clock?" She penciled in the time and said, "I'll meet you up in the tearoom."

After concluding the phone call, Ashleigh buzzed Catherine Bannister on the intercom. "Give me about five more minutes and then bring the file on Walt Adams."

Not bothering to return the receiver to the cradle, Ashleigh pushed the button for her outside line and dialed Danielle's number yet again. The answering machine clicked on after the fourth ring. While the recorded message was still playing, she spoke over it. "Please, pick up the phone. Danielle or Ruthie, please—"

As the recorded message ended, someone picked up the phone.

Ashleigh held her breath.

"Mrs. Norman's residence," a hesitant voice answered.

"Is this Ruthie?" Ashleigh asked.

When the woman confirmed that it was, Ashleigh introduced herself and said, "Danielle asked me to pick up some papers for her. Could you leave the key?"

"Didn't Miss Norman tell you where it's kept?" Ruthie asked. There was an unmistakable ring of suspicion in her voice.

"It was a pretty bad connection," Ashleigh lied. Then she took a chance and said, "She said it was outside the house, but we were cut off before she told me where."

Reluctantly, Ruthie told her where to find the key—in a planter just outside the front door.

"Thank you," Ashleigh said quickly, before hanging up and buzzing Betty. "Please don't make any more appointments for me today."

Danielle Norman's disappearance had hit Bentleys Royale like a tidal wave. In little more than twenty-four hours, the rumor telegraph was well out of hand, tapping out whispered hearsay and speculation in the stairways, the corridors, the small offices, the stockrooms, even the restrooms of the department store—any nook or cranny where people could put their heads together.

At the Bentley's corporate offices, the situation was simply a flash flood—a minor glitch that caused a sudden uproar and then died down quickly. For Conrad Taylor, however, Danielle's disappearance was an unrelenting firestorm that, for the time being, he was forced to shove to the back burner.

In Mark Toddman's spacious corner office, the CEO had touched on the subject briefly, but he had more pressing issues to discuss. Conrad watched Toddman pace back and forth along the same narrow path, threatening to wear a rut in the carpet. The relentless pacing was playing hell with his power of concentration. When he rose to escape it, however, Toddman stopped, met his eyes expectantly, and casually leaned back against the curved edge of his desk.

"I've initiated a twenty percent cut in expenses for the next six weeks," Conrad said. "To be accomplished without a negative impact on customer service," he quickly added. "And I've developed a plan to position ourselves for the future."

Toddman gave a quick nod. "I assume that includes the Royale division."

"Yes." Conrad paused. "Short range, we can't squeeze as much out of their budgets." He sympathized with the challenges of the smaller division. He knew that Jerome had cut out as much fat as could be expected, and that his executives already wore several hats.

Toddman cradled his chin with his cupped right hand, the knuckle of the index finger resting momentarily on his upper lip. His focus seemed to be far beyond the windows. "The cuts we discussed?"

"Mainly."

"I wish there were other alternatives." Toddman shook his head. "But we sure as hell can't go to Consolidated with our tail between our legs, explaining all those good and valid reasons why we fell short of our profit plan. No way to take excuses to the bank. Exceeding our sales plans and retaining our lead in market share is all well and good, but our stockholders look to the bottom line. We need a concrete plan."

He rose from the edge of the desk and thrust his hands deep into his pockets. "This last quarter, every time we overcame the obstacles and thought we were on a roll, the competition dropped the price in one of our major target areas. And now the Broadway is having another midnight sale, and the May Company has moved its early-bird sale up from nine AM to eight AM. With the current everyday sales climate, it won't be long before the after-Christmas sale becomes a nonevent." He paused. "Hell. Why am I spouting off to you! You know the score."

He pointed to a copy of the *Los Angeles Times* spread open on the sofa below the wall-to-wall bookcase. "Did you see this?"

Conrad nodded. The Robinson's preseason ad for twenty percent off had caught his eye. A lightweight Evan Picone blazer was the focus of the illustration. Inclining his head toward the paper, he said, "I figured that would create havoc." Then he frowned. "Unfortunately, there's ample supply in both divisions—stock that has yet to be shipped to the stores."

Toddman began to pace, but stopped short of the windows and spun around. Deep ridges appeared in his forehead.

Mark Toddman was a mover and a shaker in every sense. Tall and lean, with piercing hazel eyes, he'd been on the fast track since his first days in retailing. And as with most motivated young retail executives on the rise, he'd done a fair amount of job hopping—all upward movement—within the Consolidated Department Stores outfit from coast to coast. He had reached his present position two years before and was still a few years shy of fifty. "Did you notice Bentleys Royale's assortment mix in Picone?"

"Afraid not. I only noticed that particular blazer because I was shopping for a birthday gift for my sister."

"Have a comparison run, by style and color, in Picone, Jones of New York, and . . . let's see, how about Anne Klein?"

"Do you mind?" Conrad gestured to the four-inch-square memo box on Toddman's desk.

Toddman nodded. "This is exactly what we talked about the other day. There's a viable spot for both divisions, but there's no point sending buyers from both divisions to New York, Europe, Asia, et cetera, if they select the same assortments." He pushed a sandy lock of hair off his forehead. Giving a dismissive wave with the back of his hand, he changed the subject.

After running through how they could best weather the current "every day" sale storm spreading from coast to coast, they concluded their touch-base. Conrad slipped into his pocket the memo where he'd jotted down the vendor names. "I'll get the specifics down in writing and go over it with you before the management meeting."

Toddman nodded. "It's a shame, but it would take nothing short of a miracle for Bentleys Royale to pull its bottom line up sufficiently in the next six weeks to retain total autonomy. And it sure as hell won't be easy for Jerome to swallow that pill. No one's crazy about relinquishing power."

Conrad agreed and was about to take his leave when Toddman said, "By the way, have you broached the possibilities with him?"

"Yes. Strangely enough, I think he's more willing to consolidate the two buyers' positions than to lose either his Sales Promotion or his Personnel head."

"I thought as much. Actually, when it comes to Ashleigh McDowell, you'll have to battle James O'Brien as well. Since Ashleigh's been at Bentleys Royale, there have been far fewer personnel fiascos."

CHAPTER
23

In the center of the seventh-floor office complex, Conrad stopped at the bank of cubicles and scooped up the messages from his secretary's tidy desk. He walked the few steps into his office, sank into his high-backed desk chair, and thumbed through a healthy stack of pink memos. He stopped when he came to one from Ross Pocino, and immediately punched in Ferrari's extension.

Pocino was on the line within seconds. "Hi, boss. Police have come and gone. Forensics people are taking their own sweet time, but my buddy down at Rampart just delivered some mind-blowing news. It seems this Danielle Norman dame's got credit cards up the wazoo, and they're all spent up to the max."

"Get a list of the credit cards and purchase details," Conrad replied.

"In progress as we speak . . . One thing we already know is that she's got 'em in *all* the major department and specialty stores—more than the ones you saw in her purse."

"Thanks, Pocino. I'd appreciate getting the list as soon as possible."

"Right, boss. Pronto. But hang on to your hat—you ain't heard nothing yet."

Several minutes later, when Conrad disengaged the phone, the evidence of a full-blown and elaborately planned scheme had begun to stack up, and it pointed a finger straight at Danielle.

Leaning back in his swivel chair, Conrad gazed absently up at the ceiling. *Why did Danielle have all those store credit cards?* Most retail personnel confined the majority of their purchases to the store where they worked, since they garnered sizable discounts. *Danielle could be extravagant, and she loved unique and beautiful things, but to forgo a savings of thirty percent or so . . . ?* Conrad stared out the large corner window. *There I go again, evaluating Danielle by my standards.* He shook his head sadly as he recalled Danielle's rationale. When she wanted something, she wanted it *now.* Reason and logic simply did not apply, it seemed—not in her personal life.

Still, in spite of the mounting evidence and this strange detail, he just knew in his heart that she was not involved in crime, that she would not take advantage of her position for personal gain. The Danielle he knew was fiercely loyal to Bentleys Royale and honest to the core. She didn't even cheat on her income taxes.

Conrad dialed Danielle's home number, then swiveled his chair toward the windows. Through the dull haze enveloping the city, he watched a steady stream of traffic moving slowly down the crowded streets. The answering machine immediately clicked on. He didn't leave another message.

At the moment, there was nothing he could do for or about Danielle, but if he didn't get his own act together, he could kiss the presidency of Bentley's good-bye. While rumored to be the leading candidate to fill this powerful position, he knew that he was a long shot. Granted, this had been the carrot that Consolidated, the Bentley's conglomerate, had held out to lure him from Buffum's, the beloved group of family-owned department stores headquartered in Long Beach, which had been taken over by an Australia-based firm. But no one had predicted that the spot would open so soon.

Conrad had called Ralph Lerner, the CEO of Consolidated, the moment Toddman had informed him that the current Bentley's president was resigning to start his own business. Lerner had made no guarantees, but Conrad had been assured that his hat was in the ring. Now it was up to him. Bentley's would not run with a lame duck at the helm for long.

Stepping over to the shelves, he pulled down the three large black notebooks that housed the fourth-quarter expense registers and carried them to the round worktable in front of the floor-to-ceiling windows. No one was going to hand him the presidency on a silver platter. Consolidated had come after him due to his record of results—results that landed squarely on the bottom line. It was once again time to prove himself. He must get results and get them fast.

Success could be as fickle as rain in Southern California, and the nearer the top, the more dependent he was on others. Yet the ultimate responsibility for all decisions in his arena—good, bad, and disastrous— was his alone. And now that major retailers were actively competing to gain market share by dropping prices at ever-increasing speed, the crippling blows to profits were inescapable. Expense control was the key to survival.

As he pored over the expense plans for the remainder of the fourth quarter, squeezing a little here, a little there, the task seemed monumental and hardly worth the effort. At the end of a few hours, he gave up on his open-door policy. Poking his head around the corner of the doorjamb, he said, "Edith, I need about an hour alone. Completely alone. Call me only for an emergency."

As the door clicked behind him, he recalled Churchill's definition of an emergency as nothing short of the armed invasion of the British Isles.

About an hour and a half later he totaled the savings by store, pleased to find that the small economies here and there added up to close to a quarter of a million dollars over the next six weeks. *Not too bad—not bad at all.*

Then Conrad turned his mind to the inevitable executive cuts and changes at Bentleys Royale that must be faced to make a difference for the long haul. After running her own show at Bentleys Royale, Susan Thomas, the Sales Promotion director, would balk at becoming a part of the Bentley's Sales Promotion staff. On the other hand, although Ashleigh was now a big fish in that prestigious but relatively small pond, she was young and bound to enjoy the bigger arena. And in no time at all, she'd most likely fill James O'Brien's shoes. *And very nicely at that,* Conrad couldn't help but think.

Ashleigh's meeting with her headquarters personnel director was interruption free, as she'd requested, but it was difficult for her to give her undivided attention to Catherine's dilemma. Nor had it been easy for Catherine to understand that what Mr. Jerome said was not always precisely what he meant. Ashleigh's mind kept returning to Dean Delaney and his aborted message regarding Danielle and Jeff Bradley.

As Ashleigh had suspected, there was little documentation on Walt Adams's late arrivals, so Catherine could not be expected to blindly follow Jerome's dictate and fire him. What was expected was a plan of action, which she helped Catherine put together.

The minute Catherine slipped out through the connecting door Ashleigh punched the intercom. "Betty, did you get in touch with Dean Delaney?"

"He dropped in while you were with Catherine, but said he couldn't wait. He was going out to the DC."

Ashleigh's heart sank. *Why didn't you interrupt me?* she wanted to shout. But Betty had only been following her instructions. "Did he leave a number where I could reach him?"

"No. He said he'd call you tomorrow." Betty quickly added, "Miss McDowell, I need to talk to you."

"I'll be right there." Ashleigh needed a moment to herself. Pulling her organizer to her and opening it, she checked the afternoon schedule. Laura Cameron at one o'clock—something about her divisional merchandise manager—and a special management meeting at two, and miraculously nothing else had crept onto the pages of her calendar. *Good. That should get me out of here and to Danielle's well before dark.*

This would be her last chance to look around Danielle's before the police began their search. After finding Danielle's handbag, Pocino was certain the wheels would be in motion by morning.

Ashleigh stood up, rotated her shoulders to relieve some of the tension, and then opened the door between her office and Betty's.

"I thought you'd never get out of there!" Betty announced as she handed over three phone messages. "Ms. De Mornay called twice. She sounded upset."

"Betty, I need to leave early today, so unless there's a real emergency, don't schedule any more appointments. I'll return Viviana's call now."

Ashleigh walked back into her office and pulled the door closed. It was twelve thirty. She would see the fashion director before lunch in hopes of limiting the time span of their meeting.

Viviana was not happy when Ashleigh informed her that she would need to come now or wait until morning. "Well, in that case, I guess I'll just have to stop working with my staff on our booklet for Monday's Trend Show for the associates and come now."

Ashleigh ignored her martyred tone, accepting none of the guilt the long-winded fashion director intended.

"Good. I'll see you in about five minutes."

That out of the way, Ashleigh picked up her outside line and dialed.

With nearly everything in Ashleigh's well-ordered life out of kilter, what she needed more than anything else was someone to talk to. Someone who did not work for Bentleys Royale but knew its cast of characters. The only person who fit that bill was Beverly Hoffdahl, her best friend.

After several rings, Bev answered the phone, her voice rising above the background noise of *Sesame Street*.

"Oh, yes, yes, yes," Bev said enthusiastically. "You couldn't have picked a better weekend. Ed and the boys will be at an Indian Guide camp, and Elizabeth and I are on our own. We'll have the house to ourselves and plenty of time to talk. Besides, by Friday night I'll need someone over the age of two to chat with."

This was a relief—especially since Ashleigh had already told Mrs. Wainwright about her plans to visit Palm Springs that weekend. She was about to give Bev a rundown on Danielle's disappearance when lights flashed on Ashleigh's other two lines. "I've got to run."

Bev laughed. "Nothing has changed, I see."

"Not much. But I sure do miss you."

"I don't know how you do it." Ashleigh could almost see the mirthful shake of Bev's head as she added, "I miss you too—but not that loony bin of yours. I'm afraid I just wasn't cut out to be a personnel director."

"Maybe not, but I wish you weren't so darn far away . . . But enough of feeling sorry for myself," she quickly added. "See you Friday night." Smiling, she put down the phone.

The intercom buzzed, and Ashleigh flicked the switch. "Ms. De Mornay is—never mind," Betty said. The line went dead.

At the same moment, Ashleigh's door swung open and Viviana sauntered in. "Five minutes on the dot," she said, turning to close the door behind her, not a single strand of auburn hair out of place. She slid into a chair opposite Ashleigh.

Viviana's makeup, as always, was done to perfection, and her wardrobe included nothing but the highest-quality garments from top designers. She placed her black leather Filofax organizer on the table. Grasping one thin hand with the other, she said, "It's freezing in here! Do you mind if I turn the heater on?" Without hesitating, Viviana flipped up the switch to the infrared heater, a supplement to the building's antiquated heating system.

"Sorry I can't offer you some coffee," said Ashleigh.

"I'm hyper enough without it." Rubbing her arms briskly, Viviana said, "Ashleigh, have you talked to Adele Watson?"

"Yes. This morning."

"Did she talk to you about Walt Adams?" Viviana sounded agitated.

"No, but I know she spoke to Mr. Jerome about him," Ashleigh replied.

"That bitch," said Viviana, her pale skin coloring to a rosy glow. She paused, most likely surprised at her own use of language she considered vulgar, and further straightened her perfect posture. "Do you know what she told Mr. Jerome?"

"I believe I got a fairly accurate quote."

"Well, Ashleigh, you know I would never pass along a bad apple!"

You certainly would, if it were in your best interest, Ashleigh thought. She kept quiet.

"It's a shame. Walt was one of my best display people. Then about six months ago his health gave out, and I couldn't depend on him." She glanced at Ashleigh. "I told Adele Watson the God's honest truth when she asked me about him, but she went ahead and had him transferred to furs. I don't appreciate her telling Mr. Jerome that *I* pulled a fast one." She scoffed. "She should talk!"

Despite her sometimes self-serving ways, Viviana was not an outright liar, nor was she malicious—whereas Adele Watson, Ashleigh had discovered, was both. She sympathized as best she could, but she had barely managed to calm the fashion director when Betty buzzed to tell her that Laura Cameron was on her way to the security counter.

Viviana rose. "I know you've got to go, but I need to talk to you. How about tomorrow morning?"

"I'll be in about seven thirty."

"I'll meet you at eight, if that's okay."

Ashleigh nodded, grabbed her handbag from the credenza, and picked up her organizer. This would be a working lunch. The two women walked out of the office and down the corridor together.

At the elevators, Viviana said in a conspiratorial tone, "You know, Ashleigh, Danielle isn't the first Fine Apparel buyer Adele has destroyed. In fact, she's the third in just over a year. That woman is downright evil!"

Viviana watched Ashleigh disappear behind the double doors, wondering if the personnel maven realized the extent of Adele Watson's manipulative skills. *It's hard to tell with that one,* she thought.

Ashleigh was so cool-tempered and discreet. It seemed that little escaped her, yet she never commented on or confirmed rumors, no matter how widespread. It was unnerving. And her propensity for giving everyone the benefit of the doubt was maddening. Viviana even suspected that Ashleigh might know of her own clandestine affair with the man upstairs.

She stepped off the elevator on the third floor and paused in front of the mirror on the square pillar above Swimsuits, smoothing her sleek auburn hair. Gingerly, she wiped the corner of her mouth, removing an inconspicuous smudge of lipstick, and strode through the doorway leading to the Fashion offices.

At the sound of the phone, she looked around the reception area. It was deserted. Irritated, she glanced down at the instrument on her secretary's desk and saw that one of her own lines was blinking.

With a surge of anger, she grabbed the receiver. "Viviana De Mornay." It took every grain of self-control she possessed, but somehow she managed to sound unruffled and professional.

"Mr. Jerome would like you to come to his office right away," Méchie said officiously.

Viviana wanted to object, but did not. "I'll be right up." She dashed into her office and rummaged through her cosmetic bag until she again came across her lipstick and a small tube of foundation. Then turning to the mirror beside her desk, she flipped on the light and began to touch up her makeup.

After making sure there was no trace of shadows beneath her eyes and every hair was in place, she picked up her organizer and hurried toward the fifth floor. At the elevators, she spotted her secretary and the fashion coordinator, their faces flushed, laughing. *As if they have nothing better to do.*

The moment they saw her, the laughter stopped. Both women, speaking at the same time, tried to explain that Susan Thomas had asked them to meet with her.

Viviana impatiently gestured them to silence. Then, icily, she drew herself up to her full five-foot-eight height and said, "You don't work for Sales Promotion. You work for me." She curtly added, "During store hours, the Fashion offices are never—and I do mean *never*—to be unattended." She straightened the lapels of her cream-colored Armani suit jacket and glared at the two young women. "Is that perfectly clear?"

They nodded, and Viviana turned and hurried on her way.

Outside the closed door to the president's office, Viviana paused.

"Mr. Jerome will be right with you," Méchie's voice rang out from her desk in the adjoining room.

"But you asked me to come right away."

"He shouldn't be long." Then smiling, she shrugged. "Chris Ferrari slipped in right after I called." Then with a raise of her brows, she said, "The door just banged closed."

Viviana looked at her watch. "I have no time to wait around," she protested, though she knew full well that was exactly what she would do.

Méchie shrugged helplessly and reached for the ringing phone.

Viviana tossed her Filofax onto one of the upholstered chairs and stood at the window, looking down at the street below. Her thoughts drifted to David Jerome and the way it had once been between them.

Soon after she'd arrived at Bentleys Royale, Viviana had fallen blindly and hopelessly in love with him. She had longed for each new day and the anticipation of being close to him. She had been in her late twenties then, away from home and in a big city for the first time, and she had entered and become part of the vital, fascinating world of fashion. She was completely awestruck when David, having guessed her feelings, made love to her for the first time. Even now, three years later, she remembered the way it had been.

It was early evening when Méchie poked her head in to let them know that she was leaving for the day. Viviana, seated beside David, was commenting on the fashion trends for the upcoming season. Sketches were spread before them on the management table.

When they heard the door click shut at the end of the corridor, David rose, strode across the room, and locked his office door. And then, without speaking a single word, he took Viviana by the shoulder and turned her to face him. His kiss left her breathless. Her response was unexpectedly passionate, without pretense or reserve.

Moments later he led her to the blue velvet couch in the corner of the dark-paneled room. Her awakening, her erupting passion and total lack of inhibition, surprised even her.

It was the beginning of a time unparalleled by any other part of Viviana's life, before or since. Day after day, week after week, they contrived to meet surreptitiously, stealing what minutes they could. At times their affair took on the characteristics of a game of skill. At other moments it seemed as if life and love were created just for the two of them.

Viviana closed her mind to doubts, choosing to enjoy the here and now. Yet instinctively she had known that someday it all must end. And still she had cherished the small hope that budded inside her.

Several months after their affair began, she felt that a strong, unbreakable bond had grown between them. But a week later, in his office where it had begun, the romance ended. As president of Bentleys Royale, he had an image to preserve. He needed to clear the past to make way for a future—a future that she would no longer share.

After telling her how far she had come, David said, clearly and precisely, "You are a beautiful and sophisticated woman with your feet squarely planted on the ground." Though he paused momentarily, his eyes never left hers. "You are a quick study and a natural in the world of high fashion. My faith in your fashion expertise is unshakable."

He appraised her again with a meticulous eye, gazing from the simple, understated earrings she had chosen to accent her Armani suit, right down to her Bruno Magli shoes. "You have acquired fine taste. Your wardrobe is impeccable, as is your ability to anticipate and translate fashion trends."

Confused by the rapid change from what was so very personal to his cool analytical appraisal, Viviana held her breath. She waited for the loathsome *but*. Then hearing the beat of her own heart, she drew her hands from his.

He stepped back, then said, "I would like you to become the official fashion merchandising director for Bentleys Royale."

Just last month, he had refused to elevate her title, saying titles were meaningless. *Why now?* she thought.

"Before you say anything, it is only fair that I tell you that from now on, our relationship must be purely business—nothing more. It won't be easy for either of us . . . But my offer is sincere."

He reached out and, lightly touching Viviana's chin, tilted her head up, forcing her downcast eyes to meet his. "Will you accept?"

"No," she said, "I can't." Her eyes were dry, but she feared that wouldn't last long.

He nodded. "I understand. But Viviana, you have more than just yourself to think about. If you change your mind, I want you to know—"

"I won't," she said. Her heart sank. Why had she told him about Mason? He and he alone held her most guarded secret. She regretted her blind trust, regretted telling him of her beautiful, broken son. David knew she had given birth before she reached fifteen. He knew that Mason was severely autistic and had been institutionalized since birth. But he did not know the whole truth. Her parents did not know the whole truth. Not a living soul, other than herself and her late brother knew the whole truth. Had her parents allowed her to keep the child, as she'd begged them to do, her life would have been very different. It had taken her years to realize that they had done what was best for her. Her guilt was palpable, however, and her penance had been taking Mason from the state-run facility and providing for him at the Hillside Long-Term Facility.

She left David's office knowing that her days at Bentleys Royale had come to an end. But after a week of soul-searching, she had been unable to resist the prestige and the power of the position that the president had offered. Besides, she had to think about her son.

At first, her return had been difficult, and a sense of what might have been was never far from the surface. Yet sadness and private tears had never soured into embitterment, and in the end, Viviana's love for David Jerome had turned into respect and a shared loyalty for Bentleys Royale and all it stood for.

CHAPTER
26

David Jerome sprang to his feet, slinging the papers across his desk. "Damn it, Chris! I asked *you* to handle this. Not Central!"

"I understand." Ferrari pushed back his chair and rose to face the president. "I've been working on the figures. But it takes time."

"I don't care how long it takes. I want those figures on my desk before you leave tonight." Jerome's palm slammed down on the desk, toppling the crystal clock. "Is that clear?"

"Yes." His voice faltered, and Jerome saw beads of perspiration pop out on Ferrari's forehead. "I'll do my best, but—"

"But what?"

"The figures generated on yesterday's reports don't match the ones we have for today, or even the day before yesterday." Ferrari frowned and shook his head. "Either the computers are spitting out garbage or, more than likely, someone is feeding them garbage. I'm not sure if I can get it all together by tonight."

"Alright." Jerome set the clock upright, frowning as he noticed the time. "But I want those figures, along with your analysis, on my desk no later than nine o'clock tomorrow morning." Impatiently, he watched Ferrari gather the computer reports at the pace of a snail. "Was there something else?"

"Could I skip the management meeting this afternoon?"

Jerome folded his arms, as if cradling his anger. "I believe we've had this conversation before." His tone was metallic.

"Sorry," Ferrari replied. "I just thought that . . . well, I could use the time."

"I know exactly what you thought." Jerome cleared his throat. "Somehow you'll find the time to be a part of the management team *and* still get your work done like the rest of us."

As Ferrari walked out, Jerome punched the intercom button. "Please call Store Planning and tell Jerry Cohen I've been delayed." He glanced back at the clock. "I'll be in his office about one forty-five, and I'd appreciate it if he could have the blueprints for the Beverly Hills store."

The mere thought of having this store again slip through his fingers was gnawing at Jerome. A store in Beverly Hills had been his dream—a dream shared by his management team and the buyers. He was convinced that Bentleys Royale's patron profile was ideally matched to the demographic of the Rodeo Drive area. Now, far greater issues stood in his way than the insufficient parking issue that had been raised earlier. Still, he refused to give up the dream. Somehow Bentleys Royale would not only survive the current crisis—it would grow.

Switching his thoughts back to the present, Jerome said, "Move the management meeting up half an hour, and send Viviana in."

As usual, he had mixed feelings at the prospect of seeing Viviana De Mornay. Sometimes, even now, he had a strange nostalgia about her, even though the physical desire had evaporated long ago. He wondered at his own intensity back then. *How could I have let it happen?* He thought he might never understand.

Chapter
27

An unnatural silence filled the hallway in front of the security counter. Ross Pocino, holding a small boy in his arms—Ashleigh guessed the child to be about four years old—stood rigid next to the counter. He spoke through clenched teeth to Ann, a young security agent who now manned the counter. Anger reddened his face, but his voice remained low as he shifted the dark-haired child in his arms. Carefully balancing him on the high counter, he pulled out a wad of Kleenex from his jacket pocket and gently wiped the little boy's tearstained face.

Ann bristled and raised her eyes to the ceiling.

Ashleigh stopped a few feet short of Pocino. Associates paused in silence when she asked, "What's the problem?"

Pocino glanced toward her. "Miss McDowell, I'd like to speak to you," he said, his tone tense.

Then turning back to the boy, he whispered something into his hair. The boy looked up to the burly man and gave him a timid smile.

"I can't believe what this dame's telling me." Pocino nodded in the direction of Ann, who stood stiffly behind the security counter. "I've got a lost kid who's bawling his eyes out while his mom's wandering willy-nilly around this goddamned store." Tossing his head in the direction of the security agent again, he continued, "She refuses to make an announcement over the loudspeaker! I'm banging my head against a wall of ice here. I need to find this kid's mother." He fixed Ann with a steely glare. "This highfalutin store has a heart as cold as its marble walls."

"Hold it," Ashleigh said, looking from Pocino to the child. Tears ran down the little boy's soft skin, and he clung tightly to Pocino's coat sleeve. "We'll find his mother."

"What do you propose to do"—he eyed her with skepticism—"without upsetting the status quo?"

The sound of Laura Cameron's slim heels clicked through the corridor. Ashleigh looked up. "I'll be right with you," she said to Laura.

As the VP of stores gravitated directly to the child, Ashleigh turned back to the security counter. "Ann, please page the boy's mother."

"But, Miss McDowell, I just told Mr. Pocino that Mr. Jerome doesn't want the voice page used while patrons are in the store."

"I understand," Ashleigh said, "but for this situation we'll need to break that rule."

Looking at the girl's troubled face, Ashleigh wondered, *Why is common sense so uncommon?* Then she added, while reaching for the phone, "I will take full responsibility, but right now I'd like you to page the mother. I'll explain to Mr. Ferrari."

Pocino said, "Not in. Tried to get in touch after I was reminded that Bentleys Royale did not use the voice page when there were 'patrons' in the store." He enunciated the word *patrons* as if it left a foul taste in his mouth.

"Please make the announcement," Ashleigh repeated, before joining Laura Cameron.

Ashleigh and Laura made their way to the back section of the restaurant, where Laura immediately plunged into her rhetoric on the negative effect of jerking her new divisional out of the La Jolla store to fill Danielle's position.

The waitress appeared, filled their cups with coffee, and asked, "Will it be your usual?"

As soon as the woman was out of earshot, Ashleigh glanced around and smiled. "Somehow I never envisioned becoming a regular at Tiny Naylor's."

"What it lacks in ambience, it makes up for in convenience," Laura said with a shrug of her narrow shoulders. A frown quickly replaced her smile as she continued to pour out her frustration. "Just once, I'd like Mr. Jerome to give some thought to the suburban stores. He seems to forget that they're seventy-three percent of our total sales and profit. Yet the Central organization is always his number one priority."

Ashleigh broke in. "Laura, before you go any further, let me fill you in. The buying position isn't officially open. But we have to be prepared, since there isn't an experienced assistant in place." Not giving Laura the opportunity to interject, she went on. "Your divisional is happy in her present position."

"She told me so—but you know how quickly these young people change their tunes when they think they can bypass a step on the ladder." Laura hesitated before she asked, "Did you tell Mr. Jerome that she wanted to stay in place?"

"Not yet, but I will."

Laura's eyes met Ashleigh's. "Don't say it. I know; it's a matter of timing."

Ashleigh nodded.

"There's a phone call for you, Miss McDowell." The waitress smiled and pointed in the direction of the pay phone in the front of the busy restaurant.

"Is there no escape?" Laura laughed as Ashleigh rose.

The receiver dangled from the pay phone. Ashleigh pulled it up by the cord, fully expecting to hear Méchie's crisp tones. Instead, she heard a rapid flow of disconnected monologue from Viviana De Mornay.

"Hold it." Ashleigh smiled patiently into the phone. "I'm lost. It's pretty noisy in here."

"Sorry. I wouldn't have called you during lunch, but the boss wants me to go to New York immediately to work with Adele Watson on selecting assortments for Danielle's department." Viviana groaned. "Anyway, Méchie got me a flight that leaves at five fifteen. I'd hoped to be excused from the management meeting this afternoon, but no such luck."

Ashleigh transferred the receiver to her other ear, wondering why Viviana couldn't have left a message with Betty or talked to her at the management meeting. "So, obviously I won't be seeing you in the morning," she interjected, thinking, *Viviana must have more on her mind than our appointment.*

Rather than respond, Viviana whispered, "Ashleigh, I hate talking about this over the phone, but I have to make a beeline home after the meeting, and there's something I think you should know. I meant to mention it when I was in your office, but I got sidetracked. I was in La Jolla yesterday, and I noticed something odd." She paused again. "The amount of Lady Adrianna merchandise there seemed excessive. You know Jeff Bradley is the rep for that line and—" Cutting off suddenly, she said, "That will have to wait. I've got to run."

"That was Viviana De Mornay," Ashleigh said as she slid back into the booth. "Mr. Jerome has asked her to meet Adele Watson in New York to edit the Anne Klein collection." Viviana had said there was even more she had to tell Ashleigh, but the rest could wait until she got back.

"God help her!" Laura smiled. "Viviana will blow her cool if Adele goes after this year's fifty-dollar blouse again."

"Somehow they'll muddle through. They're both pros."

Laura's brows lifted. "Always the diplomat."

"Well, I thought Viviana made her point at last management meeting when she challenged Adele's quest for this season's fifty-dollar blouse."

"I'm afraid Adele refuses to consider inflation."

The waitress reappeared and automatically refilled Ashleigh's coffee. Laura placed a hand over hers. When the waitress walked away, Laura asked, "Surely Viviana didn't call you here just to let you know that she was going to New York."

Ashleigh sighed. "No. She was concerned over the amount of merchandise Danielle had in La Jolla."

"I don't agree." Laura handed the daily sales flashes to Ashleigh. "Just look at this. Their sell-through in Better Sportswear is phenomenal." She shook her head. "It would be a shame to lose Danielle Norman. She has that rare taste level that's so critical to the success of that department." Then, making sure that Ashleigh hadn't overlooked the fact, she added, "Even if my La Jolla divisional were ready, she doesn't have that level of taste." She paused to let the impact of her words settle, then said, almost to herself, "Danielle Norman is one buyer who's truly responsive to the stores, and it's not fair that Adele is allowed to destroy her."

"Viviana implied that Danielle was under Jeff Bradley's influence. Do you think she might be investing too heavily in his line?"

"No, I don't agree. Lady Adrianna is a good, salable line, and we're certainly not overstocked." Laura adjusted her oversized glasses. "I saw Jeff in Palos Verdes just yesterday," she said with a thoughtful frown. "In fact, I stopped him to discuss the Lady Adrianna assortments in PV. With the vast Asian population there, we can't keep enough petites in stock."

"How well do you know Jeff Bradley?"

Laura looked thoughtful. "Reasonably well. I was general manager in the Woodland Hills store when he was our Men's Furnishings buyer."

"I know his background, and I've seen him in the store. I just don't know much about him. A nice-looking man. He's gay, isn't he?" Ashleigh asked.

Laura shrugged her shoulders, seeming not at all taken aback by the question. "Probably. I know there were rumors to that effect, even though he was married with a couple of kids, I believe. As I recall, he and one of our display associates shared a condo after Bradley's divorce. Which I guess is neither here nor there." Laura lifted her glasses from the bridge of her nose, as if stretching her brain to remember every detail. "He's creative, has well-developed taste, though he tends to be somewhat hyper. Except for those narrow-set eyes, he could almost be described as pretty, and he's always meticulously well groomed."

Suddenly, the image of Jeff Bradley in a slightly rumpled gray pin-striped suit flashed in Ashleigh's head. Laura's description fit perfectly and jarred something in her mind that the passport photo hadn't. She was sure now that she'd seen him this week. She'd run into him at the elevators. And this time he hadn't had that fresh-from-the-shower look. In fact, now that she thought about it, that baby face of his had needed a shave. *Oh, God.* Was that Monday? Or was it yesterday—the day that Danielle failed to show up in New York?

Back at the store, Ashleigh saw that she had just enough time to make a quick phone call and drop off her handbag before the management meeting. Or at least she thought she did until Betty came running down the corridor to meet her.

"Mr. Jerome wants to see you," she called breathlessly.

"Any other messages?" Ashleigh asked as she continued down the corridor and turned into the reception room, Betty at her heels.

"He said he needed to see you right away." Betty looked worried as Ashleigh stopped to check the message holder.

"Okay, I'm on my way." She passed her handbag over to Betty. "Please put this away for me," she said, and headed back down the corridor. No time now. *But I've got to find the time to call Dean Delaney at the DC and find out what he knows about Danielle and Bradley!*

She hurried to the elevators. To her relief, the instant she touched the button, the light flickered and the doors slid open.

Ashleigh arrived on the fifth floor at the same time as Ferrari and Don Horowitz, divisional merchandise manager for Menswear.

"Just what we need. Another meeting!" Horowitz groaned, and he flung open the door to the short corridor, stepping aside for Ashleigh.

"Watch it, Horowitz. No need to play Sir Galahad here in Petticoat Junction." Ferrari laughed derisively. "Got to stick together. Equal career opportunity, equal pay, and equal opportunity to open doors."

Undisturbed by Ferrari's theatrics, Ashleigh said, "Thank you, Don," and stepped into the pre-meeting cacophony. Most members of the management team had arrived ahead of them, nearly filling the narrow corridor and spilling over into Méchie's office.

The door to the president's office was closed, and two of the DMMs were seated on the built-in bench on the right-hand side of the corridor, engrossed in conversation.

Ashleigh edged her way to Méchie's office, unconsciously taking roll. Other than Adele Watson, who was still in New York, Susan Thomas was the only one missing.

Viviana De Mornay, with her back to Méchie's desk, stood stiffly, cradling her organizer and tapping the tapered toes of her Maud Frizon shoes in an agitated rhythm. She repeatedly looked down at the diamond pavé watch on her slim wrist, appearing lost in her own thoughts—about her upcoming trip, Ashleigh presumed. Packing was no small endeavor for the fashion maven. Viviana took time to plan each outfit so that it was flawlessly accessorized for her grand entrances into the showrooms of New York. And since she had been named by *Women's Wear Daily* as one of the top fashion merchants in the industry and a credit to Bentleys Royale, her meticulous planning had become a fetish.

The massive door to Mr. Jerome's office swung open, and Susan Thomas hurried out, averting her eyes and not stopping for a word with anyone. Ashleigh caught a glimpse of her tearstained face beneath her light brown hair and knew it must have been another of those sessions Susan had spoken to her about. From week to week the pressure points changed—a misprint in a newspaper ad, an apostrophe left in *Bentleys Royale*, or more likely, Ashleigh imagined, something to do with the upcoming Salute to Hollywood promotion that would culminate with a black-tie dinner dance in the store next week. These colossal affairs never failed to ignite a confrontation between the president and the sales promotion director. Susan's standards were every bit as high as his, but the two were often on different channels over details.

As the rest of the management team began to file into the president's office, Jerome strode toward them and raised his hand, stopping them in their tracks. Catching Ashleigh's eye, he said icily, "I'd like to see you first." Then addressing the others now jammed together in the corridor, he said, "Excuse us. This will take only a moment."

Squeezing through the retreating group, Ashleigh tried to figure out what was wrong. For Mr. Jerome to require the entire management group to stand by, it had to be terribly important.

When she was barely inside the office, he pushed the door with such force that it banged as loudly as if he'd pressed his infamous button. Slowly, he turned to her. His posture was rigid as he stood with his back to the door. It seemed an eternity before he spoke. Finally, he removed his glasses and said, "Ashleigh, I understand that you left Ross Pocino alone with a small boy after having the mother paged."

"Yes." Ashleigh stared at the unfamiliar scowl.

Mr. Jerome flipped the back of his hand in an upward motion. It moved so swiftly that Ashleigh stepped back, feeling as if he had actually struck her rather than the air between them.

"How on earth could you leave Pocino alone with a lost boy—especially with his mother on the way?" His voice was filled with tension.

What was he saying? Ashleigh did not comprehend at all. Finally, she blurted out, "Is there something I should know about Pocino? I don't understand."

A look of incredulity crossed Jerome's stern face, and he leaned back against the door. "You don't know?" His voice softened.

Shaking her head, Ashleigh felt the heat rising to her cheeks.

"I apologize. I thought you must know."

"Know what?" Her voice rose, her impatience undisguised. Suddenly she felt inundated by mysteries.

"Pocino had a son . . . a boy around three, maybe four years old." He hesitated. "It seems that the child and his mother were separated in a crowd at the West Covina Shopping Mall. To make a long story short, the child was kidnapped and murdered. Pocino quit the LAPD, and he and his wife were divorced within a few months."

Ashleigh sank down onto the arm of one of the chairs in front of the president's desk. The look on Pocino's face as he held that little boy was etched into her memory. Mr. Jerome didn't have to tell her; she could imagine what happened when the child's mother had appeared.

Amid the rattle of coffee cups, the management staff took their customary seats around the large oval table. Ashleigh sat on the near side facing the patio, midway between Jerome and the foot of the table, where the five smokers banded together—as far away from the Benevolent Dictator as possible.

As best she could, Ashleigh forced thoughts of Danielle from her mind so she could concentrate on the issues at hand. Her organizer had barely touched the table when she had to jerk it back out of the path of a well-marked best-sellers report as it sped down the center of the table from Jerome toward Don Horowitz, not quite reaching him.

All conversation came to a halt as Jerome took his seat at the head of the table. "We'll discuss this after the meeting." Jerome glared at Horowitz, then tossed his red pencil on the table.

Horowitz's round face colored as he reached for the papers and said, "Yes, sir."

Ashleigh cringed as a cold look of disdain passed from Jerome to the red-faced DMM. Except for the rustle of bodies adjusting position in high-backed chairs, an awkward silence permeated the room. *Why does Horowitz continually do things to irritate Mr. Jerome? Why can't he just say yes, when he knows that the use of* sir *is one of the president's hot buttons?*

Susan Thomas slipped into the chair beside Ashleigh, her composure intact. A quick trip to the powder room had done wonders.

Jerome gave Susan a fleeting glance, but his attention didn't rest on her long enough for Ashleigh to read between the lines.

"Now that everyone's here, we'll get started." Jerome cleared his throat. "I must be downtown by four." The fact that he had not removed his jacket was a clear signal that he had no time for one of their marathon sessions.

He looked around the table. "Does anyone have anything to add to the agenda?"

As usual, there was no written agenda. After sitting in on Ashleigh's time management sessions, the president had tried her idea of having a prepared agenda. It worked well for a short time, but soon fell apart. He'd said, "Theoretically, the idea is sound, but we're just too damned busy for all that nonsense." And that had been that.

Now, directly to his right, and out of turn, Viviana De Mornay said, "I'd like to discuss the Salute to Hollywood evening. It seems—"

"It's on the agenda."

Susan Thomas glared over at Viviana. The battle between the fashion director and the sales promotion director—both dedicated to the image of Bentleys Royale, both experts in their fields, and both fiercely competitive—had been raging for months. Susan had located a replica of King Kong and had arranged to have it hoisted to the roof of the store, to herald the Salute to Hollywood affair.

Having dismissed the issue for now, Jerome began his eye-to-eye contact with each member of the management team, traveling clockwise.

Laura Cameron tidied a small stack of papers and glanced around the table. "The remodel of the May Company in Woodland Hills is due for completion on the first of next month. I'd like to discuss the strategy to combat their reopening activities."

Jerome nodded and jotted down a reminder on his agenda.

When the president came to Ashleigh, she shook her head. "I have nothing to add to the agenda but would like to make an announcement."

"Go ahead," he said, leaning back in the armchair and hooking his thumbs in his waistband.

"Executive review packets will be ready tomorrow and can be picked up from Betty. Please leave your schedule for the next three weeks with her." She paused. "Let me know when you are out of town or unavailable during that period." She looked to the head of the table and, reading Jerome's unspoken question, said, "I have given Méchie the review documents and statistical information for the management team's self-reviews."

"Thank you." Jerome nodded. "Thank you very much. Have you asked Méchie for my schedule?"

"Yes."

"Ashleigh?" It was Laura who spoke.

Ashleigh looked toward the vice president.

"Are you going out to the stores to conduct training sessions?"

"Yes." This morning she had asked Betty to schedule La Jolla and Palm Springs for this Friday and Saturday. Conveniently, they were the stores Danielle had visited Monday, before her disappearance. *Don't think about that right now,* she admonished herself.

Jerome said impatiently, quickly pulling the discussion back to agenda items, "If you have more questions about this, talk with Ashleigh after the meeting."

Ashleigh leaned back in her chair. She willed herself to detach from her personal emotions. Mr. Jerome counted on her to be his thermometer of overall morale, and it was her job to stay tuned in. What was not voiced was often more important than what was. But today it was nearly impossible to concentrate on group dynamics.

Jerome's eyes flashed over to Susan. She shook her head.

"Sally?" he said next to Conrad Taylor's secretary.

Sally's dark hair accented alert eyes, which bored into his as she spoke. "Just one question." She didn't wait for his nod. "How long will we be out of business for the setup of next Saturday's gala?" Sally Greenfield, one of the most territorial of the DMMs, had been at Susan's throat over her menu selections as well as disrupting to her merchandise presentation ever since the last promotion. Ordinarily the menu was not an item on anyone's priority list other than Susan's and her sales promotion staff. However, following the fiasco of the permanent blackberry stains on the carpeting of the handbags area from the hors d'oeuvres' station in that department, it had risen to the top of Sally's. Cutting her off before she went into specifics, Jerome said, "We'll discuss the Salute to Hollywood setup when we get to it on the agenda." He cleared his throat and took a drink of his signature hot water with lemon. "Don, do you have anything to add?"

Horowitz shook his head. Jerome's questioning eyes rested next on Ferrari.

"Yes," Ferrari said. "We had a conference call from Conrad Taylor today. He said that we must reduce our expense budgets by twenty percent, effective immediately."

Bodies shifted. Eyes met. Shoulders lifted. Suddenly all of them were muttering either to themselves or to a neighbor.

"That's one of my agenda items," the president said, raising his voice above the din. The profits of Bentleys Royale, along with those of Bentley's and other West Coast retailers, had taken an unprecedented nosedive over the holiday season. He raised his arms in a quieting gesture. "We'll take this one step at a time. We have insufficient time right now to fully discuss all the options. However" —he leaned forward, bracing his hands against the edge of the table so firmly that the blood seemed to drain from his fingers— "we are close to seventeen percent below our profit commitment. To retain our autonomy . . ." He paused, making eye contact with each member of his team in turn. "With only six weeks remaining in our fiscal year, we must take action. Reduce expenses now. Not tomorrow or next week. Each of you must look over your own areas of responsibility. Be ruthless. Pinpoint and implement all possible reductions at once." Another pause. "Furthermore, by nine o'clock tomorrow morning, I want a list of at least three additional cost-savings opportunities from each of you on my desk. Is that understood?"

Jerome made individual eye contact around the table. Behind the assenting nods he received, the management executives wore hollow expressions.

CHAPTER
30

Ignoring the apprehensive gazes from his management team, Jerome continued, "Now, before we talk about the sales promotion, I'd like to put an end to speculation concerning Danielle Norman." He looked sternly over steepled fingertips at each person in the room. "We must be circumspect when it comes to this matter."

Circumspect, circumspect, circumspect, thought Ashleigh. *There's that word again. What does he really mean by that?*

"I'm counting on your professionalism in quelling any and all rumors. Understood?" The room fell silent. Heads nodded, their faces showing discernible ambivalence.

"There is nothing to be gained by jumping to conclusions." Jerome picked up the folder next to his cup of water and flipped through the papers, then shut it and tossed it back on the table. "Better Sportswear, if the input is correct, is considerably overbought. Unfortunately, it is now widely known that Danielle Noman did not arrive in New York as scheduled, and no one knows where she is."

Ashleigh felt numb. Her stomach twisted and turned as if she were on a roller coaster. She quietly refilled her coffee and shifted her attention to the individuals responsible for the fate of Bentleys Royale: Viviana De Mornay bit her bottom lip and drew her folded arms in tighter. The DMMs, Ferrari—nearly everyone in the room gave each other knowing looks. Only Laura looked directly at Jerome. And only Susan seemed surprised. As usual, she was the last to hear the latest rumor, so submerged was she in the world of sales promotion.

Jerome took it all in, then concluded by saying, "That's all I can tell you. The reputation of this buyer is on the line, and I trust that everyone in this room will curtail the gossip. Until we have all the facts," he said, lifting his cup to his lips, "don't listen to speculation. Squelch it."

Taking a long, slow drink as he studied the expressions of those around the table, he said again, "Is that understood?"

Again there were answering nods.

Ashleigh was certain that Jerome's warnings would prevent few of her peers from seeking more information. They were inquisitive, free-thinking individuals, and in the sanctity of her office, questions were bound to crop up. But Jerome had unknowingly given her an out—a way to sidestep having to share her conflicting thoughts about Danielle and her whereabouts. Unfortunately, this was only a small consolation. Still remaining was the problem of how to find out what had actually happened and how she could help the troubled young buyer.

"Before we move on," Jerome continued, "I need the assurance that you are monitoring and keeping on top of the open-to-buy in your divisions." He looked at each of the DMMs. "We must stay on plan. No exceptions—I want no more surprises."

Sally spoke out. "Mr. Jerome, I have a problem in handbags. Saks broke their sale on Fendi."

"We'll discuss it after the meeting." He shifted his eyes, taking in the entire group in a single scan. "Are there any other problems?"

The merchandise managers shook their heads.

Ashleigh's eyes shot from Sally to Don Horowitz as he said, oblivious to the fire he was sure to ignite by passing the onus onto his buyer rather than taking responsibility, "I'm not sure. I asked Peter to check into that on Friday."

As the meeting droned on with discussions of merchandise availability and housekeeping and maintenance details, Viviana surreptitiously checked and rechecked her watch. Apparently no longer able to contain herself, she asked at last, "Could we please discuss this King Kong situation?"

David Jerome did not answer immediately. He squeezed another lemon into his cup and added more hot water as the room started to buzz. He had spent many a sleepless night visualizing King Kong mounted alongside Bentleys Royale's historic tower. Inadvertently, that decision had been taken out of his hands a little over a month ago when he'd come down with pneumonia while in France. In the four days during which he'd been hospitalized and out of phone contact, the CEO had given the go-ahead for this abomination.

If only I hadn't given the appearance of being open to that harebrained idea when it was first suggested. Jerome berated himself now. Toddman had thought it a wonderful promotional idea, and with the precarious state of holiday business, Jerome had not wanted to immediately squelch any "out of the box" idea that might add to the bottom line. However, he'd never had any intention of uniting King Kong and Bentleys Royale in any fashion. Although he had not prevented Susan and her group from getting all the relevant information, he'd been certain his management team would vote it down. If not, he'd been prepared to use his power of veto. Now it was too late to do anything other than give the appearance that the project had his wholehearted support. And he would place the onus for success or failure on no one but himself.

The fashion and sales promotion mavens, each at the edge of her chair, exchanged hostile glares. While Viviana and Susan both had a keen sense of entrepreneurial pride in Bentleys Royale, they remained highly competitive and were often at odds.

Jerome held up a hand. The room again fell silent. Looking directly at Viviana, he said, "We all know how you feel. You've made it abundantly clear. I don't care to hear about it again—the decision has been made." He gestured to the sales promotion director to proceed.

Susan smoothed her skirt and leafed through a manila folder. "This is a drawing of King Kong. It's from a professional balloon company we found in San Diego." She pulled out the drawing and handed it to Laura Cameron to pass around the table. Before anyone could challenge her, she said, "There isn't any closer source. It's been thoroughly checked."

Ashleigh smiled. Susan was learning how to stave off objections. Apparently, the King Kong issue was not the one that had brought the woman to tears prior to the meeting. She obviously had the president's full support on that issue—a fact that surprised Ashleigh. She agreed with Viviana, and would have bet that Jerome would be as violently opposed to the union of King Kong and Bentleys Royale as their fashion director was. But she'd been wrong.

"He will be several stories tall," Susan was saying.

"Precisely how tall?" Jerome asked tersely.

Susan looked down at her notes. "Fifty-two feet." She looked around the group, stopping just before she reached Viviana at the opposite corner of the table, next to Jerome. "We wanted to have him actually hanging on to the tower, but the cost was prohibitive, so he'll be hoisted to the roof and placed next to it, right at the base. He'll be seen from several blocks down Royale Boulevard and from the north as well."

"Wonderful," Viviana murmured under her breath. "Just what we want our patrons to visualize when they think of Bentleys Royale."

Jerome's brows pinched together. "Did you have something to say?" he challenged.

"No. Apparently I'm alone in my concern for the Bentleys Royale image."

Jerome folded his arms firmly and squarely in front of him, color staining his well-defined cheekbones. "Are you saying that I am not concerned with Bentleys Royale's image?"

Viviana appeared shaken. "Of course not. I just thought—"

"I appreciate your point of view," Jerome said, his expression softening. Picking up the picture that was being passed around the table, he continued, "But I'm afraid on this matter, you must refocus. King Kong symbolizes Hollywood; it is not meant, in any way, to symbolize Bentleys Royale."

"This promotion has generated a lot of enthusiasm," Susan interjected. "We've already heard from Gregory Peck, George Burns, Peter Falk, James Stewart, Kenny Rogers, the Gabor sisters, and a host of other celebrities."

At this news, Viviana sat woodenly; she was still unable to wrap her mind around the ungodly uniting of King Kong and the specialty store, particularly the fact that David could think it was a good idea. *It just isn't Bentleys Royale,* she thought. She'd done everything in her power to derail it—even arranged a surreptitious meeting with the Bentley's CEO, intent on sabotage. Knowing Toddman's priorities and his commitment to the bottom line, she'd gone to the meeting armed with all the relevant facts and made her dramatic presentation. Her Oscar-worthy performance focused on the enormous cost of the King Kong replica, and she'd thought this had gotten the CEO's attention. But apparently it was a done deal.

Ashleigh gazed down at the drawing being circulated of the larger-than-life King Kong balloon. Her thoughts drifted amid the murmurs and smiles around the table. The battles over image and expense faded. It all seemed so inane. Her mind wandered at last to the forbidden topic, and she found herself visualizing a life-size King Kong charging ahead to rescue Danielle, their own damsel in distress.

CHAPTER
31

Viviana De Mornay leaned forward and looked out the window as the jet climbed steadily up through the darkened sky above Los Angeles. The city lights faded, and she rested her head against the seat.

Her irritation over missing the five-fifteen flight was a thing of the past. A strong and unexpected feeling of bittersweet nostalgia washed over her. Over the years, David Jerome had achieved so much. But he was now threatened with losing what he held most dear: the autonomy of Bentleys Royale, the embodiment of his alter ego. She should resent his single-minded dedication to the store, but she could not. She had learned to love and respect his ideals, and no matter how often he brought her to the boiling point, in some ways she would always love him. The urgent longings had faded, and yet her feelings went deeper; she wanted to protect and shield him. More than anyone in her life, he had given her a sense of value. She had learned to value herself, her work, her principles.

The inevitable challenges of working with Adele Watson in New York, though an annoyance, were not insurmountable. She would see to it that the assortments for Better Sportswear were up to Danielle's standards. *Adele doesn't intimidate me.* She would see to it that Adele's perennial quest for profit at the expense of quality was derailed. She would make sure the department achieved both.

But she would think about that later, not tonight. Tonight was hers and hers alone, and she planned to make the most of it.

A faint smile played around Viviana's mouth as she thought of what awaited her in New York. This thought cheered her, and she relaxed in her seat, the built-up tension of the past few days diminishing. Eager to slip into the waiting arms of Philip Sloane, she tucked a pillow behind her neck so that she would not crease her hair.

She had met Philip three months before, when he'd come to Los Angeles during Bentleys Royale's British Promotion and the culminating black-tie extravaganza. A host of stars and other celebrities were among the guests who had welcomed Princess Margaret to the city. And since that first night, their affair had raged on without intermission—dining and dancing and loving from coast to coast. She stayed with him in the Beverly Wilshire when he came to Los Angeles, and he had her picked up in his white stretch limousine when she arrived in New York. Whenever they were separated, they talked daily on the phone.

Philip Sloane was handsome and charming, and wealthy beyond her imagination. If she played her cards right, and she planned to do just that, the life she had always dreamed of would be hers. Though recently separated, Philip could give her the kind of life she had once hoped to share with David Jerome—only better.

The fact that he was a bitter enemy and archrival of Mitchell Wainwright only heightened her excitement. Remembering now the rage and jealousy that she had been obliged to conceal when Ashleigh had coolly snatched Wainwright from her, she had to smile. If the recent blurb in the *Wall Street Journal* was accurate, the Sloane conglomerates were outperforming Wainwright Enterprises by a good margin. As for the rumors connecting Philip to the Mafia, she was sure those were nothing more than vicious lies—sour grapes over his successes.

Viviana pulled the gold compact, one of Philip's endless gifts, from her Fendi handbag. She checked for telltale signs beneath her eyes and quickly reached for her concealer. Gently patting a dab on the dark circles, she smiled to herself. He had money, and he was not afraid to flaunt it. And oh, the things that money could buy! It was enough to center her dreams and hopes on.

And Philip was certainly generous with it. That familiar little Tiffany's box never failed to give her a thrill, to make her feel important and special and loved. She would never fall victim to true love again. She had loved David too much, and that had made her weak. *Being* loved—now that was the ultimate power. She would be more than the love object of this powerful man; she would become his wife. Philip's power thrilled her to the core, and she could picture herself on his arm. This time, whatever it took, she would not lose.

CHAPTER

32

At the employee security counter, Ashleigh picked up the attached pen and signed herself out—an annoying new procedure about which she had serious doubts. Executives who were too busy to listen for the warning bells at lockup time would be the very ones who would forget to sign in or out. "If the security staff relies on these sign-in sheets," she had said, "more—rather than fewer—executives could end up being locked in the store. And your security staff could incur more, rather than less, overtime." But Ferrari had paid no heed to her challenge. So, since stating her view, she had gone along with the plan. Only time would tell.

Ashleigh pointed to the three video monitors to her left and in front of the security officer on duty. Her name tag read JENNY. "Did anyone tell you how important it is to keep an eye on these?"

The girl nodded. "I'm sorry, Miss McDowell. I know I shouldn't have been reading a book, but nothing seems to be happening."

"I realize it's not easy to stay alert, but it is extremely important." Remembering the events leading to the purchase of the sophisticated and costly system, Ashleigh asked Jenny if she knew why the cameras had been installed.

She shook her head. "I just started on Monday, and my boss is on vacation."

Ashleigh made a mental note to talk to the security manager. It certainly wasn't the girl's fault that she had not been given the proper guidelines. Despite her rush to be on her way, she began, "About a year ago, during the Christmas season, an elderly couple was mugged and robbed in the underground parking area. Shortly after that, there was an attempted robbery of the handbag buyer and her assistant." Ashleigh had heard several versions of this story, but she shared the facts she was sure of: that an armed guard came on the scene just in time to prevent the robbery, and that the would-be robber got away.

"An armed guard?" The girl's eyes widened.

"Yes. We generally hire outside security to escort associates to and from the nearby church parking lot where they park during the week before and after Christmas. We use the same service in Fine Jewelry." Ashleigh went on to tell the girl, who was now looking from one monitor to the next, that the three-camera system was purchased to observe the staircase as well as the underground area. Then she glanced up at the clock. It was five until five, and it would soon be dark. She said good-bye to the young girl.

Outside, Ashleigh looked up at the sky as the door closed silently behind her. In fact it was already dark, with ominous clouds forecasting heavy rains. She quickened her pace, slipped into her coat, and hurried toward the stairs leading to the underground parking, hoping the rain would hold off. Suddenly, a memory filled her thoughts: that of the shrubbery surrounding Danielle's house and the unsettling crunch of branches breaking underfoot. Perhaps she should wait until daylight came the next morning.

Don't be stupid, she told herself. *Whoever or whatever was in those bushes last night would hardly return.* Still, an involuntary shiver coursed through her.

Pulling out from the covered parking area, Ashleigh was temporarily blinded by the sudden downpour. She swiftly slipped her foot from the accelerator to the brake and leaned forward, straining to see out the window. As she proceeded, the wipers scraped fitfully across the windshield, and huge drops drummed rhythmically on the rooftop and splattered against the glass. Rolling to a stop at the traffic light on Seventh and Vermont, she looked into her rearview mirror and noticed a dark blue car behind her. A Karmann Ghia.

CHAPTER
33

There aren't many of those around, thought Ashleigh, remembering the one she had seen being pulled over by the police car just the night before. *Could that be the same car?* They were so rare that it was unlikely she'd see two in as many days, and both the same color.

The rain diminished as quickly as it had begun, and Ashleigh's thoughts moved on to other things. She switched the windshield wiper knob to DELAY and turned the stereo on. She struggled out of her coat. This was her last chance to look around at Danielle's. Tomorrow the police would surely be there. She prayed that Ruthie had left the key for her and tried to dispel her sense of foreboding. Switching the radio from station to station and finding nothing she wanted, she slipped a Julio Iglesias tape into the cassette player and turned the volume up a notch.

At the next stoplight, she slid open the tortoiseshell clip at her neck and ran her fingers haphazardly through her hair, shaking her head so that her hair fanned out around her shoulders. She enjoyed the freedom from her business image. If only she could free her thoughts with so little effort.

A jarring revelation washed over her. *When Danielle needed me most, I was too objective—too damned professional—not the big sister she needed. I wasn't there for her.*

Suddenly the clouds seemed to open up again. Raindrops thundered on the car's rooftop, hit and skipped across the windshield. Flicking the wipers to full power, Ashleigh concentrated on the road. The headlights blurred into starlike images.

It was on a night just like this that Dan was killed.

As if on cue, the rich, mellow tones of Julio Iglesias filled the car: "If I ever needed you, I need you now . . ." Ashleigh's mind spun back in time, and with the back of her hand she wiped away the tears trickling down her cheeks.

Only three days before their rehearsal dinner, Dan's mother had called to tell him that his sister, Danielle, would not be attending their wedding.

"I'm afraid Danielle's had a rough go with our so-called . . . *stepfather* . . . while I was at the university," Dan had told Ashleigh, his fists clenched. "Mom blames Danielle for the breakup of her . . . relationship."

Ashleigh didn't ask questions. That could wait. Instead, she had said, "Let's send Danielle an airline ticket. Maybe she'll be able to make it after all." And before he could object, she'd pulled out the check Grandpa Charles had given them for a wedding present.

Now, the day before their wedding, Dan called from LAX. "Sweetheart, Danielle just had me paged. The airport bus she was on broke down, and she missed her flight. It's another two hours before her plane is due."

"Don't worry," Ashleigh replied. "If you're a little late, you can meet us at the club, and I'll asked Reverend Price if we can move the rehearsal to after dinner. Since he will be there for both, I'm sure it won't be a problem." She was too happy and too excited to let anything upset her. While she was still on the phone, Gran scurried into the room.

"You'll have a lifetime to tell that young man how much you love him." Gran smiled. "But right now I need you." She handed Ashleigh a checklist of last-minute details. Ashleigh nodded and said her farewell over the phone. "Okay, Dan. Love you. Drive carefully."

Dan and Ashleigh had met and fallen in love while attending the University of Washington in Seattle, and now they planned to begin their lives where Ashleigh had grown up, in Long Beach. Since Dan's mother lived in Atlanta, neither Ashleigh nor her family had met her. But from the moment Dan had introduced Mrs. McIntyre two days earlier, Ashleigh had noticed that he had not been himself.

Irene McIntyre appeared much older than her forty-two years, and her forehead seemed to be creased in a perpetual frown, except for those moments when Dan was in sight. At those times, her face lit up.

But when Dan was not near, his mother was inscrutably unfriendly. Mrs. McIntyre appeared ill at ease with Ashleigh and her family despite all their efforts to make her feel at home. The night Dan's mother arrived, Grandpa Charles had tried his best to lighten the mood by offering a toast. But Mrs. McIntyre had retreated to the guest bedroom, leaving Ashleigh, Dan, Gran, and Charles to clink their glasses and wonder what was the matter.

Now, after finishing Gran's list of to-dos, it was time for the rehearsal dinner. At quarter to six, in an unexpected downpour, Grandpa Charles delivered Ashleigh, Gran, and Dan's mother to the door of the Long Beach Yacht Club. The rain had dampened none of their spirits—except for Mrs. McIntyre's. But that could hardly be blamed on the weather.

Even Charles, a tall, aristocratic man with thick silver hair and appealing laugh lines, was unable to break through Irene McIntyre's glacial manner, but he tried his best, gallantly offering his arm to escort her upstairs to the quarterdeck. For a moment the woman stood motionless, then she wordlessly took his arm and stiffly walked up the wide staircase to join the wedding party.

The setup for the rehearsal dinner was simple and elegant. Ashleigh was filled with love as she cheerfully greeted her bridesmaids and ushers, and was quickly engrossed in lively conversation. She didn't even notice when Charles was called out of the room.

A few fateful minutes later, Charles returned to the quarterdeck, his face grief-stricken. "Ashleigh . . . darling," he said, his voice unsteady. The effect was instant; the entire group immediately fell silent.

He took her hand and led her to a spot just outside the door. With his eyes fixed briefly on the highly polished floor, he pulled her to him. And she knew.

Something terrible has happened.

Charles didn't speak for a few seconds, but it seemed an eternity.

Ashleigh pulled away. "Grandpa Charles, tell me! What's wrong?" Her eyes filled with tears. "It's Dan! Is he alright?" Charles took her in his arms and smoothed her hair. Gran was nowhere in sight.

"Darling, there has been an accident. A very bad accident, I'm afraid. They've taken Dan and his sister to Memorial Hospital."

Hope burning inside, she'd asked, "He's alive?" She hadn't even asked about his sister or about his injuries. All that she wanted to know was that he wasn't dead.

"Yes, he's alive. But Ashleigh—"

"Please, I just want to go to him. Now."

"Yes, darling. We'll go right away," he said tenderly. "Get your coat, and I'll get the car as quickly as I can." He paused. "But first I must tell Dan's mother. She'll want to go with us."

Gran came up the stairs with Ashleigh's coat folded across her arm. Her eyes were red, but she held her chin high as she took Ashleigh into her embrace. Her voice was steady. "Ashleigh, Charles will take you to the hospital. I'll take care of things here and meet you there as soon as I can."

Loud, anguished cries filled the alcove where Charles had gone. Mrs. McIntyre had pulled away from him when he'd tried to comfort her. She looked at him with incomprehensible loathing.

The short ride to the hospital seemed unbearably long. And before the car came to a full stop, Ashleigh shot out and ran through the swinging doors to the emergency room.

CHAPTER
34

Mrs. McIntyre followed Ashleigh through the broad electronic doors, staying close by her elbow. At the glassed-in counter at the far end of the room, Ashleigh felt her stiffen and turned toward her. Dan's mother was glaring in the direction of a gangly blond teenager who walked slowly toward them.

Ashleigh immediately recognized Danielle from the pictures that Dan had shown her. Now she noticed a large dark spot on the girl's forehead, the beginning of a nasty bruise. Her concern over Dan had overshadowed all else. She had forgotten all about Danielle.

Everything around Ashleigh seemed to move in slow motion. It was a long, tense moment before Danielle stood beside them, her shoulders sagging and tears glistening in her eyes. Before she had a chance to speak, her mother snapped, "What in God's name happened?"

Despite her own anxiety, Ashleigh was shocked by the older woman's tone. It was so different from Dan's, which was so gentle and caring. In spite of the five-year difference in their ages, Dan and Danielle were close, and Ashleigh knew the siblings shared a great deal of love. It was evident in the way he talked about her and in her letters to him, which he'd read aloud to Ashleigh. And now to find that their mother was so . . . Ashleigh, who'd been surrounded by love all her life, had no understanding of the woman before her.

Tears began to stream down Danielle's pale face. Charles, who had returned from parking the car, strode up to join them, and intuitively assessing the scene, slid his arm around Danielle's shoulder. He introduced himself and then Ashleigh to Dan's sister.

Danielle went through the brief introductions in a daze, and then looked to her mother; there was no sign of affection from the older woman. Danielle's face, with tears rolling down her cheeks, told its own tale. "Mother, I . . . I don't . . . don't know what happened," she stammered. "I was lying down in the backseat."

With a look of pure contempt, Mrs. McIntyre challenged her. "Why were you in the backseat?"

"Mrs. McIntyre." Ashleigh's voice rang out. "Please. We're all upset, but there's no need—"

"Young woman, that will be enough." Mrs. McIntyre glared at Ashleigh, then turned back to Danielle. "Well?"

Danielle's gaze strayed from her mother's hardened features, and she stared down at the floor. Her voice unsteady, she said, "I wasn't feeling very good so Dan told me to try to catch a short nap before . . ." She cupped her hands and lifted them to her eyes as she struggled to regain her composure. It seemed as if a full minute had passed before she spoke again. Mrs. McIntyre made no attempt to conceal her irritation.

"We hadn't gone very far," Danielle went on, "when Dan said . . . I didn't really hear what he said . . . Then there was a terrible crash . . . and . . . and there was blood all over." She hesitated, then gulped for air.

Ashleigh's legs felt like damp rags, but she stepped forward and reached for Danielle's hand. "Come, sit down, Danielle," she said softly, trying to hold back her own tears. She led her to the large sofa near the reception desk

Mrs. McIntyre stood stiffly nearby, staring toward the double doors that led to the intensive care unit. From the corner of her eye Ashleigh saw Grandpa Charles talking to the woman, the usual warmth drained from his handsome profile.

It seemed like another world, a million years ago, since Ashleigh had set off for the rehearsal dinner in high spirits, so filled with the joy of life. She still didn't know what had happened to Dan, nor did she know why his mother looked at her with such disdain.

Finally the doctor, a short and serious-looking man, appeared through the swinging double doors and walked toward them. He wore green scrubs, paper booties covering his shoes, and a cap, which he pulled quickly off his head as he approached the small group. His face was grim.

Ashleigh jumped to her feet, as did the others. The doctor looked at each of them, his eyes finally resting on Charles. Mrs. McIntyre quickly stepped in front of Charles and said, "Doctor, I'm Mrs. Irene McIntyre, Dan's mother." She towered over the much shorter doctor.

The doctor took a step back and smiled without mirth. "Hello, I'm Dr. Wells." He looked from Mrs. McIntyre to Charles, who in turn introduced himself, Danielle, and Ashleigh.

Then softly, Charles said, gesturing with his head to Ashleigh, "My granddaughter and Dan were to be married tomorrow."

Dr. Wells's eyes filled with compassion. "He is in stable condition," he said.

Ashleigh was shaking, her eyes flooded with tears. "Is he going to be alright?"

"We hope so. However, right now we would consider his condition to be critical. He has a number of contusions—some bruises on the head and chest, multiple fractures, a collapsed lung, and may have some internal bleeding."

Ashleigh paled. "What does all that mean?"

Dr. Wells took a step forward and steadied her by the elbow. "Your young man has had quite a jolt. But he's strong, and it appears he has a lot to live for."

"I want to see my son. Now." Mrs. McIntyre bristled, trying to step between Ashleigh and the doctor.

Dr. Wells held his hand up as he finished speaking to Ashleigh. "We will know a lot more in the next couple of days." Then, addressing them all, he said, "I can allow only one visitor at a time."

"Well, I'm the boy's mother."

"Just one moment . . . " Charles spoke up.

"It's alright, Grandpa Charles. Let her go in." Ashleigh said, biting back the tears and wrapping her arm around Danielle.

Then for what seemed like an eternity, Ashleigh paced the corridor as Dan's mother went in to see the man she loved so deeply, the man she was about to marry. She prayed with all her might that he would not die. In her heart, she was terrified.

Finally Mrs. McIntyre returned, her face contorted with pain. "Danielle," she croaked, "you should have stayed in Atlanta. If you hadn't come—after I told you not to—this wouldn't have happened."

Once again Ashleigh was stricken by the abrasive woman's insensitivity, her downright cruelty to her daughter. She froze, but only for a fraction of a moment. Then all thoughts of anyone or anything other than Dan vanished. "I need to stay right here until Dan is out of danger," she said, hastily kissing Charles on the cheek before dashing toward the door to the ICU. Though Dan was unconscious, she vowed she would not leave his side.

She tiptoed into his room and stood by his bed. He looked so pale and vulnerable. The white dressing covering the gash above his left eye was stained with blood, and beside the bed were bottles of liquid on tall stands. Transparent tubes ran from the bottles to one arm, bruised where the needle had been inserted. Cords attached to suction cups, about the size of quarters, ran from his chest to overhead monitors. His bare chest rose and lowered slowly as she reached for his hand, kissing his cool fingers. No one asked her to leave; she wasn't sure what she would have done if they had. *He can't die,* she thought,. *We have so much to live for.*

Hours later, when a plump, matronly nurse walked into the room and told her that Dan was to be moved the next morning from intensive care to a private room, she was filled with new hope. Still, she didn't leave Dan's bedside but waited impatiently for more news.

She was staring out the window, unseeing, when Dr. Wells walked through the door at six fifteen the next morning. She sat motionless as he approached her and sat down beside her.

"Don't let your hopes soar too high," he said sadly.

Ashleigh felt as though she'd been punched in the stomach. "But the nurse said that he was leaving intensive care. She said he was being taken to a private room." She searched the doctor's face, imploring him to give her some thread of hope, no matter how thin.

"Yes, that's correct. He will be moved later this morning. We've done all that we can for him in intensive care. He has a steady heartbeat now, but we are not removing the monitors. His lungs are clear, so we have removed the chest tube but will continue with the feeding tubes." He paused. "What I am telling you is that he seems to be responding very well, but only time will tell."

Dr. Wells was gentle and compassionate, but Ashleigh heard little and could assimilate even less of what he said. She told herself that surely doctors must always give the worst-case scenario. Regardless, she knew she would have to wait for the news that he was out of danger.

For the next two days she sat for long hours by Dan's bedside, whispering softly, encouraging him to fight for his life—a life that was as precious to her as her own. He was briefly conscious at times, but Ashleigh could not tell if he was aware of her presence. In between, she wandered about the small room, gently running her hand over his few personal belongs. Holding his watch, she was mesmerized by the steady sweep of the second hand.

On the third day, she sat quietly by her fiancé's bedside, holding his hand, afraid that if she left him, he might die. Finally he opened his eyes and murmured her name, his voice barely a whisper. When his eyes fluttered closed again, she was frightened, until they opened again and he weakly squeezed her hand.

"Ashleigh," he repeated, ". . . love you so much . . ." His next words were so soft, she couldn't understand. He mumbled something about Danielle, and then it was clear: "Please, help Danielle. Don't let them hurt her anymore."

She didn't want him to talk. It was as though he were saying good-bye, and she would not let him. She simply would not let him. She wiped his brow, and with her fingers laced in his, she said in a voice as soft as his, "I love you too. And we'll look after Danielle. Both of us, together." *Don't you dare leave me.*

She held his hand and watched him as his eyes closed again. "That's right," she said. "Try to sleep, darling." He looked so peaceful as he slept.

She sat back in her chair and raised her eyes to the bottles beside his bed. They dripped in a slow but steady cadence. Still holding his hand, she drifted off, exhausted by the strain of the past three days.

When she awakened, the room was cold and quiet. Dan's hand was cold in hers. Dim light drifted in from the corridor, and her eyes flew wide open. *He's gone.*

For the first numbing moments she could not breathe. How could fate be so cruel?

Gently she tucked his hand in beside him, stood up on trembling legs, and then kissed him softly on his cheek. With a last look, through eyes blinded by tears, she left the room and closed the door behind her.

She learned later that Dan's death certificate listed cause of death as a pulmonary embolus. The words were meaningless. Dan was gone.

Ashleigh shook her head, trying to dispel the cascading memories, and blinked back the tears that threatened to further blur her vision.

From the center lane of the Santa Monica Freeway, she saw the sign for the Bundy Drive turnoff. Checking her rearview mirror, she maneuvered her way lane by lane to the far right, just in time to catch the turnoff.

The shrill squeal of tires behind her told her that she was not alone.

CHAPTER
35

Ashleigh forced herself to concentrate on the rain-soaked street ahead of her. She drifted into the slow-moving traffic on Bundy Drive and tried to make out the car behind her. Unable to see clearly through the rearview mirror, she rolled the window down partway and peered hard into her side mirror. The street was brightly lit, but through the pelting rain the image was unclear. Still, she thought she could make out the color. It was a dark or royal blue.

The car was still behind her when she stopped at the second traffic light. It was a Karmann Ghia. *That's the same car I saw before.* Ashleigh fought back panic. *This is no coincidence. I'm being followed.*

She tried to downplay it in her head, but she didn't know anyone with a blue Karmann Ghia. Nor could she think of any reason why someone would be following her. Surely Mitchell wouldn't have her followed. *Or would he?* A shiver crawled up her spine. Mitchell kept a detective agency on retainer—he claimed it was for business purposes only. However, he had confessed that he'd had his former wife followed after she'd become unreasonable in the midst of their divorce proceedings. Ashleigh's fear flashed to indignation.

On impulse, she pulled her car into the Shell station on the corner of Bundy and Olympic Boulevard. The blue Karmann Ghia continued down the street.

Ashleigh let out a breath that she hadn't realized she'd been holding. Although the gas gauge registered half full, she pulled up to the full-service bay. "Please fill it," she said, "but don't bother checking under the hood." She wanted time to settle her jangled nerves—but not too much time.

The rain had waned to no more than a light mist, but it was now fully dark. She didn't like going alone to Danielle's, particularly at night, but whom could she have taken with her? *If only Beverly hadn't moved to Palm Springs*, she thought. Taking her heavyweight flashlight from the console, she placed it on the passenger seat.

Ashleigh signed the charge slip and turned the key in the ignition. She prayed that she wouldn't have trouble finding Danielle's house in the dark—and prayed even harder that Ruthie hadn't forgotten to leave the key. Before pulling out into traffic, she looked in each direction—the blue Karmann Ghia was nowhere in sight.

Danielle's tree-lined street seemed even darker than it had been on her first visit. *That night with Pocino,* she thought, and then reality smacked her squarely between the eyes. *That was only last night*. The streetlamps seemed somehow dimmer and farther apart now. Or was it just her imagination?

She drove slowly down Ohio Street, hoping she hadn't already missed the house. She hadn't remembered it being this far from Bundy.

She was about to stop the car and look for the memo paper tucked in her handbag, where she had written the address, when the small house came into view. The same dim light peeked through the crooked shutters.

But this time there was a metallic-gold Jaguar parked across Danielle's driveway—an XJS.

Ashleigh approached slowly, pulled in front of the Jaguar, and parked directly just past the pathway to the house. Her eyes moved rapidly from the front door to the garage, trying to take in as much as they could. She thought she saw movement near the side door to the garage, but she couldn't be sure. It was too dark, and the path beneath the archway linking the house and garage was partially obscured by a thick covering of bougainvillea.

Unsure of what to do, Ashleigh turned off the headlights and sat silently, peering into the darkness. Then she reached for the flashlight and hit the automatic door locks.

As Conrad Taylor stood beside the garage door, fumbling with the keys, trying to find the one that fit, he noticed a white Thunderbird approaching. He hadn't expected to see anyone here tonight. He had counted on being alone.

The car slowed, then eased around his Jaguar and parked in front of the house. The headlights flicked off. He stood for a moment and watched for someone to get out. When no one appeared, he slipped the keys back into his pocket and walked boldly toward the Thunderbird.

From under the dim glow of the streetlamp, he saw a thick mane of blond hair glistening through the rain-streaked window. As he drew closer, large, dark eyes met his.

Conrad heard the click of the door locks as he reached the driver's side of the car; then the door swung open. Smiling, he held out his hand. It was Ashleigh McDowell. She pulled the strap of her handbag over her shoulder and slipped out from behind the wheel.

Making light of the awkward situation, he said, "We meet again!"

"Thank you," she said skeptically, shifting the flashlight to her right hand before taking his and allowing him to draw her to a standing position.

As she straightened to her full height—about five six or seven, he guessed, since her head came just below his chin—for a second he just looked at her. She was so beautiful. He noticed that the rain droplets sparkled and virtually danced through her hair. She looked down, then back into his eyes. Her expression was quizzical. *I'm still holding her hand,* he thought sheepishly.

"Oh, sorry," he said, releasing her hand—the large diamond engagement ring on the hand wrapped around the flashlight winked up at him. Quickly forcing his mind into gear, he asked, "What brings you here?"

When she didn't respond, he saw her eyes focused on the key ring that he'd absently taken from his pocket.

"Are those Danielle's keys?" Her voice was hesitant, and she took a short step backward, putting more distance between them.

"Yes, they are."

"Did you talk to Ruthie?"

"Ruthie?" He gave her a puzzled look.

She took another step back, eyeing him suspiciously, and began to explain. As Conrad listened, the pegs began to fall into place for him. But Ashleigh's suspicion didn't wane.

"If you didn't talk to Ruthie," she quizzed him, "how did you know about those keys?" Her voice was becoming more shrill than usual, and her expression was starting to take on a note of sheer terror. Her fingers tightened around the husky flashlight.

For a moment Conrad's eyes locked with hers. Recognizing her fear, he kept his distance, but he had no intention of being backed into a corner. "Hold it," he said. "Calm down, and I'll tell you about these keys—why I have them, why I'm here." His voice had a defensive edge. "But first, I'd suggest we get out of the street."

Conrad took Ashleigh by the elbow, steadying her as she stepped across the flowing rainwater along the curb. Even with her long legs, she narrowly missed the outer edge of the enormous puddle flooding the gutter.

Now safely on the sidewalk, she disengaged herself and turned, still holding the flashlight as if it were a weapon, peering into the darkness around her before her eyes met his once more.

"Obviously, we both have more than a casual interest in Danielle, so we may as well level with each other. I knew Danielle quite well when we were both at Buffum's, and I know the part you and your grandmother played in her life. But I haven't seen much of her since she left Buffum's . . ."

Surprised that Conrad knew so much about her relationship with Danielle, Ashleigh relaxed a fraction. As he spoke, his clear blue eyes shone with sincerity, and Ashleigh felt foolish for challenging him in such an accusatory tone.

"One night, about a year ago, when Ted Norman started knocking Danielle around, she called me in tears and asked if I could come to the house. Ted had taken off with her car keys, and she said she was afraid he would come back." He hesitated and shook his head sadly. "I'll never forget the way she looked that night. I wanted to beat the hell out of that bast—"

Conrad shoved his hand deep inside the pockets of his Burberry raincoat. Sudden fury raged in his eyes. "Sorry, but that night was a nightmare. A Hollywood set couldn't have depicted the violence any more graphically."

"Danielle's eyes were already black by the time I arrived."

Ashleigh didn't want to hear any more, but she knew she had to listen.

"When she got out of the hospital, she stayed at my condo and kept in contact with Bentleys Royale by phone until she could cover the damage to her face with makeup. She stayed about a week, then got a restraining order and had the door locks changed. I've had these keys ever since." He gave a wry smile. "I guess you might say I became sort of her big brother."

Ashleigh flinched. Danielle had lost her real big brother in that terrible moment five years ago. *Does Conrad Taylor know about Dan?*

Conrad ran his fingers through his damp hair, dislodging a slender twig. He noticed that Ashleigh seemed to be taking in his muddy shoes and damp trouser legs. "Pocino told me about the noises you heard last night," he explained. "I'd be willing to bet that someone has been in those bushes, and quite recently." He pointed to the tall shrubbery to the right of the porch. "Is that where you heard the sounds?"

Her eyes flickered, and she nodded her head. Conrad saw in her expression a mixture of fear and expectation. "I arrived a little before that last downpour and just about covered the entire outside area," he continued. "It was damp, but I saw enough broken branches to suggest that someone could have taken cover there." He paused thoughtfully. "I can't figure out why anyone would choose that particular location—unless maybe you and Pocino caught someone snooping around the house." He held up a hand. "And before you ask, I have no idea who that could be or why. Just one in a growing string of mysteries."

She looked in the direction he pointed.

"It's too wet to show you now, but that's the only bit of shrubbery that has a mass of broken branches on the underside." He made a motion with his hand. "Whoever it was probably crept in from back there, maybe taking cover when you and Pocino drove up." He pointed into the darkness where he'd explored earlier.

"First, let's check the garage for Danielle's car."

Ashleigh shook the dampness from her hair and carefully lifted her feet from one cement stepping-stone to the next, spanning the large gaps between the stones of the pathway alongside the house and garage. Conrad held on to her elbow all the way.

A few paces from the garage door they stopped, and Ashleigh stepped aside as Conrad pulled out the key chain. He tried all three keys. None of them seemed to fit. Holding the key ring up to the light cast by the moon, he said, "It has to be one of these." He retried the first key; it didn't fit. He had more luck with the next one. He heard the lock turn, but it took a moment or two before he could push the warped door open.

The cement floor of the garage felt cold and damp through the thin soles of their shoes. Before Conrad's eyes fully adjusted to the darkness, he could make out only a yellow car.

A muffled cry slipped from Ashleigh's lips, and her hand flew up to cover her mouth. She stood rigidly beside him, staring at the yellow VW bug. He reached out and gently grasped her arm again. His other hand skimmed the surface of the wall near the doorframe, searching for the light switch.

Through the damp fabric of Ashleigh's cashmere coat, he felt her tremble, and something stirred within him—a feeling that he cast aside at the very moment of awareness. Anyone within the world of retail was simply off limits. Besides, if those articles in the *Long Beach Press-Telegram* were to be believed, Ashleigh was engaged to one of the wealthiest and most eligible bachelors in Los Angeles County. Conrad knew he was better off dismissing any inkling of attraction when it came to Ashleigh McDowell. He'd have to just nip that one in the bud.

Ashleigh felt the warmth of Conrad's gentle hold on her arm. She peered into the darkness of the garage until a dim light flicked on. She looked around the wooden structure and saw that the pegboard paneling was bare—not a single tool in sight. Cupboards and shelves were stacked with boxes, all neatly labeled with a burgundy marking pen.

"If Danielle left town, she sure left a lot behind," Ashleigh said softly, her voice lacking conviction. In her heart, she knew Danielle had done no such thing.

Conrad tried the door to the VW. It swung open. He flipped back the driver's seat and reached for something on the backseat: a black notebook and a couple of file folders. He thumbed through, then he handed the stack to Ashleigh.

"These look like Danielle's open-to-buy plans," he said.

Ashleigh recognized the notebook. It was from the buyer training class on business planning. Leafing through the folders, she saw the plans. *But for what season?* She couldn't tell. *They must be dated,* she thought, but she couldn't decipher the mass of digits.

Noticing the strong set of Conrad's jaw as he scanned the garage, she asked, "Can you tell if these are the latest of Danielle's revised plans?"

"Here," he said, reaching for the papers. "Let me take another look." His forehead creased as he scrutinized the report. Holding his wrist up to the light, illuminating the face of his watch, he made a quick calculation. "Yes, they were done on the twelfth . . . That was Sunday." After a momentary pause, he added, "Just three days ago."

And just yesterday she was due in New York, Ashleigh thought as Conrad popped his head into the car again. When he emerged this time, her eyes widened. He held an alabaster-colored raincoat, which he had taken from the passenger side of the front seat.

"Look at this, will you?"

For a moment she couldn't speak, but then softly she said, more to herself than to him, "I didn't think she would do it."

"Do what?" he asked with a puzzled frown.

"Sorry. It's not important."

"What's not important?" he insisted.

Ashleigh's mind was in a whirl, but knowing how she hated that "Oh, never mind" response from others, she said, "Last month, during the fur promotion, Danielle was in my office when Dory Brown, our fur buyer, came dashing in with that coat. I told Dory that I had no need of a fur-lined raincoat, but Danielle fell in love with it. She slipped it on and began to rationalize how cold it was in New York and how versatile the coat would be for her buying trips. Then she came to her senses." She paused. "At least I thought she did. She said there was no way that she could manage it, even at forty percent off and with her executive discount—"

Ashleigh stopped in midsentence as Conrad folded the coat over his arm. "The fact is, whether or not she could afford it, she did buy it." His words hung in the chill night air.

With endless questions running through his mind, Conrad unlocked the front door to Danielle's house. Why had Ashleigh come here? And why alone? What did she expect to find? *Hell, I might ask myself the same questions.* He did know one thing: His picture of Ashleigh McDowell and the life he had imagined her to lead—both personal and professional—was beginning to blur.

The front door groaned and creaked as he pushed it open and stepped inside. But when he turned, he saw that Ashleigh was not behind him. She was kneeling beside the planter.

"What are you doing?" he asked.

"Just checking on the key." She smiled. "It's right where it was supposed to be."

A vision of Ashleigh out here on her own, digging in the planter for the key, flashed in Conrad's head, and before he knew it, he had reached down and yanked her to her feet. "Whatever possessed you to come here alone?" He surprised himself with his angry tone and was stunned momentarily by the defiant gaze emanating from her brown eyes.

Distracted, he did not register the car parked a few doors up the block, which was now easing silently out of sight—headlights off.

Being jerked to her feet caught Ashleigh by surprise. Glaring uneasily at Conrad, she quickly pulled herself together.

"I'm not sure how much Danielle told you about our relationship," she said.

Conrad's face softened. "I don't think she left much out," he said quietly. "She told me about you and her brother." His voice faltered as he said, "Danielle . . . Danielle was crazy about her brother, and I don't think she ever let go of the guilt she felt over his death."

"It was an accident." Ashleigh's voice was no more than a whisper.

"That's what I told her. But it didn't seem to make any difference."

Ashleigh slipped past Conrad into the entryway. "It isn't much warmer in here than it is in the garage," she commented, rubbing her folded arms. This trip was bringing everything back. All of the pain she'd worked so hard to put behind her. She didn't want to discuss Dan's death.

A few paces to their right stood a round table, covered in a paisley cloth that matched the window coverings and the sofa. A small lamp on the table dimly illuminated the living room.

Conrad flipped on the overhead light and said, "Let me go turn up the thermostat."

Ashleigh remained in the living room while he strode through the adjoining dining room and disappeared down a narrow hallway. It appeared that he knew his way around, which was oddly disconcerting. She wondered if he had been there more often than he had implied. Was his relationship with Danielle really a "brotherly" one, or was there more to it than that?

She recalled reading an article in *Glamour* during her university days that said there was no such thing as a purely platonic relationship between a man and a woman. It had caused quite a stir with her roommates, producing some lively and heated discussions. Ashleigh had been a defender of the premise that a man and woman *could* have a relationship based solely on friendship. *So why am I feeling so uncomfortable about Conrad Taylor's "big brother" relationship with Danielle? And why hasn't Danielle ever mentioned him to me?* She caught her breath. *Oh, God.* Was Conrad the man Danielle had told her about when she'd been an assistant manager at Buffum's?

Back then, Ashleigh had given Danielle advice that she hadn't asked for: "Keep your personal and your career lives totally separate," she'd told her. Danielle must have followed this advice, because she had met Ted Norman soon after.

Ashleigh's mind splintered off to thoughts of Danielle's abusive ex-husband and to all the things that Danielle had kept to herself. She shook her head but couldn't brush away the painful thoughts. Danielle was a bundle of contrasts and contradictions.

It seemed that those contrasts and contradictions extended to the young woman's house, and it rattled Ashleigh. The carpet was threadbare in places, and the furniture had definitely seen better days. Every piece was either makeshift or of decent quality but quite old. The phrase "early Depression" came to mind as she walked through the living room. Yet when she stopped in the doorway of the dining room, she smelled Lemon Pledge and saw that everything sparkled. The china cabinet, buffet, and oblong dining table were solid mahogany, of high quality, and looked new. Selected pieces of Lalique and Steuben decorated the table and buffet, and the cabinet was populated with a full set of Baccarat crystal, surrounded by decanters and miscellaneous pieces of Waterford.

Ashleigh knew that Danielle had begun to make her mark in the merchandising world, and had been rewarded with an income well above the average. But a forty-five-thousand-dollar salary could stretch only so far. Ashleigh couldn't help but wonder how on earth Danielle could have afforded it all.

When Conrad came back into the dining room, Ashleigh didn't look up. She seemed engrossed in the contents of the china cabinet, her eyes wandering across each of the neatly arranged shelves of crystal and Lladro porcelain pieces. He watched as she picked up a small crystal object from its velvet display box and held it gingerly, staring down at her hand as if in a trance and slowly turning the smooth, egg-shaped object over.

Conrad stepped closer and saw that it was delicately sculpted in the form of a rather flat rabbit. "What do you call that?" he asked. He could see no use for it. It was obvious that the piece couldn't even stand up on its own.

Ashleigh's head snapped up.

He realized that she must not have heard him reenter the room.

"A few weeks ago I couldn't have answered that," she replied, attempting a smile and looking down, rubbing the smooth surface. "It's a hand cooler. At the Steuben reception, the rep told us the story behind it. In days gone by, the ladies would keep these in their hands when they wore gloves so that when they took their gloves off, their hands would be dry and not feel clammy."

Conrad smiled distractedly.

Ashleigh didn't return his smile; something else had caught her eye, and now she just stared down past the hand cooler. It was a set of Lalique butterflies.

Conrad saw the tears glistening in her eyes. He knew the significance of the butterfly to Danielle, and apparently so did Ashleigh.

When a tear trickled down her cheek, he took a step closer, but stopped himself a few inches short of the spot where she stood. As she attempted to discreetly wipe away the tear, the large diamond glittered on her third finger. To Conrad, it was like a huge neon light flashing, *Beware*.

CHAPTER
38

Ashleigh heard the groan of the outdated heating system, but she felt none of its warmth. She could feel Conrad's eyes on her, but he kept his distance.

Pulling herself together, she looked down at her watch. "I didn't realize it was so late." Even though she had no idea what she was searching for, she wasn't willing to leave before having a complete look around. "Are you in a hurry?"

"No, take your time." He smiled and thrust out his arm in a dramatic gesture, ushering her down the hallway toward the back of the house.

The first bedroom had no carpet and no curtains, although the closet was crammed full of Danielle's clothing. There were blackout shades on the windows, and the only furniture was a card table piled high with computerized statistical sheets, a single folding chair, and a bookcase loaded with thin romance novels and a couple of black binders. Ashleigh felt slightly uneasy with Conrad close behind her, watching her every move, and yet she had no desire to be alone.

In the second bedroom, Ashleigh stood in front of the open door of the closet for what seemed a very long time. There was no question that this was the one Danielle used. The closet was full—crowded, in fact— the same as the first. Ashleigh scanned the closet floor and the overhead shelves: handbags, shoes, empty shoe trees, a few odd garments that had fallen to an empty space on the floor. Something was missing. But what? She'd never been in Danielle's house, and yet . . . She couldn't shake the feeling. Unsatisfied, she turned around and caught a glimpse of Conrad slipping something into his pocket.

"What was that?"

Conrad hesitated before answering. "Just my notepad," he said. "Have you found anything?"

"No, not really," Ashleigh answered breezily. But she hadn't missed the uneasy flicker of Conrad's eye or his abrupt change of subject.

She turned back to the closet and pushed a few hangers to the side, then saw two Vittadinis and a Krizia outfit from the new spring line—not yet worn. The resource tags hung from the sleeves. Her eyes traveled from one item to the next. Finally, she stepped back and turned to Conrad. "This looks like a designer's boutique."

Glancing around the room, Ashleigh saw that Danielle's decorating mode was the same as the one she'd used in the living room. She had achieved a coordinated look by incorporating a round table identical to the one in the living room—inexpensive, prefabricated—which she had draped with a circular, floor-length tablecloth. The pastel butterfly print on a stark white background also decorated the windows and bedspread. Similar wallpaper was hung directly below the chair rail—loving, time-consuming details in a room where the paint was faded, even transparent in spots. But the cleanliness and attention to detail spoke of Danielle's love for her home.

"Ashleigh?"

She felt strange and somewhat disconnected as the volume of Conrad's voice reached out to her. "Yes," she answered, still searching.

The next moment Conrad was standing in front of her, firmly holding on to both of her arms.

Not certain how long she had stood silent, she finally found her voice. "There's something missing. Something important."

With a quizzical raise of his dark brows, he released his hold on her arms and said, "Like what?"

"I don't know," she snapped, more in frustration than anger.

But suddenly she knew what she'd been looking for. Clasping her hands together, she cried, "Her luggage! There isn't any luggage in either of the closets." And yet there was plenty of space for it in the wide, uncluttered section of the closet floor, and it was this that sang out to her.

They checked the hall closet and then rechecked both bedrooms. There was only a small Louis Vuitton overnight bag. The larger suitcase and garment bags were nowhere to be found.

"How about the trunk of the car?" Ashleigh asked.

"I don't have any car keys," Conrad lamented. "And with the trunk in front, there's no access through the backseat. It would have to be forced open, and I don't think I should do that."

"No. Of course not." She gave another cursory glance around Danielle's bedroom, her eyes settling on the fur-lined raincoat that Conrad had draped across the single twin bed. She slowly sank down beside it, absently shaking her head.

"What's wrong?" Conrad sat on the dressing table stool across from her.

"What's *not* wrong would be more to the point," she said, and she stood up.

Conrad followed her to the living room, turning off the lights along the way.

"I'll just pick up my handbag," she said, walking over to the sofa. She leaned down, then abruptly straightened and took two small steps to the end of the sofa.

A red light flickered on Danielle's answering machine. Conrad saw Ashleigh hesitate for an instant, then press the playback button. The tape began to rewind.

"A couple of those messages are bound to be mine," he said.

"I also left a couple," she replied.

Conrad's heart sank. He would have to tell Ashleigh the whole truth about his relationship with Danielle. She might think him a grade-A jerk, but there was no point pussyfooting around. Not after she heard his voice on the machine.

And yet to his surprise, the machine played back only two messages—one from Méchie and the other from Dorothea Sable. *What happened to the ones I left?* he asked himself, and he realized that Ashleigh was wondering the same thing about the messages she'd told him she'd left.

Conrad stared down at the answering machine.

Breaking the silence, Ashleigh asked, "When did you call?"

"Yesterday." He'd called again today but left no message.

Ashleigh nodded as she dropped down on the couch and picked up the answering machine. She inspected the various function keys. "Mine is nothing like this one." She glanced up and added, "Do you think we can retrieve the earlier messages?"

Conrad knelt beside her. "Let me take a look." He reached for the instrument and popped the lid open. He took a moment to study the instructions posted in the cassette compartment. "I don't think we can retrieve them on this machine, but maybe Pocino and his buddy can do something with it." He held the machine directly under the lamp. "I used to have one of these Panasonics. When it was on its last legs, the tape began playing messages that I had thought were long gone."

He removed the tape and slipped it into his pocket. "I'll take this and see if the past messages can be retrieved." He rose, then hesitated, and pulled the tape out again. "Obviously, someone's picked up Danielle's messages." He turned the cassette over in the palm of his hand.

"Do you think someone came into the house?"

He took a second to consider. "That might explain the man . . . or woman . . . in the bushes. Or Danielle could have picked them up through her remote code."

Ashleigh stared down at the worn carpet. Her eyes met his. "It wasn't Danielle."

Conrad agreed. "I know. As hard as it is to accept, I know she's in trouble. But did someone come to the house? Maybe that's who was here when you and Pocino dropped by. If so, why didn't he just remove the tape?" He held the cassette up to the light so that Ashleigh could see the original Panasonic label.

"You know," he continued, "Pocino gave me the thorough rundown on this Bradley fellow, and it's not pretty. I can't imagine Danielle getting herself involved with someone like him. You were right about those Personnel records skirting the real grounds for his termination."

Ashleigh's eyes met his.

Conrad went on. "Bradley was heavily involved in vendor kickbacks. All small-time, and relatively insignificant dollar amounts—not worth spending time in court to either initiate a case or defend it."

But, they both knew, certainly enough grounds for termination.

Danielle was vulnerable, Ashleigh realized. Could she have been open to ideas planted by someone like Bradley, schemes that might produce a short-term profit for her department? If so, had her participation put her at risk? Brushing her hair back from her face, Ashleigh said aloud, "Conrad, I'm frightened. Is Bradley a violent man?"

Conrad shifted his weight and leaned against the back of the armchair. "He has no police record. There's no reason to think he's been involved in any type of violence. In fact, Pocino thinks Bradley's a real lightweight—with a questionable lifestyle. A certain . . . preference."

"Meaning . . . ?"

"He's been known to frequent some of the more popular gay hangouts."

"If that's the case, it's clear he's not the new man in her life—if there even is one."

"I intend to find out for certain. We're convinced that Bradley's involved here, that he's gotten her into something shady, but maybe . . ." He paused. "Just maybe Danielle's business situation and her disappearance are totally unrelated."

"Unrelated?" Ashleigh repeated.

"There's someone else who has a violent history with Danielle, remember? Someone who might have a motive."

Ashleigh gasped.

Ted Norman.

CHAPTER
40

Conrad and Ashleigh paused beside her car. Black clouds blanketed the sky, but for the moment there was no more than a light drizzle.

Shifting the reports he'd retrieved from Danielle's car to his other arm, Conrad said, "If you don't need to get home right away, how about stopping for a bite to eat? Maybe we can make some sense out of what we have so far."

Ashleigh glanced down at her watch. She felt as if she were on an emotional roller coaster. "I could use a cup of hot coffee." She wanted to know what Conrad thought about Danielle's disappearance, about what kind of danger she was in. *Is she even alive?* She pushed the thought away as quickly as it had surfaced. She hadn't asked Conrad this question for fear of what he might say. Instead, she was focusing on the fact that Danielle had been missing for less than forty-eight hours. She was clinging to hope.

And yet . . . A vision of Danielle's fur-lined raincoat flashed before her. *If she had left for New York, surely she would have taken that coat with her.* Ashleigh felt her body turn to liquid. She quickly put the thought out of her mind.

Unfamiliar with Danielle's neighborhood, she suggested the Hamburger Hamlet on Wilshire Boulevard, where Pocino had taken her the night before. The location—en route to Bentley's headquarters—was ideal, since Conrad planned to stop by his office before heading home.

Unlike the night before, Ashleigh noted as she waited in the entry, the restaurant was quiet, not crowded at all. There was not much to occupy her. *What is keeping him?* she wondered.

Conrad rushed in a good five minutes after she had arrived. When he asked for a booth in the back, Ashleigh did not miss the urgency in his tone. The moment the waiter left their table, Conrad leaned across it and asked, "Do you know anyone who drives a blue Karmann Ghia?"

She stared at him, those words echoing in her head. *Blue Karmann Ghia, Blue Karmann Ghia.*

When she failed to respond, Conrad said, "I don't mean to frighten you, but as I followed you here I noticed a blue Ghia following a few car lengths behind you. He made the same wrong turn we did, so I know you were being followed."

"I don't know anyone with a blue Karmann Ghia," she said, and then she told him about seeing the same car earlier that night and the night before.

"I took down the license number." He withdrew a folded paper from his breast pocket. "I'll have Pocino get in touch with his police buddy and have it checked out."

"Did you see the driver?" she asked.

"Not a good look. All I could make out was light hair, hanging well below the collar, but I'm fairly certain the driver was male. By the time I was sure that the car was following you, we were in front of the restaurant. He must have seen me, because he sped up and peeled around the corner about two blocks east of here. When I turned the corner, there was no sign of the car—not even taillights. Then I heard a car roar past in the opposite direction. The headlights were turned off, but I could see from the streetlamps that it was the same blue car." He shrugged. "I'm afraid I don't have much experience in the chase."

"Conrad, none of this makes a bit of sense," Ashleigh said, shaking her head. "What possible motive could anyone have for following me?"

"I've no idea. But you were followed. No doubt about it."

"But why?" she asked. "I'm not a threat to anyone."

The waiter reappeared, ready to take their order. Without opening the menu, Conrad ordered the number eleven, a bacon cheeseburger. "How about some of their famous rice pudding to go with your coffee?"

She nodded—it was exactly what she wanted.

As they spoke, time seemed to fly. They shared everything that they'd learned about Danielle in the past day and a half. Ashleigh wanted to tell him more, but she held back. Her instincts told her that he cared about Danielle, yet she felt that he wasn't being completely up-front with her. She wasn't sure she could trust him.

Breaking into her thoughts, Conrad said, "Ashleigh, you asked me what I was doing at Danielle's—why I had a key. What I told you was the truth, but only a small part of it." He looked down. "You deserve better."

Ashleigh's finger trailed along the rim of her cup, her eyes intent on Conrad's as he opened up to her about his secret involvement with Danielle. She detected a trace of vulnerability, which he doggedly tried to conceal. His candor relieved some of the uneasiness she'd felt earlier, but as his story came to an end she still felt there was a lot he wasn't telling her—she was sure of it.

Conrad rose as Ashleigh slipped out of the booth, excusing herself to go make a phone call. The scent of her hair lingered in the air. He was definitely attracted to this beautiful, sensitive young woman, but it was all too ironic. Here he was, explaining the difficulties he'd had when he'd mixed his personal and professional lives once before, and simultaneously thinking about Ashleigh above and beyond their professional relationship. No, he would not do it again. Besides, she was engaged.

Jolted back to his senses, he returned his thoughts back to Danielle.

When Ashleigh returned, she was smiling. It occurred to Conrad that she looked more relaxed than he'd seen her since Danielle had vanished.

"Looks like all is well," he said.

"How I could have gone without that wonderful man in my life, I'll never know," she said as if thinking out loud.

Mitchell Wainwright is a very lucky man. "Hope your fiancé doesn't mind—"

"Oh, no," Ashleigh broke in. "Mitchell is in Atlanta. My phone call was to my . . . to Charles." She hesitated before giving a quick explanation. "I was brought up by Charles and my grandmother. Gran died last year. That's when Charles came back into my life."

"Charles is your grandfather?"

"He and my grandmother were more like a mother and father to me." She paused again. "My parents were killed in an accident when I was an infant."

Conrad looked her in the eye. "I'm sorry."

Ashleigh smiled. "I never knew my parents, but my own parents couldn't have been more loving or supportive than Gran and Charles."

"But you didn't see him until after your grandmother died? May I ask why?"

"That's a rather long story."

Conrad glanced at his watch and gave Ashleigh a warm smile. "This place doesn't close for another hour and ten minutes."

CHAPTER
41

Ashleigh was too keyed up to go home and drop into bed. She wanted to tell Conrad about Charles. But not quite everything.

"While my grandmother and Charles were unable to marry, no one was untouched by the love they shared," she said wistfully. Conrad Taylor didn't need know to why Charles had been trapped in a loveless marriage. She stopped and looked up at him. *Does he really care?*

"Please continue," he encouraged her.

She concentrated on how to explain what she herself had never come to terms with. Mentally assembling what she had pieced together from what she knew and what Charles had filled in this past year since they had reunited at Gran's grave, she began, "My grandmother was a nurse at Harriman Jones Hospital . . ."

As she told Conrad of those early days, Ashleigh's imagination was flooded with images of Gran and Charles and the generation in which they'd lived, and she found herself telling far more than she had intended. But she wasn't ready to tell Conrad that Charles was C. G. Stuart, the man with the vision and the dream that had become Bentleys Royale. *Nepotism had nothing to do with my rise to the management team of the stores he created,* she reminded herself. She did not want to give the impression that it had.

Finishing her story, Ashleigh took a sip from her water glass and met Conrad's gaze. Almost to herself, she murmured, "I couldn't have asked for a more loving father figure, though obviously I made their lives more challenging."

"Because of their ages?" Conrad asked.

Ashleigh shook her head. "I never thought about their ages. They seemed forever young, even when I was a teen. Gran was only eighteen when my mother was born, and my mother not quite nineteen when I came along." She paused and smiled up at Conrad. An image came to her of Charles and Gran—his heart-stopping good looks, her dark eyes dancing with the love of life ingrained in her—as vivid now as they had been throughout her young life. The two of them had given her so much. "They were gorgeous, and I loved introducing them to teachers and friends. Charles is now eighty-six, but has always seemed decades younger . . ."

"Will there be anything else?" the waiter asked as he refilled their coffee cups.

Ashleigh's eyes shot down to her watch. "I'm so sorry. I must be boring you—"

"Not at all." Conrad leaned forward, shaking his head. "Did Charles have children of his own?"

"Yes, a daughter, but she was no longer a child when Charles and Gran met and fell in love." She'd never met Caroline Stuart, but she knew a great deal about her.

"It's such a shame that Charles didn't have the courage to terminate his marriage."

Ashleigh shook her head. "That's what I thought. But that's not the way it was. In the end, it was my grandmother who wouldn't hear of his proceeding with a divorce. I didn't know until this past year, but Charles again put his divorce in motion about the time I graduated from college, and he and Gran planned to marry as soon as it was final."

"They didn't tell you?" Conrad's voice held a note of disbelief.

"They were on the verge of telling me their news when I announced that Dan and I were getting married. They decided that their news could wait."

Conrad frowned. "So what happened?"

"I never knew about any of this until after Gran died. But when Charles's wife found out about his plans to remarry, she called my grandmother. She told Gran that she was terminally ill with a severe heart condition, that she needed Charles at home with her, and she pleaded with Gran not to take Charles from her. She told Gran that their affair was the cause of his daughter's attempted suicide." Ashleigh sighed. "Gran was a softhearted woman. She told Charles she could not be the cause of any more pain. He also felt the weight of responsibility and moved back to Hancock Park—reluctantly. He purchased a two-bedroom condo for Gran, close to the First Christian Church, then closed the house in Naples."

"Were you living with them at that time?"

"No, I was in the executive training program at Bentley's and lived in my own condo." She didn't want to think about that period in her life. Instead, she continued her story. "In the last two years of Gran's life, Charles called her once a week—every Monday. They still shared the dream that someday they would be together." Ashleigh's throat constricted as she remembered that familiar masculine voice she had heard on the answering machine the day after Gran died. It was on a Monday. It was Charles. "I should have known . . . but I never noticed when Gran began putting three pansies in those shallow dishes again." She quickly explained. "Gran loved pansies, and for as long as I can remember, she put three of them in flat bowls around the house—one for me, one for her, one for Charles. After Charles left, there were only two."

Ashleigh lowered her eyes. "The final irony is that Mrs. Stu—Charles's wife, who was ten years older and in extremely poor health for years, died two weeks after Gran." She told Conrad about seeing Charles at Gran's grave. "He reopened the Naples home about a month after his wife died. I've always loved him like a father, but he's also a good friend."

She stopped abruptly, taken aback at how she had confided so much in Conrad Taylor—a virtual stranger before the past two days. Until Danielle's disappearance. "Please do not mention my trip to Danielle's to anyone," she said.

He smiled. "Understood. I'm not exactly anxious to have my involvement broadcast on the eleven o'clock news either."

They laughed, and again Ashleigh checked her watch. "Look at the time. I'm afraid we've missed the eleven o'clock news." Her face returned to a serious expression. She said, "I really must go." *Even if I don't want to,* she admitted to herself, realizing that she liked this man more than she wanted to. More than she could afford to.

Conrad noticed a sudden change in Ashleigh's expression and sensed her fear, knew she was thinking about the blue Karmann Ghia.

"I'll drive you home," he said. "I have monthly parking across from Central's office building. We can park your car there."

"No. I live too far from here."

"Then let me follow you."

"No," she repeated, the diamond on her left hand casting a rainbow of delicate color as she pushed stray tendrils of hair from her cheek. "I live in Long Beach."

"Long Beach?" He smiled broadly at her incredulous stare. "So do I. What area?" Inexplicably he felt his stomach tighten, expecting her to say Park Estates, the location of the frequently photographed Wainwright estate.

"Belmont Shore."

"Well, you're not going to believe this. We're neighbors. I live in Naples, at the Portofino."

"Very close neighbors," Ashleigh said. "I'm in the condos diagonally across from the Portofino, on the other side of the bay."

"When I came out here from Boston eight years ago, I worked for Buffum's," he explained. "With the corporate offices in Long Beach, it was the ideal location."

"It must have been difficult to give up that easy commute," Ashleigh said.

"At times, but I really don't mind. I enjoy being near the ocean. And the complete separation between my personal and professional lives suits me." His eyes held hers as he drained his cup. "How about you?"

"Sometimes that thirty-mile commute is my only time to be alone and collect my thoughts."

Conrad was tempted to ask about Mitchell Wainwright. It was obvious what attracted the notorious corporate raider to Ashleigh. She was not only beautiful, but when she let go of that Bentleys Royale façade, her sincerity and openness were contagious. The thought of her in the arms of Mitchell Wainwright seemed incongruous. He was surprised to find that it troubled him.

Conrad followed close behind Ashleigh the entire 28.3-mile drive. Meanwhile, Ashleigh willed herself to stop thinking about Danielle—and about why someone would want to follow her. She was tired of thinking about things that frightened and confused her. She preferred to live in her tidy, logical world and was not accustomed to either of these emotions. Until yesterday, she had been convinced that for every question there had to be an answer. But now there were only deeper and more baffling questions.

Pulling up to her condo, she reached for the garage door opener and pointed it at the far door. Then she looked back over her shoulder, forced a smile, and waved good night to Conrad. Swinging into the parking structure, she heard a single sharp blast from a car horn and turned her head. Conrad pulled to a stop and parked his car beside the driveway.

"Ashleigh," he called as he sprang from his car. "Wait."

"What's wrong?" she asked as she rolled down her window. "You didn't see anyone, did you?" She had continually checked her rearview mirror and had seen no one. Still her heart thudded.

"No, but I'll walk you to your door. I'd rather not watch you disappear into that dark hole," he said, indicating the entrance to the parking structure.

Ashleigh turned to look in the direction he pointed. A couple of the lights were burned out, and those that remained were dim. As her eyes adjusted to the darkness, she felt an aura of misgiving. "Thank you. If it's not too much trouble, I'd like that." He waited as she pulled into her stall, and then opened her door.

Two yellow lights flickered on either side of the elevator. As she scooped up her handbag and organizer, he asked, "Is this parking area always so dimly lit?"

"No, there are usually a couple of lights near the entries. Even so, it's never been very bright."

"It should be a lot brighter in here, particularly at night. It's downright dangerous." As they climbed the cement steps beside the elevator door, he added, "Someone could fall and get hurt."

Ashleigh smiled at his fatherly tone. "You're right. I'll look into it tomorrow. I'm not too fond of dark places, particularly now."

They reached her door, and she turned around. Conrad was so close that she felt the heat from his body and stepped back, stumbling on the threshold. He caught her by the elbow, steadying her, and when she regained her balance, he let go of her arm and widened the distance between them.

"Do you have a dead bolt?" he asked.

She nodded. There was nothing left to do but say good night and lock the door.

Once inside, Ashleigh heard his retreating footsteps, and then the hum of the elevator. She wished she could just fall into bed, but knew she was too keyed up. Instead, she took a shower. As the hot water pulsated over her body, she felt the fatigue lifting and her thoughts becoming more coherent.

It was twelve fifty when Ashleigh finally slipped into her peach terrycloth robe and padded toward the kitchen across the deep pile of the white carpet. She had a clear view of the Portofino from the window above her immaculate blue-and-peach-tiled sink. She wondered which condo belonged to Conrad and took comfort from knowing he was near.

For the best part of an hour, she worked on her presentation notes for the meeting she'd scheduled in La Jolla for Friday. Then, too tired to clean up, she left everything on the low coffee table and headed for the bedroom, treading wearily across the living room to turn off the light.

The fresh, clean smell of the smooth sheets gave Ashleigh a sense of luxury. But as her head hit the pillow, disturbing thoughts filled her mind. The normal sounds of the night, even the settling of the building, were magnified.

Though she drifted off quickly, she woke again and again throughout the night, in half-hour intervals. Butterflies and burgundy borders filled her dreams. Then a disturbing vision of Conrad in Danielle's bedroom, slipping something into his pocket drifted through her mind, and she bolted upright.

Viviana's travel alarm sounded at five in the morning. She snatched it up and disengaged it quickly. Cautiously, she raised herself on one elbow and glanced at Philip, still sleeping soundly.

Viviana lifted the covers and slipped out onto the carpeted floor without a sound. Hardly daring to breathe, she looked down at the sleeping man, his brown hair tousled and a look of contentment on his face. She padded softly down the hallway to the guest bath, resisting the temptation threatening to pull her back into bed. She had an eight o'clock appointment at the New York Ambassador with Adele Watson. While Philip was proud of her and her considerable talent, she must be careful not to make him jealous of her commitment to her career. It was her identity, and she realized that and no matter how much money she had, she could never give up the quest to be known as the very best fashion authority in the world.

Though Philip was thirteen years her senior, his testosterone was at its peak after a good night's rest. She had read that interesting tidbit in last month's *Cosmopolitan*, the only periodical she read other than those devoted to fashion. She wasn't sure how valid the theory was in the case of Philip, since he was always an eager and terrific lover—gentle enough to let her know how much he cared for her and demanding enough to make her feel irresistible.

This time she didn't intend to take a single chance. She wanted to be Mrs. Philip Sloane. To accomplish this, she knew instinctively that she must make him believe that he was her number one priority. And she knew just how to do it.

After going through her morning routine, she snapped on her earrings and adjusted the three-way mirror to check the back of her hair. Satisfied, she turned to the full-length mirror on the door and made a complete circle. She checked her hemline, frowning at her plump ankles that were impossible to fully disguise without the benefit of very high heels.

Stocking-footed, she stood on tiptoes to get the effect. *That's better,* she thought. Overall, she was pleased. The simplicity of the gold earrings, the beige silk crepe suit by Giorgio Armani, and the plain, bone-colored pumps would make a clear statement: elegance, taste, and quality.

"Ah, if it isn't my barefoot contessa," Philip said, giving her a roguish smile. "Did you sleep well?"

Viviana hastily skirted the large bed, picking up the shoes she'd hurriedly discarded the night before. "Yes. I had a wonderful sleep." She raised a flirtatious brow as she slipped into her pumps, surreptitiously stealing a glance at the clock. *Not much time to spare.*

"You were certainly up bright and early this morning."

"Do you mind?" she said, then instantly slipped in, "I'd much rather have stayed in bed with you."

She crossed the room to join him.

"I know," he said, "but we must occasionally forgo some of our wanton pleasure for the world outside."

"Wanton?" she repeated with a frown, embarrassed.

Taking her two slim hands in his, he pulled her down on his lap. "Deliciously wanton, I should say." He kissed her forehead, then turned her loose. And with a light pat on her bottom, he said with a lustful smile, "Off with you, if you don't want to be terribly late. It's nearly seven thirty. Let's have some coffee. Then I'll drop you off at the Ambassador."

She felt heat rise inexplicably to her cheeks. *What's wrong with me?* She struggled to put away that thought but couldn't smother it. Shouldn't Philip be begging her to stay for another romp in the hay? She knew it was irrational, but she couldn't help but feel disappointed. Why was he so ready to let her be on her way?

It was sometime after four twenty-five before Ashleigh finally fell into a deep sleep. She woke with a start at the sound of the morning hubbub of Belmont Shore. Springing from her bed, she grabbed the alarm clock. She'd forgotten to set it. It was nearly six o'clock, a full hour after her usual waking time.

Barefooted, she raced across the floor to the closet. She reached for the David Hays suit in red silk—the one with the champagne-colored miniature rectangular design—and frowned as her schedule for the day flashed through her mind. Remembering the ten o'clock management meeting at Bentley's headquarters, she impulsively returned the suit, replacing it with the new emerald green St. John dress. Dorothea had been right. The dress fit perfectly, and she knew the deep green suited her. Moments after she'd slipped it over her head in her office and smoothed down the skirt, she'd reached for the phone and charged it to her account.

At six twenty, Ashleigh backed her car out of the parking stall, then glanced across the seat and realized that in her haste she'd forgotten her organizer—one item she could not afford to leave behind. She quickly pulled back in, slipped the gear into park, and ran to the elevator. When the elevator doors opened, she stepped inside and pushed the button for the third floor.

As the doors began to slide closed, a deafening explosion shook the building.

Ashleigh thrust her arm out just in time to stop the closing doors. Slowly they reopened, and she saw a widening slash of yellow light. She took a cautious step forward, then froze, staring at her car.

The white T-Bird was engulfed in flames.

It was a long moment before she managed to force herself to move beyond the elevator. Ghostlike shadows danced along the gray cement walls, reflections of the flickering flames. Ashleigh stared at the shattered glass strewn across the garage floor beside the car and in the empty stalls on either side of hers. Clutching her arms around her midsection, she was mesmerized by the flames leaving their angry black marks along the wall. She scarcely noticed the small group of residents gathering in the entry until she felt a hand on her elbow.

Jerking her head from the sight of the flames, she turned to see the wizened custodian beside her.

"Are you alright?" he said.

"Oh my God." Hearing the panic in her own voice, she bit down on her lip.

"What happened?"

"I don't know," she answered in a daze. "I forgot something and was going back to get it . . . I guess I shouldn't have left the motor running."

He gave her a curious look. "Leaving the motor runnin' wouldn't cause nothin' like this!" He jerked his head toward the car and the dwindling flames.

"Yes . . . I know . . . you're right," Ashleigh agreed, her voice barely above a whisper. But she didn't want to consider the shocking alternative.

Viviana paused at the curb in front of the Ambassador Hotel. As the door to the limousine clicked softly in place, she surreptitiously glanced around to see who might be observing her grand arrival. Then, leaning down into the open window, she give Philip Sloane a fleeting kiss, followed by her practiced smile—seductive, but with a certain degree of wide-eyed innocence. Leaning even closer, she whispered, "Tonight at seven?"

She was pleased with the boyish grin that spread across Philip's face as the long white limo pulled slowly from the curb.

It was eight AM on the dot when Viviana walked into the coffee shop. She spotted Adele Watson at a booth next to the window and glided toward her, head held high, not missing a single admiring stare that came her way.

Adele glanced up at Viviana, then at her watch—a habit that infuriated Viviana almost as much as the phony smile and chatter that were sure to follow.

True to form, Adele smiled sweetly. "Good morning, my dear," she said. "I tried to get in touch with you last night, and again this morning, but I was told that you weren't registered."

In spite of herself, Viviana felt a flash of heat rise from somewhere around her neck. It was none of Adele's business where she stayed, as long as she did her job, which she always did. Viviana prided herself on always being on time.

To avoid appearing defensive, she carefully formulated her response, but before she had a chance to deliver those well-chosen words, Adele said, "I was hoping perhaps we might have met a little earlier to go over the strategy for Anne Klein." Then with a flick of her wrist, she said, "Oh well, somehow we'll manage."

Adele smiled sweetly, but Viviana did not miss the cutting edge. *Jealous old biddy,* she thought, but wisely decided not to be baited.

"All I want is a cup of tea. I see you've already ordered, so we have plenty of time." Viviana signaled to the waitress. "Anne Klein is only five minutes from here, and nothing has changed since I went over the current trends with you and your buyers just last week." She paused thoughtfully. "We know how much we have to spend, so all we really need to decide on is the assortment, which we will need to do while we are in the showroom." She spoke in a congenial tone but could see that her words had hit the mark.

Adele's struggle for control registered on her pinched face "Until we actually edit the line, it is not prudent to commit to our numbers in stone. Danielle's little disappearing act doesn't surprise me one bit. She might have pulled the wool over many eyes, but I know my business."

If Adele wants to play one-upmanship with me, Viviana thought, *she'll find herself the loser.*

As Adele spewed out one platitude on top of another, Viviana wanted to scream. "Look, Adele, I don't know what's happened to Danielle, but she was one of the best."

"Oh, my dear, please don't get defensive," Adele said, her voice saccharine. "I don't deny that Danielle Norman has fine taste, but it takes a lot more than that to make a profit. And profit is the name of the game, isn't it?"

There she goes again, thought Viviana. Adele had a way of twisting things and talking down to just about everyone. Viviana was well aware that the number-one priority of any retailer was the bottom line. She forced herself to listen until she could get the conversation back on track. Appraising the large, expensively dressed woman across the table, she noted, as she had many times before, that Adele hadn't the foggiest idea of how to make a quality fashion statement for herself, let alone for Bentleys Royale. *God help her poor defenseless buyers.*

As Adele droned on, Viviana glanced down at the assortment recap for Better Sportswear. The commitment in Lady Adrianna was excessive, and it was out of character for Danielle to go overboard with any vendor. Fiddling with an earring, she realized that if what she was beginning to suspect was true, and she still couldn't reach Jeff Bradley by the afternoon, she would have to bring David Jerome completely into the picture. The depth of merchandise she'd seen in La Jolla from Bradley's line was not reflected on this sales and stock sheet for Better Sportswear.

As it struck her that it might already be too late for Danielle to salvage her career, a wave of nausea washed over her. *Danielle Norman had more taste in a single blond curl than Adele Watson would ever have. Yet this evil woman had been allowed to push and destroy one talented buyer after another. Where would it stop?*

CHAPTER

46

The shrill blare of the fire trucks still rang in Ashleigh's ears. Only vaguely did she remember the custodian running up to her and the other residents milling about. The paramedics had at first insisted she be taken to the hospital, but she had refused. Luckily, she hadn't been anywhere near the explosion. After the police and bomb squad had arrived, she had signed the various information and release forms and the ambulance left the scene.

Now, alone in her own condo, she waited for the police to come upstairs to interview her. Someone—but she couldn't remember who—had said they would be there any minute. She couldn't even remember who had walked her back to the condo, only that everyone seemed to think she was in shock. *Well, I probably am,* she reasoned. *But there's no need to stay home and dwell on what just happened.* There was a corporate management meeting at ten, and although she no longer had any illusions of arriving on time, she was determined to be at that meeting.

Pulling her thoughts together, she crossed the room, slowly lowered herself into the chair beside the phone, and mechanically dialed the number to Mr. Jerome's office. Méchie picked it up on the second ring.

Steeling herself to sound normal, she said, "I've had some car trouble . . ." Then she hesitated, her nails absently strumming on the phone table. "I'm afraid I will be a little late to the management meeting." She paused for Méchie's acknowledgment before asking, "Is Mr. Jerome planning to stop by his office before he goes downtown?"

"No," Méchie responded. "He has an eight thirty appointment with Mr. Toddman, so he's going straight to the corporate offices."

"Please leave a message with Mr. Toddman's secretary. I'll get there as soon as I can, but I'll have to rent a car first." *I have too much to do to rely on taxis,* she thought as she hung up.

She would tell Mr. Jerome in person what had happened. Then she must make it clear to him that she could not be objective about Danielle after all. Whatever the consequences, she must be up-front about that.

Next she called Mitchell's hotel in Atlanta but learned that she had just missed him; he had a lunch with Mr. Updike, owner and CEO of Updike Publishing Company. Though Mitchell's explanation was vague, she knew that he and Philip Sloane, his strongest rival, were vying for the Updike acquisition. She didn't understand all the nuances of leveraged buyouts, but according to the *Wall Street Journal*, these two "major corporate raiders" had personal reasons for gaining control of the small publishing house. She had no greater knowledge of Mitchell's motivation than she did of Sloane's.

She quickly jotted down the number where he could be reached, then thumbed through the Yellow Pages until she located the number for Hertz. Just as an efficient-sounding woman answered the phone, Ashleigh's doorbell rang. She asked the Hertz woman to hold, laid the phone down, and went to the door. She felt gooseflesh rise on her arms as she reached for the knob. "Who is it?" she asked.

Two police officers identified themselves, and she opened the door. "How long do you think this will take?"

Neither man answered immediately. Then the stocky man with black wavy hair spoke up, rubbing his thumb along his jawline. "No more than half an hour, ma'am?" His voice rose at the end, as if it were a question.

"I'll just be a moment," Ashleigh said, and she returned to the phone. But today's management meeting was not one she intended to miss, for any reason. She had to hear for herself what the CEO had to say about the probable year-end results. The fate of both divisions hinged on those results. She did not want it to be secondhand news.

After making arrangements to pick up the car at the Long Beach airport, she turned her full attention to the police officers. She told them about her being followed the night before, but could shed no light on who had followed her or why. The fact that someone had planted a bomb in her car shot fear through every fiber of her body, but there too she was at a loss. It was all incomprehensible. She seen enough movies and read enough novels to know that there had to be a motive, but she could not think of a single one, nor a single person who might be out to do her harm. By the time the officers left, there was no doubt in her mind: Her car had been tampered with, and by someone who certainly knew his way around explosives.

CHAPTER

47

Ashleigh stood in front of her condo waiting for the taxi that would take her to the airport. She didn't have any time to spare. It was already nine twenty. She looked across Second Street to the Portofino, desperately wanting to talk to Conrad about what had just happened. But he would already have left very early that morning.

Catching herself, she looked away, focusing her mind on the yachts moored in the bay. Today, as they bobbed up and down, Ashleigh was not soothed. To her raw nerves, the wailing of the riggings as they scraped against their masts seemed unusually mournful.

She stood with her back against the building and scanned the street. There was no sign of a Karmann Ghia. Nothing seemed out of order. But she couldn't deny the magnitude of this morning's events.

For the past two days she had felt as though she were playing the role of someone else—a role that was unreal and alien to her. She felt a vulnerability she hadn't known for years. Someone was trying to harm her. It was clear that she was physically in danger. Why and from whom, she had no idea.

After Ashleigh deposited the rental car beside the sign marked 50¢ PER HALF HOUR/$10 MAXIMUM PER DAY, her hand shook as she gave the keys to an attendant. It seemed that she'd spent as much time looking in the rearview mirror as she had looking straight ahead. After a tense forty-five-minute drive, her nerves were on edge.

She steeled herself and raced toward the corporate office building. By ten fifteen, she was creeping into the mini-auditorium, headed toward a straight-backed chair beside Laura Cameron and the other Bentleys Royale executives.

The familiar words of Mark Toddman echoed through the room. "We must tighten our belts and recoup our losses. I'm not going to dictate how you do it; this group is bright enough to figure that out. And I don't need to tell you that although we exceeded our sales plans by three-point-one percent, the profit picture is far below expectation . . ."

Making her way down the row of chairs, Ashleigh felt the critical eye of Mr. Jerome on her. He was seated at the far end of the row. Either Méchie had been unable to forward her message, or he'd chosen not to accept it. She should have known he wouldn't consider car trouble an acceptable excuse. Why hadn't she told Méchie that her car had been blown up? Surely that was a good enough reason for being fifteen minutes late. *I have no reason to feel guilty,* she thought. *And yet . . .*

She attempted to focus her attention on the meeting, but felt the unsteady rhythm of her heartbeat when Conrad Taylor's head turned briefly in her direction. She silently took her seat beside her peers.

Conrad sat in the front row, just a few feet from the lectern. Although he had instantly returned his attention to Toddman, she hadn't missed the quizzical tilt of his dark brow. *I must talk to him.*

When Conrad took the microphone, his message was clear. Not only had Bentley's Department Stores and Bentleys Royale blown their profit commitment, but the holiday season that typically generated eighty percent of annual profit had been a financial disaster.

"We know what eroded this year's gross margin," Conrad declared. There was an uncomfortable silence. Eyes stared down at the carpeted floor, avoiding direct contact as Conrad's voice echoed through the room. "No one predicted the change in the retail climate of Southern California. I don't need to remind you of the part we all played, with one major retailer after another dropping prices and beginning the traditional after-Christmas sales weeks ahead of schedule. We might say it started with the colossal pre-Christmas sales initiated by the May

Company and Broadway, and spread quickly through the retail community. The domino effect took over."

Conrad cleared his throat and took a large gulp of water from the half-filled glass on the table to his left.

The majority of the top management of Bentley's Department Stores and Bentleys Royale were merchants responsible for sales and profit and therefore for the fate of the entire West Coast Division of Consolidated. Aware of their level of discomfort, Ashleigh waited for Conrad to continue. Brows furrowed and jaws were set tight. A background of chairs creaked as bodies readjusted their positions.

Ashleigh felt the tension spread throughout the room, and she found it difficult to concentrate. Her head filled with visions of the dark-blue Karmann Ghia, her own white Thunderbird in a cloud of smoke, and Danielle's yellow VW. Dancing through her mind were the fur-lined raincoat, burgundy pens, butterflies, phony vendor receipts, the LV handbag, and all of Danielle's crystal ware. A throbbing certainty began to pound in Ashleigh's head: *Danielle could be dead.*

". . . and the challenge is how to maintain our gross margin as well as our share of market. I believe that in this room we have the intelligence and the talent to make it happen."

Ashleigh was rocketed back to the present by the thunderous applause in response to Conrad Taylor's challenge and vote of confidence.

"Now, that's the good news." His forehead creased in a frown as he continued. "We are seeing a tough year ahead for most apparel-based retailers, particularly major department and specialty stores. Bentley's and Bentleys Royale will continue to feel the impact of consumer reluctance to spend. Our number-one priority at this time is to recoup fourth-quarter losses. We must be proactive, tighten our belts, and drastically reduce expenses. Effective immediately, each store and each budget center must reduce expenses by a minimum of twenty percent."

Looking in the direction of the Bentleys Royale management team, he said, "Customer service areas—excuse me, *patron* service areas—are not to be touched." There were murmurs throughout the room. "Other areas, however, must be targeted for major reductions. In many sales support areas, we have become fat and overstaffed. This is not a popular concept, but nevertheless it's true. Some carefully executed pruning must be set in motion."

He shook his head sympathetically. "Many of these reductions will be temporary. When our gross margin reaches or exceeds plans, we will reevaluate." It was little consolation.

After the meeting, Conrad, engrossed in conversation with Mark Toddman, walked out of the mini-auditorium without a backward glance.

Ashleigh watched as the two men disappeared through the heavy doors. Then, turning her head, she saw Mr. O'Brien just three feet away from her.

"Ashleigh," O'Brien said, "could you spare about twenty minutes?" Not pausing, he added, "I'd like to talk to you in private."

There was an awkward silence as Ashleigh scanned the room for Mr. Jerome. She spotted him near the lectern, talking with someone she did not recognize.

"Yes," she responded. Her hands felt clammy, and she tried to pull her thoughts together. "Do you want to see me now?"

He nodded. "If it's not inconvenient, I'd like you to come up to my office."

In fact, it was terribly inconvenient. She needed to talk to Mr. Jerome, and she had to call Mitchell again. And then there was Conrad Taylor.

Not for the first time that day, Ashleigh reined in her thoughts. Her mind stopped reeling, and her thoughts crystallized. She knew what she must do.

CHAPTER

48

Conrad Taylor stepped back into the crowded auditorium and scanned the room, his eyes darting from one group to the next. But Ashleigh was gone, and so were the other Bentleys Royale executives. *They must have slipped out the east door,* he thought as he hurried down the corridor, past the associate security counter, and out through the massive double-glass doors at the entry of the corporate building.

"Mr. Taylor," David Jerome called, walking away from a small group of his colleagues. Jerome wore a pink shirt with his three-piece Oxxford suit, a shade lighter than Conrad's, and the familiar pin-dot tie. His appearance was no more casual than his greeting.

"Yes, Mr. Jerome." Conrad smiled and approached the older man, his eyes continuing to survey the sidewalk leading to the parking lot. There was no sign of Ashleigh.

When the two men were face-to-face, Jerome said, "Conrad, I have another meeting back here at four. Could we meet sometime before then?"

"Sure, David." He pulled a small leather-bound Day-Timer from his inside pocket. "I think I could arrange to be free by three or three thirty."

"Three thirty would be good. And, Conrad, would you gather all the statistical information you have so far on Danielle Norman's departments? I realize this is no big deal to corporate, but the effect on Bentleys Royale could be devastating. That three hundred thousand or whatever it turns out to be will make a hell of a dent in our profit picture."

Conrad nodded his understanding.

Then Jerome's look changed to one of grave concern as lines cut deeply into his forehead. "There's something . . . *out of kilter* about

Danielle Norman's disappearance," he said quietly. "If you knew her like we do, you'd know there has to be something . . ." His face colored. "What I mean is, something's just not kosher."

As the door clicked softly behind them, O'Brien motioned Ashleigh into one of the armchairs while he lowered himself into the other. He turned to face her, noting that she looked pale and drawn. He was particularly fond of Ashleigh McDowell, and this deeply concerned him. *Damn it,* he thought, *don't let her be another casualty in the Royale division.*

Ashleigh had brought a semblance of sanity to the Personnel department's decisions and practices within the specialty stores. While the president had retained his own unique ideas about how to run his business, as a result of her counsel he had made far fewer irrational promotions within the organization. O'Brien wasn't willing to go back to square one. He needed Ashleigh, and he needed her at her best.

"Mr. O'Brien," she began in her clear, unwavering fashion, "I'm glad you asked me to see you."

He looked at her skeptically and folded his arms in front of him. His agenda for this meeting was clear, and he was impatient to get started.

"Mr. Jerome told me that you asked if I could be objective in regard to Danielle Norman."

Somewhat taken aback, he said, "Ashleigh, I didn't say anything to your boss that I wouldn't say to you. I realize that you are a professional, but your personal ties to Ms. Norman would make objectivity difficult for anyone."

She cut him short, shaking her head. "Mr. O'Brien, what I want to tell you is that you were right to question my objectivity."

As she leaned forward, he noticed the pain in her widening eyes.

"I thought I could be," she went on. "But no matter how objective I may have been in the past, I can no longer remain so."

"I don't want to hear that." He pushed back his chair and began to rise, but stopped when he saw the determined set of her jaw.

"Please," she said, "let me finish." Then she paused, as if she wasn't sure how to tell him what was on her mind.

When the secretary arrived with two mugs of coffee—black for her and cream and sugar for him—he watched her, saw her hand shake as she reached for the mug. The secretary disappeared behind the closing door, and Ashleigh took a long, thoughtful sip, then shifted in the chair.

When she began to speak, her eye contact was direct, her voice determined. "Before I see Mr. Jerome, I want to know if it would be possible for me to take a brief leave of absence."

CHAPTER
49

A light tap on his office door broke Conrad's concentration. He looked up from the stack of reports. "Yes," he snapped.

The door slowly swung open, and Ashleigh poked her head in.

He sprang from his chair, the reports that had seemed so important moments before forgotten.

"Is this a bad time?" She remained just inside the doorway.

"Not at all," he said, ushering her in and closing the door behind her.

"I just have a few minutes." She hesitated, looking vulnerable. Unless he was mistaken, she'd had barely a wink of sleep.

"You weren't followed again, were you?" He pulled out one of the armchairs from in front of his desk and gestured for her to be seated.

She shook her head, and the next thing out of her mouth shocked him: "Someone planted a bomb in my car." She instantly added, "I wasn't hurt. But my car is beyond repair."

Questions filled Conrad's mind, but Ashleigh held up her hand and quickly began filling him in. Alarm sliced through him then, as a picture of Ashleigh behind the wheel of the flaming Thunderbird suddenly flashed before his eyes.

"Conrad, were you able to get any information on that Karmann Ghia?"

Conrad was having trouble making sense out of what had happened, let alone who was responsible or why. He felt as if he'd been punched in the stomach. He could no longer deny that he cared for this woman—cared a great deal.

When at last he broke his silence, he spoke slowly, his tone calm. "Pocino had the license number checked by his buddy." He didn't bother to tell her the problems Pocino had had in tracing the plate. "The plates belonged to a black Buick Riviera, not a Karmann Ghia."

Ashleigh furrowed her brow. "Could you have miscopied the number?"

"No," Conrad replied with certainty. "I double-checked. The number I gave Pocino was the number on that car." He softened his tone. "The police contacted the owner of the Buick. He had no idea that his front license plate was missing." He paused. "When I described the car and asked Pocino to check on the license number, he said he remembered seeing a Ghia parked on the street beside Danielle's driveway the night he drove you there. He said it could have been blue."

Ashleigh stared up at him, her dark eyes wide.

"Whoever you heard in those bushes had to have transportation. And think about it: Danielle's car was seen Tuesday morning at Bentleys Royale, so someone had to have returned it to her house. The Ghia was his ride back. So I'd say there's more than one person involved in her disappearance."

"Ross didn't say anything about a car that night. Was it still there when we left?" Then answering her own question, she said, "It couldn't have been. I would have noticed a Karmann Ghia." She leaned forward as if to rise.

Placing his hands on her shoulders, Conrad said, "Slow down. I'm not sure when Pocino noticed the car. You can ask him later. He said it hadn't seemed important at the time." He rotated his shoulders, but it did little to relieve the tension. "Karmann Ghias are rare these days, so even with stolen plates—the Buick's or new ones, it shouldn't be difficult to trace."

It sounded logical, but he hadn't a clue where to start. There was something strangely out of sync. The use of stolen plates had the ring of a professional, but driving a Karmann Ghia for surveillance, or whatever it was, seemed ludicrous.

"Did you tell the police about last night?" he asked.

"A little. I told them about being followed last night. But when they asked if I had any idea who it was or why, I said no." Shaking her head as if to clear her mind, she added, "And that's the absolute truth. I didn't tell them about Danielle's disappearance, though. They would've thought I just sounded neurotic . . ."

Conrad wanted to reach out and touch her as her voice trailed off. "Ashleigh, if you're neurotic so am I. I don't know what's going on. I don't know if it has anything to do with Danielle's disappearance or not. That car being at Danielle's points in that direction, but the person in the Ghia may have just followed you there."

"But why?"

He hesitated before saying what had kept him up half the night. "Your fiancé's business dealings tend to breed powerful and potentially dangerous enemies."

So do his personal dealings, she thought, recalling the bad blood between Mitchell and his former wife. "But I have nothing to do with hostile takeovers. And what about the signs of someone hiding in the bushes at Danielle's?"

"That does point back to Danielle's disappearance," he agreed. "Whatever the motivation, it's obvious that you are in danger." He rose and began pacing back and forth in front of the large window, watching the traffic glide by. Then he turned back to Ashleigh.

With a sigh, she pulled herself to her feet. "Nothing adds up. I've never been more frightened in my life."

"God knows you're entitled." He frowned. "How about police protection?"

Ashleigh shrugged. "They said they'd keep an eye on my condo and the parking area."

"That's not good enough." He stepped toward her.

Her eyes narrowed. "I hate this. I hate being scared. I hate jumping every time I hear a noise in the hall, or bracing myself whenever an elevator stops on my floor."

"That's my point. You need protection." He hesitated. "Ashleigh, for the moment, set thoughts about Danielle aside. I'm not sure how to . . . how to say this . . ." He faltered. "And you may think it's none of my business, but I want to help you."

"What are you trying to say?" she demanded.

"Alright, I'll just blurt it out. Do you have any information that could be considered damaging by anyone—whether inside or outside of Bentleys Royale?"

Without a second's hesitation, she said, "Of course I do. It's my job to keep notes on every executive in the organization, and I sit in on every review, with the exception of Mr. Jerome's and my own. I have volumes of information that people would prefer remained sealed between the covers of my big black notebooks. Like that old cliché, 'Never to see the light of day.'"

She paused briefly, then said, "But there's nothing that I alone know. And it's certainly not the kind of information that would cause some-one to blow up my car in an attempt to silence me." She shuddered and breathed deeply. "I've thought of every possibility and there's noth-ing . . . nothing that I know of."

Conrad saw no other option. His thoughts went back to Mitchell Wainwright and the unorthodox type of business venture he was pio-neering. Perhaps that *did* involve the kind of information that someone would want to silence.

CHAPTER
50

After Ashleigh left, Conrad again closed his office door, but he found that he was unable to concentrate on the reports piled high on his desk. *Why would someone be following Ashleigh? And what about the car bomb?* If it were a distraught executive—someone out for revenge—it was far more likely that the target would be that troubled person's boss, not Ashleigh McDowell.

As he continued to speculate, he could come up with no link between Danielle's disappearance and the danger Ashleigh was in. It made no goddamned sense—until his mind traveled back to Mitchell Wainwright. He didn't know a lot about the corporate raider's business dealings, but he did know that Wainwright's new weapon of corporate destruction was the leveraged buyout. And that world was inhabited by a host of the nation's most volatile personalities. Unbidden, Medley Originals drifted through his mind. *Medley Originals was Wainwright's first hostile takeover. It was also one of Danielle's vendors—one that accounted for thousands of dollars of her overbought status.*

Like a corkscrew, Conrad's mind twisted back again to Ashleigh. *She won't be safe until we find out what in blazes is going on.* He jabbed the intercom button and said, "Please page Ross Pocino."

Placing his elbows on his desk, his head supported between his hands, he tried to piece together what he knew about Jeff Bradley. *Too damn little,* he realized. He reached for a sheet of memo paper and jotted down a reminder to have Pocino check into the make of Bradley's car.

That settled, Conrad's thoughts shifted back to Ashleigh. She had to be protected. He picked up the phone and dialed information. "I'd like the number for the Long Beach Police Department, please."

CHAPTER

51

It was nearly twelve thirty by the time Ashleigh reached her own office. She walked into the abandoned reception area and gathered her messages from the black Lucite rack on her secretary's desk, then went straight into her office, shutting the door behind her. Although Betty was away from her desk, she would know when she saw the closed door that Ashleigh wasn't to be disturbed.

First, she dialed Mr. Jerome's extension and asked Méchie to set up an appointment with the president for the afternoon. Mr. O'Brien's advice had been prudent; the president would never agree to an LOA. Besides, she could no more walk out on Bentleys Royale than she could turn away from Danielle.

Next, she picked up her private line. Somehow, she must reach Mitchell. Cradling the phone between her head and shoulder, she sorted through her messages and saw that he had returned her earlier call and left another number to call after three o'clock. Ashleigh looked at her clock; it was now close to three thirty in Atlanta, so she dialed the new number. It was the Atlanta Hilton.

Mitchell answered on the second ring. "Hello, darling. Good to hear your voice. I rescheduled a meeting so I wouldn't miss your call."

Ashleigh stiffened at the sound of his voice. His *everything's wonderful* greeting had the same effect as cat claws on a slick surface. She went on as if he'd said nothing other than *hello*, and attempted to take the chill out of her tone. "Mitchell . . ." She hesitated, suddenly feeling foolish. She knew that he was not responsible for the explosives in her car. He wouldn't hurt her. It made no sense. But nothing she could think of did.

"Yes, darling? What's wrong? Are you alright?"

"Yes," she said, in a stronger, more confident voice. "Mitchell, some-one has been following me."

After a long few seconds he said, "What do you mean? Who's follow-ing you?"

"I don't know."

He laughed. "I don't blame them." Then, as if it had just struck him, he said in an incredulous tone, "Ashleigh, you don't think I've had you followed, do you?"

"I don't know what to think."

"Why would you think I'd have you followed?" He sounded angry and offended.

"I'm sorry. It's just that you're the only person I know who has people followed."

"Look, Ashleigh, I don't know what's going on, but I certainly didn't have you followed." His voice was harsh and impatient. "Tell me what's going on."

When she tried to tell him, he stopped her abruptly. "Why in the hell did you have to go to Danielle Norman's house a second time? Wasn't once enough?"

Ashleigh tightened her grasp on the receiver, and her voice rose as she said, "Sorry I bothered you. Good-bye."

"Wait. I didn't mean to raise my voice." Mitchell sighed. "I guess I'm losing my perspective. Chris Ferrari had me pulled out of an extremely important meeting yesterday, asking about purchases Danielle made from Medley Originals. What kind of idiot is he, anyway?"

"Mitchell, Chris Ferrari is no idiot," she said defensively. "I don't know why he asked to talk to you, but I imagine Mr. Jerome told him to start at the top."

"Well, it's a hell of a waste of time. I'm no merchant, and I'm certainly not involved in the day-to-day running of Medley Originals. Jerome is well aware of that fact. I know nothing of those insignificant purchases."

Ashleigh shifted the phone to her other ear. "Ferrari should know bet-ter. I referred him to the general merchandise manager, where he should have started in the first place."

Ashleigh sighed in frustration. It seemed that Mitchell was always putting her on the defensive. *Should I even tell him about my car?* she said to herself.

Mitchell fell unexpectedly silent. Then—calmly, softly—he said, "I didn't mean to unload on you."

Her mind drifting, she drew circles interlacing more circles on her yellow pad.

"Ashleigh, I'm concerned. The fact that someone may be following you scares the hell out of me."

"Wait, Mitchell, there's more." Tears filled her eyes. She could handle his anger. But his concern broke down her defenses. She suddenly decided to tell him everything. She began with the Thunderbird blowing up.

"Hold it . . . Your car was blown up? Where?" He stopped his barrage of questions as abruptly as he had begun it.

Her throat felt dry, and her hand was unsteady on the phone. As she attempted to fill him in, he broke in repeatedly with a litany of unanswerable questions.

Finally she asked one of her own. "Why would anyone put a delay switch on explosives in a car?"

"A delay switch?" he parroted.

"When I asked why the car hadn't blown up when I started the engine, the policeman told me that it would depend on the explosives, but that it was probably rigged with a delay switch." By now her bisecting circles covered the entire page. "I wasn't thinking too clearly at the time, and I didn't ask why."

"I'll look into it."

She let the pencil drop from her fingers. "Forget it. I don't know what difference it makes."

"I don't know what's going on, but I'm damned sure going to find out. And I'll be on the next flight into L.A."

"No!" The word was out of her mouth like a shot. "I'm going to La Jolla tomorrow and then to Palm Desert. I'm going to spend the weekend with Beverly. And, Mitchell, nothing has changed between us since two nights ago."

"Not now, and not over the phone. We'll discuss it when I get back," he said emphatically. "Now, let me make sure I understand what has happened. First you tell me that you've been followed. Then you tell me that your car was wired with explosives. And you're going to keep pursuing this, going to keep working—and you don't want me to come back to L.A. to make sure you're okay?"

Anxious to bring the conversation to an end, she said, "Mitchell, whether you like it or not, I have to find out what's happened to Danielle." She was prepared for his angry retort, and when it didn't come, she was relieved. So relieved that she decided to ask a favor. "While you're in Atlanta, could you find out if an Irene McIntyre still lives there? She isn't listed in the phone book."

"Dan's mother?" His raised voice blazed through the lines.

"And Danielle's," she countered. Detaching from his animosity, she asked, "Please, Mitchell, will you try to help?"

"Ashleigh, your own life is in danger. I'll be damned if I can figure out why—"

"Will you help?" she repeated.

His voice traveled through the line, straining for control. "Alright. I'll see what I can do, but there are conditions." Sensing her readiness to protest, he quickly added, "Conditions to assure your safety."

Ashleigh heard the click of his familiar gold lighter and imagined him lighting up. By this time of day, he was probably at the end of his second pack or even beginning his third.

"You told me that Danielle had a stepfather, didn't you?"

Ashleigh had no trouble anticipating his next question. "Irene chose to keep the name McIntyre." She hesitated, remembering what Dan had told her. "I don't believe she was ever legally remarried. And I don't know what her situation is now. But if you find her, I'd like you to find out if Danielle has been in touch."

He sucked on the cigarette and exhaled. "Is that likely?"

"No. Her name isn't even listed as next of kin in Danielle's Personnel file. But Mr. Jerome asked me to call." She thought of the woman with distaste "I don't have her number, and I would prefer not to have to talk to her if I can avoid it."

"I may be able to locate her through voter registration. But if she can't be found that way, is it important enough for me to use other means?"

"Like what?" she asked.

"There are ways. Utility companies have fairly accurate records, which can be tapped. I'm asking how far I should chase this lead, since it's clear you think it's another dead end."

"Please, do what you can."

By the time they ended their conversation, Mitchell had made his position clear: He was opposed to her trying to find out what had happened to Danielle. But she was sick of discussing it and would not back down. Despite initial protests, she had at least agreed to turn in the Hertz rental and use the Mercedes—an engagement gift she had refused to accept. And yes, she would meet with Dick Landes, the private investigator Mitchell had on retainer.

Furthermore, Mitchell had thwarted each of her attempts to make it clear that there was no future for them together. He refused to discuss it, refused to accept that she would not change her mind. But she would not. She had felt something for him—so charming, so attentive—but it was more akin to plugging a hole in her heart than it was to true love. Now that she had realized this, there was nothing to be salvaged.

With all Mitchell currently had on his plate, she hadn't actually believed that he'd been responsible for having her followed—but now that he had vehemently denied it, she was left with the same haunting questions: Who was? And why?

Chapter

52

For Ashleigh, the two days since she'd learned that Danielle had gone missing seemed to have passed in a blur. The personnel director was out with chicken pox, of all things, and the clerical was on vacation, leaving only the assistant in the headquarters Personnel office. Ashleigh's time so far had been divided between the urgent and necessary aspects of her own position and those of headquarters Personnel.

Having been away from the day-to-day running of a personnel office for the past few years, Ashleigh had scarcely managed to clear her calendar from one o'clock to two for her lunch date with Naomi Wainwright.

She stepped out of the elevator on the fifth floor and looked up at the large clock above the concealed door to the associates' cafeteria. It was exactly one o'clock—right on time. She turned and walked rapidly past Mr. Jerome's office toward the reservations line.

Naomi Wainwright, who was just a few paces ahead of her, swept into the famous tearoom without a backward glance. Heads turned as the stunning, aristocratic woman glided across the floor. Her classic Chanel suit, with a pearl-pink jacket and straight black skirt, complemented the petite woman's slim figure.

Lawrence, the dapper maître d', rushed forward to greet her. "Mrs. Wainwright. What a pleasure to see you." He gave her one of his most charming smiles.

Naomi smiled warmly. Then, spotting Ashleigh, she turned, stretching up to give her an air kiss, a gesture that always made Ashleigh uncomfortable—now more than ever. Forcing a smile, she greeted Naomi.

Naomi held her head high as they were led to their table. After a bit of small talk, the area of conversation with which Ashleigh felt most inadequate, they ordered lunch from the leather-jacketed menu.

Mitchell's mother got right to the point after announcing her intention to do so. "We haven't had much of a chance to get to know each other, and I plan to remedy that, beginning right now."

Ashleigh felt a quiver in her stomach as the older woman smiled and patted her hand. If only she could change the course of this conversation, turn it in any other direction, but her brain seemed to have shut down.

"I must tell you," Naomi continued, "we've seen such a change in Mitchell. A very positive change, I might add. I don't want to sound melodramatic, and as much as I dislike clichés . . . You have been the best thing that could have happened to him, especially now." She paused expectantly. "I don't know how much Mitchell has told you . . ."

About what? Ashleigh didn't want to listen. "Naomi, Mitchell and I haven't had much time to talk about anything lately, and there are several things he and I need to get settled between us." *If only I could just tell her the truth.*

Naomi stiffened a little, but her expression did not change. "I'm sure you'll be able to sort things out with that spirited son of mine." She smiled again. "Ashleigh, I'm afraid that the Wainwright men present quite a challenge. Mitchell is just like his father and his grandfather—strong-willed and dynamic men. They tend to be controlling. However, they aren't really so difficult to handle once you learn how." She smiled and took a sip of water from the crystal goblet. "Mitchell is awfully proud of you."

A tall, dark-haired girl ascended the stairs to the modeling ramp that ran the length of the tearoom. She wore a suit from the David Hayes collection. Relieved to have an excuse to turn the conversation to safer, less personal grounds, Ashleigh opened her mouth to comment on the model and her outfit. But it soon became clear that Naomi had a plan of her own.

Leaning across the table, she confided in a low, throaty voice, "Ashleigh, I wanted to talk to you without Mitchell hovering about." For a split second, she appeared uncomfortable. "I'd like our little talk to be strictly between the two of us. Mitchell is very tight-lipped, and he'd be furious with me for discussing these things with you. But I think you should know."

Ashleigh didn't want to hear. Whatever it was, it could no longer concern her—she wanted to put a stop to this. "I don't think . . . ," she began.

Naomi looked down at her hands and began to twist the large emerald dinner ring on her right hand. She appeared to be searching for just the right words. "Has Mitchell told you about his son?" she asked at last. Her solemn blue eyes met Ashleigh's big brown ones.

"I know that he has a son," she answered. "Mitchell told me they had a falling-out, and he no longer sees the boy. He made it clear that he didn't want to discuss it."

Naomi sighed and stared across the room at everything and nothing. "Yes, I know." Then she added, "Is that all he's told you?"

"Yes?" Ashleigh said, turning her reply into a question.

Naomi's face was expressionless. "I was hoping that perhaps he might have confided in you." She took a slow, thoughtful breath and said, "Mitchell doesn't seem able to let anyone get too close. If only he could." Again looking uncomfortable, she went on. "Out of the blue, Mitchell told us that he planned to disown Anthony."

Her words sounded as if they had been taken from a Victorian romance novel. But Ashleigh saw the pain mirrored in the woman's eyes and heard the strain in her voice.

"I'm sure he cares for him. Although they have never been . . . well, what you'd call close." Naomi heaved a sigh, a worried expression on her face. "Ashleigh, I have no idea what prompted him to remove Anthony from his will—if, in fact, that is what he's done. The boy is his only son—his only child—my only grandchild."

Another model glided down the long ramp. Ashleigh noticed that she wore a Blackwell cocktail suit, fully accessorized with hat and gloves. She longed to focus her attention on that instead of on the conversation at hand.

But Naomi gave only a perfunctory glance toward the model. "Anthony is only twenty-three," she continued as she turned the stem of the water goblet between her thumb and index finger, "but he's been in trouble since his early teens. He wasn't quite ten when Mitchell and Diana—the boy's mother—divorced. Although it wasn't a particularly bitter divorce, I'm afraid that it was very damaging to the boy. At first Mitchell saw the boy on weekends, but that didn't last."

She told Ashleigh of the problems with visitation and how weekends had slowly tapered off when the boy preferred to be with his friends on weekends anyway. "Mitchell continued to support Anthony financially, though he seldom saw him—until he started getting into trouble. Mitchell was the one to go to the police station when Anthony was arrested for forgery, and then again on two assault and battery charges. Mitchell had him out on bail with not as much as a single night in jail, and he hired a top criminal attorney. The boy was given no more than a heavy fine, which Mitchell paid, along with damages for the forgeries. Both charges of assault and battery were dropped."

Naomi's eyes met Ashleigh's again. "I'm afraid Mitchell made things all too easy for Anthony. The boy has never had to take responsibility. But he can be so sweet and loving, and I honestly believe that getting in trouble is Anthony's way of getting attention from his father. Sadly, Anthony is a victim of too much money and too little direction."

Ashleigh nodded throughout Naomi's monologue, on the one hand wanting desperately to halt the conversation, and on the other wanting to know more. She realized how much Mitchell's mother must need to talk about this heartbreaking issue.

"About six months ago," Naomi said, her eyes brimming with tears, "Mitchell arrived at the house for dinner and announced that he no longer wished to consider Anthony his son. He even insinuated that perhaps he wasn't the boy's real father, which is absurd—though he lacks Mitchell's height, Anthony is a mirror image of his father." She took another sip of water. "Mitchell told me that I could handle my relationship with Anthony in any way I wished, but that he didn't want to hear any more about him—not ever." Naomi's silver-blue eyes were damp and glistening, but she sat straight in her chair, her hands folded in front of her. "I've tried—oh, how I've tried—to get Mitchell to tell me what happened! I know he's hurting. Otherwise he wouldn't be so angry."

Finally Ashleigh tried to interrupt once again. "Naomi, I don't want to be rude, but I'm uncomfortable talking about this."

"Oh! Why, of course you are, dear," she said. "I'm truly sorry. I hadn't intended to surface all the family skeletons. I'm just so upset . . ." She made a gesture with her hand, as if to erase her words. "Please forgive my rambling. I shouldn't have bothered you."

The woman looked so upset that Ashleigh felt she should say something, but before she could figure out just what, Naomi said, "What I really wanted to talk to you about was Diana."

"Diana?"

An energetic waitress in a black uniform with the familiar white ruffled apron appeared and silently placed their lunches in front of them, while a busboy refilled their water goblets. Naomi, with the salad trio of chicken, turkey, and shrimp, eyed Ashleigh's tuna boat, a half cantaloupe filled with tuna, and continued, "Diana, Mitchell's former wife, is program chairman for the Assistance League, the service organization that's sponsoring the Salute to Hollywood dinner dance."

"Yes, so I've heard," Ashleigh said.

"Ashleigh, I don't think you understand. Diana and Mitchell were completely wrong for each other. She was involved in everything—adored all the social affairs. Mitchell, on the other hand, hated the stream of nightly parties, the foundation dinners and social events and charity galas. It was a source of irritation in their marriage, and while I don't believe there is any such thing as a good divorce, theirs was not particularly traumatic. They both wanted out."

Ashleigh's mind wandered as Naomi continued. She thought of all the organizations that Mitchell supported and was involved with. What Naomi was saying didn't ring true.

Her mind snapped back abruptly when Naomi again grasped her hand, this time saying, "Ashleigh, you must understand. Anthony is her only son—her only child. Diana holds you responsible for Anthony being threatened with disinheritance."

CHAPTER

53

Wainwright clicked the phone button once. With the phone still gripped in his hand, he dialed the hotel operator and gave her the number to the Landes Agency in California. He paced restlessly on the veranda, the long silver phone cord dangling behind him.

The secretary, recognizing his voice, switched him straight through.

Skipping the customary greetings, Wainwright said, "Dick, I'm late to an important meeting, but I wanted to get hold of you first. I need you to protect my fiancée." He gave Landes Ashleigh's number and a general idea of what she had told him. "Ashleigh is not one to overreact. In fact, the exact opposite. There's no question that she's been followed; she has no flair for dramatics." *She's too preoccupied with her damnable career for any attention-getting nonsense.* "I know she isn't as together as she pretends. She's frightened, but she's also stubborn as hell and bent on finding out what's happened to that missing buyer I told you about. I need you to find out as much as you can as well, and you'll have to provide twenty-four-hour protection. I'm afraid that hardheaded determination of hers could get her into a lot of trouble—or worse."

Wainwright answered Landes's questions and filled him in on what little he knew.

"Assign as many agents as you need to have her protected round the clock," he ordered. "I don't want her out of sight until the person responsible for the car explosion is in custody." Absently, he tapped another cigarette on the gold case that Ashleigh had given him for Christmas. "And give the Bentley's security honcho a call—that heavy-set fellow who got himself in some kind of jam when he worked for the

LAPD. You said he came to you for a job before he went to work for Bentley's . . . ?"

"Ross Pocino?"

"Right. Find out what he knows about the buyer's disappearance. The only thing I know is that she made some unauthorized purchases from Medley Originals, and Ferrari—"

"Head of operations?"

"Right. Apparently we aren't the only vendor involved in this scheme. There may be a lot more, but Ferrari's keeping that to himself."

Wainwright gave a humorless laugh when Landes suggested that perhaps Ashleigh might fill him in, saying, "One thing you need to know about Ashleigh McDowell is that her blinding sense of professionalism takes priority over damned near everything else." He instantly regretted his hasty remark to the P.I., and added, "Ashleigh has a lot of responsibility, and she takes it seriously. I respect her for that, but I'm afraid it's quite unlikely that she'll be candid about what's going on behind the scenes at Bentleys Royale. The only thing I could get out of her was that it appeared there were irregularities in the missing buyer's department. Don't think she'd have offered even that if she hadn't known that I'd been questioned already by their operations man and that Medley Originals was somehow involved."

Wainwright paused and cleared his throat, then said, "I only care about the situation at Bentleys Royale as it relates to Ashleigh. Now, if you don't have any questions, I'd like the number to your Atlanta office."

He jotted down the number and terminated the call. Before making the next call, he decided to check the phone book to see if there was a listing for Irene McIntyre. There was not.

Crossing the room, he picked up the Ronson table lighter from the circular coffee table. Unbidden, his thoughts returned to Ashleigh and their confrontation. It seemed a long time ago, and yet he realized that less than forty-eight hours had passed since he had stormed out of her condo. He shook his head, trying to dispel the vision of his ring in the palm of her hand. But it kept repeating like a merchandising video set on perpetual replay. She was the most infuriating woman he had ever known—so goddamned independent and driven . . . *Yes, driven—there's no other word for it,* he realized. She had been one hundred percent in the wrong Tuesday night. He had made a point of the importance of getting to that special symphony performance on time, but somehow she had maneuvered him into a defensive position—a position he avoided at all costs.

Invariably on the offensive, Wainwright was known for turning the tables in his business dealings—always landing on his feet. He prided himself on doing it with finesse. But somehow Ashleigh managed to turn the tables on him, and even now she would not reverse herself. Stupid pride or just plain bullheadedness, he couldn't be sure. Still standing, he turned the gold cigarette case in his fingers and traced the initials, tastefully etched in the lower left-hand corner. Like Ashleigh herself, elegant rather than ostentatious, the engraving was discreet and delicately rendered.

Suddenly too frustrated to stand still, he strode through the open doors to the veranda and looked down on the gardens below, but saw nothing except his own rage. It had taken him more than a year to get that ring on her finger, and he wasn't about to let her go back on her word. She didn't give a damn about the Wainwright name, money, or power. But her sense of honor was something else. He would make that exaggerated sense of honor of hers work for him; he would use it to his advantage. She might not know it now, but by this time next year she would be Mrs. Mitchell Wainwright. And eventually she would forget about a career. Her role as his wife would be her sole, full-time job.

54

The moment Conrad saw Ashleigh walk through the double doors of Hof's Hut restaurant in the marina he began to weave his way through the crowd toward her.

"Glad you could make it." He smiled. In a cobalt blue cashmere sweater and black wool pants, with her hair swirling casually around her shoulders, she seemed to fit right in with the groups of college kids jammed in the waiting area.

Conrad took hold of Ashleigh's elbow and guided her past the first two booths to their left.

Ashleigh stopped short, then leaned close to his ear. "Oh my God! That's Jeff Bradley."

"Where?"

"The third booth back." She gestured in the direction of a table for two.

"You mean that guy with the dark, wavy hair?" Conrad craned his neck, trying to see over the top of the menu. "Are you sure?"

Ashleigh nodded. *Could he live nearby?*

"Well, what are we waiting for?"

The next instant, the face darted behind the menu. It seemed Mr. Bradley did not want to be seen. When they stopped next to the table, the dark-haired man still hid his face behind the menu. There was no evidence that he had eaten—only two unfinished cups of coffee on the table.

"Jeff?" Ashleigh asked hesitantly.

The menu came down. "Why, hello, Miss McDowell," he said, a surprised look pasted on his ghostly pale face.

Conrad, looking intently at the man, caught a flicker in his eyes. *Like a rabbit that has just been cornered.*

"Have you seen Danielle Norman since Monday?" Ashleigh blurted out.

"Last I heard she was going to New York." His tone implied, *Why do you ask?* "But I heard through the grapevine that she never showed up." A spasm of coughing erupted, and he covered his mouth.

"You were scheduled on the same Monday-night red-eye to New York," Conrad said carefully. "Apparently, neither of you made the flight."

Bradley stared up at Ashleigh, then shifted his eyes to Conrad.

"Look, Bradley," Conrad said, "do you know anything that might help?"

"Wish I did," he replied, signaling to the waitress. Then, turning his focus to Ashleigh, he said, "Came down with this rotten cold and had to cancel. Had no idea Danielle was scheduled on the same flight. She never mentioned it."

Pocino told me he was a no-show, thought Conrad.

When the waitress appeared, Bradley asked for his check. "Hadn't realized it was so late," he said. "Got to run."

Though everything about the man seemed less than straightforward, there was nothing more they could say or do. As they were shown to their table, Conrad handed Ashleigh a small pile of papers. "These are the purchase orders I wanted you to look at," he said. He hesitated as Ashleigh took her seat, and remained standing, keeping his eye on Bradley.

When Bradley paid his bill and headed for the door, Conrad said, "I'll be right back."

Quickly moving through the crowd, he rushed outside just in time to see Bradley folding himself into a beige Volvo—not a Karmann Ghia.

CHAPTER
55

Aware of the minutes ticking away, Viviana smiled warmly at the showroom rep. "I've always favored Sonia Rykiel. And this season's line is one of your best. You have a winner. I'd stake my career on it."

Adele, seated on one of the folding chairs beside a six-foot ramp, gazed over the top of her half-glasses. "My dear, would you mind leaving us alone for a few minutes so that we can talk over the appropriate level for our commitment?"

As the young woman walked away, Viviana looked down at the clipboard Adele held firmly in her hand. Attached to it were the worksheets they had pondered earlier, weighing all the factors, discussing and agreeing on the selections and appropriate stock levels. As Viviana stared at the scratched-out numbers on the paper, her mouth went dry. Not daring to speak, she closed her eyes, counting slowly to herself. Adele had changed the numbers, eliminating one of the three most salable skirt styles. Then she'd had the audacity to add units with the trumpet hemline, though she had not openly disagreed after Viviana had given her the rationale for bypassing that style.

Adele had the last word on any order for Fine Apparel; Viviana was simply a consultant. And yet Viviana's own performance was evaluated on the overall quality of fashion and on the statement made in each and every department of the store. Thinking about the fate of this division in the hands of this loathsome woman hurt her right down to her Ferragamo shoes.

"Adele," she said, not yet in control enough to look her counterpart in the eye, "I am fully aware of our profit priority, and with that in mind, I selected the units and appropriate stock levels to make a profit. We agreed on them before I placed a single mark on that form." She took a step back from the tall, ungainly woman and turned to face her straight on. "You can't sell from empty rounders." Her voice was low and controlled, belying the churning in the area of her recently diagnosed ulcer.

Adele sprang to her feet. "I told you I appreciate your input, but ultimately this is my responsibility. And as you know, Danielle has left us in a very precarious position—a real predicament."

Finally losing all semblance of control, Viviana cried, "If Danielle Norman had an ounce of support, there would *be* no predicament."

"Don't raise your voice, Viviana. It's most unbecoming," said Adele with more than a hint of patronizing emphasis. "I have to live with the backlash, and so do my buyers. Due to the treachery of Danielle Norman, the buying power of our entire division has been jeopardized."

CHAPTER
56

At six o'clock Friday morning, Ashleigh ran up the circular staircase of Charles's home in Naples, heading straight to the library. "Good morning," her voice rang out. "I just have a few minutes, but, I wanted to see you before I left for the weekend."

Charles looked up from his *Business Week* and laid the magazine in his lap, open to the article he was reading. The headline was upside down, but it was in such bold type that she had no trouble reading it.

CORPORATE ENTITIES IN PERIL—
CORPORATE RAIDERS PHILIP SLOANE AND MITCHELL
WAINWRIGHT SPAR FOR POWER AND CONTROL

Charles greeted Ashleigh warmly, but his smile failed to reach his deep blue eyes to set off that sparkle that was so infectious. "Have you seen these articles?" he asked, revealing the cover of *Business Week* and pointing to the current issues of *Forbes* and *Newsweek*, splayed in front of him. The business wars between Mitchell and Philip Sloane were featured on two of the three covers.

"Afraid so," she replied.

"They've each got their own slant, but none is flattering." He flipped back to the article in *Business Week* and read, "Recently published news of mergers and takeovers opens questions of intent. Unsavory marriages that wind up with division spin-offs—their eventual demise benefiting the greedy few with no regard to the workforce . . ."

Ashleigh knew there were even more negative articles in *W*, *Women's Wear Daily*, and the local newspapers, but she didn't mention them.

"Well"—he smiled—, "when you're hot, you've got to be prepared for the heat."

"I'm sure you're right, but I bet Mitchell is fuming. Quickly changing the subject, she said, "I'll be staying with Bev in Palm Desert," and handed him a slip of paper listing the phone numbers where she could be reached.

"Yes, darling. You told me." There was now a sparkle in his eye as he said, "Give Bev my love."

Ashleigh leaned over and kissed him on the cheek. "Take care of yourself. I'll call."

Charles made his way down to the kitchen, his mind reeling.

"Just in time," said Mary, Charles's nurse and long-term companion. "I just brewed—" She stopped short. "What's wrong?" she asked.

"Nothing," he responded all too quickly.

Mary said nothing at first, just held his gaze. "Is it Caroline?"

She knows me all too well, thought Charles.

His daughter was a constant source of worry. He shook his head and pulled out a chair at the kitchen table.

While Mary poured him a cup of tea, he tried to find the words to express how he felt. "Did you get a chance to speak to Ashleigh during her whirlwind visit?"

"No more than a greeting, I'm afraid." Mary looked thoughtful. "I know she has a lot on her mind and she—"

"Mary," Charles interrupted, "Mitchell Wainwright is not the man for Ashleigh. I know it deep in my soul."

Mary sat down beside him and silently looked into his eyes once again. Finally, she spoke. "I understand, and I don't disagree. But Ashleigh has a good head on her shoulders. She will figure that out for herself."

She will indeed. Charles took a sip of the piping-hot tea and tried to relax. *I just hope it's not too late.*

CHAPTER
57

The buzzer blared, and Ashleigh struggled to open the door of the La Jolla store's employee entrance with her free hand. The door, equipped with the latest security system, was virtually impossible to open with only one hand.

In the distance she saw the black Ford Escort. It made her feel safe to know that the Landes Agency was keeping an eye on her as well as looking into Danielle's disappearance, but she wished that the P.I. was close enough to help with the door. *Or is that against the rules?* she wondered.

Setting the documents on the edge of one of the nearby planters, she glanced around. It was eight fifteen AM. The parking lot was nearly deserted—no one in sight. She smiled as she looked up at the large gold letters that spelled out BENTLEYS ROYALE. The exterior blended into the Santa Fe motif of the mall, yet it retained the distinctive ambiance of the specialty stores.

Despite the warnings of both Jerome and O'Brien to leave well enough alone, Ashleigh had to find out why Danielle had felt it necessary to come here when her time was so limited. Hadn't she been concerned about making her flight to New York? Danielle had been missing for three days now, and Ashleigh was clinging to a thin thread of hope. Even the faintest of possibilities had to be explored.

She rang the bell a second time and pulled the door open as the buzzer again sounded. Then she looked back at the pile of papers she'd left on the planter and momentarily pondered how to keep the door propped open and retrieve them.

"Good morning, Miss McDowell," said a middle-aged man in a beige uniform, clean and freshly starched—the maintenance engineer was just arriving. "Looks like you could use a hand." He picked up the papers while she held the door open.

Ashleigh smiled. "Thank you."

As she walked through the door of the training room, she saw that it was set up with a review packet placed on the seat of each of the wood chairs—the typical training room variety, with pallets that pulled up to form desks. The divisional manager, Sue Barns, had arranged for coffee and Danishes.

Ashleigh walked to the front of the room and placed her notes on the podium. A moment later Sue bounced through the door, her face radiating enthusiasm, her ponytail bobbing.

"Good morning, Ashleigh. Is there anything you need?"

Shaking her head, Ashleigh returned her friendly greeting. The bubbly redhead smiled. Glancing up at the large round clock on the wall above the four computerized registers used for training the sales associates, Ashleigh asked, "Do you have a few minutes before the meeting?"

"Certainly. I'm scheduled on the late shift, but I came in early for your meeting and to make sure that everything was set up for you."

"Good. Could we go into your office for a brief touch-base?" Noticing the divisional's anxious expression, Ashleigh added, "I want to make sure I didn't misunderstand your career parameters."

An oversized desk, with a stack of computer printouts and the *Beat Yesterday* book opened on the top, dominated Sue's office. Sue nodded toward the two chairs in front of her desk and slipped into the chair beside Ashleigh's, her eyes wary. When she spoke, there was a nervous ring to her tone. "Can I talk to you confidentially?"

"Of course." Ashleigh was suddenly certain that Adele Watson had gotten to Sue and in her sweet-as-honey tone had asked her not to mention whatever it was she had wanted to say.

Sue stared down at the brown carpet. Tears welled in the corners of her eyes. "I told you why I couldn't be a buyer. I just got engaged and we can't move to Los Angeles. At least not for a while," she admitted. But Mrs. Watson told me that if I wasn't prepared to become a buyer *now*, I was wasting a valuable training spot, because I would never be a general manager." Sue struggled for control. She moistened her lips and blurted out, "If no one knows what's happened to Danielle Norman, why is Mrs. Watson already trying to replace her as if she's . . . ?"

As if she's gone for good, Ashleigh finished in her mind. It was a fair question, though she didn't want to think of the real repercussions.

"I believe Mrs. Watson is just exploring the options," she managed. But the more Sue told her, the more convinced Ashleigh was that her instincts were right on the money. Adele Watson had to be stopped.

After the meeting with La Jolla's management team, Ashleigh stayed in the training room answering questions. She would have remained considerably longer, but the general manager's secretary called her to the phone.

It was David Jerome, sounding out of sorts. "Adele Watson is returning from New York this evening and would like to meet with the two of us first thing in the morning. She says she has been trying to reach you for the last two days and that you have not returned her calls."

In a voice that belied her anger, Ashleigh said, "She called Wednesday after six thirty in the evening and again Thursday morning before six o'clock—our time. I picked up both messages when I came in Thursday and returned her calls then. She was not in, and she did not call me back."

"I see," he said. His voice was filled with irritation, but Ashleigh was confident that it was not directed at her. *Adele Watson has a way of hitting a nerve with most everyone,* she reminded herself. Her constant manipulation was tiresome, and she seemed determined that her unjustified accusations of age discrimination be heard. The president himself was the target of much of her backstabbing, and Ashleigh suspected that he was well aware of it.

When Jerome remained silent for what seemed a long time, Ashleigh asked if Méchie had given him the intrastore envelope marked PERSONAL—the one she'd left the night before, detailing the backgrounds of potential candidates for the buyer position.

"Yes, I have it. Thank you. It's quite complete, but I'd like the three of us to go over it tomorrow morning." He paused. "Could you come in at nine thirty?"

Ashleigh held her breath for an instant. "I have a meeting with the Palm Springs team tomorrow morning."

He was silent.

Her heart sank. "Would you like me to reschedule the meeting?" she asked.

"No," he replied curtly. "I assume you will be in on Monday." His tone was unsettling.

When Ashleigh hung up, she called Betty for her messages, returning only the urgent calls before going down the escalator to La Jolla's Better Sportswear department.

She talked briefly to the sales associates who were on the floor, then asked one of them to let her into the manager's office. A petite, silver-haired associate punched in the door code and opened the door to the stockroom, which doubled as the manager's office, pointing to the desk in the far corner. Ashleigh dodged through the maze of hanging clothes and the rolling racks. The manager was at her desk. She gestured for Ashleigh to sit on a folding chair beside her.

Take this slowly, Ashleigh told herself. Later she could subtly ask about Danielle's visit in her department four days ago. First she asked, "Do you have any questions on performance reviews?" After exhausting that subject, she said, "How is business?"

"Not so hot until this past weekend," the manager said. "But now that we've got something to sell, it's phenomenal. And Danielle has been terrific. A couple weeks ago, she gave a training session for the sales associates. They'd been kind of depressed with business down, but Danielle perked them up. She's the best. We all love her visits. She was here again on Monday, but I didn't see her. It was my day off."

Ashleigh tried to conceal her surprise.

"I hadn't heard that she was coming,"the manager continued. "If I'd known, I would have come in."

Ashleigh listened, occasionally nodding her head while the manager told her about Danielle's visit.

Later, as she walked through the department with the manager, she noticed that while some of the designer assortments were limited, there was no apparent shortage in the selections of Lady Adrianna or Medley

Originals. She fingered through the collections. "I haven't seen some of this merchandise in L.A."

"Isn't it sensational?"

When Ashleigh didn't immediately respond, the manager added, "Danielle brought it in on Monday."

"A hand-carry?" The words involuntarily slipped from Ashleigh's lips.

The manager sheepishly nodded.

Ashleigh sighed inwardly. She could no longer deny that Danielle was guilty of manipulating her inventory and sales performance. Specially equipped trucks delivered merchandise twice a week; Ashleigh had noticed a Bentleys Royale van at the loading dock when she pulled into the parking area that morning. Obviously Friday was one of La Jolla's delivery days, making Tuesday the other. Yet Danielle had hand-carried merchandise to the store less than twenty-four hours before a scheduled delivery, on a day when she must have known the manager wouldn't be in. Hand-carries were frowned upon and authorized only for emergencies—for instance, if there were insufficient merchandise to cover an advertised sale.

It didn't make sense. Ashleigh had to ask herself, *Why would Danielle hand-deliver merchandise the very day she was to fly out to New York?*

CHAPTER
59

The guest room of Bev's Palm Desert home felt like Ashleigh's private oasis. Her friend's warm domestic touches were scattered around the cozy room, as they were throughout the comfortable home. As she kicked off her shoes, she felt more like herself than she had in days.

The yellow print wallpaper beneath the wainscot border, the matching comforter and dresser chair—it reminded her of an upscale version of the loving touches Danielle had added to her small dwelling.

Don't think about that now.

Ashleigh tossed the clip from her hair onto the top of the dresser, and bending at the waist, she flung her head forward and began raking the brush though it briskly. She then slipped into the jade green quilted robe she'd purchased earlier in the day in the La Jolla store, tying it around her waist.

Heaving a sigh, she glanced in the mirror and frowned at the dark circles beneath her eyes. She hadn't had a decent night's sleep that entire week—not since Danielle's disappearance. She shrugged to relieve the tension, then flipped off the light and padded down the carpeted hallway.

Walking past Elizabeth's room, she heard Bev's soft voice reciting "Hickory Dickory Dock" to the two-year-old, then retraced her steps and peeked in. *What a lovely cover portrait for* Parents *magazine,* she thought.

Tiptoeing by once again, she noticed the fresh flowers arranged in various pots and vases, which left their welcoming fragrance in each room, even the kitchen. In the family room, she picked up a cup and saucer from the coffee table and poured some tea from the steaming pot. Mesmerized by the flames of the cozy fire, she sank into the corner of the cushioned couch, enjoying the few moments of solitude while she sipped her tea.

"Well, at last we can talk," Bev said as she walked into the room and put another log on the fire.

Ashleigh drew her legs up beneath her. "It's so peaceful here."

"Not always. But it's a far cry from the pressure of your domain. Six months at Bentleys Royale were more than enough for me." Bev smiled, setting her cup on the table as she dropped down on the sofa. "How's Grandpa Charles?"

"He's sharp as a tack. Did you know he's on the board of directors for three organizations besides Bentley's?"

"Does he still have the live-in housekeeper?"

"Not the one you met a couple of years ago," Ashleigh said. "He has a new one, an RN named Mary. She looks so much like Gran, it gives me a start every time she comes to the door."

"Gee, he must be in his eighties by now," Bev said, shaking her head in disbelief.

"He'll be eighty-six in August."

The two women had much to share, and with Ed and the two boys off at camp, they had been able to start catching up through dinner. As usual, they seldom finished a complete thought before another topic surfaced. Ashleigh had purposely postponed telling Bev about Danielle and Mitchell until the day's interferences were behind them and the time was right. And that time was now.

As Ashleigh thought about where to begin, Bev said, "Now, let me get a good look at that rock!"

"It's in the bedroom," she said looking down at her bare finger. "And if I hadn't been so spineless, I wouldn't be wearing it at all."

"You, spineless? Crazy, maybe, but not spineless," Bev teased. Her eyes met Ashleigh's. "Oops, lousy timing. I can see that there's trouble in paradise." She curled her legs beside her and said, "Ashleigh, what's wrong?"

"I don't know how to . . . " Ashleigh began. "No, I'm making it more complicated than it is." She clasped her hand in front of her and said, "I can't marry Mitchell."

Bev's eyes grew wide. "Well, that's getting straight to the point."

"I've made a big mistake," Ashleigh said. "I realize now that I was selling myself short just to have a man on my arm. I don't love Mitchell. Maybe I never did."

"Wait a minute. Back up." A puzzled expression dominated Bev's face. "Have you told him?"

"Yes, but he didn't listen. He was so angry that I'd gone to Danielle's and missed the special symphony preview honoring their patrons—"

"I assume Mitchell is one of those patrons?"

Ashleigh nodded, "A major contributor. It's a good business write-off."

"Wait a minute. How is Danielle involved?"

"Oh, there I go again, making things more confusing than they already are."

"Let's get some more tea, and I'll try to keep it simple."

While Bev clattered around in the kitchen, Ashleigh tried to organize her thoughts. Thank God, expressing her feelings was far from taboo with her friend.

Their cups refilled, Ashleigh began again. She wanted to tell Bev all that had happened, in chronological order, but one explanation triggered another and it continually got jumbled. At least Bev knew the cast of characters, even though she had been at the headquarters store for only a short time. When Ashleigh got to the part about Jeff Bradley, Bev interrupted her.

"Wait a minute! I know him. But he can't be the man in Danielle's life. He's gay."

"That's been insinuated." Ashleigh brushed the hair back from her face and leaned forward. "Do you know for sure?"

"Sure. Don't you remember when all hell was breaking loose with Viviana De Mornay and that display guy?"

"Walt Adams?"

Bev nodded and repeated, "Don't you remember?"

Ashleigh was temporarily at a loss. Where was this path leading? "Yes, vaguely. In fact, Walt's in trouble again." Suddenly, the details came crashing in on her. "Oh, no!"

"Oh, yes!" Bev said. "Jeff Bradley was Walt's lover. They'd lived together for two or three years. Don't you remember? I told you about their big domestic squabble."

"The silver!" Ashleigh's voice was barely above a whisper. "It was about splitting their silver collection." An icy chill enveloped her.

"Are you sure he's involved with Danielle's disappearance? Maybe he's bisexual," Bev said with a raise of her brows.

It was a long few seconds before Ashleigh spoke. With tears threatening, she said, "Danielle's dead. I know she's dead."

Staring at her friend, her jaw set firmly, Bev said, "Don't you think you're jumping to conclusions now? You said she'd only been missing since Tuesday morning." She stared up at the ceiling as she bent each finger in turn. "That's only three days."

"You don't understand, Bev. Her career was everything to her, and this trip to New York was the only chance she had to save it." Ashleigh struggled to tell her friend the rest.

Bev was wide-eyed. "Oh my God, Ashleigh, I do understand."

"If Mr. Jerome finds out I'm still asking questions, he'll . . . I'm not sure what he'll do, and I don't want to find out. But I can't stop. It just doesn't seem to be anyone else's priority."

Bev stood up abruptly, almost upsetting the low table in front of the sofa. "Ashleigh, you've got to stop it."

Ashleigh looked at her friend in stunned silence.

"I don't know what's happened to her," Bev continued, "but I tend to agree with that bear of a security director. She's no innocent victim. I think down deep you know it too."

Ashleigh held up both her hands. "I know she's far from innocent, Bev, but I'm sure what she did was to save her job."

"Ashleigh, I'm a lot more concerned about you than I am about Danielle, damn it. We'll talk about that later. Right now . . . You've lost all perspective. You're about to throw away a career that most any woman would give her eyeteeth for—and not only that, but you're also going to dump the bachelor of the century!"

"Bev. Please—"

"No. Let me finish." Bev's eyes flashed. "Please, just hear me out. You've found something wrong with every man you've dated since Dan died." She grasped one of Ashleigh's hands. "I don't mean to be cruel. You know how much I cared for Dan. And I know you resented what Mitchell said. But he's right. Dan is dead, and you're still alive. You've got to go on with your life, and you can't just throw in the towel when a man has a few needs of his own. You've built such a thick wall around yourself that only a strong man, one like a Mitchell Wainwright, would even attempt to penetrate it." Her voice softened as she sat down on the edge of the couch. "You'd never respect a man who wasn't strong. But there's a price to pay. A man needs to feel that he's number one in your life."

Ashleigh blinked back her tears and smiled. "Bev, you're beginning to sound like Laura Cameron."

"An excellent role model, if you ask me."

"She claims all you have to do when duty calls is show your man you'd rather be with him than doing anything else and he'll kiss you as you fly out the door. Of course that works for her since she and Max share a deep love."

"Your greatest obstacle is your darn sense of duty."

"Sometimes I think you know me better than I know myself. But it's more than that. Dan is no longer the barrier. I'll never forget him, but I let go a long time ago. The problem is, I can't marry a man I don't love."

Bev slipped her arm around Ashleigh's shoulders. "Of course you can't. And I'm not saying that you should marry Mitchell Wainwright. I'm just saying you shouldn't make any decisions right now. Things are too intense, for both of you—it's not the time for rash decision making. It's not fair to either of you."

"That's almost exactly what Mitchell said. But from you it doesn't sound so self-serving and actually makes a lot more sense."

But when she told her friend about the white roses, Bev's face paled. "That insensitive bastard."

Ashleigh raised an eyebrow. But her amusement vanished as she began to revisit the agonizing lunch with Naomi Wainwright.

Bev leaned forward and said, "I'm beginning to think that the life I lead is pretty dull."

Ashleigh glanced around the cozy setting and laughed. "If this is dull, dull looks pretty good to me. Anyway, I'm certain that Naomi had no idea that I'd broken off our engagement." Again she caught the flicker in Bev's eyes. "Or *attempted* to break off the engagement. And that's not the worst of it. Naomi said that she wanted to talk to me about Diana, Mitchell's former wife." She paused. "Actually I think she wanted to warn me."

CHAPTER
60

Bev's eyes widened. "Hasn't Mitchell been divorced for a long time?"

"More than fifteen years," Ashleigh answered. "And this is no love triangle. Diana is remarried."

"Happily?" Bev asked with a dramatic leap of her eyebrows.

Ashleigh shrugged. She had no idea. "Next week there's a big promotion," she said. "You know, the usual black-tie dinner-dance type of thing, with the Les Brown orchestra."

Bev leaned forward. "One of those big extravaganzas like the one the Share organization hosted last year with all the stars?"

"Exactly. The buyers on the second floor are already having their customary fits over the business they think they'll lose by having their departments torn apart, not to mention the impractical finger foods that stain their carpets."

"Ah, yes," Bev said, "I remember it well. "

"Well, it's sponsored by the Assistance League, and Diana is the program chairman."

"Of all the . . . " Bev started to say, before faint cries of "Mommy . . . Mommy!" sent her scurrying to little Elizabeth's room.

Ashleigh leaned back, her thoughts turning to Dan and the promise she had made. His last words echoed in her head: "Please, help Danielle. Take care of my little sister. Don't let them hurt her anymore." She didn't know whom she meant by *them*, but Dan had told her months before that their mother had never shown any warmth or love for Danielle, that she couldn't be trusted. *What did that mean?* It was a question that had never been answered.

Ashleigh's eyes flew open as she felt a hand on her shoulder. She looked up and saw Bev tightening the sash on her pink quilted robe. "Elizabeth wants to know if you'll come to the park with us tomorrow."

Ashleigh smiled. "Sounds wonderful. I should be through at the store by eleven."

"Great!" she said with an impish glimmer in her eye. "I already told her you would." Bev plopped down on the couch, then focused on Ashleigh's empty cup. "I'd be up all night if I drank that much caffeine."

"As you know, I'm a bit of an addict, but it never seems to keep me awake." She set her cup on the table. "Don't feel bad if you need to creep off to bed, though. I'd like to stay up for a while." Ashleigh didn't need caffeine. She had plenty on her mind to keep her awake.

Conrad fastened his seat belt as the plane taxied down the runway. When the plane lifted off successfully, he began to relax—but not for long.

Thoughts of the mystery surrounding Danielle's disappearance plagued him. All hell had broken loose with the various players in Bentley's Central Purchasing. They had discovered an increasing number of irregularities in Danielle Norman's department. Bills had been paid ahead of the usual 30-/60-/90-day schedule. Reports indicated that merchandise had been received from the fictitious vendor La Salliano, and yet not a single scrap of merchandise bore a La Salliano label. At the same time, no major shipments of Lady Adrianna or Medley Originals were recorded as received. Nevertheless, there were significant sales increases under their classification numbers.

He had to face the facts: Danielle was in serious trouble. The kind of trouble that he was sure she couldn't have initiated on her own.

Immediately after Ashleigh had called him early that morning, Conrad had sent Pocino to the stores Danielle had visited the day before her disappearance, to take cursory inventories. If Danielle had hand-carried merchandise to La Jolla, it was a safe bet that she'd done the same in Palm Springs.

Conrad hadn't missed the bemused look on Pocino's face when he'd said, "Be discreet." *Discreet* wasn't a word in Pocino's vocabulary. Yet Conrad knew that the security chief could be counted on. Pocino would be tight-lipped as always when it came to an investigation.

Conrad stared down at the city lights. It had taken him longer to drive through the Friday-night freeway traffic from Los Angeles to Long Beach than it would take now to fly to Palm Springs.

The rattle of the rolling refreshments cart broke into his thoughts. The airline stewardess gave him a cheerful smile when he ordered a scotch and soda. Opening his small bag of peanuts, he reflected on his motivation for this trip. Earlier that evening, around six o'clock, Pocino's third call from Palm Springs had been put through. "The shit's really hit the fan," the security chief had said. "We just busted that shoplifting ring, the one that's been making the desert circuit—two white chicks and the three black guys. And guess what?" His pause wasn't long enough for Conrad to interject. "They grabbed a whole rack of Lady Adrianna merchandise."

The phone line crackled, and Pocino said, "Can you hear me?" Then he continued, "Most of it had never been checked in. Another thing: The damned price tags on the remaining Lady Adrianna units aren't in our typeface."

Conrad was about to ask how they knew the stolen merchandise wasn't checked in, but in another beat it was obvious. He'd already checked the stores' stock and sales sheets. At that time, it had seemed imperative for Conrad to take a look for himself. Now it seemed irrational.

The *FASTEN SEAT BELTS* light flashed on, and the pilot announced their descent into Palm Springs.

Conrad pulled the shade of the small window fully open and looked down at the stream of widely spaced headlights moving in all directions. What could he possibly expect to uncover that Pocino couldn't have done just as well without him? Sure, the fact that Ashleigh had scheduled her review training sessions in Palm Springs this weekend was a plus, but he was clear on his real motivation: He had to find out for himself as much as he could about Danielle's disappearance, and to do that, he needed all the facts. And that meant this plane ticket would never appear on his expense account, nor would his hotel bill.

This was personal.

Bev's concern only deepened when Ashleigh told her about the Karmann Ghia and the explosion that destroyed her car, but she still kept her usual sense of humor. "My God, this is beginning to sound like *As the World Turns*," she exclaimed.

Ashleigh drew her knees up in front of her and clasped them with both arms. "More like a B movie, I'm afraid. I just hate to think of Danielle . . ."

"Ashleigh, you seem more concerned about Danielle than about yourself. Someone is following you—someone has blown up your car!" Bev's voice was shrill. "My God! You could get yourself killed."

"I *am* terrified, Bev. I find myself spending as much time looking in the rearview mirror as straight ahead. But at least I'm not alone."

"What do you mean?"

"Mitchell arranged twenty-four-hour protection. He has a detective agency on retainer."

"You mean there's someone outside the house right now?"

"A black Ford Escort," Ashleigh said.

Bev jumped up from the couch and ran toward the window. She lifted a few blades of the venetian blinds and then she turned back toward Ashleigh. "Are you sure they're the good guys?"

Ashleigh nodded. "I sure hope so."

"Don't they ever go to sleep?"

Ashleigh shrugged. "I assume they work in shifts. They have my schedule, and I'm supposed to tell them of any changes."

"This is unreal. And somehow it's all connected to Danielle." Bev kicked off her slippers and drew up her knees, her arms pulling them tight against her chest. "What I don't understand is why you think of her as the victim and not the culprit. Not in terms of her disappearance, maybe, but look at what's happening in her business!"

"I wish I knew." Ashleigh shook her head. "I just can't imagine her taking that road, not with all she wanted to do in the fashion industry, with all she had to prove. She's a good person. Plus I just don't think she had it in her to think up this sort of criminal activity."

"Right, and doesn't a buyer need the DMM's approval for purchases? And isn't there a special code to get them into the system?"

Ashleigh nodded. "But those codes are leaked more often than we'd like to believe."

"Okay." Bev pursed her lips and said, "But doesn't that show up on some kind of a computer printout?" Again Ashleigh nodded and Bev scowled. "So how could it help her business?"

"Quite simply, if buyers don't have enough fresh merchandise, there's no way to make their sales plan, which is their report card, so to speak. Any smart buyer will try to get more merchandise. If unable to get approval, a desperate buyer might try other means."

"But how could she get away with it?"

"There's a slim chance—*if* the buyer can generate enough sales to justify the purchases."

"Even if they sold more, wouldn't they be in trouble?"

"Buyers tend to be dreamers. They buy what they think will sell, and expectations often exceed reality. There's a whole system to take care of those unrealistic expectations—it's called 'markdowns.'" Ashleigh knew she digressed, but maybe talking it out with Bev and answering her friend's questions would help clear her own circular thought process and provide them both with answers. "But in their best-of-all-possible-worlds scenario, the merchandise will *blow out*."

Noticing her friend's raised eyebrows, she added, "It goes something like this. Open-to-buy is calculated at retail. That means the selling price rather than the purchasing price of the merchandise. When a thousand dollars' worth of merchandise is sold, the open-to-buy is increased by a thousand dollars."

"Good God, how do they keep up with it?"

"There are a jillion computerized reports." Ashleigh unfolded her legs and rose from the couch. "At this point, no one knows which of her department's purchases are real and which are phony." She sighed. "But poor Danielle really had nowhere to turn. Adele Watson reduced her open-to-buy. That meant she had less new seasonal merchandise to sell. As she told me, she couldn't sell from empty rounders and shelves. Adele gave her no support. She may have thought this was her only way to get merchandise in stock — her only way out."

"I had a few run-ins with Adele myself." Bev wrinkled her nose to indicate her dislike. "She's a real two-faced . . ."

Ashleigh supplied, "Conniving bitch?"

"Right. She had a way of making you feel no bigger than a match-box." Bev shook her head as if trying to dispel an unpleasant image, then frowned. "I thought you said that a DMM's review is based on the results of her buyers, so . . ."

"So why would Adele sabotage Danielle's business?" Ashleigh finished her friend's question. "I don't really know, but I have some strong suspicions."

"Like what?"

"Adele is no dummy. She's a shrewd merchant. And yet, while she's responsible for Moderate and Better ready-to-wear and Fine Apparel, her expertise is in Moderate."

Bev smiled. "*Moderate* always seemed like a misnomer at Bentleys Royale. I could never understand how Bleyle and Evan Picone could be considered 'moderate.'"

"It's all relative, I guess." Ashleigh shrugged. "Anyway, since the Moderate division is the most profitable, the Better and Fine Apparel buyers have a tough time under Adele. Particularly those strong-willed ones like Danielle. Adele supports only those buyers who do things her way." Suddenly she thought of something. "Viviana De Mornay says that Adele forces her buyers to shy away from top-quality merchandise and that she is jeopardizing the reputation of Bentleys Royale . . ."

Seeing the quizzical look on Bev's face, she broke it down further. "Quite simply, Adele controls the dollars for her entire division. She can divide the money in any way she sees fit. The Moderate division brings in the largest bottom-line profit; Adele's own performance is evaluated on bottom-line profit. So that's where she invests her open-to-buy dollars.

"Danielle built her reputation on quickly assessing an entire collection and selecting the finest pieces for her division. She's refused to lower her standards, and I'm not alone in thinking that this was her downfall with Adele Watson."

Bev looked puzzled. "Moderate makes more money?"

Ashleigh took a few seconds to consider this before responding. "Not exactly. Most of the merchandise is marked up fifty-two, even fifty-five percent, while more expensive merchandise is often marked up considerably more—up to two hundred percent on some imports that can't be purchased by the competitors. But it is risky. There's a smaller market for the more expensive merchandise, and the markdowns are far greater."

Bev threw her arms out wide. "You've got my head spinning. But I still don't understand how Adele could benefit by sabotaging Danielle."

"I'm far from having all the answers."

"Okay, I think I've heard enough about the insidious Mrs. Watson. But how can you be so sure that Danielle isn't the one behind the shenanigans in her department?"

Ashleigh shook her head. "She's obviously used poor judgment, but she couldn't have been the one to set up a phony vendor. That would take someone with a lot of computer savvy."

"You think Bradley's involved?" Bev asked. Then she added, "I'd be surprised if he knows much about computers. But what do I know?"

Ashleigh began pacing the floor again, her arms crossed loosely in front of her, frustrated with her limited knowledge of the system.

"Enough already." Bev gave a short laugh and said, raising her eyebrows, "I'd rather hear about this Conrad Taylor who has popped into your life."

The moment Conrad stepped out of the rented Buick he heard a familiar nursery rhyme from his childhood.

Ring-a-ring-a-roses,
A pocket full of posies;
Ashes, ashes, we all fall down.

An explosion of giggles carried across the grassy park area as he jogged toward the children's playground. And there she was—Ashleigh McDowell, clad in designer jeans and a crisp peach-colored shirt, not tucked in but belted around her slim waist. Her hair flew in a soft cloud around her shoulders as she twirled a small child and laughed. She looked like a teenager, her usual "sophisticated executive" image cast aside, oblivious to anyone but the little girl. He'd never seen her look so relaxed, so free of care.

Drawing closer, Conrad noticed an attractive brunette, her short hair cut in soft waves, sitting Indian-style on a blanket on the lawn. The woman was smiling as she watched the antics of Ashleigh and the little girl.

Ashleigh didn't look in his direction.

"Hello," he shouted.

She turned and, after registering a look of surprise, motioned for him to join them. As he approached, the child tugged at her pant leg.

"More, more," she pleaded, and Ashleigh scooped the girl up in her arms.

The woman on the ground looked from Conrad to Ashleigh and rose to her feet, smiling.

The child's mother, surely, he thought.

Still holding the little girl, Ashleigh introduced Bev and her daughter, Elizabeth. Bev shot her a knowing glance, when Conrad said, "It was great to find that Ashleigh also had business in the Palm Springs store this weekend."

Elizabeth squirmed in Ashleigh's arms, not at all happy about the intrusion. Bev reached for her daughter, but Elizabeth clung tightly, her arms wound around Ashleigh's neck.

Conrad smiled and winked at Bev, and in no time at all, he and Elizabeth were off to the play area.

Ashleigh was anxious to find out what Conrad had learned earlier that morning at the Palm Springs store, but it would have to wait. Besides, she had enough on her hands, with Bev firing one question after another about the handsome vice president, whom she referred to as "eye candy."

A dark cloud eclipsed the sun, and Ashleigh was immediately chilled. She retrieved her sweater from the blanket, her eyes lingering on Conrad with Elizabeth atop his shoulders as they walked leisurely back toward them.

When Bev announced that it was time she got Elizabeth home for a nap, Conrad set the child on the ground and asked, "Would you three lovely ladies care to join me for dinner tonight?" He knelt down to the little girl's level and took her two small hands in his, then looked up at her mother.

"Thanks, anyway, but I'm exhausted." Bev replied with a sigh, then pleaded, "But please . . . please take Ashleigh. I've got to get some sleep before I collapse." She made a dramatic gesture, resting the back of the hand on her forehead.

Ashleigh laughed. "Very funny. We could make it an early night."

"Yes." Conrad rose, scooping Elizabeth up in his arms. "I could pick you up after Elizabeth's nap."

"Thanks, I'd love to, but I'm really beat."

In spite of little Elizabeth's reluctance to say good-bye, they could not persuade Bev to change her mind.

"Well?" Conrad smiled, and looked at Ashleigh.

Ashleigh turned to Bev. "Would you mind?"

"Absolutely not. I'm not up to another of our all-night marathon tea-and-chat sessions," Bev said, "but Conrad, please come to the house around seven or seven thirty for cocktails or a glass of wine."

He nodded and said, "Thanks. Sounds good to me."

As they walked toward Bev's station wagon, Ashleigh searched through her handbag for the small memo pad she always carried. By the time Elizabeth was belted into her car seat, she found it and scribbled her friend's address. Handing Conrad the paper, she pointed to the black Ford Escort parked on the circular side street and asked, "Would you tell the agent that I'll be with you this evening? He'd probably appreciate the night off."

CHAPTER
63

That evening, after a leisurely glass of wine, Bev repeated the directions to Don O's and said, "It's just a short ride. Ten minutes at the most." Ashleigh and Conrad would be right on time for their dinner reservations at eight.

As Conrad went to say good night to Elizabeth, Bev caught hold of Ashleigh's arm. "Must you wear that ring tonight?"

Ashleigh glanced down to her hand and nodded ruefully. "Just until Mitchell gets back."

"Too bad."

Ashleigh had to agree. But she knew that not wearing it would be like making an announcement—directed especially to Conrad.

Outside, the air was cool. "Look at those stars," Ashleigh said as she looped the belt of her coat and pulled it tight around her waist. "The sky is so clear. I can see the constellations."

"That's what I like best about the desert," Conrad said, opening the passenger door for her.

As he slid behind the wheel, he realized it was time to stop talking about the weather and start pooling their information, but when he looked across at Ashleigh, he was distracted by her dark liquid eyes. He felt a tug at his heart when he thought of them filling with tears at Danielle's house the other evening. *Damn it, I have to stop thinking of her as being so vulnerable!* It was too easy to want to take her into his arms and comfort her. But just showing up at the management meeting yesterday, only hours after her car had blown up, was sound evidence that the woman had guts.

He took a breath and brought her up to date on what he'd learned from Pocino, telling her only what she needed to know—no more, no less.

"Conrad," she said with a quizzical look, "I'm not sure I know what Pocino was saying about the price tags. Is there only one machine in the Distribution Center for making those?"

"No," he said. "There are a several machines in the DC, and others in the stores, but they are all the same make, and the print is nearly identical on all of them. The tickets on the stolen merchandise, on the other hand, were most likely direct from the resource."

"Lady Adrianna?"

Conrad nodded. "About the only time our own tickets aren't used is when a buyer anticipates that a shipment needed to cover an ad won't arrive in time for ticketing. In that case, arrangements for the vendor to ticket the units with our retail price are made in advance. As a rule, this makes the merchants uneasy. There are enough slipups when they're done in-house."

Ashleigh shook her head in disbelief. "Isn't it ironic that those shoplifters chose Danielle's merchandise?"

"Not really, if you stop to think about it." He braked quickly at the stop sign, and his arm automatically shot out protectively across her midriff. "Sorry." He smiled and then continued, "Shoplifters go straight for the high-ticketed merchandise. As Pocino so aptly commented, it was a piece of cake with that rack of Lady Adrianna just a few yards from the back entrance. They ran out with all but two of the skirts. It's a professional shoplifting ring. We don't suspect any inside conspiracy, just poor judgment in placing the T-stand in such an accessible pathway."

"Was it the same gang that hit Saks a week or so ago?"

"Pocino said it's the same M.O. He's been in touch with the security honchos of the other major retailers, and he's compared notes. The storewide shoplifting statistics are staggering. Of course, we don't know how much is internal versus external, or even how much might be merely a paper loss."

Conrad grinned as he swung into the shopping center, spotting the sign for Don O's in the far corner. "I'm glad Bev told us about this place. Can't remember the last time I had chicken and dumplings."

After dinner, they moved into the cozy bar area. The music stopped, and couples on the small dance floor began drifting back to their tables.

Ashleigh smiled across the petite, round table that separated them. Conrad signaled to the waiter and ordered a gin and tonic for Ashleigh and a scotch and soda for himself.

When the music started up again, soft and low, he asked, "Would you like to dance?"

"I'd love to." She rose, and he followed her to the dimly lit dance floor. She moved into his arms, and he felt her body anticipating the music and his every move. Her hair brushed lightly against his face, and he breathed in the fresh, subtle fragrance.

The music was romantic, the stuff of years gone by, and the lyrics were sung by the slim, dark-haired musician: *I see you walk away, beside that lucky guy.*

Conrad held Ashleigh close, but not too close. *How beautiful she is,* he thought. Composure, strength of conviction, and utter femininity. He noticed again the simplicity of the dress she wore and how right it was for her. Her gold jewelry, understated and elegant, earrings evident only as her curtain of hair swayed from side to side.

As the song ended, he deliberately shifted his thoughts to the conversation he knew they must have. They moved from the dance floor, and taking her arm, he gently guided her to their table.

She looked at him directly as she slipped into her chair, and he noticed the subtle shadow of her lashes as she took a sip of her gin and tonic. He was about to speak, to open his mouth and tell her the whole story—his whole story—when she reached out and brushed his hand briefly, softly.

"There's something I've needed to tell you," she said.

Ashleigh decided that she had to trust someone, to let down her guard. There was no one else. She had to take the risk.

"Conrad, I know that you are aware of my relationship with Danielle, but—"

"Danielle told me just about everything," he broke in. "Her brother's death was a living nightmare for her. Though it was years later when we met, the pain was still raw and intense."

"Conrad, I'm not one to jump to conclusions, but I know if Danielle were alive, she'd call." She had to avert her eyes as she felt them fill with tears.

Conrad had not missed the tears that now trickled down Ashleigh's smooth cheek. He reached across the table and, taking her hands in his, said, "Ashleigh, I wish there was something I could do—something I could say . . ."

Watching her blot the thin trail of tears with the back of her fingers, he said, "I know how Danielle felt—how she *feels* about you."

Her dark eyes gazed back at him questioningly.

"She idolizes you."

Withdrawing her hands from his, Ashleigh said, "I wasn't there for her when she needed me most."

"You're being pretty hard on yourself, aren't you?"

"I promised that I would look after her."

"Danielle is a grown woman with a mind of her own," he reminded her.

"You don't understand." Her voice rose. Then, just as suddenly, she fell silent, and it seemed a long time before she spoke again.

"I've never met anyone as vicious as Danielle's mother, and for no apparent reason, she was particularly hostile toward her own daughter."

She doesn't know, he thought. *She really doesn't know.* Resisting the urge to reach out for her again, he said softly, "Ashleigh, Danielle was abused by her stepfather."

A look of horror flashed in her eyes. "You mean . . . sexually abused?"

"Danielle's mother walked into her bedroom late one night . . ." He flinched. The image never failed to hit him squarely in the gut, just as it had the night Danielle had told him. Seeing the pain register on Ashleigh's face, he knew he need say no more.

"I didn't know. Neither did Dan, or he would have told me."

Conrad nodded. "Just like those stories you read in the newspaper, Danielle said she was too frightened to tell her mother when it first began, and her brother was away at school. Somehow she felt guilty— like she must have done something wrong." He sighed and lifted his glass. "And that mother of hers told Danielle that she was wicked, that she was driving the poor man beyond his power to resist."

Ashleigh covered her face with her hands. It was quite a long time before she lifted her chin. "I thought that Danielle had told me every- thing. I thought we were close."

"It was too painful for her to talk about. She didn't want you to think badly of her."

"But she told you." Ashleigh blinked back the tears.

He nodded. "Danielle told me that you and your grandmother were her salvation."

Biting down on her bottom lip, she said, "I wish I'd known. No won- der she was driven to be the very best. Perhaps the nightmares that sur- rounded her were the very things that made her strong."

He shook his head. "But what a hell of a price."

When Ashleigh excused herself and left the table to freshen up, Con- rad sat back. *Perhaps I've told her enough,* he thought. Then he shook his head. *No. I've gone this far. I have to tell her the rest.*

When Ashleigh returned from the powder room, dry-eyed, Conrad stood up and gave her a warm smile. The table was small, with just enough room for their drinks, so Ashleigh placed her velvet evening bag under her chair before she slid into it.

Moments later, in the center of the dance floor once again, Conrad slipped his arm around her and gently pulled her to him. Amid the soft and romantic music, she found herself making comparisons between Conrad Taylor and Mitchell Wainwright.

"What brought you to Long Beach?" she asked.

He smiled down at her and answered, "I'm afraid my story isn't all that interesting. I was married in my last year of graduate school."

So, he had been married at one time. Ashleigh was not at all surprised to learn this.

The music stopped and they returned to their table.

When they were comfortably seated once again, Conrad picked up his scotch and soda and continued. "My wife—rather, my former wife—was pregnant and wanted to stay in Boston, but when I decided on the Buffum's executive training program offer, she was a good sport. Naturally we settled in Long Beach, since that was where Buffum's was headquartered."

The waiter stopped by to ask about another round. When he'd departed, Conrad continued, "Something went wrong. The baby died when Anna was nearly full-term." His face contorted.

Ashleigh was silent. She looked at his downcast eyes, reading the quiet agony as it spread across his face.

Conrad swirled the amber liquid in his glass, then raised his eyes to hers. "Anna was too far along, and they couldn't take the baby. She had to go through the delivery."

His voice faded, and he looked thoughtful. Then he shifted his focus. "Anna's very much a family person, close to her parents, and she'd never been far from home before." He set his glass down. "Anyway, we had the funeral for the baby in Boston. It was a boy," he said just above a whisper.

Pushing his shoulders back and straightening his posture, he seemed once again in control. "Anna wanted to stay there for a couple of weeks, which turned into a month. She came back to Long Beach for two weeks—maybe less. She was in a state of depression. Although the cause of death was unknown, and there was no reason why she couldn't deliver a healthy child, she said she had to move back to Boston. She wanted me to come with her, but I couldn't. Anyway, that's how I felt at the time."

"And now?"

"I didn't really know the answer to that question myself until recently. Something happened . . . " His eyes drifted, and his voice became difficult to hear above the music. "For months after Anna left, I asked myself if I'd been fair, if going back to Boston could have saved our marriage. At first I rationalized my decision, and at the same time blamed myself. Then guilt turned to anger."

He shook his head slowly, and his eyes brushed hers fleetingly before he looked away. "That baby was mine as well as Anna's, and losing him hurt like hell. But I don't think Anna, or her family, ever thought of *my* loss." He set his glass down firmly on the table and stared for a long moment at Ashleigh.

She reached across the table and laid her hand gently on his arm. "It must have been terrible for both of you."

He gave a simple nod of acknowledgment.

"You said something happened recently?" she probed.

"Let's talk about something else. I have no right to unload on you."

"Please, go on," she said softly.

He glanced down at her hand on his arm. "I saw Anna when I went back for my sister's wedding." He looked thoughtful and took another sip of his scotch. "She hasn't remarried. I guess I knew from the beginning that it could never be the same, and yet there was always that lingering doubt. But just being in the same room, seeing that melancholy look in her eyes, the grief as raw and as deep as it was the day we found out that our baby was dead, I knew." He shook his head as if he were trying to dispel an ugly image. His gaze was directed across the room, or perhaps somewhere even farther away.

Ashleigh wondered if he had forgotten she was there. She knew somehow that he was talking about things that he had kept inside for far too long. She didn't know what to say; she just reached her other hand across the table. He took both of her hands in his and looked deep into her eyes. The people around them seemed to vanish.

Finally he spoke. "That's when Danielle and I started seeing each other outside the store."

CHAPTER
66

Ashleigh closed the door softly behind her, then leaned back against it until she heard Conrad's car pull away.

A flood of memories had crashed in on her when Conrad had made his confession, and her head ached with self-recrimination. How had she not seen it before? That man Danielle had told her about—the man she was seeing from Buffum's—was Conrad. *That romance must not have been a serious one and it obviously died on its own. I should have just kept my mouth shut.*

Peering out through the window as she turned off the exterior light, she felt a tug of unease. The now-familiar black Ford Escort was absent.

Bev had left a light on in the entry. Flipping it off, Ashleigh noticed a glow from the opposite end of the hallway leading to the family room. *Bev must have left it on.* Turning toward the lighted room, she slipped off her shoes and tiptoed down the tiled corridor. The cold seeped into the soles of her feet.

"Ashleigh, is that you?" her friend's voice rang out.

She hurried toward the family room, where she found Bev waiting. "How come you're still up?"

"Waiting for you, Cinderella. It's past midnight, you know." Looking down to Ashleigh's stockinged feet, she added, "And I see you've stepped out of your glass slippers."

Ashleigh laughed softly. "You're too much. You said I'd kept you up far past your bedtime last night, so what's the story?" She looked over at the domed clock on the mantel. "Oh, I get it—you're in training for when the kids become teenagers."

Bev placed her hands on her hips in a mock reprimand. "I can sleep anytime. It isn't too often I have a chance to be an on-scene observer in the proverbial love triangle." She smiled and walked toward the kitchen.

Ashleigh followed, noting a large saucepan of hot chocolate on the front burner of the stove, and two cups and saucers set out on the sink beside a small plate of shortbread.

"Bev, I thought you weren't up to another 'marathon' session!"

"Okay, okay, you got me. Hey, I'm living vicariously!" She poured the cocoa into the cups and said casually, "Mitchell called at about eleven."

"Oh." Ashleigh sighed. "I'm sorry. Did he wake you?"

"No, I had to get up anyway—to answer the phone."

"Very funny! Eleven o'clock our time?"

"About that. Anyway, after the call I was wide-awake, so I thought I might as well read until you came back and I could find out how you've managed to capture not one, but two of the most eligible bachelors on the West Coast!"

"Hardly," Ashleigh scoffed, a bit distracted. "Did he say where he was?"

"Didn't you say he was in Atlanta?"

"Yes, but it would be two o'clock in the morning there. What did he want?"

Bev put the pan back on the burner. "Obviously, he wanted to talk to you."

Ashleigh smiled, but she was still puzzled. "I'm surprised he would call so late. I'm sorry," she said again.

"Forget it." Bev gave a dismissive wave of her hand. "As I said, I can always sleep. Now, tell me about that gorgeous Conrad Taylor."

"There's not that much to tell. And if you're conjuring up some sordid love triangle, you're way off base," Ashleigh said. "Do you mind if I slip into something more comfortable?"

"Go ahead." Bev picked up the tray. "I'll take our goodies into the other room." She paused and with a lift of the brow, added, "And if you want coffee, you're on your own."

"No problem. Hot chocolate sounds great. This is a night of special treats—real chicken and dumplings, and hot chocolate that doesn't come from a little square packet."

Bev sighed. "Do the men in your life know that the kitchen isn't your forte?"

As she answered Bev's never-ending questions, Ashleigh realized just how much she had missed her friend, who was always supportive but also willing to play devil's advocate.

"What time is Mr. Wonderful picking you up tomorrow?" was one of Bev's last queries.

"I'm picking him up at the car rental office," Ashleigh replied.

"Ah yes, the rental. So, what kind of car do you plan to get to replace the T-Bird? Or will you be keeping that little beauty out front?"

"No, I think I'll get another Thunderbird. I'm just driving the Mercedes until I get a chance to buy a car of my own." She added thoughtfully, "I must admit that I'd never thought much about a security system until a couple of days ago, but it has helped settle some of my jangled nerves. I still check the backseat before climbing in, though."

"And so you should."

"I hate borrowing the Mercedes, especially now, but it isn't being used by anyone else . . ."

"Well, you sure look good in that car. Ever think about getting one of your own?"

Ashleigh swished the idea through her mind but rejected it just as she had in the past. "As much as I like the Mercedes, and even though I can get one at cost through Wainwright Motors, I really can't rationalize the difference in the price. Besides, I have other expenses. I like nice clothes, and I'm thinking about making some property investments."

"Providing for your old age?" Bev didn't smile; she looked troubled.

"Heaven forbid," Ashleigh said. "Is that what you think?"

"I don't know. It just seems that you guard that damnable independence of yours so fiercely that . . . that . . . Oh, I don't know. I told you last night: That wall you've built around yourself is getting way too thick. And it's not just Mitchell. Tonight you had a perfect opportunity to let Conrad know that your marriage to Mitchell was far from a fait accompli. But did you do that?"

Bev clasped her hands together, pausing to let the words sink in. "I think you're afraid to depend on anyone—to let anybody get too close. You've learned that art of detachment only too well." Her gaze penetrated so deeply, Ashleigh felt naked. Bev went on. "Separating emotions from business may be a part of your survival at Bentleys Royale, but no relationship can withstand it." She looked down at her folded hands and fell silent.

Ashleigh wanted to tell her it wasn't true. She *did* want to love again. A career wasn't enough; she wanted more—a lot more.

Bev slid her arm around her friend's shoulder. "Ashleigh, I'm sorry. I've said too much."

"No," Ashleigh said, her eyes damp. "You may be right. I didn't think it was true, and I don't want it to be true, but I'm afraid it might be." She gave her a weak smile. "I must confess my mind is muddled. And Conrad Taylor has nothing to do with it. Until last week, I hardly knew him."

Bev gave her one of those familiar skeptical looks.

"Okay, I'm attracted to him, I admit it. But if I were truly in love with Mitchell—" She paused. "I don't buy that *other man* or *other woman* syndrome. No one can convince me that any third party can destroy a good relationship."

Ashleigh swirled the remaining hot chocolate in her cup. "Events in recent weeks have brought things to a head, and I was convinced Mitchell Wainwright is not the man for me. But Mitchell's been so darn supportive since . . . Well, in the past few days. I know he cares about me, and now I'm not sure . . . I'm not sure of a lot of things. Maybe I just haven't given him a chance. I thought it was him, but it's probably me." She stopped abruptly. "Do you want to go to bed?"

Bev shook her head.

"Good," she smiled faintly. "I think I need to talk this through. Before this whole thing with Danielle came up, things were rapidly going downhill with Mitchell and me. I felt he was asking too much. He wanted me to be someone that I wasn't—someone whose total life revolved around him. Oh, Bev, you know me! I just don't think I can be that person. Or that I'd want to be." She took a thoughtful pause. "But one thing he said to me is now registering loud and clear. He said that I was never totally 'there' with him. That there was a part of me that was always somewhere else." Ashleigh hesitated. "Does that make any sense? Is that what you're trying to tell me?"

Bev started to nod, when suddenly Ashleigh's mind shot back to Mitchell's late phone call.

"Bev," she asked with trepidation, "just what, exactly, did Mitchell say when he called?"

Her friend looked surprised at the question. "It was a person-to-person call, so I didn't actually speak to him. I just told the operator that I expected you soon."

Ashleigh froze. She felt the color drain from her cheeks.

"What's wrong?" Bev looked puzzled.

Ashleigh answered faintly, "Mitchell never calls person-to-person."

"Maybe he had his reasons."

Almost in a whisper, Ashleigh repeated, "No, even when I've asked him to, he emphatically refuses—says it's tacky." She closed her eyes and felt the room close in. "Bev, that call wasn't from Mitchell."

Conrad's mind circled through the kaleidoscope of the week's events, landing back on what had passed between him and Ashleigh that evening at Don O's.

The uneasiness in Ashleigh's manner when they'd said good night now flashed before him. She'd said nothing—at least not in words. It was her dark eyes that spoke as she silently scanned the street. Where was his head when he'd agreed to tell the detective to take the night off? After he'd walked her to Bev's door, his mind had filled with thoughts of her, not the danger that surrounded her. He was already fifteen minutes down the road.

What an idiot I've been!

He would have to go back to Palm Desert.

Ashleigh was frightened. She couldn't deny that, and yet as she mulled things over, she wondered if she was becoming paranoid. There had been no sign of anyone following her since Wednesday night, and that was three days ago.

Before Bev said good night, she and Ashleigh checked the windows and all four doors. They even double-checked the alarm system, which was not the type that merely made noise in hopes of frightening a burglar away, as in Ashleigh's condo. Instead, it was wired directly to a large security organization.

In the guest room Ashleigh turned on the bedside light, determined to cast apprehension aside. Yet the phone call still troubled her. She knew it couldn't have been Mitchell, but hardly anyone else knew she was there. She'd talked with Charles and the P.I., Landes, earlier in the day, and she'd been with Conrad—except for the few minutes when she'd gone to the powder room.

She shook her head, trying to stop the inescapable path of her thoughts, and climbed into bed. Thumbing through the pages of an old issue of *Sunset* did little to distract her from the sounds of the night—all magnified in the silence surrounding her. Leaves rustled. Branches scraped across the window glass. The house creaked as it settled. All the little noises kept her nerves on edge.

She looked over to the dresser clock. It was just after three, and still she couldn't sleep. She tried another magazine, the Christmas issue of *Better Homes and Gardens*. It was no use.

Ashleigh checked the bookshelves. She and Bev might be kindred souls in many respects, but Ed's novels had far more appeal, particularly for the distraction she now craved.

Ashleigh remembered seeing Frederick Forsyth's *Day of the Jackal* on the bookshelf in the family room. She liked Forsyth; it wasn't Tolstoy, but it would do.

She flipped on the hall light and tiptoed down to the room at the opposite end of the house.

On her return, with book in hand, she reached to flip off the light—and then stopped suddenly. She noticed a large manila envelope on the floor, directly below the mail slot. It hadn't been there when she'd come in after being dropped off by Conrad.

She thought about ignoring it, but picked it up on impulse. Nothing was written on the envelope, and it was sealed. Puzzled, she tossed it on the long, thin table that sat in the entry and returned to her room. After about half an hour, the print on the pages of the novel began to blur and Ashleigh could no longer keep her eyes open. She closed the book and snapped off the bedside lamp. Though her eyes were tired, her thoughts were not quiet. Who could have slid the manila envelope through the mail slot in the middle of the night, and why? She would ask Bev about it in the morning.

Conrad awoke at four AM. It was pointless to linger in bed. Throwing off the covers, he found that his first and recurring thoughts were of Ashleigh.

When he'd driven back to Bev's the previous night, the sight of the familiar black Escort at the end of the cul-de-sac had relieved his mind. The P.I. had not taken the night off after all, so Conrad had made a U-turn and returned to the tennis club where he'd stayed on his previous trip to Palm Springs. Now he wished he had stopped and talked to him.

Whether Ashleigh believed it or not, whoever had followed her had to be the same person who planted the bomb in her car. But he wasn't any closer to solving this mystery than he was to figuring out Danielle's disappearance. He didn't know how or why, but he felt that Danielle had to be dead. There was no other explanation. Ashleigh had expressed that feeling the night before too, but neither of them wanted to fully admit that it must be true.

Since Danielle's disappearance, unexplained figures had appeared on, and then disappeared from, the merchandise information sheets of the Better Sportswear department. And Danielle just couldn't be the one responsible. That kind of dishonesty wasn't in her, and besides, she didn't have the know-how to make it happen.

His mind flashed back to Ashleigh. Maybe someone thought she knew more than she did—something incriminating. But what? Whether or not this had any relationship to Danielle Norman, Ashleigh's life was in danger. And if someone wanted to kill her, he'd try again.

I can't let anything happen to her.

Recalling Ashleigh's candor last night, Conrad was aware of a large gap in the conversation. She had made no mention of Mitchell Wainwright—not once. He recalled now that when he'd asked if they'd set the date, she'd merely changed the subject. Was she afraid of Wainwright— afraid that he might be the one following her? Did she have cause to be frightened of him? Conrad had to find out. And to do that, he had to find a way to win her trust.

CHAPTER
68

Ashleigh awoke with a start. A dim light filtered through the mini-blinds as she struggled to orient herself. She looked at the travel alarm on the bedside table; it was not quite seven, but she wide awake. She stretched, listening for signs of life in the house. Only the sound of birds broke the silence as she slid out of bed, walked to the window, and opened the blinds.

The black Escort still was not there.

After donning her robe and slippers, she walked down the hallway. She smelled the coffee before she reached the kitchen. Then she saw that the round table was set and orange juice filled a white pitcher. Pouring herself some coffee, she looked out the window and watched as Elizabeth toddled behind Bev from one potted plant to the next. In her small hand, the girl carried a tiny watering can—identical to her mother's larger one. Her face radiated pride as she imitated the watering of each plant.

Later, at breakfast, Ashleigh realized that she felt much better in the light of day; surely there was nothing suspicious about the manila envelope, otherwise Bev would've said something. She also felt somewhat guilty about dominating the conversation for the past two nights, so she was glad to engage Bev in an hour or so of light conversation about her family and life in the desert.

Finally Ashleigh said, "I'd better take a shower and get dressed."

"You aren't leaving before lunch, are you?"

"No. Conrad has to work with the operations manager today and has an early dinner meeting, so we won't be leaving until around seven." She was halfway to her room when she heard Bev call her name. Bev was right behind her when she turned.

"Here," she said, handing Ashleigh two manila envelopes. "You must have left these behind." She grinned sheepishly. "Sorry, I opened this one." She held up the larger envelope. "It had no name on it, but it was on the entry table. I didn't know what it was until I looked inside. Then I saw the smaller envelope with your name—misspelled, of course!"

The torn, unmarked envelope was the one Ashleigh had picked up early that morning. In the upper left-hand corner of the smaller envelope was a butterfly, drawn freehand with a burgundy felt-tip pen. The perfectly formed letters A S H L E Y, pasted squarely on a ruler-straight pencil line, looked like they'd been cut out with a stencil from the comic section of a Sunday newspaper.

Her heart dropped to her slippered feet.

"What's wrong?" Bev said. "You're as pale as the walls."

Ashleigh didn't respond, but turned and walked slowly down the hall toward the guest room. Bev followed.

Sinking down on the bed, she gazed at the envelope in her hand as she explained its arrival. "This wasn't on the floor beside the mail slot last night when I came in. I'm absolutely sure of that."

"Then how on earth did it get on the entry table?"

Ashleigh explained picking it up and setting it there. The two women stared down at the large burgundy butterfly. Then Ashleigh tore into the sealed flap of the smaller envelope. Inside was a single piece of lined paper folded in thirds. Bev sat down beside her. Neither spoke as Ashleigh carefully unfolded the paper, torn from a legal-size yellow pad. Her palms were damp, so she smoothed the paper with the back of her hand.

The author of the cryptic message had painstakingly cut out individual phrases, words, and even single letters to form other words. Unlike the front of the envelope, a black-and-white section of newspaper had been used. Portions of the print were underlined with burgundy ink.

```
Stick to personnel you're not helping Dani-
elle Norman. You are putting her in danger. She
wants you to stop two trips to her home are two
too many. If you don't back off now, more than
```

<u>a car could be destroyed</u>. Wainwright's men can't
protect you. There's no black Ford outside your
door now. Perhaps Wainwright found out about
<u>that other man</u> and is making better use of his
detectives he's done it before!

STOP BEFORE IT'S TOO LATE!!

Ashleigh leapt up from the bed, thrust the note into Bev's hand, and
darted across to the window.

Bev sat silently gaping at the note. "Is this some sort of a joke?" she
asked with a frown.

"If it is, it's a sick one." Ashleigh jerked on the cord, raising the blinds
and revealing the clear plate-glass window. She pressed her face to it,
feeling the coolness on her forehead, and peered out at the street of the
quiet suburban neighborhood. She saw a next-door neighbor mowing
his lawn. Two women, apparently just returning from church, stood on
the sidewalk, engrossed in conversation.

Outside, everything looked peaceful. A perfectly normal Sunday.

Still in her robe, with her hair uncombed, Ashleigh replaced the receiver as Bev hovered beside her.

"Well, what did they say?"

"They'll be here within the hour." Ashleigh ran her fingers through her tangled hair. "Obviously, it's not much of a priority for the Palm Desert PD. I get the feeling they were just humoring me—" She broke off, her mind racing. "I'd like to call Mitchell. Do you mind?"

"Of course not." Bev pulled out the straight-backed chair next to the telephone and gestured toward it.

Ashleigh dialed the number for the Atlanta Hilton. Listening to the successive rings, she calculated the time difference, though she felt as though her brain had ceased to function: nearly ten AM. But it really didn't matter what time it was—he wasn't answering. Just as she was about to give up, a response crackled across the line.

"Wainwright."

She heard voices in the background and hesitated.

"Mitchell, I need to talk to you when you are alone."

"I'm alone," he said. In seconds, the other voices had faded. "That was the TV. What's wrong? Were you followed again?"

Ignoring his question, she asked, "Did you call last night?"

"I had every intention of calling, but by the time—"

She cut him off abruptly. "I hadn't expected you to call. But someone placed a person-to-person call to me last night." She told him all that had happened. And he listened, this time without interruption.

When she had finished, the line was silent for a few seconds.

"Landes called me yesterday afternoon," said Mitchell finally, "and told me that you had said he needn't stick around. That you were being taken care of. Is he back on the job now?"

"Not unless he just arrived." She switched the phone to her other ear. "It's my fault. When it appeared that no one was following me from Long Beach to La Jolla, or to Palm Desert, it seemed pretty silly to have him sitting outside my door."

An awkward silence followed. Then she heard him clear his throat and knew he was most likely getting his temper in check.

"Didn't it ever occur to you that having a private investigator around could be one hell of a deterrent?" He was talking to her as if she were a dull child.

"Yes, that occurred to me." Ashleigh tried in vain to control her own temper.

"Hey! Truce! This is no time to argue," Mitchell offered apologetically.

"You're absolutely right. I'm sorry," she responded. "And I would like to have Dick Landes or one of his agents back on duty when I get home."

"When you get home?" Mitchell's voice rose. "How about now?"

Ashleigh selected her words carefully. "That won't be necessary. Bentley's VP of operations and finance is here this weekend. He's driving back with me."

"Conrad Taylor?"

"Yes." *He knows darn well that's who I mean.*

"How nice."

"Mitchell, everything is under control," she said with more confidence than she felt. "I have to go. I'm not dressed, and the police are due soon."

"I sure would feel a lot better if Landes or one of his agents were with you, darling."

The sudden change in his tone was unnerving. *Why does he have to pretend that nothing has changed between us?* She wished she could avoid taking advantage of his protection, but she was on foreign ground and didn't know what else to do.

"Stop worrying. Mr. Taylor will be with me, and he'll be on the look-out for the blue Karmann Ghia."

A gasp came through from Wainwright's end of the line. "What did you say?" When she did not reply right away, he said, "Is that the car that followed you? You never mentioned the make."

Ashleigh frowned. "I thought I did . . . Why, do you know someone who owns a Karmann Ghia?"

"It's an unusual car, that's all," he replied, with a trace of hesitation. Then he told her that he would call later that evening.

It seemed to Ashleigh that he was in an awful hurry to say good-bye.

CHAPTER
70

Mitchell Wainwright swung the car into the Hertz lot at the Atlanta airport, rolled up to a uniformed attendant, and placed the paperwork in the man's outstretched hand.

Spotting the waiting taxi, he grabbed his bags and ran straight to the car door, which was held open by the driver.

"Mr. Wainwright?" the driver asked.

Wainwright nodded and slid into the backseat. "Delta. And step on it." He gave a wry smile. The words that had just rolled off his tongue echoed in his head like something from a movie—but he sobered quickly. "My flight leaves in less than an hour."

Following Ashleigh's call, he hadn't taken time to call anywhere but the airport. *Thank God for the age of electronics and the cellular phone.* He pulled the large, awkward instrument from the case, prayed for reception, and punched in Randall Updike's number. When the exchange answered, Wainwright asked that they reach Updike as soon as possible.

"Tell him that Mr. Wainwright had to fly to California unexpectedly due to a family emergency, and I'll be in touch to reschedule the eight o'clock meeting set for tomorrow morning. Monday," he clarified.

He waited for the woman to repeat his message, then disconnected and punched in the digits for Landes's car phone. There was too much interference; the call wouldn't go through. Frustrated, he pushed the phone back into the case.

Before the taxi came to a full stop in front of the Delta terminal, Wainwright picked up his other bag and jumped out, thrust a twenty-dollar bill in the driver's hand, and turned and raced into the airport. Not slowing his pace, he glanced up at one of the screens to check the gate number and sprinted toward his plane.

By the time he reached the departure area, the final boarding call was being announced. He walked straight onto the plane, checking in with the stewardess and carrying both bags. It had been a close call.

The five-hour flight had given Wainwright sufficient time to formulate his plan. With a car agency and a limousine at his disposal, it seemed ironic that he should find himself en route to the Hertz counter. But he was in a hurry, and tonight he could not call on Donald, his longtime chauffeur—not this time. This was something he had to do covertly.

Inside the rented Buick, Wainwright switched on the light and once again set up his cellular phone. Then he dialed Landes's car phone.

No answer.

Reaching around to the backseat, he picked up his sports jacket and withdrew the address book from the inside pocket. He thumbed through the pages until he found Landes's home phone number, and he punched it in.

No answer.

Wainwright wanted to slam the phone down. Instead, he looked up the number for the Landes Agency in Long Beach. The answering service picked up.

"Tell him to call Mitchell Wainwright as soon as possible," he said, and left his cellular phone number.

He checked his watch. It was now after eight. It was a safe bet that Ashleigh wouldn't be home for another couple of hours. He dialed her number and left a message that he'd call again tomorrow night. Hopefully, she wouldn't call and discover that he'd left Atlanta. He didn't want to talk to her until he got things sorted out.

But where in the hell is Landes? He dialed the detective's car phone again and listened to the eternal ringing, then started up the car and threw it into gear.

He could be at Belmont Shore in under an hour.

CHAPTER
71

Turning off the 605 and onto Studebaker, Conrad looked across the seat at Ashleigh, who had fallen into a restless sleep just outside of Riverside. As he watched her head swing from side to side, he knew how frightened she must be.

Whoever had sent that note knew a lot about Danielle but not much about Ashleigh, not even the spelling of her name. Nor was this person aware of the closeness of her relationship with Danielle. *She wants you to stop,* the message had said. Conrad pondered this. *If there is any truth to the warning, perhaps Danielle is still alive.* It was the first ray of hope he'd felt since finding her handbag nearly a week ago.

It was fortunate that his unusually early rising had allowed him to stop at Bev's before heading to the store that morning. He had arrived just before their encounter with the two Palm Desert police officers and was glad he'd been there for Ashleigh, even though he knew he could have handled things a lot better. He marveled at the dispassionate way in which she had avoided becoming defensive. At the same time, he wondered, *What came over me?*

He wasn't in the habit of losing his cool, but the moment the first officer began talking to Ashleigh in that patronizing tone, he'd seen crimson, lost control, and exploded. *Ashleigh McDowell is not the type of woman to create a situation just to get attention,* he'd wanted to shout. While the officer hadn't said anything like that, he'd sure as hell implied it. And yet she'd taken his insinuation in stride and remained calm—at least outwardly.

At the red light on the corner of Westminster and Studebaker, Conrad stepped gently on the brake, trying not to wake his companion as he rolled to a stop. She had grown calm, but noting the gentle rise and fall of her breathing, he was again troubled. *She's holding something back.* Whatever it was, she hadn't told the police, he knew that—and she hadn't told him everything either.

Under the brightened illumination of the streetlamps, he noticed how pale and exhausted Ashleigh appeared. Her hair was loose and splayed across the headrest, and her wan coloring blended with the cream interior of her fiancé's car. In spite of all this disarray, Ashleigh McDowell was the most captivating woman he'd ever known. And yet what did he really know about her?

The car lurched forward when the light turned green at an intersection, and Ashleigh's eyes sprang open. She pulled her coat up around her neck and looked around. Her lips turned up in an attempted smile, and she lifted her hand to cover her mouth as she tried unsuccessfully to stifle a yawn. Sliding back against the seat, her posture now erect and color flowing back into her cheeks, she said, "Sorry I was such rotten company."

Conrad just smiled. He hadn't thought that at all.

Ashleigh was fully awake by the time they reached the Pacific Coast Highway. They rode in a companionable silence. She had appreciated Conrad's sticking up for her when that short, pudgy policeman with the balding head had taken the whole affair as a practical joke. The officer had done nothing to conceal his skepticism when she'd asked to make a copy of the note so that the Palm Desert PD could keep the original. If it hadn't been for the calm, professional manner of the second officer, things could have gone a lot worse. The trim, nondescript man quickly took the lead and made two copies of the crude note for her. He was polite and took the matter seriously, assuring them that he would follow through with both the LBPD and the LAPD.

Ashleigh looked toward the neon sign at the side of the Hyatt Edgewater, which honored its employee of the month, but she was more aware of the strong, chiseled features of Conrad Taylor, his profile outlined against the blazing background of lights.

Conrad drove past his own condo and stopped in front of the door to her underground parking. Turning toward her, he asked, "How do you feel?"

"Fine," Ashleigh lied. At the skeptical raise of his eyebrow, she added, "Well, considering." Then it dawned on her. "Your car is still at the airport."

"Don't worry about it," he said. "I'll call a cab from your place, if you don't mind."

She nodded. "I'd rather not go to the airport now. But why don't you drop me off and take the car home with you? You can pick me up again in the morning and I'll drop you off at the airport."

Conrad smiled and agreed, before a shadow of concern crossed his face. "Ashleigh, I don't like the idea of you going upstairs alone."

She adjusted her position and pushed the garage door opener, which she'd taken from the glove compartment. "Landes said he would have one of his agents here within the hour. I'll be fine once I'm inside the condo . . . but if you don't mind, I would like you to walk me to my door." She wasn't thrilled about being alone either.

Conrad had no intention of leaving before the agent arrived, even if that meant waiting in his car outside the condo. He would double-check that a private investigator from the Landes Agency was assigned to be there that night. According to Pocino, Landes had said that he was not on duty outside Bev's the night before, nor were any of his agents. So who did the black Ford Escort belong to, and why had it been there? It was more than a coincidence, Conrad was sure of that. *Can Landes and his agents be relied on?* he wondered.

As Ashleigh pointed him in the direction of her parking stall—now marred with black smoke stains left by the explosion—he saw a flicker of fear in her eyes. It caught him completely off guard. Suddenly, he realized all that had happened to her in the past week, and he felt a rush of compassion.

The light through the leaded glass at the top of the paneled oak door seemed unusually bright as Ashleigh placed her key in the lock, and he heard the first tumbler click into place. She appeared perplexed.

"Is there something wrong?"

"I always double-lock the door. I guess . . . I guess I'm getting forgetful. " She smiled up at him, still looking troubled.

The door swung open. Ashleigh gasped and dropped her overnight bag, which thumped as it hit the floor.

CHAPTER
72

Conrad steadied Ashleigh, drawing her close. With her garment bag draped over his other arm, he shoved the door fully open with the toe of his shoe.

For as far as he could see, the condo was flooded in harsh light. To the right of the marble entry, he saw the living room. The table lamps at each end of an L-shaped couch were aglow, as was the shaded wall light directly above the center cushion of the sofa.

His arm still around Ashleigh's shoulder, he felt her body stiffen. Releasing his hold, he followed the path of her gaze and took a step forward, then cocked his head around the corner of the alcove to their left.

Beneath the brightly lit crystal chandelier, lying on the polished walnut dining room table, were sections and scraps of cut newspaper and a small pair of scissors, the blades spread apart. He moved toward the table. It was obvious that someone had cut out letters and words from the colored comics as well as the black-and-white newspaper sections, just like the words on the crude note.

Conrad threw the garment bag across the back of a dining room chair at the end of the rectangular table and scanned the clutter. His instinct told him not to touch anything. He looked at the date in the upper margin of the top newspaper. With the face of his thumbnail, he shifted the position of a few more sheets and again checked the dates. They were all the same.

The fact that the macabre note was constructed here in Ashleigh's condo told him two things. Number one, someone was aware that she would not be here. And number two, that person's—or perhaps those persons'—intention was to scare the hell out of her. Through his head, unbidden, shot the thought *Mission accomplished.*

Still standing just a few feet inside the door, Ashleigh tried to suppress the thickening in the back of her throat. Her eyes darted between the living room and the dining area, and then beyond. Everywhere she looked there was hideously unnatural light.

She forced herself to move toward the table. Conrad looked up from the pile of cut-up newspapers and said, "Look at the date on these papers."

She started to pick up one of the sections, but he stopped her. "Don't touch anything until after the police arrive. I don't think they can get much from this mess. If there were any prints, they probably wouldn't show on newsprint, and the scissors have probably been wiped off. But still . . ."

Ashleigh looked down at the sections on top and then back at Conrad. "This is last week's paper. Is that important?" she asked.

"I'm not sure. But it does mean that this could have been done any day since you left for La Jolla." He shrugged. "I'm grasping at straws."

Inspecting the rest of the condo, they discovered that lights glared from every room: the bathrooms, the bedroom, the study, even the closets. Ashleigh started to turn off the bathroom light.

"Don't touch anything," Conrad demanded again, this time in a harsh voice. "I'm calling the police." Then, gently taking hold of the hand with which Ashleigh had reached for the switch, he said more softly, "The chance of getting any good prints is remote, but . . ." He didn't bother to finish the thought; instead, he guided her back toward the living room.

She looked up at him. "I don't know what to say. This is unreal. This kind of thing has never happened to me before. And now, within the span of a week, police officers have had to come to my condo for a car explosion and now this."

Wordlessly, he wrapped his arms around her. Resting her cheek on his shoulder, her thoughts temporarily halted. The bright lights seemed to dim, and for the moment she felt safe and secure.

When Conrad released his firm hold, Ashleigh did not step away. Instead, she remained leaning against him, her breathing unsteady.

Taking a half step back, he guided her to the couch.

She sank down into the corner of the sofa and glanced around again at her surroundings, then back to Conrad. She felt the color rush to her cheeks and was frightened by her unexpected response to him. Then, as if those brief moments of intimacy had never happened, she rose from the couch and asked, "Would you like some coffee?"

Conrad didn't answer immediately, and when he did, his expression was bemused. "Yes. I think we could both use a shot of caffeine." He hesitated, looking toward the open door. "I'll take your bags back to the bedroom and call the police." He hesitated again, as if deep in thought, and then spoke with confidence. "Before they arrive, we'd better talk this out."

Ashleigh scooped out the coffee beans. Noticing the blinking light on her answering machine, she punched PLAY. It was a brief message from Mitchell. She frowned. She'd told him she wouldn't be home before ten that night, but he'd called at eight. She pushed the button marked TIME. It was correct. But Mitchell was a night owl, usually not taking the moments for his personal life until the evening was well under way. So why would he call so early?

Seconds after Conrad disappeared in the direction of the bedroom, he reappeared, interrupting Ashleigh's thoughts and disturbing her composure. "The police are on their way," he said.

The coffee made its final percolating cough, and Ashleigh filled the thermal pitcher and placed it and two cups on the white wicker tray. She carried the tray out to the coffee table and knelt down to fill the cups. "Black?" she asked, more as a means of confirmation than as a question. Somehow she knew that he took his coffee just as she took hers.

It seemed like hours since she had unlocked the door, but of course it had been only moments. And yet so much had changed.

Conrad nodded, noticing the sturdiness of the cup and the sensible size of the handle in contrast to the subtle feminine pattern. He waited patiently for Ashleigh to settle against the soft cushions in the corner of the couch before he began to speak. Despite her attempts to conceal it, fear and confusion filled the room, and he realized that he would have to be careful not to push too far.

"Ashleigh, who besides yourself has a key to this condo?"

Her eyes looked straight ahead. "My cleaning lady, the lady next door, and—"

"Mitchell Wainwright?" he filled in.

Her eyes met his with a flash of indignation. "Yes, Mitchell has a key, but he's in Atlanta."

"I'm not trying to pry."

Her eyes softened. "I'm sorry. I know you're not . . ."

Conrad leaned forward, picked up his cup, and moved closer.

Ashleigh began again. "I'm trying to make some kind of sense out of this. There's no sign of . . . forced entry." She smiled wanly. "I think that's what they call it."

"You mentioned the lady next door."

"Yes, Mrs. Nix. She's lived here since before these apartments became condos. She takes in my mail and any odd papers that are left down in the mailboxes, and waters the plants when I'm away. Not a likely suspect."

"Could she have let someone borrow the key?"

Ashleigh considered the question. "No, I don't think she would do that. But I'll ask her tomorrow."

"Good. Now, how about your cleaning lady? Do you trust her?" Conrad asked. Then he muttered, more to himself than to her, "Of course you do, or she wouldn't have a key." Making direct eye contact, he apologized. "Forgive me. I didn't mean to sound like another detective. Just trying to see what we might be able to piece together."

"Go ahead," she replied. "I appreciate your help."

"Has the cleaning lady worked for you long?"

After exhausting the safe questions, Conrad could no longer avoid asking about Wainwright. He was about to do so when the intercom shrilled.

Ashleigh set down her coffee cup and went to the phone. The police officers identified themselves, and she buzzed them in, saying, "I hope these aren't the same officers who were here a few days ago."

Time was running out, and Conrad realized he must ask a very direct question before the police walked through the door. "Ashleigh, could

Mitchell Wainwright in any way be mixed up in this? What I mean is—" he attempted to clarify—"according to the media, Wainwright is involved in a number of so-called hostile takeovers and has some rather formidable enemies."Although he was aware that he was treading on dangerous ground, he couldn't stop now. "Could any of this be some sort of misplaced revenge?"

Wainwright's rented Buick screeched to a halt in front of the Byzantine-style gates. He lowered his window and leaned toward the call box. "Mitchell Wainwright to see Mrs. Lane," he announced curtly.

"Is she expecting you, sir?"

At the sound of the ostentatious voice, he exhaled audibly. "No. Please, tell her I'm here."

A brief silence followed. "Mr. Wainwright. It's past ten o'clock."

His voice rose. "I know what time it is." His former wife rarely went to bed before the eleven o'clock news, which had little to do with a genuine interest in the world and local affairs. This was Diana's fuel for cocktail dialogue—her entry into the clusters of prominent men and a handful of influential women. "I choose to spend my time with people who can talk of more interesting aspects of life than children, grandchildren, and the most effective spot remover," she'd once informed him.

"Yes, Mitchell. What do you want?" Diana's voice sliced through the intercom.

"I wouldn't be here if I didn't need to speak to you."

"Why didn't you call?"

"Been trying for the past half hour," he shouted, "but all I get is a busy signal on both your goddamned lines!" He ground his cigarette in the open ashtray. "Are you going to buzz me in?" Not waiting for a response, he pushed the electric window control to close the window and put the car in gear. The gate slid open.

As he swung around the circular drive, a full blaze of light flooded the house and grounds. Diana had done well for herself, he surmised, as he took in her Lakewood Country Club Estates mansion. It was reminiscent of the White House—or perhaps Mottell's Mortuary, as Anthony had once described it.

What mattered most to Diana Ciano Wainwright Lane was money—well, that and position. Even as a young woman, she had been careful to date only men who could provide both, Wainwright recalled bitterly.

Diana stepped out, closing the door behind her. Clad in a red velvet robe, she stood resolutely beside one of six enormous pillars, her arms folded aggressively in front of her. Her jet-black hair hung loose around her slim shoulders, and her green eyes shone.

The crunch of gravel broke through the silence of the cool night as Wainwright made his way around the car. He braced himself as he mounted the stone steps to the broad porch.

Like so many times before, he could see the fury—in her face, in her entire body—building to an uncontrolled rage. His failure to return her umpteen calls since his confrontation with Anthony a few weeks before had fueled that eternal fire. *I knew her so well,* he thought. Cold and self-centered, but still a beautiful woman—a fact that never failed to jar him.

For a moment neither of them spoke. Both grappled silently for control—biding their time, not wanting to be the first to break the silence. Finally Wainwright said, "Sorry I didn't return your calls. I've been up to my—"

"Too busy to discuss your own son," she said caustically.

"My son. That's a laugh. He doesn't even use my name," he scoffed. Lowering his voice, he added, "For which I should be grateful, I suppose." With the same instinct that served him so brilliantly in business, he suppressed his emotions and continued. "Look, Diana. This is not the time to discuss Anthony."

"When is the time?" She stepped forward, her arms still tightly folded in front of her.

He didn't have time for a verbal duel, but he wasn't prepared to just walk away as he had done often times before. He needed some answers. "First of all, I haven't taken any legal action regarding Anthony and his precious inheritance, but unless he can sort himself out, I intend to." He held up a restraining hand as she began to bristle and bluster. "I won't do anything until after you've had your say. But not tonight."

Diana's eyes bore into his. "Then what brings you here?"'

Wainwright wasted no more time. "Does Anthony still live in that apartment in Horny Corner?"

"Horny Corner?" she repeated with a frown.

"Forget it. It's just a nickname." No point in telling her it was one of Long Beach's centers for dispensing drugs. "In Belmont Shore?"

"Yes."

"Do you know where he is now?"

Hands on her hips, Diana asked, "You're asking me if I know where our twenty-three-year-old son is at"—she took hold of Wainwright's arm and held his wristwatch up to the light—"ten twenty on a Sunday night?"

"Cut the histrionics. I need his phone number."

Her dark brows shot up. "You don't have his phone number?"

"If I had the goddamned number, I wouldn't be asking you for it." He ground out the words through gritted teeth.

"I have it inside. Would you like to come in?" she asked icily, nodding toward the house.

"I'll wait." He leaned back against one of the pillars.

She started to turn, then stopped abruptly. "Why do you want his number?" She glared. "Just last week you wouldn't return his calls or mine."

Wainwright was not listening. He had only one thing on his mind. "Diana, is Anthony still driving the Karmann Ghia?"

CHAPTER
74

Outside the monstrous complex housing Anthony's apartment, Wainwright climbed back into the car, slamming the door behind him. He looked out on the bay, his powerlessness threatening to drive him mad.

It was nearly midnight, and no telling when Anthony might show. *But I'll be damned if I'll budge before confronting the miserable little reprobate,* thought Wainwright.

He shifted in his seat, trying to get into a more comfortable position, and his eyes wandered across the street to the water's edge, where a group of five young men huddled together. Their clothes were a blur of various shades of black, and they wore sneakers with creative zigzags and stripes. The two on the far side of the circle, facing him, held half-smoked cigarettes—marijuana, it smelled like.

They seemed to take turns shooting skeptical glances his way. Finally all five shifted their eyes in Wainwright's direction. Even though he'd removed his sports jacket and tie, he clearly looked out of place there. The blond teenager with narrow shoulders, wearing a black leather jacket with large silver studs, pointed with his chin toward the Buick. In unison, the boys strode toward him.

Curiously unafraid, Wainwright watched them advance. They did not appear to be armed with any sort of weapon. As they approached the three-foot cement wall that separated the sandy shore from the street, he scanned the interior of the car. He picked up the sturdy umbrella on the passenger seat next to his suitcase, and flinging open the door, he heaved himself out of the car.

Wainwright's eyes remained fixed on the advancing group. Cautious, he restrained himself from making any rapid movement. He held the knobby-handled umbrella in the hand that rested unobtrusively just inside the open car door. He'd be damned if he'd let this band of low-life punks intimidate him. Not one of them was close to the six-foot mark. Their strength, if any, was in numbers—certainly not in brawn.

With a casual air that appeared forced rather than natural, Wainwright called out, "What's happening, guys?"

The group was halfway across the street when his voice reached them. Taking a drag from his cigarette, Wainwright maintained eye contact with the skinny blond he assumed to be the leader.

"Not much," the blond responded, taking in Wainwright's six-foot-two frame, from his head on down to his half-brogue shoes.

Wainwright's grip tightened on the umbrella.

Shifting his gaze from Wainwright to the group and then back to Wainwright, the blond asked, "Looking for someone?"

Gesturing toward the building to his right, Wainwright again adopted a casual air. "My son lives here."

"So?" asked a teen with a stud earring in his left lobe.

"He's not home. I just got into town, so I thought I'd wait."

"What's his name?" asked the leader. His question was echoed by a heavyset fellow with curly red hair, who wasn't more than five-four. The other two—Hispanics, each wearing an earring in his left ear—remained silent but looked on with interest.

A young man wearing an earring did not necessarily denote homosexuality, or so Wainwright had been told. He seemed to remember that it depended on which ear the ring was worn in . . . But it was beyond him. Why would any normal male want to wear women's jewelry?

"Anthony," he said congenially. *No point in antagonizing these punks, earrings or no.*

The group remained in the middle of Bayshore for several more minutes before moving in closer, until they were just a few feet away.

"Maybe you ought to come back tomorrow," the blond leader said.

Wainwright quelled a sudden desire to lash out at the pimply-faced youth. Reason dictated that he not make the kid look small in front of his gang. "Yeah? Well, if he doesn't show soon, I'll do just that."

The anxiety of the moment was rapidly supplanted by tedium, and Wainwright was relieved when the small group finally climbed back over the retaining wall, sauntered across the sand to the damp area in front of the bay, and headed in the direction of Second Street. He wondered how Landes and his cohorts managed this type of bullshit day in and day out. He could've just had the agency find Anthony—it probably would've been a hell of a lot easier—but using them was too risky. They were capable of uncovering more than he was willing to share—things he hadn't come to terms with himself.

Still standing beside his car, he distractedly tossed the unnecessary umbrella back onto the passenger seat and stretched his tense muscles, peering off into the distance. The curve of the road obscured his view, as he'd known it would. *Besides,* he reminded himself, *Ashleigh's apartment would remain out of sight from this side of Second Street no matter where I stood*. He wasn't ready to tell her of his suspicions. At least, not until he knew a hell of a lot more than he did now.

As he eased himself back into the car, the umbrella caught his eye, and he was aware of the uneven beat of his heart. Now that it was all over and he had a chance to think about what might have happened, the full impact of his recklessness hit him. He was in good shape, yes. But at forty-nine he had been a fool to think that he could outmaneuver a gang of hopped-up kids.

This is all getting to be too much. His thoughts ran rampant as he fumbled for the seat adjuster. *What am I doing here?* He, the master of mergers and acquisitions, had walked out on a multimillion-dollar deal in the heart of full-swing negotiations. Philip Sloane was breathing down his neck, yet here he sat in a rented car in the high-rent district of the city's low-life swingers.

With the seat at full tilt, he leaned back against the headrest, thinking of the consequences of delay. He took his cigarette case from his jacket pocket and shifted his thoughts to Diana. What the hell had happened to her? Pushing in the cigar lighter, he remembered what she'd been like back in the days when they first met.

Wainwright was twenty-four and Diana barely nineteen and in hot rebellion against her middle-class roots. In their first years of marriage she was everything he had expected. Wainwright was the center of her world, and she had been in awe of him and of the wealth and power that surrounded him. And though hesitant at first, she soon became an accomplished and gracious hostess. Then, right after Anthony started kindergarten, she began to change. She spent more and more time in pursuit of her own identity. She lost much of her charming passivity.

Inadvertently, Wainwright's thoughts shifted to Ashleigh, and like a quick plunge into the icy bay, it hit him. *Bentleys Royale is the center of her world, a world that is unlikely to ever revolve around me.*

He glanced back up at Anthony's apartment; it was still dark. Absently he cracked his knuckles, one at a time. Leaning back in the seat, he closed his eyes, striving not to think about Ashleigh, and not to think about Anthony and his shattered dreams for the son who was no longer his.

CHAPTER

75

Early Monday morning, Ashleigh set her handbag and organizer on Betty's desk, opened the right-hand drawer, and felt for the key to the file cabinet. Opening it, she fingered through the folders for a second, then a third time. Danielle Norman's records were not there.

The shrill ring from one of the phone lines pierced the silence of the reception room. She answered it just as Betty walked through the doorway—it was Conrad. Ashleigh nodded to her secretary. "Excuse me," she said as she moved aside, giving Betty room to maneuver to the other side of her desk. "Let me change phones." She pressed the HOLD button and placed the phone back in its cradle.

"Betty, have you seen Danielle Norman's file?" Ashleigh asked after a perfunctory greeting.

Betty nodded. "Catherine must still have it." Betty told her she'd called the personnel director when Ted Norman had barged into her office on Friday morning, threatening to go straight up to Mr. Jerome.

"What did he want?" Ashleigh had talked to Ted Norman the day after Danielle disappeared. He'd told her they hadn't been in touch for months.

"He said something about needing information on *his wife's* profit sharing and savings."

Suddenly remembering that she had left Conrad hanging on the phone, Ashleigh said, "I'll be right back. " She dashed into her office and picked up the phone.

"Conrad?"

"I'm still here." She heard a click that signaled he'd transferred the call from the speaker to the receiver. "Just came from Central Purchasing," he said. "I've pulled the original purchase orders from Danielle's department and would like you to take a look. I doubt that Danielle wrote more than a small portion of those recent orders. Can you get a sample of her assistant buyer's signature?"

"Yes, I . . ." Ashleigh heard the sound of shuffling papers on the other end of the line and then a voice in the background.

"Sorry, I'll have to call you back." *Click.*

Before she had a chance to consider the abrupt end to Conrad's call, the sharp buzz of the intercom interrupted her thoughts.

"It's Mr. Jerome." Betty said. She glanced down at the flashing red light on line one. "And Catherine wants to see you right away. Ted Norman is in her office."

Betty didn't have to say another word. Ted's voice thundered through the adjoining door to the Personnel offices.

Suddenly there was a loud crash followed by the sound of shattering glass.

Ashleigh dropped the phone and sprang to her feet. Her desk chair banged against the credenza as she rushed to the door. It was locked. Fumbling with her keys, she heard the chaos in the next room.

The lock turned, and she flung the door open. All eyes turned toward her as she stepped into the room. Ashleigh glanced around quickly. Catherine looked up from a stooped position alongside her desk. She held the base of her desk lamp and was picking up a jagged piece of ceramic tile. Her assistant swept the smaller pieces and scattered fragments of the bulb into a white plastic dustpan.

Ted Norman leaned against the doorframe of Catherine's small office, his arms locked in front of him. The dissipated man stared at Ashleigh through red-rimmed eyes. "It's about time you graced us with an appearance." The speech of this once-attractive man was slurred, and he looked years older than he had the last time Ashleigh had seen him.

Too angry to be frightened, Ashleigh fixed him with an icy glare, but she felt heat rise to her face as he gave her a lusty head-to-toe appraisal. Getting her emotions in check, she said dispassionately, "Come into my office."

"Thought you'd never ask. " He grinned, and running his fingers like a comb through his unkempt hair, he strode through the door.

"Would you like me to come with you?" Catherine stood beside her desk, a worried expression on her round face.

"Not right now, thank you," Ashleigh replied, quickly adding, "but stand by."

"Don't call me, I'll call you." Ted grinned again, this time in Catherine's direction.

Gathering every ounce of her waning self-control, Ashleigh closed the door behind them and gestured for Ted to take a seat as she slipped between the credenza and the table. She sat directly across from him.

Ted leaned toward her, both elbows on the table, the slack skin of his chin resting on white knuckles. A look came over his face that might have appeared sinister had his eyes held a trace of sharpness—a flicker of life. They did not. Instead they reflected the essence of a dead soul.

Ashleigh did not wait for him to speak, nor did she make any attempt at diplomacy or even common courtesy. She felt nothing but contempt. "I understand you've been asking questions about Danielle's profit sharing."

Ted Norman sat motionless, his unfocused gaze resting just above Ashleigh's head. "You—you're . . . damned right I have. Sh—She owes me."

Ashleigh rose to her feet and leaned toward him. "She owes you nothing." Her hands gripped the edge of the table as she glared down at his dull eyes. "Just what exactly do you know about Danielle's disappearance?"

"Like I told you on the phone, I don't know nothin'!"

Ashleigh wondered at his stuttering and the strange inflection he was using, as if he were uneducated, which she knew was not the case. "Then why are you here? Why were you here on Friday?" She remained standing, her eyes boring into his—a power position she seldom employed.

Mopping his sweaty brow with the back of his hand, Ted pushed back in the chair and, patting down his hair, cleared his throat. "Now you settle down!" His macho demeanor restored, he rose to his feet and gestured for her to sit. "I'll tell you the way it is."

Ashleigh's eyes flashed, and she gripped the chair back more tightly. "Don't try to bully me." She maintained her penetrating gaze. "My God, look at you! I can smell the alcohol on your breath, and it isn't even noon."

Ted sat down as suddenly as he'd stood, and the belligerence disappeared from his expression. "Truce!"

The intercom blared. Not taking her eyes off Ted Norman, Ashleigh punched the button.

"Is everything alright?" Betty's voice filled the room.

"For the moment." Her eyes still pinned on Ted, Ashleigh asked, "Did you let Mr. Jerome know that I was detained?"

"Yes. He asked that you call as soon as you can."

Ashleigh tapped the intercom button and sat back in her chair.

"As I was saying before we were so rudely interrupted . . ." Ted began. His speech was becoming more coherent. "I've no idea what's happened to Danielle. She's most likely gotten herself in over her head. She always did spend a hell of a lot more than either of us made."

Ashleigh had to admit to herself she knew the unfortunate truth of his statement.

"After your call, I heard about Danielle from some . . . mutual friends." He grinned sardonically. "When they confirmed that she'd flown the coop, I figured I'd better make sure I got my share of the house. Maybe more than what might be considered my share if she's skipped town."

"What mutual friends?" she scoffed. "And if you know nothing about what's happened to Danielle, why are you asking about her profit sharing—as if you don't expect her to return?"

He stared blankly at her and straightened his back against the chair.

"Were you at her house within the past week? Do you still have a key?"

"Hold it, lady. Is this some kind of inquisition?" He leapt to his feet. "You're sure as hell barking up the wrong tree if you think I had anything to do with Danielle's disappearance."

"Sit down, Ted," Ashleigh snapped. "Danielle would not take off, leaving her house and everything else behind. You know better than that."

He sank back down in the chair. "Maybe she did, maybe she didn't. Who knows what's going on in that pea brain of hers? I sure as hell don't. But it's not her house. She was supposed to sell it and give me half. She owes me."

Ashleigh's pulse quickened in anger. She leaned forward and began to rise until Ted said, "Okay, okay," and gestured for her to remain seated.

"Look, I haven't seen Danielle for weeks," he went on. "She took out a goddamned restraining order to keep me out of my own house."

"So you weren't there last Tuesday night?"

"Didn't I just get through telling you I haven't been to the house?"

"Why are you asking about her profit sharing?" Ashleigh asked a second time.

"Jesus Key-rist. That bitch took me for everything I had. She got to be such a big shot that after I lost my job, she wouldn't give me the time of day."

"Stop evading the question!"

"Told you I haven't seen her for weeks. Yet you think I'm involved in her disapp—"

In a low voice, Ashleigh said, "I know she didn't walk out on her life of her own free will."

Ted scowled. "Open your eyes, Miss McDowell. There was a hell of a lot she didn't tell you. Or me! Sure as hell didn't know what I was getting into. Her and all her psychoses." With a wicked smirk, he lowered his voice. "Ever tell you how she got rid of her stepdad?"

Ashleigh's breath caught in her throat.

Ted was still talking, but she'd missed part of his rhetoric. With his next words, she tuned back in. ". . . but I'm not about to lose my share of the house."

She wanted to shout that she didn't give a damn about his share of the house. "Ted, let's begin again. Obviously our concerns for Danielle are not the same. I understand that you two were very much in love in the past, and for a while you made her very happy."

He shook his head. "Why don't you ask me how happy she made me?" An insipid grin dominated his face.

Taken aback, she was tempted to mention his posters filled with butterflies and protestations of love when he'd been courting Danielle. But what was the point?

He folded his arms boldly in front of him. "Now, let's get a few things out in the open. Things like, I know the whole story about you and your grandmother. And I know how paranoid Danielle was about not looking bad in your eyes—not being what she called 'professional.' She had you on some goddamned pedestal."

His words whipped across her with another stinging reminder of how she had failed Danielle. "Ted, this isn't getting us anywhere."

"Wait! Still my turn," he said. "You know, we're still married!" He tipped back in his chair, smirking through thin, chapped lips. He laced his fingers behind his head, and his eyes locked with hers.

Ashleigh wanted to contradict his lies, but stopped herself. The Normans' property settlement was in limbo. Was it possible that the divorce was too?

CHAPTER
76

Ashleigh escorted Ted Norman through the reception room and watched him start down the corridor. Betty, her head cocked to one side, cradled the phone and said, "Mr. Taylor is on line one."

"I'll be right with him. Please ask Méchie if Mr. Jerome is free."

Betty began to punch in the president's extension as Ashleigh turned and walked slowly to her phone.

Conrad launched right into what was on his mind. "I now have the bulk of Danielle's purchase orders. I'd like to get your impression." Then he paused. "I hate to involve you, but I need your help, and I'm concerned for your safety. I want to get to the bottom of this." He hesitated again. "I'm tied up until six," he continued, "but if you are free this evening, I could come over there by quarter after."

Ashleigh wavered. "I have a meeting with Mr. Jerome and Adele Watson at five thirty to go over Danielle's performance review, and I have no idea how long it will take."

"Her performance review?" he repeated. "Isn't that an exercise in futility?"

Ashleigh tried to think of a rational response to what she considered an irrational process.

"I'm afraid so," she replied, the reality almost more than she could endure. "But Adele Watson wants to replace Danielle as soon as possible, and Mr. Jerome said he needed to have all the loose ends tied up."

"And a written document ties up all those so-called loose ends?" His voice rose. "That's bizarre. We don't know if she's dead or alive!"

"I know," Ashleigh said softly, not trusting herself to say more.

"Ashleigh?" Conrad's voice rang in her ear.

"Yes, sorry." She shifted the phone to her other ear. "I'm not sure when I'll be free."

"No problem. I have a mountain of work to do on budget revisions, so I can use the time. I'll just work here and you can give me a call when you're finished. We can have dinner over at the Sheraton Townhouse—or the Biltmore if you prefer."

Budget revisions. The words echoed in her head. Just how many executive heads would roll with his next proposal?

"I'd rather not stay in L.A. How about Hof's, the one on PCH where we saw Bradley last week? Let's say eight?"

"Sure . . . eight o'clock at Hof's."

Ashleigh thought she detected reluctance, but she ignored it.

"I'll bring the paperwork, and we can compare the signatures." He paused. "By the way, Pocino had LAPD see what they could get off that cassette from Danielle's answering machine. There's nothing there, other than what we heard . . . And, Ashleigh, I need to talk to you about something else. There are a few things I need to explain more fully than I did the other night."

I thought he was extremely candid. What on earth does he need to explain more fully?

CHAPTER
77

The hazy, reddish light penetrated Wainwright's closed lids. He heard the gentle lapping of the bay upon the sand and the muted cawing of seagulls.

Neither asleep nor fully awake, he shifted uncomfortably in the seat of the rented Buick. Then his elbow banged against the armrest, and he bolted upright behind the wheel. Momentarily disoriented, he shifted his glance from Alamitos Bay to the large terra-cotta apartment complex to his right. The New Orleans–style ironwork trim made the building stand out among the casual bayfront properties. And the peaceful calm of early morning left no hint of the clandestine meetings and activities for which this vicinity was known.

Taking a few moments to collect his thoughts, he pulled down the visor mirror and ran a comb through his hair. He checked the adjacent parking areas again for the Karmann Ghia, climbed out of the rented car, and strode purposefully toward the apartments. The Ghia was not in sight.

Wainwright mounted the stairs, taking two at a time. At Anthony's door, he simultaneously rang the bell and banged on the door while trying to peer through the narrow slits of venetian blinds on the window to his right.

"Whaddya want?" The waxy voice came from somewhere inside the apartment.

Wainwright announced his presence, but when no one appeared he resumed hammering on the door with the brass knocker. Finally he saw a shadowy figure emerging from somewhere beyond the doorway and heard an angry voice.

"Jesus Christ. Don't you know what time it is?"

"Anthony?" Wainwright glanced down at his Rolex and saw that it was five o'clock in the morning.

The door cracked open, and Anthony sleepily tried to focus his gaze. When his blue eyes widened with recognition, all traces of drowsiness vanished and he hurriedly tied the belt of his purple velour robe around his waist.

"Dad?" His voice held a note of caution. He glanced over his shoulder at the disheveled apartment. "Just a second . . ." He tried to suppress a yawn, covering his mouth with the back of his hand. "I'll be right with you."

Filled with disgust, Wainwright stood outside. Through the partially opened door, he watched his son as he scurried around the room picking up beer cans, full ashtrays, and articles of clothing strewn about the room. He shook his head. *It must have been one hell of a party*. But when? He'd arrived before midnight, and the apartment had been dark. Anthony must have been there—probably too spaced out to answer the phone or come to the door.

As Anthony threw his assembled pile onto the bedroom floor and quickly pulled the door closed, Wainwright gave the apartment door a shove and stepped inside. "If you've finished your housekeeping chores, I'd like to speak to you."

Anthony whipped around to face his father, and with the same cutting edge, he said, "Yes, sir."

In the deafening silence, Wainwright reached into his coat pocket and pulled out his gold cigarette case, his face contorted in anger.

Anthony's eyes, fixed on his father's, blazed in challenge.

"Anthony—"

"Don't call me Anthony. The name's Tony."

Taking out a cigarette and tapping it on the closed case, Wainwright ignored the juvenile request. "Where's your car?" His eyes scanned the untidy apartment. They stood in the living room beside a high counter separating it from the kitchen. Wainwright looked at the closed door of the bedroom, the open one to the bath, and then at Anthony's rigid form.

"What did you say?" It was more of a challenge than a question.

"You heard me. Where's your fucking car?"

For a nearly imperceptible instant, Anthony averted his eyes, then boldly stared back at his father. "What the hell gives you the right to storm in here—"

"Cut the crap. Answer the question." Wainwright lowered himself onto the arm of the sofa.

Anthony walked behind the kitchen counter and leaned forward on his elbows. "Thought you never wanted to lay eyes on me again."

Wainwright began to rise.

"Okay . . . okay. I've nothing to hide. If you're talking about the Ghia, it was stolen."

"When?" Wainwright was now on his feet.

"Two, maybe three weeks ago," he said. "Why this sudden interest in my car?"

Wainwright cut in angrily. "Is that the truth?" He hoped to hell it was. The whole idea of suspecting Anthony was preposterous. *He hates my guts, but why would he follow Ashleigh? What could he hope to gain? But a Karmann Ghia? How many of those are still around?*

"Why would I lie?" Anthony's face relaxed. Like a chameleon, his expression changed to one of incredulity and hurt, and indignation. "Has my car been found?"

Wainwright wanted to believe him but was wary. Anthony possessed the dubious gift of being a consummate liar, and his injured expression generally rendered an accuser confused and chagrined. Glancing down at his unlit cigarette, Wainwright pulled out his lighter. "Have you reported it to the police?"

"Of course. Do you think I'm some kind of an idiot?"

Wainwright said nothing as he lit the cigarette and mounted one of the barstools.

"What's this all about, anyway?"

"I'll give it to you straight. Ashleigh . . . my fiancée has been followed by a blue Ghia, and her car was blown up in her own garage, which is less than two blocks from here."

Anthony stood upright and pounded a clenched fist into the flat of his hand. "I can't believe it! After telling me you never want to see me again, you march into my apartment at dawn and accuse me of stalking your girlfriend!"

"I'm not accusing—"

"It sure as hell looks that way. It's time for you to leave."

Wainwright saw the shift of Anthony's eyes toward the bedroom. Now unable to control his rage, he slammed his hand down. The counter shook and dishes rattled in the sink. His voice boomed angrily. "Are you afraid we might wake that little faggot in your bed?"

Anthony's venomous stare caused him to take a step back.

"Sit down, Anthony." In a more conciliatory tone, Wainwright added, "Please," and gestured toward the couch.

Standing his ground for a moment, Anthony eyed his father skeptically. Then he walked around the counter and plunked down on the couch.

Wainwright turned and took a seat in the armchair facing the young man. It was like looking at a picture of himself at a younger age, in one of the family albums. But every time he thought about his son's lifestyle, he was paralyzed with anger and shame. With regret, he realized that physical attributes were all that they shared—the only thing they had in common.

Anthony crossed his legs, but his attempts to look casual and unconcerned were clumsy and didn't ring true. The rhythmic twitch in his eye had not escaped Wainwright's scrutiny.

"Nothing has changed between us. I told you I want nothing more to do with you until you get yourself straightened out." He felt a wave of nausea wash over him again, and his voice wavered. "I make no idle threats. Unless you pull yourself together, you're no son of mine, and you won't get one thin dime from me—not now—not ever."

Anthony flashed a ray of pure hatred, but remained silent and riveted to his seat. He folded his arms in front of him, and his balled fists were tight, turning his knuckles white.

Unflinching, Wainwright continued. "I wouldn't be here now if it wasn't for this situation. Which I hope to God is merely a coincidence."

Anthony shot to his feet. Standing over his father, he said through clenched teeth, "I don't give a fuck about your goddamned money. There are things your money can't buy." He thumped his chest. "And one of them is me."

Wainwright sprang from the chair and gave Anthony a shove. "You little . . ."

Regaining his balance, Anthony took a step back. "Money's all you've got. You've never been a father! You abdicated that role long ago."

Even as he seethed with rage, Wainwright knew that what his son said was true. *I could be at fault for not being around when his troubles began. But not Anthony's choice of lifestyle—that couldn't be my fault. Could it?*

The two men stood glaring at each other. Finally Anthony broke the silence and took the offensive. "Maybe you'd better find out what your fiancée has been up to. She must be involved in some heavy stuff." A grin dominated his unshaven face. "I suggest that you start by asking her a few questions."

Wainwright, with no pretext of civility, boomed, "I'm *not* questioning Ashleigh. I'm questioning *you*. And with your track record . . ."

Hearing stirrings from the bedroom, he left the sentence unfinished, turned on his heel, and departed, letting the door bang shut behind him.

Ashleigh stopped abruptly in front of Mr. Jerome's closed door. To her right, with a phone tucked under her chin, Méchie motioned with her free hand that she should go straight in. The secretary continued writing on the pink memo pad, giving no indication of the president's mood. He'd sounded less than amiable when Ashleigh had returned his call moments before and told him about her conversation with Ted Norman.

Mr. Jerome glanced up when Ashleigh walked in. He continued thumbing through an inch-high pile of reports as he nodded toward the armchair across from him.

She slipped silently into a chair facing his desk and placed her organizer on the overhang.

Following their brief greeting and before Mr. Jerome had an opportunity to ask any questions, Ashleigh told him about the threatening note she had received in Palm Desert.

The president listened politely to Ashleigh, his chin propped between his thumb and forefinger, before interrupting her. "There's more to this than you're telling me."

She pushed herself back in the chair and met his eyes. She could not continue to function with half-truths. "Mr. Jerome, you asked me to distance myself from Danielle's disappearance, but I can't."

"Ashleigh, please . . ." He held up his hand, a familiar gesture. His eyes glinted with anger, then quickly cooled. She could not read his expression. "May I see the note?" He extended his hand.

"The Palm Desert police have the original." She slipped a paper from her organizer and handed it to the president. "This is a copy." She explained as much as she thought he would want to hear. She wasn't sure he was really listening, and yet he had proven time after time that he missed little.

Jerome read the note, and after what seemed a long pause, he tossed the paper on his desk. Finally his slow, measured words began to flow. "While you remain on the payroll of Bentleys Royale, I expect you to act in a professional manner. I don't accept that you are unable to leave Danielle Norman's disappearance in the hands of professionals. But your actions thus far . . . Ashleigh, not only have you jeopardized your objectivity, it's clear that you are in physical danger."

He rose slowly, gently kicking his file drawer closed, and walked around the back of Ashleigh's chair to the ornate fireplace. Leaning against the mantel, he asked, "Why did you go to Danielle's house a second time?"

The intercom buzz interrupted, and Ashleigh heard Méchie's insistent voice. "Mr. Toddman says he must talk with you immediately."

Outside Mr. Jerome's office, a pink-smocked sales associate was organizing the register in the Gourmet department while waitresses in black uniforms with crisp white aprons prepared their stations for the day's business.

Ashleigh stepped inside the elevator closest to the associates' cafeteria, but as the doors began to close, she heard her name called and instantly reached for the button marked OPEN DOOR. It responded to her touch at its own speed; the doors paused and then slowly spread wide apart. The breathless voice was that of Méchie.

"Miss McDowell, Mr. Jerome would like to see you again!"

Ashleigh followed Méchie back to the president's office. Once inside the office, she noticed Mr. Jerome's flushed face. He stood next to the leather desk chair, holding the phone, with an expression of extreme agitation on his face. "I'll take care of it right away," he said, and began to pace back and forth, looking down at the floor in front of him. "Thank you for calling."

Remaining on his feet, he frowned in Ashleigh's direction and said, "I can't get anyone to answer in Sales Promotion. Why would Susan allow that?" It wasn't a question. Surging ahead, he said, "Would you mind going up to the tower and asking Susan to come to my office right away?"

"The tower?"

"The tower, the roof—whatever you want to call it." Impatience iced each word.

It dawned on Ashleigh that Susan Thomas and her staff must be preparing for the controversial installation of King Kong for the upcoming Salute to Hollywood affair. She nodded. "Right away."

For a moment Mr. Jerome's face softened. "I'm sorry to have to send you." Immediately his scowl returned. "Find out if Susan got a city permit. No. On second thought, just ask her to come down to my office." As he turned away, she heard him mutter "I certainly don't want to get involved in a big brouhaha with the city."

Ashleigh waited a few minutes for the number-three lift, the only one that went to the sixth level. Wedging her organizer under her arm, she cautiously placed her index fingers on the two unmarked buttons. The elevator jolted to a halt about half a foot below the flat surface of the floor. Stepping up and across the gap, she was assaulted by the cold, stale air, bringing with it an involuntary shiver. Shifting her organizer to her forearm, she pulled her arms close to her body and headed for the door to her left—the one that opened onto the roof.

Heavy machinery banged and groaned beside her in the dimly lit structure. She groped her way past the emergency generator and the display department's arsenal of mannequins. The only light was that which managed to make its way through the dirt-caked windows. High overhead, Ashleigh saw two lightbulbs loosely screwed into old sockets, their long silver chains hanging down. It was only a few steps to the door, so she didn't bother with them. She mounted the two steps and pushed on the door, holding it as she stepped across the threshold.

Ashleigh looked up to see traces of sunlight struggling to break through the dismal gray sky, then quickly refocused on the task at hand. Heavy ropes were strewn across the loosely graveled rooftop and the square blocks of cement that formed a pathway leading directly to the famous tower. The ropes were secured to broad iron stanchions set in concrete. To her right was the immense air-conditioning unit, an addition to the original construction.

Ashleigh stepped gingerly from one cement block to the next. Above the steady drone of traffic and hum of the morning activities six stories below, she heard faint sounds of indistinguishable voices and a hint of laughter floating across the roof. Two limp black objects were floating alongside the tower, growing steadily larger and larger before her eyes.

She smiled, sensing the birth of King Kong on the far side of the tower. She checked her footing and crunched across the gravel-strewn surface. Nearing the tower, she recognized Susan's voice giving instructions to one of the San Diego balloon company's workmen.

When the group came into sight, Ashleigh glanced down again before stepping off the last bit of cement. She was now directly opposite the bumpy steel stairs of the tower itself. The worn, orange-painted steps were the same as those of the fire escape, which spanned the building's height except for the section between the rooftop and the fifth floor. That portion had been torn from the building in a driving wind earlier in the month; Mr. Jerome had exploded during last week's management meeting when Ferrari reported that the damage had not yet been repaired.

From her location Ashleigh saw that the King Kong balloon, though not yet fully inflated, was gigantic. She understood why having him straddle the tower was inconceivable. Not only was Susan's entire staff assembled, but the advertising manager, the creative director, the special events coordinator, the copy chief, and a number of people who reported to them, not to mention four men from the balloon company, were there as well. All were holding onto pieces of rope and the transparent wires that were attached to various parts of the huge gorilla.

What a paradox, Ashleigh thought. *Anne Klein, Krizia, Missoni, Vittadini, and other top designers would never have envisioned their creations in this setting!* She could just imagine a picture on the front page of *Women's Wear Daily*, the Sales Promotion executives attired in full fashion—Bentleys Royale style. Only the men from the balloon company looked like they had any business on a rooftop, let alone battling to steady the gargantuan creature teetering before them.

Ashleigh stood back from the others, waiting for an opportunity to deliver her message. Impatient, she glanced at her wristwatch; it was just after ten o'clock. She opened her organizer quickly and began to scrawl a brief note, nearly dropping the organizer to the ground. She fumbled and caught it, but something shiny and gold amid the gravel had caught her eye. Ashleigh reached for the gold object, then stared fixedly at the tiny gold butterfly on a thin gold chain in the palm of her hand. The organizer tumbled to the ground.

The gold butterfly chain was just like the one Gran had given Danielle for her eighteenth birthday.

Ashleigh felt numb. The tower loomed ominously above her. Then everything went black.

Tony slammed the door shut and turned, aware of nothing but his own rage. Listening to his father's retreating footsteps, he clenched his teeth and leaned back against the door, his face flushed.

Across the room, the bedroom door eased open about an inch, then slowly widened, and Jeff Bradley's head poked out between the jamb and the partially opened door.

Wiping the sweat from his brow, Tony gestured *all clear*.

"Your dad?" Jeff asked. His black hair dipped rakishly above his right brow as he fastened the short Polo wraparound at his slim waist and strode across the carpeted living room.

Tony nodded and turned to peer out the window, frowning as he saw his father slip behind the wheel of an unfamiliar black Buick.

"Thank God you reported the Ghia missing." Jeff gently brushed the blond hairs back from Tony's face.

"Yeah, but it sure as hell wasn't two or three weeks ago."

Jeff eyed him warily. "We can't take a chance on it being found—not with your dad and who knows who else snooping around."

Tony paced back and forth in front of the large window. "Shit. I'm not letting that son of a bitch push my buttons." He punched a closed fist into the open palm of the opposite hand and stared up at the ceiling. "Control. That is all he knows. It's his game. And this time I'll make damn sure he knows what it's like to lose. His millions will buy him sweet-fuck-all."

"Hey, Tony, love, you're scaring the hell out of me."

"Don't worry, I can handle it." As soon as the words hissed out, a plan materialized in his head, bringing a smile to his taut lips.

"Things are already out of hand," Jeff warned him.

"Don't sweat it. We've gone too far to turn back now. And don't even think about disposing of my Ghia. The bastard who just walked out that door has been on my ass for years about getting rid of it, calling it 'sophomoric' and 'inappropriate.'" He spat out the words. "Besides," he added, "even if the police find the car, they can't prove it wasn't stolen. I told you, I had gloves on when I opened the car door and drove it up to the mountains." He laughed with a boyish show of pride. "Just enough smudged prints to look like it was stolen, and just enough clear ones left behind to show that it's mine."

Jeff looked away from the beautiful blond man. He cared for Tony more than he'd cared for anyone for a very long time. And yet suddenly it was all going wrong. Things had escalated rapidly, and he didn't know how to put a stop to it. The irony of the situation made his head swim, and the words *fatal attraction* screamed through his thoughts—even in his dreams.

Tony was young, headstrong, and far too impulsive, but Jeff couldn't help but love him. And that special love, as long as it lasted, overrode all reason. The man who had just stormed out of their apartment had damaged Tony's soul, made him feel unworthy. His hurt had turned to rage—a rage that was out of control and could bring them down.

Jeff placed his hands gently on the younger man's shoulders and met his eyes. "You're right. It's too late to turn back. I know you need to report in to the DC once more to reverse the purchases in Danielle's department, but—"

"I'll be damned if I can understand why it really matters when she'll be dead within the next six months."

"It matters a great deal to Danielle, and I owe her." *She deserves to die with dignity.*

"Like hell, you owe her. That dame royally screwed us both. We owe her nothing—nada, zilch, not a solitary thing." Tony paused, then shrugged. "No point in going round and round on that again. I gave you my word, so I'll do it."

No point indeed. "We've got to escalate our departure," Jeff pleaded. "It's too risky to stay here."

"No." Tony pulled back, and Jeff's hands fell from his shoulders. "I helped you. Now you've got to help me."

"Damn it, Tony. Can't you see? It's too damn late. The game's over. We've got to get out of the country."

"No! No! No!" he shouted, like a petulant child. "The Bentley's job is over, but I've come up with a plan to put Medley Originals out of business and throw suspicion on the old man. I can't stop now." His voice quavered, and he stared down at his bare feet. To Jeff, he suddenly appeared terribly young. "It's more than the money. I just can't leave now. Not even for you."

Jeff was only too aware that it was more than money that drove Tony. He stepped back, placed a hand on his hip, and ran fingers through his hair. His voice was low and controlled. "How long?"

Tony stroked his chin and looked up again at the ceiling as if the answers were carved on the tiles overhead. "Just a few more days."

"How many?" Jeff asked pointedly. "Two, three—"

"Give me three—no, make it four days."

A heavy silence fell between them.

Finally Jeff said, "Okay, but no more." He strode across the carpeted floor to the kitchen and looked at the calendar held by magnetic clips to the side of the refrigerator. Turning, he picked up a pen from the high counter that separated the two rooms and circled JANUARY 24. He wore a worried expression. "Tony, I don't feel good about this. Your dad knows about the Ghia, and he could cause one hell of a lot of trouble."

Seeing that Tony was about to jump in, he held up his hand. "Let me finish. Against my better judgment, I am agreeing to your four days, but shorten it if you can." *Christ, I sound like that pompous bastard who just left.*

Tony bit down on the corner of his lip, an expression of chagrin flitting cross his handsome face. "Thanks for understanding."

Jeff leaned forward, both elbows on the counter, his chin resting in his hands. "One other thing." He paused and met Tony's eyes. "Ashleigh McDowell is off-limits. Thank God she wasn't in the car when that bomb went off."

Tony clenched his fists. "Hey, don't split a gut. Why in the hell do you care about that little gold digger?"

"Danielle has nothing but nice things to say about the woman. And I don't want innocent people getting hurt."

"Yeah, yeah. But that dame could be our ticket to prison. What if Danielle wasn't bluffing about that note? We can't wait to find out."

"Goddamn it, Tony, we've gone down that road before. It's been seven days. If Danielle had left Ashleigh a note, it would have surfaced by now. Besides, Danielle doesn't know anything about you. If there's any such note, it's my neck in a noose, not yours. If Ashleigh had been killed, it would be nothing short of cold-blooded murder."

Tony arched his right brow, and a grimace spread across his face. "It's a bit late in the game to develop an overblown set of scruples. Besides, I told you—you're not involved."

"How can I *not* be involved? Danielle said she spilled everything in that note. So if it does exist, the finger points straight at me. I'd be the first on a list of suspects. Embezzlement is one thing—murder quite another." He straightened and walked across the living room, sitting down on the sofa beside Tony. Putting his arm around the young man's shoulder and lifting his chin with a cupped hand, he said, "I care about you."

Tony shrugged free of Jeff's embrace and jumped to his feet. "Then get off my back." Pacing the floor in front of the sofa, he said, "I tried to play it your way." He folded his arms in front of him. "But it didn't work . . . Well, did it?"

Jeff shook his head slowly. He didn't have the answers, and he was still worried as hell over Danielle's condition. That note Tony had slipped through the mail slot in Palm Desert . . . The newspaper remains in Ashleigh's condo . . . He was afraid those measures had not frightened Ashleigh enough to put an end to her attempts to find out what had happened to Danielle. The thought of Danielle's correspondence showing up brought a cool sweat to his brow. Maybe Tony was right. Perhaps Ashleigh couldn't be intimidated. But killing her was out of the question.

"She's still poking her pretty little nose right where it could hurt us both."

"And she's your father's fiancée!" Jeff's voice was harsh. "Could that have something to do with it?"

Tony did not respond. He stopped a few feet in front of Jeff and again met his eyes. "You're the first person who's ever understood me and accepted me for myself. I don't want you winding up behind bars. I don't want to lose you." His voice cracked, but he quickly regained his composure. "I don't like the idea of murder any more than you do, but Ashleigh McDowell is a threat. You know I had no intention of killing her. I'm no expert with those explosives, and apparently—"

"There's no need to run through that again. I believe you."

"Even if there's no note," Tony continued, "she saw us get off the elevator the morning after our all-nighter in the tower."

Jeff wanted to shake some sense into him, but he knew it was hopeless. "It's been seven days! Oh, hell, there's no point in repeating." He rose from the sofa. "Just don't do anything crazy." He brushed Tony's arm as he strode across the room.

Tony followed him into the bedroom. Jeff pulled his suitcase from beneath the king-size bed, laid it on top of the bed, and began emptying the second drawer, which was filled with his underwear and socks. He wanted to reach out to Tony, but he needed time to think. *He must realize we can't be seen together. Not now.*

Turning to his partner, Jeff said, "I'll keep in touch."

Tony mumbled an *okay,* then asked, "Will you be in Westwood?"

Jeff nodded. It was the truth—but he also planned to take a side trip to check on Danielle. Fortunately, Tony seemed to be taking the move in stride. "Call me if you need anything or if you can get away earlier, but don't leave any messages. And don't use this phone." He gestured toward the bedside phone.

As he headed to his car, his mind turned to everything in their plan that had gone awry. Tony was smart, and there was no denying he was a proficient hacker. He'd broken the Central Purchasing code in Bentleys Royale's Moderate and Fine Apparel divisions, using Adele Watson's individual password. He'd figured out a pattern for decoding other divisions, and was on the verge of cracking the systems for the entire Bentley's operation. *If only Danielle hadn't caught on,* he thought. If only she hadn't panicked, threatening to destroy their entire scheme. If only she'd been able to keep that eight o'clock appointment with Anne Klein. Damn her exaggerated sense of loyalty to an organization that was trying to screw her!

CHAPTER

81

In his oceanfront home, Wainwright knotted his tie, pulled his jacket on, and glanced in the mirror for a final check.

He had secured a seat on a twelve thirty flight Monday afternoon and would be heading back to Atlanta. His cellular phone was still on its charger, and the red light had not yet blinked off. Just as he contemplated leaving it behind, his bedroom telephone gave a shrill ring. He picked it up but remained silent, waiting for the caller to speak.

"It's Landes."

"Where in the hell have you been? I've been trying to reach you since last night."

"Looking after Miss McDowell."

The lying bastard. There had been no sign of Landes's car outside Ashleigh's condo when he had swung by there after leaving Tony's. But keeping the fury out of his tone, Wainwright said, "Did you get my message?"

"Yes. I called back right away, but your line was busy. After that the phone went unanswered." There was a pause. "Sorry, we've been having some problems with the reception in that area." Landes's husky voice was polite, but not subservient by any stretch of the imagination. "Miss McDowell said she wouldn't need me until she returned home. Didn't feel it was my place to argue, but since you told me she wasn't to be out of my sight, I thought it best to use a pool car when I followed her from the desert." A muffled yawn traveled through the phone line.

"Where are you now?"

"Just left her apartment complex. I'm on the Harbor Freeway, headed for home to get four or five hours of shut-eye. Then I'll pick up my own

car and be back on the job. Billings introduced himself to Miss McDowell this morning and has followed her on up to Los Angeles."

"Billings?" Wainwright repeated.

"Ray Billings, from our New York operation. Just transferred out
here. Good man."

"Fine, fine," Wainwright said impatiently. "Look, Dick, got your fax.
Seems we're merely duplicating the work of the LAPD and Bentley's
corporate staff. So drop the investigative portion of this assignment and
just protect Miss McDowell."

"But Mr. Wainwright—"

"It's not open for discussion. Drop it."

The line went silent except for the habitual feedback from Landes's
car phone. After letting his instructions sink in, Wainwright continued,
"What I'd like you to do, in addition to protecting Miss McDowell,
is keep in touch with the police investigation and the security honcho
at Bentley's."

"Pocino?"

"Right. And keep me informed. I'll be at the Atlanta Hilton."

The red charger light finally winked out, and Wainwright, cradling
the bedroom phone's receiver between his ear and his shoulder, pulled
the cord and stowed the cellular phone back in his briefcase. Just before
terminating the call, he said, "By the way, Miss McDowell is not aware
that I left Atlanta. I prefer that she not know I was here last night. I'm
in the middle of negotiations on a sizable acquisition for Wainwright
Enterprises, and I have no time to spare. And you know how sensitive women can be." Though attempting to sound nonchalant, he nearly
choked on his own words and wondered how much of it Landes actually
bought.

"Sure, Mr. Wainwright. And before you hang up, I thought you'd like to
know what our man in Atlanta found out about that McIntyre woman."

Wainwright heaved a sigh. "Go ahead."

"An interesting case, actually."

"Dick, I'm in a hurry. Did you or did you not locate her?"

"Well, yes . . . She resides at U.S.P. Atlanta. In other words, the
penitentiary. Been there about two months. It seems that she and the

common-law husband you told us about got back together soon after the daughter ran off a few years back."

"What?"

"My man in Atlanta says the old lady came home one night and found her man in bed with a young girl who rented a room from them. Shot and killed both of them. The warden says she'll be up for parole in a few years, but since she shows no sign of remorse, he doubts that she'll ever go free." He paused, as if waiting for a response, but it didn't come. "Probably a dead end, but I'll find out if she's had any contact with Danielle at any time since the daughter left home."

Wainwright scowled. Was he expecting fate to deliver him answers on a silver platter?

Still gripping the gold butterfly in the palm of her hand, Ashleigh was halfway down the back corridor when Betty rushed out to meet her.

"What happened to your dress?"

Ashleigh gave a faint smile and decided not to mention that she may have blacked out. "I tripped."

"Would you like me to take it up to Sophie in Alterations?"

"Not right now."

"You could slip the model's coat on—I haven't returned the one Ms. De Mornay loaned you last week."

"Betty," Ashleigh interrupted. "Not now. Just get me a damp towel, please."

Betty nodded.

"Unless there's an emergency, I don't want you to schedule anyone until tomorrow." Noticing her secretary's reticent smile, she added, "Do your best."

"O-kaaayyy." Betty thumbed through the phone memos, giving only one to Ashleigh. "These can wait," she said as the bulk of the memos remained in her hand.

Ashleigh glanced at the memo. Danielle's assistant, Jan, had returned her call. Handing the note back to Betty, she said, "Jan has been waiting for the tapes on negotiating skills. Please give her a call and tell her they're here." She pointed to the top of the file cabinet. "And please make sure she signs for them." Then, looking down at the array of random piles on her secretary's desk, she frowned. "You do have a checkout sheet for the tapes, don't you?"

Betty went right to the clipboard, pulled it from beneath the pile next to her phone, and held it out. On the top sheet, below the heading *Tape Library*, Ashleigh noticed a haphazard listing of audiotapes and names. There were a few signatures, but most of the names were printed in Betty's familiar block letters.

"Please start a new sheet. Print the name of the tape and the borrower's name, and then make sure they personally sign in the third column." She was not particularly concerned about the system, nor was she bothered by the untidiness of the sign-out sheets. It had worked well for the past two or three years. She was simply anxious to get a signature from Danielle's assistant.

"Also, Betty, please call Mr. Taylor and tell him that I won't be able to meet with him tonight." She hesitated for just an instant before adding, "And ask him to send a copy of the paperwork we discussed in a transmittal envelope." She bit down on her bottom lip, her mind racing. "Unless Mr. Jerome or Ross Pocino calls, I am not here."

Betty's brows arched, but she nodded her agreement.

Out of habit, Ashleigh stopped in front of the coffeemaker. But the smell of the strong coffee suddenly made her queasy, and she continued on into her office, closing the door behind her.

No sooner had she slipped into her chair than the intercom buzzed. For a few seconds she just stared at it. Finally she grabbed the receiver. "Yes?"

"I know you don't want to be disturbed, but you mentioned Ross Pocino."

Impatiently, she repeated, "Yes?"

"Well, he's down in Mr. Ferrari's office. He stopped in here about half an hour ago, but when I asked if he had any message or wanted you to call, he said no."

"Thanks, Betty. I didn't mean to snap. I just have a lot on my mind." She clicked off, keeping the receiver in her hand and contemplated calling Pocino, but she changed her mind. Instead she dialed the number of Dick Landes's car phone. It was picked up on the second ring, and a strong masculine voice with a New York accent answered.

"Ray Billings."

She was taken aback momentarily before she remembered being introduced to the new agent earlier that morning. A thickness clogged her throat, and she repressed an impulse to hang up. She wanted to talk to someone she could trust. Someone who already knew most of what had been going on.

"Ray Billings," he repeated.

"This is Ashleigh McDowell. Could you tell me how to get in touch with Dick Landes? I don't have his home number with me."

For a moment all she could hear was the static. "I'll give you the number, but he's just gone home to get some sleep. Is there something I can do for you?"

"Not right now, thank you." She pulled out a four-inch square of paper from her note box and wrote down the number.

She hated to wake Landes, but she would have to try. She had no choice. The intercom buzzed. She punched the intercom button and Betty said, "Mr. Pocino is here."

"Please send him in." Ashleigh placed the paper with Landes's number beside the phone, pushed her chair back, and was about to rise when Pocino ambled through the door and quickly gestured for her to remain seated.

"Betty left word you wanted to see me." He moved forward, placing splayed fingers upon her oval table.

To Ashleigh's surprise, his fingernails were clean. "Ross, please sit down."

As he plunked himself into the nearest chair, she noticed that he wore an unusually serious expression. "Just making my amends to Ferrari about blasting his wife the other day," he said. "But no matter how many kids they've got, she's got to realize—Oh, damn. Swore I'd get off that soapbox."

"Ross, I understand." Her heart ached for him. She wasn't about to condemn him for his tirade against Kim Ferrari about the missing boy the previous week. She was tempted to tell him how sorry she was about his son, but she just couldn't find the words and knew instinctively that he would not want her sympathy.

He shook his head and his expression changed. "What's up?"

"I need your help," she replied.

"Stopped in earlier. Mr. Taylor told me about the warning note and about your condo. Don't know what in the hell's going on, but I'll get to the bottom of it. I owe you."

Ashleigh shook her head. What was he referring to? Perhaps her decision to step in and overrule the edict about voice pages in the store? "You don't owe me anything, but I do need your help."

"Hold it." He raised a fleshy palm. "What I owe you is an apology." His face reddened. "I've acted like an A-one jerk over this whole Norman affair. And it seems you've been right on several counts."

A flush of warmth spread through her. She knew how difficult this confession was for the burly security chief, and it eased the tension.

"But not all of them," he quickly added.

"Ross," she interrupted, ignoring his still-raised hand.

"Let me finish." He scowled first, but forced a smile. "Sorry, but I've got to get this out."

Ashleigh nodded and, impatiently waiting for him to finish, pulled the gold butterfly and broken chain from her organizer.

"We were both right"—a pause—"and both wrong regarding Norman's involvement in the shenanigans in her department, but you were on the mark in suspecting foul play, and RHD is looking into it."

"RHD?"

"The LAPD's robbery and homicide division."

"Good. They'll want to see this." Ashleigh thrust the necklace toward him.

Pocino abruptly fell silent and stretched his hand across the space between them. Ashleigh dropped the broken necklace into his open palm. He wordlessly examined the butterfly and the cracked links of the chain, remembering what she'd told him about Danielle and her bizarre world of butterflies. No point in confirming who the necklace belonged to. He saw the pain in Ashleigh's eyes and her pinched brow, and he knew that she was convinced it was Danielle Norman's.

"Where did you find it?" he asked.

After she'd explained, he took his time before asking, slowly and thoughtfully, "And you think Danielle's body is in the tower?"

She winced. "Her body?" she said softly.

"Any unusual odor?"

Ashleigh shook her head, her stomach queasy. "Not that I noticed." She hesitated, taking a breath as she tried to regroup. "Most of the buyers know the code to get to the tower, but after one look around to satisfy their curiosity, there's no logical reason for anyone other than the maintenance or display staffs to venture above the fifth floor."

"I'll take a look." Pocino heaved himself up.

She sprang to her feet. "I'll go with you."

The words *I don't think so* were on the tip of his tongue. But seeing she wasn't about to take no for an answer, he conceded. "Okay, suit yourself."

Approaching the stairs to the tower, Pocino said, "Wait here."

Ashleigh made no protest; she stood riveted in place as he climbed the dimpled orange steps and edged through the door.

Once inside the tower, he noticed the strong smell of fresh paint and saw an assortment of props spread out on the spatter newspapers near the wall to his left. There were a few mannequins and boxes of Christmas decorations, but no smell of death.

He climbed up the steep fire escape–type stairs as far as he could, which wasn't far because of the earthquake reinforcement that had been put in. The opening was too narrow for him to get through, and he was about to come back down, but he stopped. Inside the tower landing, the scaffolding made the access too narrow to climb up any farther, so he poked his head through the opening. Seeing nothing other than a bunch of white bird shit, he headed back down the stairs. That's when he saw a dark reddish shoe on the window ledge. He pulled a crumpled wad of Kleenex from his jacket pocket and picked up the shoe by the gold butterfly clipped to the front.

Even if the butterfly hadn't been a dead giveaway, he remembered Ashleigh talking about the burgundy marking pens. He was holding a burgundy shoe. It wasn't hard to put two and two together.

What surprised him was that there was no body. Someone might have been able to force a body up through the small opening, though he doubted it. But after nearly a week, it would stink like hell.

Well, he thought morbidly, *we know one place where Danielle Norman is* not.

CHAPTER 83

At seven thirty Tuesday morning, Ashleigh pulled away from the home that Charles had built for her and Gran so many years before. Charles was troubled over Danielle's disappearance, but after a short while their conversation had turned to her engagement to Mitchell Wainwright. As usual, Charles had been right.

The more she thought it through, the more it made sense. After Dan's death she'd been vulnerable to Mitchell, to his initial adoration, to his powerful sexuality.

She couldn't deny that he had made her feel like a woman again. He'd brought her back to life, making her skin tingle and her blood race. He'd been exciting, and he'd made her feel sexy, filled her with white-hot desire. But now that she'd burned through those emotions, there was no substance to the fire. Only cold ashes remained.

Ashleigh turned the Mercedes onto the 405 Freeway. *Charles is so perceptive. Such a wise man,* she thought. *He knows life—its joys and its obstacles—and in spite of it all, he has lived it to the fullest.* From the bits and pieces of that life he'd shared with her so candidly, she knew he'd had his portion of heartbreak as well as passion. He was living proof that sometimes the more difficult path is best. How had she failed to follow his example in choosing love?

"Look into your heart," he'd told her many times before. "Be true to yourself. You are the author of your own future, and you will live with what you create."

The traffic was bumper-to-bumper, but Ashleigh didn't mind. She finally had the time to look into her heart and rediscover the essential truths. The answer she had hastily come to several days before was now resolved in her mind. *I don't love Mitchell. He's not a bad person, but we are so very wrong for each other. I was just infatuated with him. There is no way I can spend the rest of my life with him.*

She hoped she could make him understand, and then it dawned on her. *Mitchell doesn't love me. He merely wants what I represent—just another Wainwright acquisition.* With that, her sense of guilt evaporated.

At eight thirty, when Ashleigh arrived at the security counter, she noticed that she was the first of the management team to sign in.

With her mind in overdrive, she thought back to the previous night—another one that allowed her only short snatches of light sleep. At around four o'clock, unable to put her mind to rest, she'd slipped out of bed and padded into the kitchen. Without flipping on a light, she'd peered out the window.

The familiar black Ford Escort was parked across the street. Beside the car, she'd noticed the faint glow from a cigarette as a stocky man in a dark suit leaned casually against the rail in front of the boat docks. The light from the streetlamp played across his rugged features. Landes had appeared to be looking straight up at the kitchen window. Her first impulse had been to step away, but for a moment she'd stood motionless in her sheer Christian Dior nightgown, assuring herself that he could not see inside the dark kitchen. Then she had reached for the phone at the end of the counter and punched in the number on her illuminated dial. Her eyes had remained fixed on the figure beside the bay, watching as he dashed from the rail to his car phone, answering before the second ring.

After hanging up, she had wandered aimlessly through her condo until daylight, losing all track of time. What Landes had to say had shaken her to the core.

All morning, Landes's words had continued to haunt her. *Why had Mitchell taken Landes off the investigation?* As unnerving as this revelation had been before daybreak, the more she thought about it now, the less sense it made. *What was Mitchell afraid the investigator might find?*

She stopped in front of Betty's hastily tidied desk, picked up her messages from the holder, and walked into her office. Distracted, she edged through the narrow aisle between her table and the étagère and slid into her chair. On Sunday, Mitchell had been adamant about getting to the bottom of Danielle's disappearance and getting on with their lives. Then, in less than forty-eight hours, he'd decided to leave everything but Ashleigh's protection in the hands of the police. Even after pondering it for hours, she was still unable to understand why Mitchell had reversed his position.

Sliding the credenza door open to deposit her handbag, Ashleigh pushed aside the tangled cord of the phone. As she did, a pink phone memo taped to the instrument caught her eye. Ashleigh recognized Betty's delicate squiggles between the narrow lines of the square note.

9:00 Mrs. Richard Lane. Hope there's no conflict! Didn't have an update of your calendar! Mrs. Lane said it's very important.

Ashleigh's thoughts quickly turned back to the note. The name rang a familiar note. Then it hit her. *That's Mitchell's former wife. What could she possibly want with me?*

She leaned forward, her elbows resting on the table, and massaged her temples in an attempt to recall the gist of Naomi's warnings about her former daughter-in-law.

Glancing at her watch, she realized that the woman would already be on the road, soon to arrive at Bentleys Royale. It was too late to divert her.

Resigned, she sank back in the desk chair and tried to anticipate what Mitchell's former wife might have on her mind.

The diamond on her left hand glared up at her. Self-reproach, increasingly near the surface, began to swell.

At the sound of heels rapidly clicking across the tiles of the corridor, Ashleigh turned her head toward the door. She was standing next to the coffeemaker, where she had just poured a cup of the steaming liquid, when the stunning Diana Lane swept into the reception area. Her jet-black hair was drawn back in a severe chignon, accenting her fine features and green eyes—the deepest shade of green Ashleigh had ever seen. Her stark white silk crepe Armani pantsuit, which Ashleigh happened to know was featured on last month's cover of *Vogue*, was impeccably wrinkle-free. The ranch mink thrown over her arm added a degree of drama—an unusual look for the early morning hours, but somehow the woman carried it off beautifully. Ashleigh felt dull by contrast.

"I hope I didn't keep you waiting," Diana said in a breathy whisper.

She was right on time, and Ashleigh suspected she knew it. Diana extended her hand and introduced herself, and the two quickly exchanged the expected greetings. Diana appeared to be taking inventory, appraising Ashleigh from head to toe with undisguised candor.

"That's a gorgeous skirt. Krizia, isn't it?"

Ashleigh nodded, acknowledging the compliment to her wool gabardine skirt in deep jade; her silk blouse was an equally deep shade of sapphire, sprinkled with jade fleur-de-lis. She had no desire to encourage idle chatter.

Diana continued, "No designer compares with Krizia when it comes to comfort in a wraparound skirt."

Again Ashleigh merely nodded. Diana Lane had not come to discuss fashion. Ashleigh was anxious to move on, but common courtesy prevailed, and Betty would not be in until eleven o'clock today. "Would you like a cup of coffee?"

"Yes. I could certainly use one." She rolled her eyes, adding, "I'd simply die if I had to make this horrendous commute every day." She scanned the small reception area, her eyes resting on Ashleigh, who had placed the two cups and saucers beside the sugar and cream service on the silver filigreed tray. With an inquiring quirk of her brow, her eyes then traveled from Ashleigh across to Betty's empty desk and back again.

Ashleigh picked up the tray without comment and ushered Mitchell's ex-wife into her office.

Standing in the doorway for a full ten seconds before stepping across the threshold, Diana commented, "What an unusual office arrangement!"

Ignoring this comment, Ashleigh gestured for her to be seated and placed her cup directly in front of her. "Betty, my assistant, did not mention what this meeting was about." *What does she want?*

Diana sat down, draped her jacket across the chair next to her, and crossed her long legs. "You have no idea?" She dropped her veil of cordiality.

"No."

"Look, Miss . . . McDowell," she said, "I don't intend to pussyfoot around. You know damn well what this is all about." She pulled a jeweled cigarette case from her Chanel handbag. "I could care less that you've found a place for yourself in Mitchell's bed. But you won't worm your way into our son's rightful inheritance."

Shoving her chair back from the table, Ashleigh rose to her feet. "Mrs. Lane, I know very little about Mitchell's relationship with his son." She made no attempt to mask her anger. "If you want to know anything about that, I suggest you discuss it with Mitchell."

An empty silence descended on the room. Ashleigh did not fill it. Finally, Diana did. "Is that . . . the truth?" She seemed to be searching for words—thrown off balance, but still skeptical.

Ashleigh opted not to repeat herself, but simply stood waiting, as if the meeting were over and Diana would soon be on her way.

When Diana spoke again, the hostility in her tone had vanished. "I have no quarrel with you. But I'm not sure where else to turn."

"What is it you want from me, Mrs. Lane?" Ashleigh asked.

"Please call me Diana." She held her chin high.

Ashleigh sank back into her chair.

"Do you mind?" Diana asked as she pulled a cigarette from her case.

Ashleigh reached for an ashtray off the étagère by way of answering. "I don't know how I can possibly help. I know Mitchell has a son, but I've never met him, and Mitchell has not discussed him with me. And as for his inheritance, I have no knowledge of that."

"I know how closemouthed Mitchell can be when it comes to anything other than his latest business deal. And as you must know, his feelings are strictly superficial."

Ashleigh found herself inexplicably defensive. *Why should I care about Diana pointing out how shallow Mitchell's feelings are?* "Mrs. Lane, I don't care to discuss Mitchell or his feelings."

"Oh, I'm . . . sorry. It seems that everything I say this morning comes out all wrong," said Diana, shaking her head.

Ashleigh noticed that she had not yet lit the cigarette she held between her well-manicured fingers. Though part of her wanted to kick Diana out of her office, she found that she couldn't shake her role as an attentive listener—even with this bitchy ex-wife of a man she didn't love and was about to break off her engagement to. When she saw tears spring to Diana's eyes and creases of pain spread across her pale face, she handed her the ever-present box of Kleenex from her credenza and settled back in her chair.

Diana took a tissue and wiped the mascara from below her eyes. "Thank you, Ashleigh," she said quickly. "May I call you Ashleigh?"

Ashleigh again merely nodded.

Sensing that Ashleigh McDowell fit none of the stereotypes of her former husband's other flings, Diana wished she could begin this conversation again. Her intention had been to take the upper hand by presenting herself as the epitome of fashion and style. But the cool blonde sitting stiffly across the table, her hair drawn back in a pure and simple French braid, made her feel like an over-the-hill hooker.

"I'm sorry, Ashleigh," she said. "I had no right barging in here assailing you. For that, I'm truly sorry. And I want you to know, despite what you may think, that I'm not the proverbial bitchy ex-wife. I'm neither jealous nor vindictive. My one and only interest in Mitchell is his intentions in regard to Anthony. Our son.

"We didn't marry for that kind of love that fills romance novels, you know," she continued. "He never told me that he loved me. But he was so handsome and had such charisma that I was awestruck. Even as a young man, Mitchell knew exactly what he wanted." She paused for emphasis. "And when he told me that he wanted *me*, I was flattered. I convinced myself that I could make him fall in love with me." She sighed. "At first we were happy, but it didn't take long for me to figure out that I was just another Wainwright acquisition. Mitchell is incapable of love. He's too wrapped up in himself and trying to measure up to his father to ever—"

She stopped in midsentence, looking into the large, dark eyes on the other side of the round table and wondering why she was spilling her guts. *Oh my God, I'm doing it again. I've never admitted this to another living soul, so why am I telling this utter stranger?* "Oh, Ashleigh, I'm sorry. Will I ever stop putting my foot in my mouth?"

Ashleigh ignored the question. "Diana," she said, "I'm still at a loss as to how I might help you."

"I'm afraid I've digressed. I've already said far more about myself than I ever intended to, so I'll get right to the point: Did Mitchell tell you why he went to see Anthony?"

"No. I told you, we have never discussed your son."

"You mean he didn't say a word to you about their visit Sunday night?"

Listening to Diana Lane, Ashleigh was even more convinced that all her reasons for breaking her engagement to Mitchell were indeed valid. But that was neither here nor there.

"Sunday night?" she repeated.

"You did see Mitchell Sunday night, didn't you?"

"No. He's been in Atlanta since last Wednesday."

Diana stared at her in disbelief. "He was here Sunday night," she said emphatically. "He came by my home around ten o'clock to get Anthony's phone number. He wanted to see Anthony for some reason. I don't know whether they actually saw each other or not, because I haven't been able to reach my son. And quite honestly, I'm worried." There was a catch in her voice, and a note of confusion. "Mitchell had some bee in his bonnet about Anthony's Ghia."

His Ghia?

Startled, Ashleigh spilled her coffee down her blouse.

As Diana's footsteps retreated down the hall, Ashleigh sank down into her chair, resting her head against the high back. "What kind of game is Mitchell playing?" she said aloud as she reached for the phone. She had to have answers.

Dick Landes responded before her fingers left the dial. Decisively, she took a deep breath and asked, "Would you please come to my office? I must see you right away."

Fifteen minutes before the store's opening time, Dick Landes sauntered through the associates' entrance. It felt strange to him, since until now he had avoided the employee areas of all six Bentleys Royale locations. They were his brother's domain, and the detective never mixed the personal with the professional.

But this meeting with Ashleigh McDowell is strictly business, he told himself as he rapidly descended the stairs. His eyes slowly adjusted to the dim lighting, and he saw that Dean's comment about this entrance lacking elegance was a colossal understatement.

He stopped at the associates' security counter and clipped a visitor's badge on his lapel. "Would you direct me to Miss McDowell's office?" he asked the buxom brunette behind the counter.

"Out those double doors and through the Gourmet department. Turn right at the first corridor. Follow the sign that says Personnel."

"Thank you." He scrawled his name on the clipboard she pushed toward him. Rounding the corner of the partition that concealed the double doors, he saw Ashleigh.

"You knew that Mitchell was in town Sunday evening, didn't you?" she said, her voice cold.

Stunned at her accusation, Landes glanced around the vacant department. "Yes," he admitted, an unexpected wave of relief surging through his veins.

Ashleigh averted her eyes momentarily; then she brought them back to meet his. "Thank you for your honesty," she said, her voice now soft. "Would you please come to my office?"

Landes followed her around the corner and down the corridor. He couldn't help but admire her aura of calm. Taking note of her straight back and her chin held high as her heels tapped smoothly over the tiles, he made his decision.

He walked through the door to Ashleigh's office. It was tasteful yet unpretentious, like the lady herself.

Ashleigh excused herself to get coffee, leaving Landes alone in the carefully appointed office. His thoughts turned to his client. *Why, all of a sudden, did Wainwright tell me to drop the investigation?* After working for the Wainwrights for years, he knew damned well that Mitchell was a highly impatient man—not the type to leave matters in the hands of the police. *So what's his game?* Landes was certain that Wainwright has something up his sleeve. And whether it was intentional or not, Ashleigh McDowell could be the victim.

He had decided he would not leave the investigation to the police after all; there were too many departments and too many locations involved—from one department to the next, and from Los Angeles to Long Beach to Palm Desert, all those cops would never be able to cooperate. With all the goddamned red tape, it could take weeks or perhaps months, and he knew only too well that they might never get to the bottom of it all. And if the police placed this on the back burner, Ashleigh McDowell might not last the course. His decision was made. Whether on or off the Wainwright payroll, he had his work cut out for him. He preferred not to lose the account, but if that was necessary, so be it.

So, what reason could there possibly be behind Wainwright's abrupt change in direction? he wondered. It was clear that the man had something to hide. Landes stroked his chin, trying to conjure up an intelligent rationale, but it eluded him.

Ashleigh had returned. Setting the tray on the table, she looked at him from beneath raised eyebrows, a serious expression dominating her fine features.

"Look. I'm sorry I didn't tell you—"

She waved off his apology. "I understand. You work for Mitchell." Then, abruptly changing the subject, she asked, "Did you know that Mitchell Wainwright's son has a Karmann Ghia?"

Landes shot forward. "You sure?" he asked, as the odd bits of information began to shift into place. He listened in stunned silence. Then he said, "I'll run this down immediately." Rising to his feet, he said, "I understand from Sergeant Flynn that you saw Jeff Bradley in the store the day of Danielle's disappearance. Is that right?"

"He was getting out of the elevator. There was a younger man with a blond ponytail, wearing Levi's, who was with him, I think." She paused. "When Pocino showed me Danielle's shoe, everything came back to me. It was on Tuesday morning—the day we discovered that Danielle had not shown up in New York. I'm sure of it because I was on my way to the fashion-update meeting." An image of the two men flashed before her. The blond man with the ponytail must be the one Conrad saw behind the wheel of the Karmann Ghia.

"Do you think those men noticed you?"

She raised her shoulders. He looked her square in the eye. "If they are in any way responsible for Danielle Norman's disappearance and the shenanigans in her department, it might explain why they would want you out of the way."

As if a dam had broken, one question after another shot in to Ashleigh's mind. *Who was the other man? Could that have been Mitchell's son? Had they been in the tower with Danielle? Do they want me dead?*

Finally she said quietly, "If only I hadn't taken so long to put it all together. Danielle's shoe and necklace were found on the roof. They must have been in the tower with her. But she was not with them when I saw them."

So how did she get out—and where had they taken her?

Twenty minutes later, Dick Landes hit REDIAL on his car phone. As he was about to replace the phone, he heard the deep voice of Mitchell Wainwright.

"What in the hell is going on?"

"I was calling to ask you the same question," Landes said through clenched teeth.

"Look, Landes, you work for me. When I ask you to keep a confidence, I expect nothing less. Is that understood?"

"I broke no confidences. Miss McDowell already knew the facts. I refuse to tell her a bald-faced lie." His fingers were clenched tightly around the phone, and he was finding it difficult to retain a professional demeanor. "She's a real decent lady."

But Wainwright wasn't listening. He appeared to have his own agenda. "If you didn't tell her, who did?"

"Hold it, Wainwright. I'll answer your question, but then I have quite a few of my own."

"It seems your ex paid a call on Miss McDowell this morning," Landes informed his client.

Wainwright was taken aback.

"Diana?" When Landes didn't respond, he said, "Ashleigh didn't mention it," and lit another cigarette, though one lay smoldering in the crystal ashtray on the desk. He had left Updike's conference table and had been given the use of the CEO's private office to answer Ashleigh's call. Now, as he looked out the wall of glass, his heart pounded in his ears.

Landes's heated tones faded in and out of his awareness. But when the P.I. said something about a Karmann Ghia and the police, Wainwright's mind snapped to attention and began working overtime. "Time out."

"Look, Wainwright. I've been on retainer for your company for nearly ten years. You know the ground rules. I don't work with half-truths. You trust me with the whole truth or you get yourself another firm."

Wainwright felt an acute loss of control. He wasn't used to being put on the defensive. Yet in the past quarter of an hour, he had been attacked, first by Ashleigh, and now by Landes. "Damn it, Dick, I had my reasons. Cool down and I'll explain."

Swallowing his pride, he stamped out his cigarette and reached for yet another. "Until late Sunday afternoon, you knew far more than I did. Ashleigh called from Palm Desert to ask if I had called her late Saturday night. We still don't know who it was, pretending to be me." He took a drag and exhaled with a sigh. "Oh, hell. You know the rest. But neither of you mentioned that the car following her last week was a blue Karmann Ghia."

"Of course I told you! It's in the report I faxed to you the very next day," Landes broke in.

Wainwright paced between the window and desk with the phone tucked under his firmly set jaw. His restrained response shot across the phone lines. "I haven't had a chance to read your report, but if you'd mentioned a Ghia of any color, it's unlikely that I would have missed it. The point is, I didn't know the make of the car until Sunday. And I sure as hell don't like the implication that I'm concealing any goddamned information that might help us get to the bottom of who's been terrorizing my fiancée." He hesitated, "No need to tell you that my . . . my son has a blue Ghia." He poured some ice water from the pitcher on the sideboard and took a thoughtful swallow.

"Mr. Wainwright, I know about your son. That doesn't explain why you left me in the dark."

Stunned, Wainwright sat down on the corner of the desk. "Just what do you mean, you 'know about' my son?"

Landes did not respond for a few timeless seconds. Then he blurted out, "That he owns the Ghia coupe, of course."

What else did Diana tell Ashleigh? "That bitch," Wainwright said aloud as he sprang to his feet. Reminding himself that he paid Landes a healthy retainer, and he owed him no more than the simple facts, he calmed down. "The instant Ashleigh told me it was a Ghia that followed her, I postponed my Monday-morning meeting. One that was damned important," he couldn't resist adding.

Forcing himself to stick to the relevant points, he continued, "I boarded a plane that same afternoon and went to see my son, Anthony." He didn't bother with the details. "It turns out that his car was stolen a couple of weeks ago."

"Did he report it?"

"Yes, and if Anthony was involved, I'd have told you. But he's never even met Ashleigh. He's got no motive."

"And yet you failed to ask me to look into it. Instead, at that same time, you asked me to stop investigating the Danielle Norman disappearance." Landes let the statement hang in the air before asking, "Where was your son's car when it was stolen? And what police department took the report?"

Wainwright heard the door open, and Randall Updike poked his head in. Wainwright covered the mouthpiece with his hand and whispered, "Be right with you."

Returning to the phone, he signed off with Landes, saying in no uncertain terms, "Talk to you later. Just remember, your job is to protect Miss McDowell. The police have a report on the stolen car, so leave that to them."

CHAPTER
87

Conrad Taylor sat back in his chair, roughly massaging the back of his neck. The budget proposal was now complete.

He scanned through the yellow sheets, rechecking the figures on the handwritten draft of his proposal. *Right on target—a seventeen percent cutback. But at what long-range cost?*

It was just past six, and darkness had done its level best to overtake the City of Angels. But L.A. valiantly fought back, dumping billions of watts of illumination throughout the city.

Conrad wearily heaved himself from the chair and looked out the window. Seven stories below, a slow but steady procession of headlights, with pedestrians darting in and out, made their way along the busy downtown streets. He wondered how Ashleigh was coping. The total futility of conducting a review of Danielle's performance made him feel a little less uncomfortable about some of his proposed budget cuts in the Royale division— but not much.

Landes shifted his position behind the steering wheel. Still holding the cellular phone, he tapped the disconnect button, then punched in Pocino's extension.

"Pocino."

"This is Dick Landes."

"Long time no see. I suppose McDowell's given you the skinny on Cinderella and her solo shoe."

Same old Pocino, Landes thought. *Hasn't changed since our days on the force.* "Right. But I'd like your perspective."

Pocino snorted. "Haven't had this much action since joining this out-fit. It sure as hell beats writing up reports on shoplifters and employee theft. Makes me miss the good old days, out chasing the bad guys. Hey, you've been on the scene since the car bomb and probably know a helluva lot more than I do. Spill what you need from me, then I've got questions for you."

"Fair enough. Where does the tower investigation stand?"

"Homicide and the forensic crew have been over every square inch of the tower and rooftop. They picked up hair samples, a blood sample from the corner of the metal fuse cabinet, and a few other odds and ends. Of course, with the entourage that was there for the resurrection of King Kong, they've got their work cut out."

"King Kong?"

Pocino explained about the upcoming event, then asked, "Any idea why McDowell is so wrapped up in this buyer's disappearance? Even returned to Norman's house the very next night after I'd driven her there. Something weird about that dame. Driven, if you ask me—maybe too much so."

"Wainwright told me that she'd been engaged to Danielle Norman's brother, and I believe the girl lived with her for a while . . . or maybe it was with her parents."

"Christ. I had no idea."

For a heartbeat Landes made no comment. But he'd already decided to bring Pocino into his confidence. "If you're up to a little moonlight-ing, I'd like to enlist your help."

"I'm listening."

"Since I'm on retainer with Wainwright Enterprises, I prefer not to get on the wrong side of the boss unless I have to. Not only because it's a lucrative account . . . Wainwright's been known to make a formidable enemy."

"That's for sure. What's the problem?"

"Wainwright hasn't been up front with me. I can't put my finger on it, but he's got something to hide—and that something might just get Ashleigh McDowell killed." He punched in the cigarette lighter. "He denies it, but I think his son's involved."

"Didn't know he had one."

"One who owns a blue Karmann Ghia."

Pocino whistled. "No shit."

"What I'd like you to do is track down the police report on that stolen car and find out what you can about the son."

"Question . . ." Pocino paused. "Why me?"

"Number one, I trust you. Number two, Wainwright asked me to drop the investigation. And while I have no intention of doing so, I see no reason for taking myself off his payroll, since I have every intention of protecting Miss McDowell as asked. And I can do that best if I'm not thrown out of the loop. Number three, you have an inside track on what's going on at Bentleys Royale."

"O-kaaayyy, but I assume Wainwright's not picking up my tab for my moonlighting."

"Right. My agency will take care of that, at the going rate. And before you ask, if you get information that would place me in a conflict of interest with Wainwright, I drop his account."

"Jesus, Landes, this white-knight crap could get damned expensive."

"It's only money. The fact is, Wainwright's son owns a Ghia, and Wainwright flew back here a couple nights ago without letting me know. It's more than suspect." He cleared his throat. "Another thing—I'd like more information on Bradley."

"Maybe I can shed a little light. How much do you know about Royale's internal shenanigans?"

"Next to nothing," Landes confessed. "My role has been to protect Wainwright's fiancée and find out who followed her and planted a bomb in her car."

Pocino took a deep breath. "To make a long story short, a computer scam was put in motion approximately two weeks before Norman disappeared. Masterful. Unauthorized purchases were put through, including about three hundred thousand dollars to a phony vendor called La Salliano.

"There are two legitimate vendors involved in Norman's larceny, or whatever you choose to call it. One is Medley Originals, owned by none other than Wainwright Enterprises. The other is Lady Adrianna, of which Mr. Jeff Bradley is a rep. It appears that orders have appeared for those vendors on the daily merchandise reports and then been backed out of the system. Little of that merchandise has been checked in. Yet it appears on the floor, while La Salliano merchandise is recorded as received, but there is no such merchandise."

"How do you know so much about the paperwork? I thought you were head of Security."

"Security is part of it. My fancy title is director of asset protection, so at times I work hand in hand with the Purchasing department. The fact is, paper losses are more of a problem than merchandise marching out the door."

"Let's not get sidetracked on the internal trivia, just those connected to the threat on Miss McDowell's life."

"Understood." Pocino cleared his throat. "Did she tell you about her conversation with Dean Delaney?"

"About seeing Jeff Bradley in the store the afternoon of the State of the Business meeting?"

"Yeah. Guess she and Delaney played phone tag for a while, but he added another piece to the puzzle." Pocino sighed in disgust. "Any vendor with an ounce of sense would know better than to try to meet with a buyer just before the annual meeting, and Bradley had to know she was scheduled on the red-eye that very night." Again clearing his throat, he went on. "Bottom line is Delaney gave Miss McDowell Bradley's private extension at Lady Adrianna—his home number as well.

"Seems Bradley's on vacation until Monday and there's no answer at his pad. Just the damned answering-machine message with his nancy voice on it." He sighed again. "At least Delaney doesn't flaunt it. I sure as hell wish more of those fellows would stay in the closet."

Though he was a little put off, Landes said only, "Let me know what you find," then gave him the numbers where he could be reached and clicked off. Now was not the time to be telling Pocino, a dyed-in-the-wool homophobe, that Delaney was his half brother.

CHAPTER
88

David Jerome waited impatiently for O'Brien just outside the vice president's office, a folded slip of paper in his hand.

"Sorry to keep you, David," O'Brien said breathlessly, and motioned him inside.

"Jim, I'll get right to the point," replied Jerome, taking his seat. "I'm worried as hell about Ashleigh McDowell."

O'Brien sat beside him in a matching armchair. "Do you think that incident with her car had anything to do with what's going on in Danielle Norman's department?"

Jerome rose and walked to the window, then turned back to the VP. "I do."

"What possible motive . . . ?" He hesitated. "How about Mitchell Wainwright? A dubious connection in his world seems far more likely."

Jerome shook his head and handed O'Brien the paper—a copy of the warning note sent to Ashleigh.

"What on earth is going on?" O'Brien got to his feet. "I told her—"

"Hold on. No point getting steamed up."

Sinking back into the armchair, O'Brien continued, "Look, my friend, this is a job for the police. We don't know how deeply Danielle Norman is personally involved, but whatever it is that's going on in her department has hit your bottom line like a Mack truck. At the rate you're going, retaining autonomy will be a stretch, never mind those long-range plans. But how Ashleigh fits in, I haven't a clue."

Jerome met O'Brien's direct gaze. "Even without this Norman debacle, in this retail climate I need Ashleigh at her best—at her very best."

"Understood."

"So, let me share my concerns." Jerome relaxed against the back of the chair. "I know you think a great deal of Ashleigh, and so do I. She's bright, and our executives rely on her and her down-to-earth guidance. I have done so as well."

"But?"

"No point mincing words. Since she became engaged, even before this situation with Danielle Norman, things have been different." The president cleared his throat and took a sip of water. "She just doesn't seem as . . . committed."

"Give me an example."

"It's more of a gut feeling." He paused. "Alright. For example, several times over the past few weeks when I've needed to discuss something with her, I find she's already gone home."

"You mean she's left work on time." O'Brien grinned. "Or do you mean that she's working less than a forty-hour week?"

"Not less than a forty-hour week." His jaw tightened. "But no executive worth his or her salt can get by on a forty-hour week. And Ashleigh McDowell certainly didn't get where she is today on any so-called forty-hour week."

O'Brien sighed. "We've had this go-round before. The battle of hours put in versus what's put into those hours will continue long after we're dead and gone. But we're not here to talk philosophy."

"No, we're not," Jerome agreed. "I may have no right to dictate how executives spend their time outside the workplace, and perhaps it makes no difference to their performance, but—"

James O'Brien laughed out loud. "It makes a truckload of difference! But don't quote me." He rose from his chair. "It's tough to be candid with all the possible—I should say *probable*—backlash from one so-called mistreated group or another." He held up one hand, fingers splayed, and dramatically tapped one finger after another as he ticked off items. "Women . . . blacks . . . Hispanics . . . gays. The list goes on."

Not missing the opening, Jerome added, "Remember the 'good old days,' when we didn't have to skirt the issues or search for inoffensive lingo to tell someone that they're expected to do the job we're paying them for!"

"Just a minute, my friend. You and I both know there's no excuse good enough to skirt the issue of getting the job done." Now seated behind his desk, O'Brien leaned forward, resting his forearms on the edge. "But times have changed."

Jerome nodded.

"Just a few years back I would've vowed that a homosexual would never be promoted to general manager in a Bentley's or Bentleys Royale store." O'Brien grinned. "Well, look at us now. You came to terms with that reality before I did. And damn it, I was wrong." O'Brien leaned back in his chair.

Getting back to what he actually wanted to discuss, Jerome said, "If Bentleys Royale is to survive, I can't have any weak links."

O'Brien's eyebrows arched. "And Ashleigh is a weak link?"

"No," he said emphatically. "Good God, no. I didn't mean to indicate—I don't want to lose her. What I want is her total commitment. I've had it in the past, and I won't take less. Particularly now, with Adele Watson trying to throw her weight around."

O'Brien pressed on. "Before we get into that can of worms, I just want to warn you: With the current budget crunch, I'm afraid Ashleigh's position is in jeopardy."

"Ross!" The urgent cry came from the associates' security counter.

It was six forty-seven—well past closing time at Bentleys Royale's headquarters store. Mr. Jerome, adamant about there being no unnecessary overtime, had issued an edict: Security personnel must see that everyone had left the store by seven o'clock. By this time, the Security staff would be uprooting lingering executives from their offices, conducting a final walk-through, and preparing to lock up for the night. After activating the alarm system, they would be on their way.

The headquarters store's security manager was on vacation and Pocino was alone in the Security office, diagonally across from the security counter. When the frantic shriek reached his ears, he tossed the sign-in sheets aside and bolted from the office.

"Come quick!" The girl's voice rose to a frenzied pitch as Pocino rushed toward her.

Gasping for breath as if he'd run a much longer distance than the few yards from the Security office, Pocino leaned hard on the high counter. "Yeah?" He took in the area in one quick sweep of his eyes, stopping abruptly at the black-and-white monitor, which the security associate had turned to face him. The monitor was fixed on the associates' section of underground parking.

He frowned, seeing nothing unusual. The girl beside him babbled incoherently, pointing to the space between his red Mustang and a white Mercedes 450SL. He strained his eyes, but the camera rotated away from the area.

"What?" Pocino flung his arms wide. "What is it?"

"There is someone who has been lurking around the underground parking for ten minuets or so who just ducked between those cars." Her eyes intent on the monitor, she pushed her hair back and leaned forward. When the camera swept back to the area between Pocino's car and the Mercedes, she pointed. "There!"

Still he saw nothing.

"I know I saw someone. He was right there!"

Glancing at the second monitor, Pocino saw Ashleigh descending the stairs to underground parking.

He checked the third monitor, which was focused on the back lot. The outdoor associates' parking area was nearly deserted. Just two cars remained.

"Where's Sam?" he shouted as he took off, racing to the exit.

"Outside somewhere," she hollered after him.

Pocino took the stairs two at a time and flipped his pager on. The second he heard the rasp of the instrument, he called, "All security agents, get to underground parking *now*!"

Ashleigh hurried down the concrete stairs, thinking about her meeting with Mr. Jerome. The review session with Adele Watson and the president to evaluate Danielle's performance had been postponed, but her sense of relief was all too brief. She was left with a cold, biting anguish. Mr. Jerome's comment had caught her off guard. The sting of his words was imprinted on her mind: *We'll wait until you're more in control.* She and the president had had their share of disagreements, but never before had he questioned her ability to cope.

She stopped, her foot poised on the last step, her head filled with the faint hum that permeated the underground parking garage. It was eerie. She waited for her eyes to adjust to the dim surroundings and shifted the strap of her handbag as she scanned the area.

Four cars remained in the garage. Other than Mitchell's Mercedes, the only one she recognized was Pocino's red Mustang. The black Ford Escort was conspicuously absent. Her heart pounded fiercely, echoing through the stillness. She considered going back to the store and waiting for a security guard to walk with her to her car. But remembering the time, she rejected the idea.

As it was, she would have to hurry. Conrad had not sent the purchase orders in a transmittal envelope the day before, as she had asked, explaining that he did not want them out of his hands. So she had agreed to meet him tonight at eight.

Ashleigh pulled her coat tightly around her, and seeing nothing out of order, she rapidly headed toward the Mercedes. It was then that she saw the Escort and began to relax.

The next thing she knew, voices were resounding throughout the garage from all directions. There was a squeal of brakes, and her arm was jerked so hard that she tumbled to the ground, landing on the cold concrete floor. Disoriented, she saw Pocino's burly form running in the direction of the parking exit, and Sam, one of Royale's security agents, rushing toward her. She could barely think, and her mind kept repeating, *What just happened? What just happened?*

Conrad Taylor stepped out of the elevator on the first floor of the Bentley's corporate office building.

"Oh, there you are, Mr. Taylor!" It was Charlie at the security desk. "I just called your office. Saw you'd not signed out yet, so I asked Mr. Pocino to hold on. He says it's important." Charlie flashed a lopsided smile.

"Thanks, Charlie." Conrad set his briefcase down and reached across the counter for the phone. "Yes, Pocino?" He frowned up at the large, unadorned clock above the security desk. It was seven fifteen.

"There's been a hell of a lot of excitement over here at Bentleys Royale," came Pocino's voice.

"L.A.?"

"Yeah. Right here at headquarters."

Conrad heard Pocino breathing heavily over the phone, and the hackles rose on the back of his neck. "Damn it, Pocino, what happened?"

Hands wrapped around the Styrofoam cup, Ashleigh sipped the hot coffee Pocino had brought her from the vending machine in the associates' lounge.

Pocino stood over her, a strained expression on his face. He didn't seem to know what to do or what to say. He shifted his ample bulk from one foot to the other, and then he cleared his throat. "Ashleigh, have you any idea who was in that car?"

She looked up at him with glazed eyes and shook her head. It was too much effort to speak. She simply sat there on the edge of the armless green vinyl couch, shivering inside her coat, and taking another gulp of the steaming coffee. Her eyes wandered aimlessly around the lounge—a cold, sterile room, not in keeping with the warm, elegant ambiance of Bentleys Royale.

Pocino ran both hands through his untidy hair, again clearing his throat. His usual sarcasm and supercop demeanor gone, he asked, "Are you okay?"

Ashleigh nodded and set her cup on the table, absently reaching for a copy of *Retail Today*.

His heavy brows drew together, forming a solid bushy line across his forehead. "Mr. Taylor will be here any minute. Would you mind if I left you here while I check the condition of your car?"

"My car?" She rose, the magazine tumbling to the floor. "What's wrong with my car?" Her voice cracked.

"Probably nothing, but we want to make sure." He smiled, stretching out his hand. "Need keys. Promise I'll bring them right back."

She searched around her. "Where's my handbag?"

"Sam picked up your things when that maniac tried to run you down. It must be over in the security manager's office." He started for the door. "Be back in a minute."

"I'll go with you." She stood up shakily.

"Are you sure?" He started to take her elbow, then stepped back and gestured her through the door. "With your security manager off on vacation, I'd like to keep this situation low-key." They continued down the corridor. "I came in about four thirty this afternoon to see what I could find out. It wasn't much. But if Bradley was in this store in the last couple weeks, he didn't sign in. I was just about to get the sign-in sheets for the past two months, to see if he's in the habit of not signing it, when—"

"Do you think it was Jeff Bradley in that car?"

"Not unless he was wearing a blond wig." Then, without warning, he stopped in midstride, his arm held out in front of Ashleigh. They were just outside Ferrari's office—twenty yards and a set of double doors away from the associates' security counter. "Miss McDowell, if that note you received in Palm Desert is to be believed, and Danielle Norman is alive despite the evidence from the rooftop tower, then her life is in danger as well as yours. I'm going to get to the bottom of this."

They made their way through the double doors, with only the squeak from his rubber-soled shoes and the click of her heels breaking the stillness.

Inside the security manager's office, Ashleigh noticed her handbag and organizer in the armchair next to the desk. She picked up the Fendi bag, and while fumbling for the car keys, she said, "Ross, are you sure the driver of that car meant to run me down?"

He nodded. The expression on his round, weathered face was serious. "The car was parked next to one of those rear pillars just inside the underground parking, diagonally across from your car. According to the agent at the monitor, the driver had been stalling around between the Mercedes and my Mustang."

Ashleigh shuddered, and lowered her eyes as he laid out his theory.

Pocino took the keys from her hand and continued. "Nobody saw exactly what happened, but my guess is that the guy heard my call for assistance from Sam's pager. The place was dead still, and sounds echo real good down there. Sam said he was just outside in the back lot." Pocino cleared his throat. "Anyway, we figure that he—the driver— made a dash for the car." He paused, and deep ridges set in across his forehead. "Must have left the engine running. No way in hell was there time to start the engine, then spin around in time to run you down."

Ashleigh placed her hand gingerly on the tender spot on her upper arm where Pocino had jerked her out of the path of the speeding car. For the first time, she noticed the streaks of dirt on the right side of her coat where she'd hit the cement floor. She absently tried to dust them off with her hand, but the black streaks clung to the fabric.

Turning her attention back to Pocino, she tried to listen to what he was saying.

"I ran after him, but he had too much of a head start. If I'd been just a few feet closer, I could've gotten a better look at the driver." He paused and added, "And I'm sure that the car was a black Ford Escort."

Conrad swung into Bentleys Royale's upper lot and parked just outside the associates' entrance. The metallic echo of the car door slamming shut broke the silence and filled the cool night air. He paused as the echo died and voices floated up from the underground parking area.

He hurried through the porte cochere and down the broad concrete stairs. At the bottom, he peered across the dimly lit structure. Three sets of eyes were fixed directly on him. Pocino stood next to two uniformed policemen beside a white Mercedes—the one Conrad had driven home from Palm Springs just the day before.

"Hi, boss," Pocino called out, motioning Conrad to join them before introducing Sergeant Flynn and his partner. The policemen wore thin rubber gloves, which they peeled off after pushing the hood back in place and locking the car doors.

As they placed a wide yellow ribbon around the area of the car, Conrad asked, "What did you find?"

"So far, not a thing," Pocino said. "Not a damned thing. No explosives, but they'll dust for fingerprints in the morning. Our perp was definitely messing around with this vehicle." Pocino shook his head. "And someone ought to tell Miss McDowell that she'd better start locking her car."

Conrad paced back and forth in the drafty corridor between the associates' security counter and the closed door of the security office where the two officers were still questioning Ashleigh. How ironic. Through no fault of her own, Ashleigh was again being questioned by the police. It was all too much.

Stopping abruptly, he turned to Pocino. "While we're out here cooling our heels, let's compile a list of everything we know about the threats to Miss McDowell, Danielle Norman's disappearance, and the covert activity in Fine Apparel."

Pocino, now seated on a high stool behind the associates' security counter, picked up a clipboard from the shelf under the counter and took a couple sheets of paper from the stack of announcements in front of him.

The outside bell shrilled. Pocino flipped the intercom on and Dick Landes identified himself. "Your timing couldn't be better," Pocino said as he buzzed him in.

When Landes arrived, he wasted no time with preliminaries. "Miss McDowell called. Told me what happened. I just spoke to my agent, Billings. He said Wainwright called and told him that he wasn't needed. That the police were giving Ashleigh round-the-clock protection."

"You mean *Wainwright* pulled him off duty?" Conrad asked.

"Afraid so. Billings should have checked with me, but—"

"Is Wainwright still in Atlanta?"

Landes nodded. "Called his hotel. He hasn't checked out."

"And are you sure about the unlocked car?" Conrad repeated. "I don't believe it. Ashleigh says she always locks it—it's not even hers, so she's very cautious."

"Nor do I," Landes agreed. "I'll look into it."

With a shrug Pocino said, "It was definitely unlocked. No sign of forced entry."

"So if Miss McDowell didn't leave it unlocked, we've got to run down who has keys." Landes paused. "Let's see. Assuming Mitchell Wainwright's in Atlanta, how about his son, Anthony? The one who just happens to own a blue Ghia?"

Pocino shrugged. "We'll soon find out." Turning to Landes, he said, "I'd sure as hell like to know exactly what Wainwright's up to," and then, looking toward Conrad, "Let's take a look at Dick's surveillance car."

Landes's Escort was parked in the upper lot next to the associates' entrance, behind Conrad's. Within a few feet of the car, Pocino commented, "I see the bad guys slipped up on one minor detail."

"Which is . . . ?"

"This car has tinted windows—the copycat version had clear glass. I'd never have seen the blond hair if it hadn't."

"Longish blond hair?" Conrad asked.

"Yeah, like the fellow you described in the Ghia the other night. I was just a few feet behind the car when he drove under the lights at the exit," Pocino explained.

"What about that Escort you saw in Palm Desert—the one outside Beverly Hoffdahl's house?" Landes asked. "Did it have clear or tinted windows?"

Conrad shrugged. "Afraid I didn't notice."

Landes walked purposefully around to the back of his car, then called out, "Pocino! What do you want to bet that the license number you got on that Escort turns out to be mine?" He looked back down to the spot below the trunk of his car. The stainless-steel frame hung at an odd angle from the one remaining screw. The rear license plate was missing.

CHAPTER
92

After once again running through a mental checklist, Ashleigh closed the top to her overnight case, picked up her garment bag from the bed, and returned to the living room.

Conrad sprang to his feet at the sound of her footsteps. Taking her overnight things, he said, "Doesn't look like you packed much."

"I'm not letting anyone drive me out of my own condo. At least not for long, but tonight I'd rather not be alone."

"Understood," he said. "Landes plans to add a surveillance camera to the hallway in front of your door, as well as a tracking device in the car."

Rechecking to make sure she had everything she needed, Ashleigh tuned out until she heard Conrad ask, "You sure I can't take you to dinner?"

"Thanks anyway, but I think I'd better head straight on over to Charles's since I didn't tell him I was spending the night."

"Come again?"

"Sorry," she said, realizing that she hadn't explained earlier. "When I called from the store no one answered. Then I remember that Charles told me earlier this week that he and Mary would be attending an anniversary party of an old friend this evening." Picking up her handbag, she glanced down at her watch. It was nearly ten. "If they're not home already, they should be any minute and I'd just as soon tell Charles about everything when I see him."

"And if he's not there?"

She picked up her handbag and flicked off the light on the end table. "I have a key."

He just looked into her eyes, not saying a word.

In another five minutes they pulled into the driveway of the Stuart residence. Only the automatic lights were on. None were visible from the second story. It was clear that Charles and Mary had not yet returned.

Instantly assessing the situation, Conrad, said, "Look, your grandfather isn't home yet, and I have no intention of leaving you here on your own. Since my place is only a heartbeat away, how about going over there and ordering in? Don't know about you, but I'm starved. Do you like Chinese?"

The moment the elevator doors closed, Ashleigh felt a fresh stab of doubt about spending the night at Conrad's. She self-consciously pushed a loose strand of hair off her face. Her eyes flitted to the small key Conrad inserted beside the button marked PH at the top of the control panel.

As the elevator slowly ascended, to fill the awkward silence Ashleigh asked, "Didn't John Wayne live in one of the penthouses in this building?"

"Actually it was his mother, but I assume Wayne spent a bit of time here," Conrad replied. "We bought it from the people who purchased it directly from Wayne after his mother died."

The elevator came to a stop on the top floor, and Conrad quickly stepped out, holding the door for her. "To your left, and watch your step."

Ashleigh glanced down at the rough surface of the sixteen-inch-square stones leading to the high double doors of his apartment, and stepped carefully in her slender-heeled pumps from one to another. Conrad held her arm firmly. "This graveled area around the stepping-stones used to be filled with water," he said with a smile, "but we heard that *the Duke* slipped off one too many times, had the water drained, and replaced it with redwood chips."

"Redwood chips?" she asked looking down at the small white stones.

"Got fed up with the fine red dust, so . . ." He shrugged his broad shoulders as he unlocked the double doors and led Ashleigh inside.

In front of them, the living room, bathed in reflected light from the outside, looked enormous. He flipped the lights on. "Make yourself comfortable, while I call Chen's for our takeout delivery."

As he turned left and passed through an open doorway into the kitchen area, Ashleigh walked into the living room and across the hardwood floor, stopping in front of the round fireplace at the far end of the large room. Through the walls of clear glass, she saw the spacious veranda that bordered the condo. It occurred to her that she had stared up at this very penthouse often in the past week.

"Now, can I fix you a drink? Or perhaps some hot chocolate to calm your nerves?"

Ashleigh smiled. *Mitchell would never have thought of hot chocolate.*

After the Chinese food that Conrad sent out for arrived, they spent the next two hours talking and eating, and talking some more. Conrad had brought the fireplace to life just before their dinner arrived, and now they sat on one of the large couches facing the fire.

"How about a glass of wine?" he suggested.

"Yes, please." Ashleigh slipped off her shoes and curled her legs beneath her.

"Ashleigh," he said, his voice floating toward her as if on a stream of smoke. She turned toward him, and he picked up her left hand. The firelight sparkled in the engagement diamond, but his eyes found hers and held them. "Why are you wearing this ring?"

To gain her composure, Ashleigh stared for a moment into her wine goblet, away from those penetrating blue eyes.

"You're not going to marry Mitchell Wainwright, are you?"

"No," she said. The truth came easily. She found she couldn't lie to him.

Conrad let her answer hang in the air for a moment. Then he said, "There's something I must tell you. Last week at Danielle's, in the bedroom, when you asked me what I had picked up—I didn't tell you the truth."

He rose and walked slowly to the music center. Ashleigh leaned forward as he picked something up from the top of the CD unit. She had known, even that night at Danielle's, that he had lied, yet she hadn't confronted him. Her heart pounded like a sledgehammer. *What is it? What did he take?*

Without a word of explanation, he handed her a snapshot. A glass of ice water thrown in her face would not have caught her more unprepared.

Ashleigh stared down at a photograph taken at Disneyland, in front of the Fantasyland castle entrance. Her eyes clouded as she looked at the happy trio. Conrad seemed unchanged, whereas Danielle looked like a teenager. And Gran appeared to be full of life.

CHAPTER

93

Conrad swallowed hard. He saw that Ashleigh's eyes were intent and glistening in the firelight. "I started to tell you the whole story about my relationship with Danielle, but I just couldn't. I know now that I merely chose the easy way out. It's not a relationship I'm very proud of."

Conrad's voice trailed off as he sat down beside her and watched her eyes turn cold. She stared at him blankly. "Please, Ashleigh. I blame only myself. Danielle and I met shortly after Anna filed for divorce. Danielle was full of life and bubbling over with enthusiasm—like a breath of fresh air in springtime. I was captivated."

Pausing, he picked up his goblet and took a slow, deliberate drink before he continued. "We even talked about getting married. That's when Danielle took me to meet your grandmother. The day we spent with her at Disneyland made me take a long, hard look at myself. I didn't like what I saw. That gentle lady didn't say a word; she didn't have to. Luckily Danielle and I came to our senses before it was too late."

Ashleigh took her eyes from his and drained her goblet.

"You make it all sound so simple . . . so . . . antiseptically reasonable." The warmth had faded from her tone.

"No, Ashleigh. It wasn't at all simple." His jaw was set firm. "I never should have asked Danielle to marry me. It wasn't just our age difference. I should have known it wasn't right—not right for me and certainly not for Danielle. She was so very young, only nineteen, and . . . and not at all ready for marriage."

Ashleigh gazed over the top of her empty wine goblet, waiting for him to continue. She saw his pain, but she couldn't stop herself from asking, "What made you decide so quickly that it wouldn't work?"

He swirled the wine in his goblet. "We talked for a long time that night after we took your grandmother home from Disneyland. What we discovered was that all we had in common was the retail business. If we'd paid attention—all the signs were there—we would have realized that our goals were poles apart." He hesitated for a long moment. "For one thing, Danielle didn't want children—definitely something we should have discussed, but we didn't. My fault again."

"But Danielle loves children."

"I'm sure you're right," he responded. "She just didn't want any of her own. It's not that she was afraid of the responsibility—she just feared turning into someone like her mother."

Ashleigh felt her throat constrict. Tears welled up in her eyes. As Conrad continued to tell her all that Danielle had revealed to him of her dreadful childhood, Ashleigh thought back to Dan's family picture albums—the ones his mother had made for him before he left for college. Danielle had been conspicuously absent.

"I guess you know all the rest," Conrad said, as he rose and pulled Ashleigh to her feet. "We can't change the past."

I know that only too well, she thought. His hands lingered in hers, and his eyes sought her approval. At last she nodded, and only then did she feel a warm glow return to her body.

"If you'll pick out a few CDs"—he nodded toward the stack on the shelf under the player—"I'll get us some more wine." When she started to decline, he placed his finger gently on her lips. "Just one," he asserted, swiftly taking charge and propelling her toward the music center.

Ashleigh stole a glance at Conrad. His face revealed nothing. She'd half expected him to make an overture, but he hadn't. And a part of her wanted him to. She could no longer deny it.

Still, her inbred sense of self-preservation made her wary. Charles had most likely returned home hours ago—she should ask Conrad to take her home now. So why wasn't she? As soon as she officially ended her engagement, her life would once again be orderly. She had no intention of jeopardizing that. But if she weren't careful, this man could turn things upside down again.

CHAPTER

94

Conrad noticed Ashleigh's pensive expression as he set their full goblets on the coffee table.

"How about these?" She handed him three CDs in plastic cases.

As he took them from her and shuffled through them, he smiled. He lifted the first disk from the case and slid it into the cartridge—a Shirley Bassey album. "One of my favorites," he said as he turned from the CD player to Ashleigh and gently pulled her into his arms.

He held her firmly, and they danced easily across the hardwood floor, beside the fireplace. The music filled the room, and she looked out through the windowed walls at the haze of lights. Slowly he felt her begin to relax in his arms, and he joined Shirley Bassey, softly singing the lyrics of "Feelings".

Conrad's voice was incredibly rich and sensual, and when the music came to an end, he did not release her.

Ashleigh felt mesmerized.

He placed his hand gently under her chin and tilted her face up to his. A protest rose in her throat but remained unspoken as her mouth went dry. She attempted to step back, but he pulled her to him, bending his face to hers, seeking her mouth. For a brief moment, his mouth crushed down on hers, hard and insistent. Then his mouth softened as he gently parted her lips.

She stopped struggling and found herself yielding to him, returning his kisses. He pressed his body into hers, and warmth spread like fire through her limbs, filling her with sensations long forgotten.

Conrad drew back abruptly, and looked into her eyes. As she gazed at him, she saw the desire in his clear blue eyes, the physical and emotional tension. A new wave of warmth enveloped her. Then his face drew close to hers, his eyes darkening, and he was kissing her again. His kisses were rough, as if they were bruising her lips, but she did not want him to stop. The mounting wave of passion obliterated her fears. Her defenses crumbled like castles in the sand.

Conrad stepped back from her again but did not take his hands from her shoulders. His mouth curved in a smile, challenging her, and he leaned forward. "Ashleigh, I want you," he whispered hoarsely in her ear. "Tell me you don't want me, and I'll stop now."

His breath was warm against her throat. She hesitated, frightened— stripped of her self-protective instincts. And yet she was incapable of drawing away. He peered deeply into her flushed face, his eyes filled with a yearning equal to her own, and a heady excitement shivered through her. It was a combination of desire and fear that made her stomach flutter as he took her hand gently in his and led her into the bedroom. She had no strength to resist, even if she'd wanted to.

Moonlight and fragments of reflected lights from the city below streamed in the windows. Conrad left her side to draw the drapes, and the room was suddenly enveloped in soft shadows. She stood spellbound until he was beside her once more.

Conrad took her face between his palms and kissed her gently. Then, reaching behind her head, he released her hair from the tortoiseshell clip. Her blond locks spilled down around her shoulders; her eyes were dark and misty. His hand moved rhythmically, caressing her hair in long strokes, and then her neck and shoulders. *She is so beautiful.*

He pulled down on the long zipper in the back of her dress, and it fell to the floor in a soft pool at her feet. She stepped out, and he guided her to the side of the bed, his eyes never leaving her face. When he discarded his shirt, he felt Ashleigh's slight hesitation before she ran her fingers down his torso. His muscles relaxed beneath her touch.

As he pressed her back into the bed, encircling her with his arms, kissing her forehead, her face, her throat, her shoulders, it seemed that the rest of their clothes magically fell away. They were in each other's arms, and he covered her entire body with kisses, caressing every intimate and erotic part of her until she gasped with unbridled excitement.

Her passion inflamed him. He wanted to possess her, but he willed himself to be patient as she ran her long, sensitive fingers up and down his back and across his chest. When she shyly kissed his neck and traced it with her tongue, he whispered, "Please. Not yet." Her body was so exquisite that he wanted to explore every part of it.

The urgency that had consumed her beside the fireplace had calmed now. It seemed as if they had all the time in the world, and she was seized by a tremendous yet unhurried curiosity as she ran her fingers through his wavy black hair and traced the shape of his ears with her tongue.

Ashleigh felt his fingers move lightly and tentatively along her hips, and an electric current shot through her like a bolt of lightning. How long could she lie still and endure his tender caresses before she went mad? Suddenly, time exploded with a pulsating passion. She was consumed with desire—and love.

For the very first time in years, there was no ghost from the past. There was only the here and now.

Dick Landes paced restlessly in front of the breakfast room table. The large Lalique ashtray was overflowing with half-smoked cigarettes, and the room reeked of stale tobacco and strong coffee. He'd been up since dawn, puzzling over what might be relevant to the case versus what was merely coincidental.

Dean Delaney appeared in his terry-cloth robe and bare feet, suppressing a yawn. "Looks like you've had a rough night." He went straight to the refrigerator and poured himself some orange juice. "Want some juice?"

Landes shook his head.

"Christ, bro, you must have been up half the night again, judging from that ashtray! I thought you'd decided to take last night off."

"Couldn't sleep. This case has me stumped. Haven't been able to reach Wainwright since he officially took us off duty. Don't know what he's trying to pull, but he's got a lot of explaining to do."

Delaney lifted a heavy brow.

Landes looked up at the kitchen clock. "If you don't get a move on, you'll be late for your meeting with the Oxxford rep. I'll tell you all about it tonight."

"Did you talk to Bradley?"

"No. I went to the address you gave me, but no one in the complex has seen him for the past week." He paused as a thought surfaced. "Do you know an Anthony Wainwright?"

Delaney squeezed his eyes shut in concentration but eventually shook his head. "Don't think so. What about him? Is he Wainwright's kid?"

Landes nodded. "We found out he's the owner of a blue Karmann Ghia like the one that's been following Miss McDowell."

As he turned and headed toward the hallway, Delaney stopped abruptly and said, "Tony. Bradley has been spending time with a young kid named Tony who I think owns a Ghia. I've met him. Don't remember the last name, but it's not Wainwright—would have remembered that."

"Describe him."

"Maybe five foot ten. Nice-looking in a rough sort of way. Muscular build, blond ponytail."

With a snap of his fingers, Landes said, "Jesus! That's got to be it." Suddenly, the dominoes began to fall into place. *Now I just have to figure out one thing,* he thought. *What in the hell was the former Mrs. Wainwright's name?*

By the time Landes finished his shower, he'd made up his mind: This would be his last job for Mitchell Wainwright. He would follow this case through, but not for Wainwright—for himself.

Landes picked up the phone and dialed his answering service for messages. Wainwright had finally returned his call and left a number where he could be reached. The P.I. quickly dialed it.

"What is it?" Wainwright barked on the other end of the phone line.

Making efforts to take rigid control of his tone, Landes told Wainwright about the attempt on Ashleigh's life the evening before.

"Is she okay?" Wainwright barked into the phone, but did not wait for a response. "Why didn't you tell—"

Landes ignored his ranting. "Why did you pull us off the case? Why did you tell Billings that Miss McDowell had police protection?"

"What?" His voice boomed across the wire. "I told him no such thing."

Landes gripped the phone tighter. "Look, Wainwright. He heard you loud and clear."

For a few long seconds, neither man spoke. Then Wainwright said, "Tell me about this conversation I supposedly had with your agent."

"First, I have a few questions for you. Number one, does your son go by the name of Tony?"

"Probably," Wainwright answered curtly.

"Number two, does he have longish blond hair?"

"Yes . . ."

"And number three, does his voice sound just like yours?"

CHAPTER
96

As Jeff peered across the sea of bobbing heads on the dance floor, his dry throat constricted. Julian's was filled with the usual Wednesday-night crowd, but Tony was nowhere in sight.

Making his way through the throng, Jeff was oblivious to the familiar din of recorded music and the greetings of friends and acquaintances. Somehow, he had to make the headstrong young man understand. He'd made Danielle as comfortable as possible under the circumstances. But he still wasn't happy about leaving her back at the Wainwright family cabin. She should be seen by a doctor. He prayed to the man upstairs, if there was any such thing, that Danielle could take care of herself until he could send help to her. He had a plan, and by God, Tony was going to listen.

His jaw clenched. *If Tony doesn't board that flight to Zurich on Monday morning, I'll leave without him.* Although officially he was on vacation from Lady Adrianna, Jeff had no intention of returning. He would stay clear of the greater Los Angeles area until flight time. And he'd see to it that Tony did the same.

He rechecked his inside breast pocket, felt the bulge of the Swiss Air tickets and the flawlessly forged passports. Tony had arranged for their new identities and the Swiss bank account through some guy called Jimmy—a contact he'd made years ago when he was involved in the drug scene.

Slowly sidling up to the bar, he ordered a Corona. Slipping a lime into the bottle, he glanced back toward the doorway before rechecking the time. It was not quite six fifty. True, he himself was about fifteen minutes late, but where was Tony? He'd gotten off work at four, and the city of

Commerce was a snap of a commute—against traffic in both directions. Hell, even if Tony had stopped by the apartment, he should be here by now. How long could it take to drive twelve blocks?

A freckle-faced kid with a thick thatch of red hair and a small hoop in his right ear caught Jeff's eye. He tilted his mug of draft beer in the gesture of a toast and waited for Jeff's reaction.

Christ, doesn't look old enough to shave or drive a car—never mind order a beer and make a move on an older man. Jeff shook his head and looked away. He'd never thought of himself as an older man, but he now felt ancient as he stretched his neck to see over the scattered groups of well-muscled young men with unseasonably tanned bodies.

As he scanned the horde of young, enthusiastic faces, he wondered if they could possibly be as happy and carefree as they appeared. Were they aware of the pitfalls that most likely lay ahead in life?

A deep, melodious laugh reached his ears, and his thoughts were swiftly aborted. The distinctive baritone quality was unmistakable. Jeff took a generous swallow of beer and swiveled the barstool in the direction of the jovial sounds of a shared confidence. He tensed when he spotted Tony emerging from the men's room, only a few yards from the end of the bar, with a young man who had the bleached blond hair of a surfer. The boy appeared to be about Tony's age, perhaps younger. Jeff had never seen him before, and he felt threatened.

Then, after what seemed like an interminable amount of time, he saw Tony's eyes scan the dimly lit area until they met his. Tony smiled and quickly cut through the middle of the small group that separated them. He didn't look back at the other young man, who was now making his way across the dance floor. Staring at the two young men, Jeff had a thought that struck him like a bolt of lightning: *Tony's foolish, cocky behavior could bring us both down.* It was one hell of a risk. One he thought maybe he wasn't willing to take.

Downing the remainder of his beer, he rose to meet Tony, who smiled at him innocently. He then wrapped his arm around Tony's broad shoulders and guided him toward the rear exit and parking lot. "Let's get out of here," Jeff said. "We need to talk."

CHAPTER
97

By Thursday afternoon, Pocino had gathered enough information to report back to Landes. He had no qualms about moonlighting on this case—this was no conflict of interest.

He closed his office door, checked the time, and then called Landes at home.

Just as Pocino was about to hang up, the private investigator answered.

"I hit pay dirt," Pocino reported. "The loose ends are coming together. Wainwright may not know this, but his son, Anthony, also goes by the name of Tony Lane. That's his stepdad's name. Not his legal name. I gather it's more an act of defiance against Wainwright than any special feeling for Lane." Pocino paused to catch his breath. "And get this: The kid's gay, and real tight with Bradley."

"Does Anthony . . . Tony . . . live in—"

"Hang on, there's more," he said, one word somersaulting over the next, "and it all ties in with Danielle Norman and Bentleys Royale. Tony Lane works at the Bentley's Distribution Center and is known as somewhat of a computer whiz. He applied for a job in Central Purchasing last fall and has filled in part-time while he's on a waiting list for a full-time opening and a transfer from the DC. Called in sick this morning, but there's no answer at his pad. Lives in Belmont Shore in Long Beach."

Pocino leaned back in the desk chair and swung his feet up on the marred desktop. Proud of what he'd been able to dig up, he pushed on without giving Landes a chance to react to the news. "Isn't Belmont Shore where Ashleigh McDowell lives?"

When Landes confirmed this, Pocino volunteered, "Would you like me to swing by his place tonight?"

"No," Landes said. "I plan to take the watch myself tonight. Mitchell Wainwright is flying back from Atlanta today, so I want to be in Long Beach, nearby." Then he added, "Since you're in L.A., could you check out Jeff Bradley's apartment on the West Side? I'll check on Tony's place again."

"Sure thing." They exchanged addresses.

"By the way," Pocino said brusquely, "is the Landes Agency in the market for a full-time agent?"

CHAPTER
98

Thursday night, after buzzing Mitchell in, Ashleigh flipped on every lamp in the living room and waited. He'd called right after he'd spoken to Dick Landes the day before. They'd talked about everything that had transpired regarding Danielle's disappearance and her own brushes with death, carefully avoiding anything personal about their relationship.

Ashleigh had spent much of the day preparing herself for this meeting. The time to get things settled between them was now, and she would not allow Mitchell to bully or manipulate her into waiting any longer.

He must know, as clearly as she did, that the gulf between their wants and needs was in conflict. It had taken her a long time to put her finger on the problem, but now she had no doubts: She did not love Mitchell, nor did he love her. There was also the issue of control— Mitchell's need for control versus her aversion to being controlled. He had accused her of wanting to be in control, and in some respects she could not deny that. However, she wanted control of no one other than herself.

Ashleigh stepped back as she swung the door open, and said softly, "I'm glad you're here. We need to talk." She carefully avoided being swept into his arms.

He stared at her with a bemused expression. "Charming. What a marvelous greeting after a nine-day absence," he commented, following her into the living room. Ashleigh watched as he headed straight to the wet bar and set the scotch and soda out on the counter, saying, "How about you?"

She shook her head and watched him surreptitiously as he ran the lemon peel around the rim of his glass. He looked tired, and there were new lines under his eyes and deep scores running down each side of his face, from his nose to his mouth. And yet for all that, he was still a handsome man.

Mitchell strode across the room and sat down on the couch. Patting the cushion beside him, he said, "Ashleigh, please relax, and sit down."

She sat down, but kept her distance. "Mitchell, I don't know how to be anything other than totally candid."

"By all means," he said. His voice was controlled, his eyes challenging.

She wanted to give him the ring, but resisted the temptation to simply hand it over to him.

"You want to break our engagement?" he said coldly, preempting her declaration.

Ashleigh nodded, relieved, but his calm manner made her uneasy. Before she had a chance to explain, Mitchell said, "Is it Conrad Taylor who's turned your pretty little head?"

"No. The problem is between you and me. I'm not blaming you. I just can't be the wife you want or need."

Mitchell set his glass on the coffee table and took hold of her wrists roughly. "What you're saying is you want more than I can give. You want love and adoration *and* total independence. Well, I'm afraid that's an incompatible package."

"You're hurting me." She stared down at his grip and twisted loose.

He let her go and rose. "Sorry." He walked to the sliding door and pulled back the drapes. When he turned back to her, his expression was hard. "Look, Ashleigh, this Updike deal is vitally important to me, and Sloane is hot on my heels. Yet I've put it on hold twice now."

"I know you have," she said, a tremor in her soft tone. "I'm sorry. And I appreciate everything you've done. I care for you and I want us to remain friends. But I can't marry you."

"You've had a rough week, and it's no time to make any decisions until all this is behind you."

"No, Mitchell." Ashleigh shot up from the couch. "I'm not going to let you make me feel guilty. You don't love me. You just want me, and I would be no more important to you than any other Wainwright

Enterprises acquisition." Even as the words spilled out, she knew that this wasn't quite true. The greatest and most insurmountable problem was the fact that she didn't love him.

He tried to take her in his arms, but she pulled away. "I admit that I've been under a great deal of stress, but I am not incapable of making a decision. And I know this is the right one for you as well as for me."

Mitchell paced back and forth, wearing an expression of deep concentration. When he stopped in front of her, he tilted her chin up toward his face, but kept his distance. "If that is your final decision, I'll accept it. However, this is no time to make an announcement. It can wait until after Saturday night," he concluded.

Knowing he must salvage some thread of self-respect, she allowed him that one last aspect of control.

Seated in the back of the black limousine, Ashleigh sighed under her breath. *This is such a farce.* She had to believe that Mitchell knew, without a doubt, that she would be returning the outrageous diamond at the end of the evening.

Mitchell leaned across her, ducking his head slightly to get a better view, and pointed a finger up toward the sky. "I see Jerome has spared no expense."

Ashleigh glanced back up at the crisscrossed beams illuminating the sky and nodded, not trusting herself to speak. The bright beams from the searchlights were seen long before the Bentleys Royale tower came into view.

As they drew nearer to the store, she looked past the four searchlights strategically focused on the fifty-two-foot King Kong who stood on the balcony surrounding the tower. Her eyes remained fixed on the tower itself. She felt numb.

Looking down at her empty palm, she pictured Danielle's gold butterfly necklace. She closed her lids quickly to dispel the vision. In the uncomfortable silence, she felt Mitchell's eyes on her. With effort, she opened her eyes and fixed a smile on her face. Before them, a steady stream of elegant cars and limos flowed from Bentleys Royale Place into the motor court. The well-organized valet attendants moved the flow of cars swiftly along.

Within moments, Ashleigh was alighting from the car, and while she waited for Mitchell to come around from the other side to join her, she glanced at the crowd lining the red-carpeted walkway in front of her. She immediately recognized George Burns. Holding on to his arm was a young woman with long red hair that fell to her waist and a gold lamé dress that hugged her slim body. But even amid all the commotion, excitement eluded Ashleigh; she felt like someone on the outside looking in. Nothing felt right.

Mitchell appeared at her side, smiling down at her. Tentatively, she smiled back and slipped her arm through his. As they made their way along the carpeted pathway, Ashleigh noticed the long formal reception line.

"How nice to see you, Lorraine," Mitchell said. He gave the woman a kiss on the cheek. Taking her hands in his, he drew back and at arm's distance gave her an admiring gaze. "And how lovely you look. Another phenomenal success, it appears."

"Thank you." The woman's eyes moved to include Ashleigh as Mitchell extended his hand to the man beside her.

"Well, don't you think it's time you introduced this lovely lady?" The man smiled, and there was a faint glimmer in his eye.

"Sorry. Frank and Lorraine Baldwin, I'd like you to meet . . . Ashleigh McDowell."

After they exchanged greetings, Mitchell added, "Ashleigh is the director of human resources for this magnificent establishment."

Ashleigh sighed her relief. *Thank God, he didn't introduce me as his fiancée.*

"Very impressive." Frank nodded and gave Ashleigh a roguish wink, then turned his eyes to Mitchell "Well, you'd better not let this one get away."

Mitchell smiled, bringing a tight knot to the pit of Ashleigh's stomach.

When they finally made their way through the doors to the entry hall, they stopped at the reception table, which was attended by three attractive women from the Assistance League, each one much bejeweled and wearing an evening gown. In front of each woman sat a file box and an alphabetical listing. Mitchell stepped forward to face the woman whose box was marked with the letters R-Z.

Ashleigh scanned the entry hall. The reception was in full swing, thronged with glamour and excitement. The ambiance had been miraculously transformed; an elegant store had become an elite party cathedral.

It was an extremely chic gathering. The crème de la crème of Southern California society mingled with movie celebrities and members of the jet set. Yet other than the special events coordinator and a handful of security agents, she saw no one she knew.

"Perfect. Just perfect."

Ashleigh stiffened unconsciously and started to move away when she felt Mitchell pull her toward him. Then she paused abruptly, hearing the sharp, cold tone in his voice. She looked first to Mitchell, noticing the firm set of his jaw, and then to the woman with the flashing green eyes who now stood beyond the table in front of them. It was Diana, her hair piled high on her head, with loose curls brushing the sides of her fine-boned face. A slim-skirted gown from the Karl Lagerfeld collection showed off her exquisite figure to full advantage.

Mitchell's eyes flashed between the two women. "I believe you've met."

Diana glared back at Mitchell, then turned to Ashleigh and thrust her hand forward—an exaggerated movement that seemed crass and out of character with the elegant image she projected. "It's nice to see you again," she said. She kept her voice low as her eyes wandered from Ashleigh back to Mitchell. Ashleigh extended her hand, acutely aware that Diana's attention was focused on Mitchell.

"I must talk to you," Diana said sharply.

He nodded and quickly took Ashleigh by the arm. "I'll call you tomorrow." Then, without waiting for a reply, he ushered Ashleigh toward the festivities in the Accessories area.

She had taken no more than three steps from the reception area when Ashleigh heard her name. It was Diana. "I'll see you Monday at ten," she said sweetly. Her smile could easily have been mistaken for one of sincerity and friendship.

Ashleigh was sure they had no such appointment.

CHAPTER
100

Mitchell and Ashleigh strolled through the Shoe Salon, and once again she noted that elegance was the order of the evening. The men wore tuxedos or dinner jackets, and the women were decked out in the latest eye-catching couture fashions, radiating undeniable stylishness.

"It's quite a turnout." Ashleigh murmured, still not seeing anyone she knew but recognizing several well-known stars.

"Yes, quite a turnout," Mitchell repeated as he looked around the room, nodding to a few acquaintances. He smiled down at her. "Now if Jerome could just open the tills, his worries would be over," he jested.

A waiter stopped and offered them champagne. Mitchell thanked him and picked up two flutes, handing one to Ashleigh.

"To better days." He smiled and tapped his glass against hers.

She forced another smile and took a sip of champagne. *If he refuses to take the ring tonight, I'll Federal Express it to him in the morning.*

It seemed as though Mitchell knew half of the guests, and he introduced her to one after another. Many of them were involved with the charity group sponsoring the event; others were business associates, and quite a number were resources who did business with the specialty store.

"Let's move on," he said, taking Ashleigh's arm. They edged slowly behind the other guests until at last they reached two long, tent-shaped carts in the center of Town and Country Sportswear.

David Jerome welcomed them warmly before turning his attention to Wainwright. Neither mentioned their mutual business crisis. Ashleigh stood aside slightly, feeling the subtle effects of her sip of champagne. She took a plate for the hors d'oeuvres that were exquisitely arranged on a bed of crushed ice around a magnificent ice sculpture of King Kong

and the Bentleys Royale tower. Reaching for a fork, she found herself
behind Eva and Zsa Zsa Gabor, who were talking rapidly in Hungarian
and popping tiny tidbits into their mouths at the same speed, oblivious
to anyone around them.

Then she heard a familiar voice call Mitchell's name.

Looking over her shoulder, she saw Adele Watson at her heels.

Ashleigh stepped out of the elevator on the second level. The music of
Les Brown rose to a crescendo above the din of the crowd. The dance
floor occupied the center of the area. A few feet away stood Viviana De
Mornay. At the sight of Ashleigh, she rushed over.

"Where have you been?" Viviana asked, quickly adding, "And
where's Mitchell?"

"Adele Watson spirited him away."

"What gall. My guess is that she's hedging her bets."

"Hedging her bets?" Ashleigh repeated.

"She called Philip while she was in New York. Surely you realize that
Mitchell and Philip are after the same publishing house in Atlanta." She
took in a rapid breath. "It's so exciting."

Ashleigh nodded, still puzzled.

Viviana clasped her hands together, then glanced around and leaned
toward Ashleigh. "Somehow Adele found out," she whispered, "and
she's determined to get her husband's book published one way or the
other. I don't know whether it's any good or not. He retired last year,
and it could be that she's just trying to launch the old boy into a new
career."

When the fashion coordinator dashed up to Viviana, in a panic over
the failure of a certain model to show up, Viviana rushed off with her,
leaving Ashleigh to wonder what was so special about the small publishing company in Atlanta.

She wandered toward the round tables of the Lingerie department,
where floral arrangements circled mink replicas of King Kong atop
hexagonal-shaped mirrors. Ashleigh wondered what Viviana thought of

these . . . then spotted Mitchell making his way toward her. As he wove his way through the small groups around the perimeter of the dance floor, she saw Conrad Taylor standing beside a statuesque young lady with long auburn hair. She wore a strapless black dress and large diamond earrings—no other jewelry. Ashleigh had to admit there was only one word to describe her: stunning.

Conrad woke with a foul taste in his mouth and a pounding headache. Slowly, he made his way across the Persian carpet and, with a sigh, reached out to open the drapes.

He'd never seen Ashleigh looking more beautiful than she had the night before. When Wainwright wasn't hovering over her, though, she'd seemed to drift away or surround herself with other Bentleys Royale executives. It seemed that she was never off duty. Not even at a black-tie dinner dance.

The drapes swung open, revealing a blue-gray sky. Conrad blinked as his eyes adjusted. The sun slanted across the empty terrace, and the shadows of the surrounding fence lengthened into a ladder of black bars stretching as far as he could see.

He slipped into his Burberry robe, pushed his feet into the well-worn leather slippers next to the bed, and headed for the bathroom, where he splashed cold water on his face and pulled a Tylenol bottle from the top shelf of his medicine cabinet. The new toothbrush he'd given Ashleigh was tucked inside its cardboard container, next to his drinking glass.

A jolt of envy had hit him squarely last night at the Salute to Hollywood party. It was hard enough imagining Ashleigh with Mitchell Wainwright, but actually seeing them together had been worse. Wainwright was intelligent and supposedly loaded with charm, but Conrad mistrusted him. It was painful to watch him beside Ashleigh, his arm around her shoulder. Conrad had not been able to keep his eyes off of them, and he was rewarded more than once when he saw Ashleigh pull away.

In the kitchen, he poured himself a tall glass of orange juice, which he carried along with his portable phone to the patio table in the southwest corner of the terrace, where he dialed Ashleigh's number.

Nicole, his companion for the evening, had commented that he seemed distracted. He couldn't deny it. But when she'd asked if she'd done anything to upset him, he had apologized, telling her that he had a lot on his mind. Then he'd forced himself to turn his attention to her for the rest of the evening, but his efforts were clearly halfhearted. Used to getting her own way, Nicole had stuck out her bottom lip like a petulant child when he took her straight home after the Bentleys Royale affair. Particularly after he told her he was too tired to come into her luxurious Westwood condo for a nightcap.

More money and free time than is good for her, he thought now.

Ashleigh's answering machine clicked on, jarring Conrad back to the present. He decided not to leave a message. He picked up his empty orange juice glass and portable phone while gazing toward Ashleigh's complex.

A black limousine pulled up in front of her entrance.

Probably Wainwright's. What's he doing there? He understood that she had been obligated to be with him the previous night, but why now?

An instant later, he saw Ashleigh emerge from the building. He wanted to call out to her, but it was out of the question. Even if his voice would carry that far, what would he say? If only she would look up in his direction . . .

He watched as she walked down the outdoor stairs to the street, toward the limo. A uniformed chauffeur opened the back door.

Conrad shook his head, stunned. He had believed Ashleigh when she'd confirmed what he already knew, that she was not marrying Wainwright. Apparently she had not ended it after all.

Ashleigh walked swiftly to the familiar limo, but stopped when she saw the uniformed man holding open the door.

"Donald's in bed with the flu, so I'm taking his place till he's up and about," said the muscular blond man in the ill-fitting gray uniform.

Ashleigh took his gloved hand and was about to slip into the backseat when the driver's voice echoed in her head. It was Mitchell's voice. She stopped abruptly, midway between the curb and the limo, and tottered on one heel. As she tried to regain her balance, she got a glimpse of the car's interior and saw that it was Jeff Bradley, not Mitchell, who occupied the rear seat.

Taking advantage of her imbalance, the uniformed man shoved her into the limo and shouted, "Keep hold of her till I get this crate in gear."

The door slammed shut. Ashleigh let out a shrill scream and pulled back, trying to free herself from Bradley's tenuous grasp as the limo lurched into motion.

As they rounded the corner and headed up The Toledo, the music blasting at an ear-piercing volume, Ashleigh sank her slim heel into Bradley's instep and grabbed the door handle, tugging it as hard as she could.

The driver slammed on the brakes, flinging her forward, then turned to face her with a cold threat: "It's locked, Princess. And if you have a single brain cell in that big-time-executive head of yours, you'll settle down before you get hurt." He lifted his hand to the rearview mirror. In it, Ashleigh saw a gun. "And I have no qualms about using it," he said with a sneer.

That voice . . . Suddenly she knew. "You're Anthony Wainwright," she said. It was a statement, not a question.

"Try Tony Lane. Here," he said, and handed the gun to Bradley. "If she gives you any more trouble, shut her up. It would be a shame to bloody the seats, but do whatever you have to do." Then he turned back to the wheel and eased the limo away from the curb.

Ashleigh sat in stunned silence. The gun that Bradley held awkwardly looked like something out of *The Godfather*. The clumsy attachment on the end was probably a silencer. She felt as if she were watching a scene from behind a plate-glass window. Her fear was muted by her curiosity, as if she'd been shot full of Novocain, but she knew that terror waited for her somewhere in the back of her mind. She shifted, pushed back her hair, and stared directly at Jeff Bradley, who tightened his grip on the gun and stiffened against the soft leather seat. With his free hand, Bradley rubbed the top of his instep, his eyes shifting from Ashleigh to Tony. His forehead was damp with perspiration.

"Please, Miss McDowell. I don't want to hurt you."

Glaring back at him, she said, "What do you want?"

Tony swung his head around. "All in good time," he shouted above the din of the music. Bradley covered his mouth and gave no response other than a loose, rattling cough. With sudden insight, Ashleigh met Tony's eyes in the rearview mirror. They were Mitchell's eyes. "It was you who left that message on my machine early this morning, wasn't it?"

"Could be."

As she sank back into the leather seat, a few of the pieces of the conundrum began to fall into place. The phone call to Palm Desert, the one to Billings, and the one again this morning. Mitchell had made none of them. Tony had.

But the latest call still mystified her. How could that have been Tony? How could he have known what to say? And why hadn't she heard the phone ring? No matter how tired she was, the phone always awakened her, and last night she hadn't switched off her bedroom phone, because she had been hoping Conrad might call. And when he didn't, she had thought of the gorgeous auburn-haired woman on his arm.

She certainly had not slept soundly last night, so it made no sense that she hadn't heard the phone. She had been perplexed when she noticed the message light blinking. Her first thought was that it came in while she was in the shower. But that thought was swiftly dashed when she'd heard the automatic date-stamp on her machine—Sunday 7:45 AM— long before she'd climbed out of bed this morning.

The heavy metal music boomed so loudly, her head ached and it was difficult to think. Covering her ears, she tried to remember every detail from the time Mitchell had dropped her off in this limousine at three in the morning.

Bradley leaned forward and shouted to Tony through the small opening where the glass had been slid back. "Turn that damned music down!"

Tony moved his head toward the rearview mirror again and saw Ashleigh's hands pressed tightly against her ears. "What's the matter? Hurting your delicate ears?"

"Come on, Tony. You know I can't stand that heavy metal crap . . ." Bradley glanced at Ashleigh. "Sorry." Then turning his attention back to Tony, he said, "Please turn it down, or at least get another tape."

It was obvious the two men were somewhat at odds. *How can I widen that gap to my advantage?* thought Ashleigh.

Tony swung the limo onto a bumpy roadway to the south of the main entrance to El Dorado Park. Reluctantly he turned down the volume as he wound along the road leading to a deserted baseball field. He picked up speed.

Ashleigh had dropped her hands from her ears and heard the spray of loose gravel as it pelted the fenders. *Where are we?* she wondered, feeling the rise of panic. *And how on earth am I going to escape from this unbelievable nightmare?*

Conrad ran inside his condo and grabbed a paper and pencil from beside the living room phone. He scrawled the numbers and letters of the license plate that he'd been able to make out as the limo had headed up The Toledo. Then he dialed 911.

The call was picked up instantly, and Conrad hurriedly gave the police officer a description of the black limousine with the darkened windows and the partial license plate number. He filled him in on Ashleigh's recent bouts with danger and informed him of the police reports by the three separate police departments.

He hung up. A surge of total impotence hit him. He had little confidence that LBPD would take immediate action. They had challenged how, from his seventh-floor condo, he could be so confident of what he had seen and what that implied. But his distance vision was excellent and he was sure of what had taken place. Considering the earlier threat and attempts on Ashleigh's life, which were on record, he reckoned the police would take action. But would it be soon enough?

Hell, he thought racing to his bedroom closet, *how many black limos can there be roaming the streets of Belmont Shore?*

By the time he'd thrown on some clothes and headed to the elevator, though, he realized that he had no idea where to begin. He stopped midstride and returned to the living room phone, dialing 411.

"I'd like the number for Mitchell Wainwright in Long Beach." With his pencil poised, he waited impatiently.

"I'm sorry, that number is unlisted," said the operator. "But I do have a number for Wainwright Enterprises."

As Conrad recorded the number, he asked, "Do you have a listing for a Dick Landes or Landes Investigations or . . ." *Oh, hell, what's the name of the company?*

Before he had a chance to shuffle through his memory, the operator said, "I have a Landes Agency on Ocean Boulevard in Long Beach."

Conrad jotted down the number and called it. The answering machine picked up on the third ring; its message included a number for his car phone. Conrad copied the number and heard the shrill beep. He spoke hurriedly, in fragmented sentences: "Conrad Taylor. Must talk to you ASAP. Ashleigh's been kidnapped. Black limo. Dark windows. Driver in a gray uniform. License number RSJ-1 something. Couldn't get the rest. Happened at about quarter after eleven. Call me at 562-438-0268."

He clicked off and dialed the other number.

The voice answered before the second ring. "Dick Landes."

"Son of a bitch," Landes said aloud. Then, marshaling his thoughts, he said, "How long ago?" He checked the time on the dashboard clock.

"Twenty minutes ago" came Conrad Taylor's voice through the phone. *Wainwright's not talking his way out of this one,* Landes thought.

"Where were you when this all took place, Mr. Taylor?" In Landes's opinion, the pieces didn't fit. "How in the blazes can you see all that from the seventh floor?"

"I saw it," came the angry retort in the space of a second.

"Okay, okay."

"And by the way, where are you? Why wasn't one of your agents there?" Conrad's voice wasn't loud, but it had a hard edge. "There was no sign of anyone outside Miss McDowell's condo, nor any sort of a tail on that limo."

Landes turned the key in the ignition. *Who does this joker think he is?* The thought passed quickly through his mind, and then suddenly it hit him: This Taylor fellow and he were on the same side; his anger should be aimed at Wainwright.

Ignoring the questions, he said, "Thanks for the call, Taylor. I'll get on it immediately."

Just as he was about to click off, Conrad's voice exploded. "Damn it, Landes. I know you work for Wainwright, but Ashleigh trusts you, and I can't just sit here on my ass!"

"Look, Taylor, nobody owns me." Landes shifted into gear and eased the car out into the light Sunday traffic on Long Beach Boulevard. "I'm my own man, and my priority is protecting Miss McDowell. I intend to do just that."

"My sentiments exactly," said Conrad, his tone conciliatory. "What are you going to do, and how can I help?"

"Look, Taylor, I've got to clear this line for an important call." Tucking the phone between his ear and shoulder, Landes swung onto the ramp for the 405 South.

"Just sit tight."

"No way! Let me be a part of whatever you have in mind."

Landes wavered, thinking at first, *What possible help could this white-collar, pencil-pushing executive be?* And yet, as he remembered, Taylor looked pretty damned fit: tall, broad-shouldered, no excess flab. As he raced down the 405, he decided he'd take the chance. *Better to have him in tow rather out gumming up the works on his own.* "Okay. But if you want to tag along, you've got to do exactly what I say—no debates."

Landes took a few moments to establish some ground rules, and they set up a meeting place. Then he severed the connection and made that important call: to Mitchell Wainwright.

The limo came to an abrupt stop at the edge of the empty baseball field. Tony cut the engine, then quickly alighted and opened the back door.

Ashleigh did not move. She looked beyond Tony to an empty station wagon a few yards away—a beige Volvo.

"Come on," he said gruffly. "We don't have all day."

"Where are you taking me?" Ashleigh's tone was commanding and icy, belying the fear that gripped her as she took in the smooth rope Tony held in his gloved hand.

Tony's smile stretched from his thin lips to his hazel eyes. "If you must know, we're taking you on a trip to the mountains." He looked past her to Bradley and gave a knowing wink. "You've been there before."

"Why— why are you doing this? What do you want?"

"Get out of the car. We'll talk later." Tony again looked past Ashleigh to Bradley and pointedly at the gun in his hand.

She slid out of the backseat and stood on the dirt-and-gravel pathway. Bradley followed. He held the gun loosely in one hand, the leather strap of Ashleigh's Fendi handbag wrapped around the wrist of the other.

Tony gestured toward the Volvo as he ran the rope slowly through his fingers. His eyes remained riveted on Ashleigh.

Wainwright heard the phone ring as he stepped out of the shower, and decided to let the answering machine handle it—though he compulsively stepped into the bedroom to listen to the message as he towel-dried himself.

"Wainwright? If you're there, pick up the goddamned telephone."

Recognizing the voice instantly, and thinking to himself, *Landes is becoming a real pain in the ass,* Wainwright seized the receiver. "What's going on?"

"Why don't *you* tell *me*?"

Wainwright frowned. "Tell you *what*?" he countered. Silence followed. "What in the fuck is on your mind, Dick?" Again there was nothing but silence. "Landes, are you still on the line?"

A simple "Yes" was Landes's only response.

In utter frustration, Wainwright asked, "Does it have anything to do with Ashleigh?"

"You know damned well it does."

"Cut the patronizing crap and spit it out. I have no idea what you're talking about!"

"Are you going to tell me that you didn't call this morning and ask me to meet you and Miss McDowell at Wainwright Motors?"

"What? We planned—" Wainwright broke off before he'd said too much. Running his fingers through his damp hair, he tried to rally his thoughts. "This is getting us nowhere. Just listen while I state the facts." Wainwright reached across the dresser to an open package of Camels. "Number one, I did not call you this morning. Number two—" He stopped short, as the thought grabbed him. "What about our code word?" *Code word,* he repeated in his head—*it sounds so damned juvenile.*

The voice that shot back was metallic and strained. "The words *Enterprises Wainwright* did precede the message."

In stunned silence, Wainwright sat on the edge of the king-size bed and tried to think coherently. Was Anthony impersonating him? But why? And, more troubling, how? Anthony couldn't have known the code word that he and Landes had worked out, nor could he have known that Wainwright had arranged to take Ashleigh to the car dealership this morning. Asking Landes to go to Wainwright Motors might have been a coincidence, but that didn't explain how he had gotten hold of the code word.

Perplexed, Wainwright shook his head, trying to clear it. More softly he said, "Tell me what you think is going on."

"First I'd like you to fill me in."

"What do you want to know?"

"Was Miss McDowell expecting you to pick her up this morning in the limo?"

Wainwright saw no harm in telling him the truth. "I planned to pick her up this morning, but not in the limo. We hadn't set a time. She was to call when she woke up. I figured around eleven thirty or twelve." He rose, and after grinding out a half-smoked Camel, asked, "What are you getting at?"

Landes sighed deeply. "It seems that Miss McDowell was expecting to be picked up, since she walked out of the condo lobby and straight to the limo, where she hesitated. When she was grabbed and shoved in, she screamed."

"Hold it! If you saw this happen, why didn't you stop it?"

"I didn't witness it."

"Then how do you know . . . ?"

"Conrad Taylor."

The name hit a nerve. "And he just stood back and watched?" Wainwright asked.

Landes explained the circumstances before delivering his one-two punch. "No way can I be second-guessing my own damned client. For me to do my job, there's got to be one hundred percent trust and disclosure."

Wainwright was shaken by this, but he'd be damned if he'd start groveling. Not wanting Landes to have the satisfaction of ending their contract, he quickly said, "I'll expect your final statement by the end of the week." *I'll handle Anthony myself.*

Then he hung up and began to zero in on where the leak could be and the action he must take. Finally it hit him. *Jesus, the limo must have been bugged.*

The old cliché *Stuck between a rock and a hard place* flashed through his mind. That's exactly where he was.

CHAPTER
105

Bradley eyed Tony warily. Where was the young man he was in love with? All he saw right now was a spoiled, mixed-up kid out for revenge. He'd tried to bring Tony to his senses, talk him out of this bizarre plan to abduct Ashleigh, but it was agree to this or forfeit his chance to check on Danielle again before their departure. Thank God, he'd managed to make a quick trip to Big Bear earlier in the week. Tony hadn't been blowing smoke up his ass—Danielle wasn't dead. So why was he playing fast and loose with Ashleigh's life? If Danielle had been dead, Tony might have figured he had nothing to lose . . . Bradley jettisoned that thought the instant it surfaced. *Tony is headstrong and reckless, but he's no murderer.* As unpleasant as this was, it was the better of the two rotten choices.

"Hands behind your back," Tony repeated.

Ashleigh did not respond. She took a step back, stopping within inches of the Volvo. She held her chin high and her posture erect, but her eyes mirrored her fear.

Bradley was vaguely aware of a feeling of heaviness in his arm. The gun hung loosely at his side like a limp appendage. It was all too much. This wasn't his scene, and he couldn't remain silent a moment longer. He stepped around Ashleigh in a wide curve and set a gentle hand on Tony's wrist. Their eyes met. "That won't be necessary. I've set the child locks on the door and I'll keep an eye on her."

"Like you did before?" Tony's eyes flashed with anger. "She might not be able to open the door, but from what I've seen, she can do some damage. I can't keep my eyes on the road and worry about what's going on behind me."

When Tony moved toward Ashleigh with the rope, she took another step backward and banged into the car. Regaining her balance, she said, "Is it alright if I take my coat off?"

"Go ahead." His eyes remained riveted on her while he unlocked the front door of the Volvo and wriggled out of the chauffeur's jacket; then he tossed it, along with the cap, into the car.

What Tony expected her to do, she couldn't imagine. But as she let the white cashmere coat slide down her arms, she saw herself slipping out of her coat in a wild flurry, knocking the thin, gangly Bradley off balance, and taking the gun. But that was for the movies. Instead, she simply folded her coat over her arm.

Tony opened the rear door of the station wagon, impatiently yanked the coat from her hand, and tossed it inside.

"Turn around," he ordered.

Noting Bradley's discomfort, Ashleigh turned to him and said, "I won't try to get away. I promise." When he did not respond, she knew that he'd gone as far as he dared on her behalf. Accepting this, she said earnestly, "If you must tie my hands, please tie them in front so I can balance myself."

Bradley nodded. "Can't see any harm in that."

Tony's face flushed. "By all means, let's make the princess comfortable."

Still, he gave in without protest, she noted, and she quickly held out her wrists before he changed his mind. She winced as Tony grabbed her hands roughly and wrapped the rope tightly around her right wrist.

He stopped abruptly, seizing her left hand. "Where's the rock?" His eyes blazed with undisguised malice.

It took her a moment to grasp what he meant. She was totally unprepared for the slap she received from the back of his hand. Her head reeled, and she would have lost her balance if Bradley hadn't reached out to steady her.

Both men spoke simultaneously.

"What did you do that for?"

"I said, *where's the diamond*?"

They stood silently challenging one another. Bradley was obviously out of his depth; the violence seemed to make him uncomfortable. Ashleigh raised her fingertips to wipe the blood from the left corner of her mouth and glanced back toward Tony. He looked as though he could demolish Bradley in a single blow.

A thought came to her: *Can I make Jeff Bradley my ally?*

She had to do something—and do it quickly.

Conrad parked his Jaguar in front of Tam's Stationers, off Pacific Coast Highway and Bellflower Boulevard. Moments later the black Ford Escort pulled in beside him.

Landes flung open the door, and Conrad slid into the passenger seat. Just a second later, Landes backed up and nosed the car onto Bellflower. "Limo's been located," he said, quickly taking charge. "Figured they'd abandon it as soon as they could."

"So, where do we begin?" Conrad asked anxiously.

Drumming his fingers on the steering wheel, Landes began to relate his plan. "First of all, I'm no longer on Wainwright's payroll."

"Think he's involved?"

"Not exactly, but he knows something. He's holding back." Landes shook his head slowly. "Dollars to doughnuts it's got something to do with his son."

The blinds were pulled down past the windowsill, with only a thin outline of late-morning light peeping around the edges. Pocino covered his head with the pillow to muffle the abrasive sound of the telephone. He wasn't on call, and he'd be damned if he'd cover for another store executive who wasn't answering his own damned phone.

When the second round of shrill sounds filled the room, he grabbed the bedside clock and opened one eye. 11:45. "Jesus Key-rist," he said aloud, and he reached for the phone, which tumbled from the nightstand to the floor. Leaning over the edge of the bed, he fumbled for the receiver, following the sounds of the muted voice issuing forth an unintelligible jumble.

"Pocino." His mouth felt like the inside of a kitty litter box, and the bedroom reeked of stale smoke and liquor.

"Hey, old buddy. It's time to rise and shine." The voice was that of Sergeant Flynn of the Rampart PD.

Pocino jolted himself awake, threw back the covers, and planted his feet firmly on the floor. *Flynn wouldn't call on a Sunday just to pass the time of day*. Blinking his eyes in rapid succession to clear the fog, he said, "What's up?"

"We may have located the body of your missing buyer."

Pocino sprang to his feet, questions tumbling out: "What? When? Where?"

"Slow down." Flynn laughed. "I'll be buggered if you don't sound like a frustrated schoolteacher outlining the contents of a paragraph."

Pocino failed to see the humor. He paced the floor, waiting for Flynn to get back on track.

"A body at the morgue is in need of ID." A pause. "And another rather interesting development. There was a break-in at Medley."

"A professional hit?"

"No, and if you're thinking about Sloane, forget it. This was a real amateur job. The offices and warehouse were trashed. Don't know what, if anything, was taken. Looks like pure vandalism."

The second Flynn clicked off, Pocino set the phone back on the nightstand and plodded purposefully across the prewar hardwood floor to pull up the blackout blinds. Taking a second or so to adjust to the light outside, he thought about strategy versus goddamned chain of command.

As usual, getting the job done took priority.

Directly behind Landes, Conrad clambered up the narrow stairway that terminated on the third and final level. They continued along the walkway to apartment 301.

Landes rang the bell and pounded on the door, to no avail. Then he tried one key after another from a small section of the extensive collection he carried on a silver ring with the circumference of a baseball.

As Conrad glanced across the bay to the Portofino and his own condo, he shook his head ruefully. *If only I'd known Wainwright's son lived so nearby.* If he had known—what? He wasn't sure what he would have done, but he would have done something.

"Got it," Landes said as the door swung open.

They stepped inside, and Conrad scanned the room. The typical bamboo-framed sofa, the Formica tables and countertops of furnished apartments, and a few odd dishes neatly piled beside the sink. Nothing struck him as particularly unusual.

Landes covered the apartment in the space of two minutes. "They're out of here," he hollered from the bedroom. "Check the trash in the kitchen while I check the bathroom."

Conrad glanced around the kitchen, and then he opened the door under the sink to find a pristine peach-colored trash container. Thank God there was only paper in it. He moved the dishes into the sink and dumped the trash can's contents onto the counter. His mind flashed back to the morning in Danielle's office and the Louis Vuitton bag that he'd emptied on her desk, with Ashleigh beside him, her eyes filled with alarm. He blinked and returned his concentration to the job at hand, fingering through the pile, stuffing the local throwaway newspapers and advertisements back into the container.

"Hey, take a look at this," Landes said as he walked into the kitchen.

Conrad frowned as he looked down at the torn scraps that Landes was attempting to piece together on the countertop beside his own diminished pile.

It was a birth certificate for Anthony Mitchell Wainwright, born June 10, 1962, at Long Beach Community Hospital.

"But why . . ."

Conrad didn't finish the question. The significance of the discarded birth certificate hit him an instant before Landes said, "Looks like our boy's leaving town with a new identity."

As Conrad returned the final scraps of paper to the container, something caught his eye: a red, white, and blue Swiss Air folder that had been torn almost in half. Landes picked it up, and deep ridges creased his forehead as he glanced at his watch. Conrad looked over his shoulder and saw that the ticket reservation was for January 20—six days earlier.

"Well, it seems they were booked under the names of Anderson and Kimble. Same day Wainwright made his covert trip from Atlanta and claimed the kid's car was stolen. So they missed that flight, but my bet is it's been rescheduled."

A long, shrill signal pierced the room, and Landes automatically reached for the pager attached to his belt.

Conrad stood wordlessly as Landes peered at the numbers in the small display window on the top side of the beeper, then turned on his heel and picked up the phone on the kitchen counter. He prayed Landes knew what he was doing and looked up at the kitchen clock. It had been close to an hour since he'd seen Ashleigh being pushed into the limo. He waited impatiently for Landes to get off the phone.

Finally, putting his hand over the mouthpiece, Landes said, "Wainwright's on the 605. He's alone, and it looks like he's headed out of town." Then he continued to talk into the phone. "Don't lose him. Tell me the moment you suspect that we might have miscalculated his destination, despite what Naomi Wainwright said. Keep the line clear. But first, call Ross Pocino"—he reeled off the phone number—"and ask him to check the destination of flight 765 on Monday the twentith at seven forty-five AM. Check on any reservation under the names of Anderson, Kimble, Bradley, Wainwright, and Lane. Then find out the names of any passengers who canceled, rescheduled, or just plain didn't show."

Conrad wondered why Landes was seeking Pocino's expertise rather than that of one of his own men. Was Pocino moonlighting? Right now he couldn't care less—all he wanted was for Ashleigh to be found and brought home safely.

Landes added briskly, "I'm fairly certain one or two passengers who were scheduled on that flight didn't make it. I also suspect they've rescheduled their flight—for today or possibly later this week. If you can't get the info, call Pocino and tell him to see if his buddy at Rampart can. And call my car phone as soon as there's something to report."

After asking for Billings's precise location, he hung up and said, "Come on, Taylor. You're in for one hell of a ride."

CHAPTER
108

Wainwright threw on a pair of well-worn jeans and a sweater and descended the stairs from his oceanfront residence to the beach below.

His mother disdainfully referred to his place as a bachelor's pad that she hoped he'd outgrow. Naomi Wainwright wasn't impressed with the spectacular panoramic view, which included the *Queen Mary*, the Spruce Goose, scenic oil islands, and a marvelous expanse of ocean. In fact, Naomi, a product of the school of old money—"Waste not, want not"—considered the condo a gauche extravagance. The Wainwright estate provided three self-contained living accommodations in three vast, separate wings, each with its own individual entrance and exit. She saw no reason why Mitchell chose to live elsewhere.

And yet at forty-nine, Wainwright couldn't imagine sharing the same address with his parents. It was ego, of course—that he couldn't deny. *But what is a man without a healthy ego?* he rationalized.

As usual, the fresh sea air did wonders for clearing his head. Feeling no compulsion to spin into action until he'd weighed all the options, he took long, decisive strides to the water's edge. He'd learned the hard way that uncalculated action could waste precious time. He didn't want to make a false move.

No doubt about it, though—Tony was involved with the recent ransacking of offices and the looting of the main warehouse of Medley Originals. He was also the one terrorizing Ashleigh.

Mysteries were rapidly beginning to unravel.

What in the hell have I done to trigger such vengeance? Kicking a slimy chunk of seaweed out of his path, Wainwright stopped abruptly at the edge of the deserted shoreline. "Hell, Anthony's not just *involved*. He's the goddamned mastermind," he said aloud.

Reviewing all that had occurred in the space of a two-week interval, Wainwright realized with a strange sense of pride that his son had to be some sort of a genius. Misguided and twisted, but a genius all the same. *And vengeful,* he added. Even before Landes called, Wainwright had known that the office damage was nothing but pure vengeance—that the perpetrator was someone who hated his guts.

That person was his son.

He jumped back as the water splashed up on his Nikes, and he tried to remember when Anthony's deviant behavior had first surfaced. Wainwright had always blamed Diana, a convenient scapegoat, but was that really fair? For the first time, he wondered if he were in any way responsible. *What did I do when Anthony reached out to me? I called him a fag, a queer, a closet queen, and threatened to cut him off without a penny.* He imagined Anthony crawling into bed with another male. The mere thought made him sick. But he had to admit that all this could've been avoided if he'd kept his opinions to himself. The threat of cutting Tony off without a dime could have been what pushed his son over the top.

A soft breeze swept across his face. He felt numb inside. It was time to take positive action.

Sprinting back across the wide stretch of dry sand toward his beachfront property, he knew what he had to do. *I've got to handle this myself. The Wainwright name and reputation are at stake.*

The Mercedes that Ashleigh had insisted he drive home the night before sat in the driveway, blocking the garage doors. With an indifferent shrug, he returned to his condo and made a quick call to his mother to confirm his suspicions. Then he went back into the bedroom and picked up a pair of heavy wool socks, boots, and his down-filled jacket. Tucking the socks inside the boots, he opened the top drawer of his nightstand and slipped the Rolex with a shattered crystal into his pocket. It had been the only shred of evidence the San Francisco P.I. that he'd hired after demanding Landes's final invoice had turned up when he sent him to Anthony's vacated apartment. He paused and stared into the drawer as Ashleigh's ring caught the light. Then he closed the drawer, picked up the keys to the Mercedes, and headed outside.

Diana had said that she hadn't seen Anthony, but she could be covering for him. *That would be so like her.* At least she'd told him that Anthony had gone to see his grandmother the night before.

When Wainwright had called his mother, she said that Anthony hadn't stayed more than fifteen minutes or so. He left the motor running in front of the Wainwright estate and took the stone stairs up to the entrance two at a time. The door swung open before he reached the top. Naomi stood just inside, in a purple velvet robe—with no makeup, and her hair far from its usual perfection.

"For God's sake, Mitchell, *please* tell me what's going on!" she cried.

The station wagon slid sideways and jerked to a stop. Ashleigh braced herself. For a split second, she felt disoriented. Her wrists were stiff and sore, and she had to raise both hands to see her watch. It was not quite two o'clock. *Three hours,* she thought. *Has anyone missed me yet?*

Tony twisted his head over his shoulder. "Don't worry," he snarled. "You have no pressing engagements for the next few days."

His words buzzed through her head. *The next few days . . . The next few days . . . What does he have in mind?*

If he's planning to kill me, what's he waiting for?

Tony jerked the keys from the ignition with a degree of drama and then pulled on a pair of high-topped boots. Springing from the front seat and planting his feet on the icy road, he called to Bradley, "Give me a hand!"

Bradley, who had changed into a pair of stylish après-ski boots at the start of their assent into the mountains, glanced at Ashleigh, then grabbed the lavender parka beside the luggage and slipped wordlessly out of the car. He depressed the lock on his door and pushed it closed the second his feet hit the ground.

The door banged shut. Ashleigh pressed herself into the corner of the backseat, wondering what to do next. Tony glared at her through the glass as he pulled on the door handle, checking the lock. She scanned the landscape behind him and saw a four-foot wall of hard-packed snow to her right, just inches from the car. *Does he actually think I'd be crazy enough to venture out in this deserted expanse of snow and ice in these high-heeled pumps?*

Ashleigh could hear the men's muffled voices from behind the station wagon; then a blast of cold air hit her in the back of the neck as they raised the hatch. She scrunched farther down in the seat and listened to them rummage in the area behind her.

"Here they are." It was Tony's voice, followed by the familiar metallic clang of tire chains. She wanted to turn to see exactly what they were doing, but with sudden clarity, she visualized the tiny transmitter concealed in her handbag and concentrated instead on getting her hands on it. Ironically, the transmitter that was given to her in case she was followed again, might now prove to be her salvation. The Fendi handbag was on the floor next to her feet. As the two men worked on the chains, she leaned as far forward as she could, but with her hands tied together, she couldn't quite reach the handbag. She slipped her foot through the strap and attempted to raise it with her ankle. The strap was too long.

Muffled voices came from the far side of the car; the men were just out of her line of vision. She twisted the handbag's strap around her ankle. Though she couldn't see what she was doing, she maneuvered her foot in circles until she judged she had just about taken care of the slack. Just as she shifted her weight to raise the handbag, the door sprang open.

Ross Pocino arrived at the Los Angeles County Morgue at precisely twelve forty-five PM, an hour after Flynn's call. He hadn't planned to be the one to identify the body. The thought of setting foot inside the morgue made him want to barf. *Shit,* he chastised himself, *I can do anything I set my mind to. I've seen plenty of dead bodies in my lifetime . . . What's one more?* But he knew things were different now. Besides, what else could he do? The police hadn't located Ted Norman, and everyone he called was, as police academy lingo had it, out of pocket.

As he walked down the sterile corridors of the city building, he felt a gnawing sensation in his gut. All he'd done since Flynn's call was talk to goddamned answering machines. He couldn't leave a straightforward message for Ashleigh McDowell, such as *Meet me at the morgue so you can identify Danielle's body.* The message he left was simply *Call me ASAP.* He left his home phone number as well as his beeper. He'd followed up with Conrad Taylor and then Mr. Jerome. He hadn't reached one single live voice. *Where is everybody?* he wondered in frustration.

Pausing outside the doorway to the medical examiner's workroom, he sucked in a deep breath. With a sudden flash of insight, he realized that he couldn't ask Ashleigh to make the identification. Not without knowing what he might find. After all, the buyer had been missing for the better part of two weeks.

Beads of perspiration covered his forehead. Withdrawing a stained handkerchief from the pocket of his cords, he mopped his brow. He fought to dispel the vision of a tiny form inside one of the huge freezer drawers, and wove his way to a wooden bench a few feet ahead. He hadn't visited the morgue since the day he came to identify the body of his four-year-old son.

The entry area, with two desks piled high with file folders, was deserted. "Anybody here?" he shouted.

"Come on in," came the reply.

Pocino forced himself forward through the open doorway.

The antiseptic stench almost took his breath away. The chief medical examiner, Larry Mancowitz, stood beside a high table on which the bloated body of a young woman was laid out. He was examining a deep abrasion above her right brow, just below the matted blond hairline. A white sheet was bunched up at the waist, leaving the upper and lower parts of the woman's pale, nude body exposed. Pocino's eyes were drawn to a long, bulging scar on her right cheek—an old wound. The certainty that they'd found Danielle Norman began to fade.

He peered around the room. About a yard from the body, on a straight-backed chair against the far wall, he spotted a pile of female clothing stacked high. On top were two stylish black boots. His mind flashed to the single burgundy shoe they'd found in the Bentley's Royale tower. Pocino sighed his relief. This was *not* the missing buyer.

CHAPTER
111

Landes pulled the black Escort into the center lane on the 605 Freeway. "What's on your mind, Taylor?"

"One hell of a lot of questions."

Landes smiled. The man was doing his level best to go along with the ground rules they'd established, but he was clearly ready to blow. Landes felt sorry for him. "Okay, fire away." He stuck his thumb under the shoulder strap of his seat belt and gave it a few meaningful tugs.

Conrad fastened his own belt. "For starters," he said, "why are we following Wainwright? Where is this destination you mentioned? And how in the hell can we catch up when he's got at least a thirty-minute lead?"

Interrupted by the squawk of the car phone, Landes inclined his head toward Conrad and said, "First, let me take care of this call."

He answered the phone and, a split second later, turned to Conrad and said, "It's Pocino." Then into the phone, he said, "Ross, I've got Conrad Taylor in the car. Mind if I put you on the speaker?"

"Hell, no," was the immediate response. "I can kill two birds with one stone." There was a perceptible pause before Pocino reeled off a second cliché. "About now I'd say the shit has hit the proverbial fan." Then he got to the point. "Flynn called this morning. That stolen van from Wainwright's outfit has turned up." He paused. "And so has a body."

Landes saw the color drain from Conrad Taylor's face.

"There's not much left of the van or its contents," Pocino went on to explain. "Haven't had a chance to check it out personally, but Flynn tells me they figure it was shoved over the edge." Then he added, "The jughead who engineered it left the gear in neutral. So it clearly was no accident."

"And the body? Is it identifiable?" Landes asked.

Conrad tensed and leaned toward the speaker.

"Just left the morgue about ten minutes ago. Couldn't get hold of Norman's husband, but it turns out I don't need him. It's not the Norman dame's body. No butterfly tattoo on the left shoulder blade, and she'd been wearing a pair of boots."

Conrad exhaled and sat back in his seat.

There was another pause. Landes thought he'd heard an uncharacteristic show of emotion in the burly security man's voice, but Pocino had recovered so quickly that he wasn't sure.

"But listen up. The van was clearly marked Medley Originals, and the woman's body was found inside one of those vendor trunks. Police figure the trunk was thrown free from the van before it burst into flames."

"Any witnesses?" asked Conrad.

"No, the van was discovered in the Hollywood foothills by a couple of Boy Scouts who were on an overnight. It seems they got up at the crack of dawn to do a little exploring on their own and got more than they bargained for. First they came across the scorched remains of the van. They found the body about a half hour later when they climbed back up to rejoin their group." Pocino gave a mirthless laugh. "The trunk had split open, giving off one hell of a potent odor. According to the scoutmaster, both boys got sick and hightailed it straight back to the campsite—didn't even care how much trouble they were in for taking off on their own."

"Pocino," Conrad asked, shifting in his seat, "does the coroner know how long the woman had been dead?"

"ME's still working on it . . ." His voice trailed off. "Another thing. Medley was trashed last night; sometime before midnight. Flynn said it was no Mafia hit—a real amateur job—and the building's still standing."

Landes broke in. "Forget about the Mafia. This has nothing to do with Sloane. And Sloane's no real Mafia man."

"You sure about that?" Conrad asked skeptically.

Landes cocked his head in Conrad's direction as he projected his voice into the speaker. "I've been on retainer for the Wainwrights far too long not to have a handle on Sloane. The tie the press hangs onto is his friendship with Frank Caroselli. But no one's been able to link Sloane with any actual Mafia dealings. I'm not saying he couldn't call in a favor from his friend, but so far he's clean. If not, Wainwright would be dead meat by now."

Further speculation on Wainwright and the mysterious body could wait. Landes's priority was getting to Ashleigh before it was too late. He brought Pocino up to date on the events of the morning.

As Landes eased the Escort into the far right lane, he said, "We're turning onto the 91 and should reach the Ontario Airport in about forty-five minutes. The Cessna should be warmed up and ready for takeoff." He glanced at the dashboard clock. "We'll probably be out of radio contact for about an hour, between fourteen hundred and fifteen hundred." He shot a look at Conrad, who was listening attentively and nodding his understanding.

"We bugged Mitchell Wainwright's oceanfront condo last night while he was at that shindig at Bentleys Royale.

"He called his mother less than half an hour ago. The gist of the conversation was that the keys to the family cabin in Big Bear are missing from the family estate—and that Wainwright was heading over there for the spare set. I've put Ray Billings on his tail."

It didn't take a genius to figure out why the Wainwright cabin at Big Bear was so popular right now—and it didn't have anything to do with the ski slopes.

CHAPTER
112

Wainwright tightened his grip on the wheel and steadily increased speed, all the while anticipating each bend and twist in the road. Searching his mind, he tried to remember when he'd first noticed the gray Nova on his tail.

A sign alerted him to the hairpin turn looming ahead. He tapped gently on the brake pedal and backed off the accelerator. The Mercedes fishtailed on the back side of the turn, near the edge of a steep drop. Beads of perspiration popped out on his forehead. Now on autopilot, he turned into the slide, then eased out of it just in time.

What in the hell am I doing? he thought. *I'm no Mario Andretti. Speeding on these icy roads is plain suicidal.*

He kept his eyes peeled for the first turnout on the winding mountain road. When it came into view, he slowly negotiated the car into it, jerked the transmission into park, and waited for signs of the Nova.

It had to be Landes or one of his agents. He wasn't sure what his game was, but if he'd taken more time to think things through, he could have predicted that Landes wouldn't stick his tail between his legs and conveniently disappear. It was his tenacity that had prompted Wainwright to put him on retainer in the first place. Now the man had turned into his worst nightmare.

Wainwright waited impatiently. As the Nova passed, he slipped the transmission into drive and eased out behind the small gray car. His thoughts turned to Ashleigh. Was it a lost cause? He had always been the one to end a relationship, and he didn't like the recent turn of events in their engagement. *With a world of beautiful and far more acquiescent women at my disposal, why . . . ?* He abandoned the thought. No point in kidding himself; he knew damned well why he'd pursued her—he'd loved the challenge—and why, now, her rejection bothered him so.

The unbidden words of his father thundered through his head: "Son, you always want what you can't have, and you value nothing once it's yours. You are destined to become a very unhappy man."

Wainwright concentrated on the Nova and the road ahead, trying to clear his mind and plan his next move. He had to find out what was going on. He wanted no outside interference.

Nearing the area where chains were required, he made his decision. He pressed the palm of his hand on the horn and signaled the driver of the car in front of him to pull over.

The car neither pulled over nor changed speed.

Frustrated and annoyed, he thought, *God, if it weren't for Ashleigh, I wouldn't be here.* Then, with sudden insight, he realized how much better off he would be had she been inside her precious white Thunderbird when that bomb went off. This thought chilled him to the bone.

CHAPTER
113

Less than a minute after the Cessna touched down at the small mountain airport, Dick Landes and Conrad Taylor alighted from the plane. Landes pointed to the silver Honda Civic Wagon with bulky snow tires beside the terminal.

Conrad was impressed with the planning and precision of Landes and his organization, and realized that this was no cheap operation. As he sprinted toward the car, it dawned on him that since Landes was no longer on Wainwright's payroll he must be absorbing the expense himself. But why? Could he afford it?

Once they were on the road, Conrad asked, "Is there a tracking receiver in this car?"

Landes nodded. "Relax. Miss McDowell's okay. I feel it . . . here." He gestured with his hand under his rib cage.

"I hope she isn't taking any unnecessary chances."

Frowning, and pulling a cigarette from his packet of Kents, Landes said, "Like trying on her own to find out what happened to Danielle Norman?" When the lighter popped out from the dash, he raised it to the cigarette and inhaled.

Conrad nodded. That was exactly what he was afraid of. He remembered her coming to Danielle's the night after her disappearance, armed with nothing more than a flashlight.

"Another thing," Landes said. "Considering that torch job on the van and the out-and-out destruction of the office and equipment at Medley Originals, I'd say that Mitchell Wainwright could be in as great a danger as Miss McDowell."

"I don't give a good goddamn about Wainwright!"

Landes gave an exaggerated shrug of his muscular shoulders. "Whoever pulled off that job, and it's a fairly good bet it was Wainwright's son, did it for nothing but pure vengeance. Why stop at taking out the fiancée when she's only the closest link to your true target?"

The sky was dark and ominous as the Volvo station wagon swung into the driveway. Ashleigh didn't know where they were, but there were double doors on the oversized garage and a semicircular path to the front door off to their left. The overcast sky gave the illusion of impending nightfall, but she knew that it couldn't be much past three o'clock.

The two-story structure looked like a small ski lodge. Lights glowed from the downstairs windows. *Is there anyone inside?* Ashleigh wondered. *Can they be holding Danielle here?*

The Volvo gave a final shudder as Tony turned off the ignition and turned to Bradley. "Wait here." Ashleigh was hit with another blast of cold air as he sprang from the car. "Jesus, it's freezing!" he shouted as he reached back into the car for his parka.

The door slammed shut. Ashleigh seized the opportunity to speak to Bradley—alone. "Would you please untie my hands, Jeff, so I can put my coat on?" She lifted her hands up to him.

Looking apologetic, he said, "Sorry, but I have to wait for Tony."

She started to object but stopped herself. "May I have my handbag at least?" As she spoke, she managed to shake the strap from her ankle.

He gave her an inquisitive look.

"My lips are terribly dry. I need my lipstick."

"Oh. Sure." He reached down and picked up the handbag.

As she started to reach for it, he smiled. "Let me help you." He opened the bag and held it out to her. Now there was no way she could rummage through without his eyes on her.. She reached into the open bag awkwardly with both hands. Her fingers immediately touched the lipstick in the side pocket where she knew that it would be, but she pretended not to find it. "I guess I'd better wait for better light."

Bradley nodded. He closed and snapped the outer flap of the bag and laid it on the seat between them.

Peering out the window, she saw Tony trudging through the knee-high snow, making a path to the door as he went. A cold shiver traveled down her arms as she glanced down at her own high-heeled pumps.

Bradley followed her gaze, then opened his door and hollered, "Need some help to clear the path?"

"Nope," Tony shouted back. "I'll go through the house and open the garage doors so you don't have to walk up." Pushing the cabin door open, he disappeared into the house. A few minutes later the garage door nearest the house rose, and Tony jumped back into the driver's seat and eased the Volvo inside.

As she swung her legs around to exit the car, Ashleigh heard the ringing of a telephone from somewhere within the house.

The phone continued to ring. Ignoring it, Bradley made a dash for the stairs, taking two at a time. He hadn't even removed his boots.

Strange, Ashleigh thought. She noticed that Tony's gaze was fixed on the French antique phone, but he made no move toward it. She was almost certain she heard the murmur of voices from upstairs, followed by the sound of a light tread across a hard surface. She strained to hear more. Who was upstairs with Jeff Bradley? *Can it be Danielle?* Her heart raced.

Tony grabbed her by the arm, rudely pulling her from her introspection, and shoved her over to the couch. "Make yourself comfortable," he said without a trace of sincerity.

Awkwardly lowering herself to the edge of the cushion, she found that a hundred questions surged through her mind. Was Danielle's one of the voices she heard faintly above them? Ashleigh was dying to ask but held her tongue, afraid that whatever she said might set Tony off. It could wait until Bradley returned.

Though afraid she might be tied up, she realized that Tony as well as she knew that there was nowhere to run. And even if there were cabins nearby, she was hardly dressed for any attempted escape. *Besides, I have to find out if Danielle is here. Has she been hurt? Is she even alive?*

At the roar of a motor approaching the cabin, Danielle bolted up against the padded back of the king-size bed. Then all was quiet. She adjusted the rope around her ankle, one that she'd tried in vain to untie, cutting into her ankle in the process. She had only enough rope to go a short distance—nearer to the window, in and out of the bathroom, to the small refrigerator beside the armchair.

She slipped off the bed and cautiously made her way to the window. Within seconds she heard the bang of the garage door. She leaned toward the window, trying to get closer. She could see straight out, but there was not enough slack in the rope to allow her to get close enough to the glass to peer down.

The click of a door lock echoed from below. She heard heavy footfalls pounding up the stairs and thundering down the hallway toward her cozy prison.

The door slid open to reveal Jeff Bradley, a worried expression on his pale features.

"Who else is here?" she asked. Danielle could discern at least two other voices as they drifted upstairs and down the corridor. Neither was very loud.

"Are you okay?" he asked, ignoring her question and staring down at her ankle. The bloody cloth he'd wrapped around it a few days before was loose and ragged.

"What do *you* think?" she asked sarcastically as she sank down into the armchair beside the large bed. *That bloody ankle is the least of my worries,* she thought.

Tomorrow would make two weeks since this nightmare began, but it felt like a lifetime. Two weeks since she had finally begun to suspect that they wanted access to those store computers, not just to save her job but to embezzle for their own benefit. Two weeks since she had decided she couldn't go through with it and everything had fallen apart. Still, she did not regret it. She had prevented Bradley and his malevolent partner from getting to the CRTs. Why the store computers were referred to by this name was a mystery, since as far as she knew a cathode-ray tube was just the monitor.

Bradley knelt down beside her and gently unwrapped her ankle. "It's Tony."

"And . . . ?"

"Ashleigh McD—"

"Ashleigh!" Danielle gasped. "Oh my God! Why? Is she alright? What did you tell her? What does she—"

"Calm down. She's unharmed. We didn't tell her anything."

"Then why is she here? Oh my God," she repeated, trying to hold back tears of frustration and fear. "Tony. He didn't hurt her—?"

"She's okay, Danielle. We didn't tell her anything, but I imagine she knows a hell of a lot, since we weren't able to get to the CRTs the night of your . . . accident."

"Accident?" She rolled her eyes.

As if she hadn't spoken, Bradley went on. "And if you actually left her a note—"

Tears spilled down her cheeks. There *was* a note, and Ashleigh would have read it by now. "But I didn't show up in New York," she said aloud, covering her face with both hands. "She must think everything I told her was a lie. She must think—" Suddenly it dawned on her: It was her fault Ashleigh was in danger. If she hadn't told Jeff and his sick friend about the note . . .

I've been so damn naïve. Everything she'd done had backfired. "I trusted you," she said through gulping sobs. "You told me that Bentleys Royale would not be harmed. You lied."

"I'm sorry, Danielle." Bradley's voice was tinged with desperation. "I never meant to hurt you. Tony reversed the stats. No one can prove that you had anything to do with any embezzlement."

"You know I'd never have given you those codes . . . Oh, what's the use? *You* know how I feel. It's Tony. I still don't understand how you could ever get involved with someone like him!"

Bradley reached out, gently taking her hands in his. "I know you don't. But it's not all Tony. It's me, too. But I never meant for anyone else to get hurt, especially you. Tony is young and impulsive and"—he was sure she'd figure it out sooner or later, so no harm in telling her now—"had the misfortune to be the only son of Mitchell Wainwright."

Danielle stared at him, feeling as if she had just been dropped out of the bedroom window into several feet of snow. It made no sense. *How could Tony Lane be the son of Mitchell Wainwright?*

". . . needed money to break away from this rat race," Bradley was saying.

"Stop!" she shouted. "He tried to kill me!"

"No, honest to God, Danielle, it was an accident." He switched to a defense of his young lover. "What you need to know is that the poor kid hasn't had it easy. He tried for years to get a single *attaboy* from his tight-ass dad, but he could never measure up." He gave an exasperated sigh. "Oh, never mind. What you need to know is, Tony reversed your overbought statistics. It will take Central Purchasing months to figure out what really happened—if in fact they ever do. Don't worry. Before we board the plane in the morning, we'll call the police to come to your rescue. Just play the role as an innocent victim. Nothing can be proved. You'll be in the clear."

Danielle did not really understand how she could end up seeming to be an innocent victim, considering the part she had played. What she did know was that she was not "in the clear" at all. Her days were numbered, and she had no idea how long she could appear to be symptom free. Already Ashleigh had noticed her rapid weight loss.

The thought that after she was gone she would be remembered as a liar and a thief was like a knife in her heart. But how could she possibly explain? More than anything, she dreaded looking bad in the eyes of Ashleigh, and as much as she loved and missed Gran, she was relieved that the wonderful woman who had given her so much would never know about this disappointment.

Jolted out of the past, she felt Bradley's icy fingers on her cheek. "I'm sorry" is all he said before pushing a cloth into her mouth and winding a wool scarf around her head. He paused, and for a moment looked confused. His eyes darted around the room, then rested on her pillows. He hastily dumped one out onto the bed, and used the pillowcase to tie her hands behind her.

"Why are you doing this?" she tried to ask, but the words were muffled by the cloth in her mouth. Then it came to her—she was no longer alone with the two men.

"Help will be here very soon," he assured her, hurrying out of the room.

She began to tremble. *What must Ashleigh think?* she asked herself again and again.

Her hands still tied in front of her, Ashleigh looked up when Bradley lumbered down the staircase, his pale, bony hand grasping the rail. He did not look at her but headed straight to the kitchen, his eyes on the floor; his mind was obviously elsewhere. When he failed to speak, she realized this was her chance. If Danielle was still alive, as they had told her, she must weigh each word and do nothing to endanger her.

"Jeff, do you think I could see Danielle?"

Once inside the cabin, Tony began to unwind. His plan had gone off without a hitch. *Nobody*, he gloated inwardly, *least of all Mitchell Wainwright the Turd, will suspect what I've done or where we've gone.* He hadn't even dared to let Jeff in on their final destination. He took a bit of newspaper from the stack beside the hearth and wadded it up, then struck a long-stemmed match from the container beside the andirons.

By this time tomorrow, we'll be long gone. He began adding dry pine logs to the fire. Ashleigh sat huddled in the corner of the sofa, her coat wrapped around her. Much of the hostility he'd felt toward her earlier had mellowed. *After all, she had the guts to dump the old man . . .*

"Hey, Tony, open the door," Bradley called from the kitchen.

Springing to his feet, Tony headed toward the swinging door that separated the kitchen from the dining room, and held it open while Bradley walked through with a tray of steaming mugs of hot chocolate and a large bowl of microwave popcorn, saying, "This should hold us until I can figure out something to rustle up for dinner."

Ashleigh shook her head, trying to come to terms with the cozy domestic ambiance. It was so out of whack with the present reality . . . But she did need something hot to drink. Shifting her position, she rotated her neck to relieve the tension as Bradley balanced the tray gingerly and knelt down beside the oak coffee table that stretched the length of the sofa.

Her wrists ached, and she was getting fed up with being treated like a piece of furniture. The friction between Bradley and Tony seemed to have dissipated since they'd arrived at the cabin, but she had no better idea of why she had been brought here than she did when their journey began.

To find out what had happened to Danielle and why these two had come after her, she knew, she must suppress her anger and choose her words carefully. Then somehow, without raising suspicion, she must find a way to activate the transmitter. Turning to Tony this time rather than Bradley, she asked, "Would you please take these ropes off my wrists?" She glanced at the three cups of chocolate that Bradley had placed on the coffee table.

Tony met her eyes but did not respond.

She waited impatiently while he just looked at her as if she weren't there. "I'd have to be crazy to try to escape in knee-high snow," she said.

The two men exchanged a glance, and Bradley gave Tony a playful wink. "As the lady says, there's no place to go."

Ashleigh held her wrists out to Tony. He untied the ropes, and they fell away one wrist at a time. She rubbed the areas where they'd dug into her skin. Remembering her grandmother's old adage *You catch more flies with honey than with vinegar,* she said, "Thank you."

Bradley sat on the floor beside the coffee table and handed her one of the cups of hot chocolate while Tony plunked himself into a large overstuffed armchair. Bradley twisted around to hand Tony his cup and to offer him some popcorn, then he scooted closer and leaned his back against the base of the armchair.

For a moment, Ashleigh's mind rested. She sat silently, curiously unafraid. She wrapped her hands around the mug and enjoyed the warmth that radiated from the cup. But after the first two sips, she broke the silence. "Now, will you please tell me why I'm here?" Her voice wavered, betraying the calm she'd hoped to project.

"You don't know?" Tony took the lead, but strangely enough there was no trace of the cryptic bites of sarcasm that had peppered his every phrase earlier.

"No, I don't." Suddenly the strain of the past two weeks overwhelmed her, and she found it hard to speak. No words came. No sentences formed. At last she blurted out, "What have you done to Danielle?"

"What have you done with the note she left with you?" Tony responded.

"Note?" She looked from Tony to Bradley and back again. "What note?" She noticed a silent communication passing between them and, seeing their relief, knew they believed her.

Her mind shifted to the tower and the butterfly pendant and the single burgundy pump. She had no more patience for subtlety. If one of the voices she heard from upstairs was Danielle's, why would they . . . ? She fell silent, a dark cloud passing before her eyes. "Did you hurt her? Did you . . . kill her?"

The two men spoke at once: "Who says we harmed a single hair on her head?" "It was an accident."

Tony gave Bradley a crushing glare.

Bradley began coughing convulsively, and Tony's anger dissipated as swiftly as it had appeared. "Relax." He placed his hands on Bradley's shoulders and kneaded his thumbs into the base of his neck. "It's okay. By this time tomorrow we'll be gone."

Bradley's words still hammered in Ashleigh's head. She shakily set her cup on the coffee table and asked, "What do you mean, 'it was an accident'?"

Bradley looked to Tony, who gave him an indifferent shrug. His eyes rested for a moment on the crackling wood in the fireplace, and then he picked up a handful of popcorn and began to tell what promised to be a long story.

CHAPTER
116

The private road, a winding quarter-mile path leading to the cabin, was covered in a thin layer of slush and ice. The snow-laden oak trees, their branches bending and touching, formed a tunnel and blocked the faint light of the overcast sky. Switching on his headlights, Wainwright spotted indentations of tire chain tracks and dropped into second gear.

Things were going according to plan. There was no evidence of the gray Nova since the Running Springs turnoff.

When he rounded the final curve to the cabin, he doused the headlights and proceeded slowly. Shifting into neutral, he glided the Mercedes to a stop and turned his wheels into a snowbank alongside the single-car path. Ten yards from the cabin, his small car blocked the pathway. There was no room for another vehicle to pass from either direction.

Conrad saw the large hunk of rubber on the road dead ahead, but before he could issue a warning the Honda hit it dead on. There was no way they could have avoided it. Now gripping the wheel, Landes skillfully avoided jerking the car and sending it into a skid. Slowly, he maneuvered the Honda to a stop beside a wall of snow at the side of the lonely mountain road.

Conrad quickly assessed the situation. Neither he nor Landes was dressed for snow. "How far are we from the Wainwright place?" he asked.

"About twenty minutes," Landes said, "but if we don't get there before dark, I understand it's damn near impossible to find the private access road." He hastily punched numbers into the car phone.

Conrad looked out through the windshield at the rapidly darkening sky, then to the dashboard clock. It was four twenty-five.

Landes listened, then punched in another set of numbers and hung up.

"What next?" Conrad asked. His gut instinct told him it was time to bring in the police. And if Landes didn't have an immediate solution, that was what he intended to do.

The phone sounded, and Landes punched the speaker button on the first ring. "Where are you?"

After a brief pause, the voice answered, "At the Boo Bear's Den in Big Bear." It was Ray Billings, who had been assigned to follow Mitchell Wainwright. He'd reported in to Landes about half an hour before, when he'd lost Wainwright's Mercedes and was forced to abort the tail.

"Get in your car and head toward Snow Summit," Landes instructed. "These damned hills . . . We've had a minor accident. If you stay on the main road and keep your eyes peeled, you can't miss us. We're in a silver Honda Civic Wagon. I'll call Triple A to have it towed into town." Landes added, "If they get here first, we'll ride together. If not, you'll need to wait with the car."

No sooner had he replaced the receiver than the phone rang again. "Landes."

"I checked with Swiss Air like your man Billings asked me to, and I've hit pay dirt." There was no mistaking Pocino's deep, husky voice through the speaker, nor his unique phrases. "You better have your shit together, because our boys are booked on Swiss Air. Departing tomorrow at 6:05 AM, flight 567—direct to Zurich—check-in time is two hours before takeoff. The tickets are registered in the names of Kimble and Anderson."

Conrad made a speedy calculation. "That means they'll head for LAX before midnight."

Jeff locked his arms around his bent legs, his profile pale in the firelight. As he began to tell Ashleigh about their night on the rooftop, Tony saw how thin and drawn he appeared. There was as little color in his face as in the ecru shirt collar just visible above his Armani sweater.

Tony glanced over his shoulder at the clock on the mantel, frowned, and wondered if it had stopped. But when he pushed up the sleeve of his sweatshirt to check his Timex watch, he realized that it was correct. *Damn.* He wouldn't be comfortable until they were in the air. And he'd feel a lot better once he could share the new travel arrangements with Jeff, but that wouldn't be until they were on their own and en route to the airport.

"I don't understand," Ashleigh said. "Why would Danielle go up to the rooftop?"

Bradley started to reply, but his words came out in a wheeze. *This is taking too much out of him,* thought Tony. He sat down on the floor in front of the fireplace, possessively placing a hand on Jeff's knee. Jeff coughed convulsively, and Tony put his arm around him. "You really need to get this off your chest? You're not in such hot shape, Jeff. Let me take over.

"We needed access to the CRTs, and we'd planned to stay up on the sixth floor until the store was locked up. We had everything down to the last detail, but all of a sudden Jiminy Cricket must have whispered in Danielle's ear, and she gave us some bullshit about not being—"

"Hold on, Tony," Jeff interrupted. "Danielle had just figured out that our scheme involved more than paper losses for Bentleys Royale, and—"

"No one is that goddamned naïve!" Tony's voice rose, drowning out Jeff's explanation.

Jeff shrugged, and Ashleigh heard him mutter under his breath, "Danielle was."

Tony ignored his partner and returned to the story, seeming compelled now to tell it. "Anyway, to cut to the chase, no way could we let her back out. Not at that point. But I didn't touch her. I just . . . She came up to the rooftop storage and display area to deliver her bombshell. I took hold of her arm—just so she wouldn't leave before I had a chance to talk some sense into her. But she pulled back, and that caused her to trip. She hit her head on the corner of the metal fuse box. She has a nasty gash on her forehead, but it's not serious."

"That's the God's honest truth, Ashleigh," Jeff chimed in.

Ashleigh sprang from the couch and started for the stairs, calling out Danielle's name, but before she'd taken more than a couple of steps, Tony grabbed her arm and spun her around. "Not so fast. Your precious little buyer friend is a-okay. And she's got nowhere to go."

Her stomach doing flip-flops, Ashleigh attempted to wrench her arm from Tony's iron grip. It was no use. The fingers of his large callused hand dug into her flesh, and the malevolent expression on his tanned face turned her nerves to liquid.

Danielle had been missing for two weeks. Had she been here the entire time? Had they given her anything to eat or drink? With a voice that belied her fear, she demanded, "Take me to see Danielle now. I need—"

"Whoa," he said, pulling her back to the sofa and giving her a none-too-gentle shove. "You're not in charge here. Your double-crossing buyer is okay, like I said. Now sit back down if you want to hear more."

CHAPTER
118

Ashleigh scrunched into a more comfortable position in the corner of the leather sofa and tried to concentrate on Tony's words, tried to understand the scheme as he laid it out. But she could not believe what he was telling her. He used Danielle's name, but the person he described was not the Danielle she knew so well.

Her thoughts raced ahead, and a more terrifying thought invaded her mind. *Does he plan to tell me everything and then kill us both?* She discarded that thought almost as quickly as it came. *If that was his plan Danielle would already be dead—and so would I.* She'd seen enough movies and read enough novels to figure out their plan. They were fleeing the country and had nothing to lose.

She could no longer listen; she could take no more of this. If Danielle had been a part of the extortion plan Tony laid out, she knew in her heart that it was not for personal gain. Maybe Danielle had been duped into believing it was her only way to save her job. The thought gave her no comfort.

The last ten yards seemed more like a mile as Wainwright slogged his way through the virgin snow. In front of the garage, beside fresh tire tracks, he stopped to catch his breath. Cold, damp snow filled his boots, and his feet were nearly frozen. He balanced himself precariously against the garage door, emptying one boot, then the other. Then he set one foot after the other in the deep tracks leading to the cabin door.

Tiptoeing onto the porch under the shelter of the second-story balcony, Wainwright kept his head low. When he reached the side window, he cautiously peered over the sill.

Ashleigh was right in front of him. She was very much alive. Her pumps lay on the floor beside the sofa, where she sat with her legs folded under her. Though he couldn't see Anthony, it didn't take a genius to figure out that he had to be just a few feet away, probably by the fire. He hoped to God Anthony's pansy friend had not come along, despite knowing that he probably was in there too.

This was hardly the scene he'd envisioned on his trek up to the mountain cabin. An inexplicable anger welled inside him. The scenario that he'd worked out during the past two hours faded from his mind. Instead, he plunged his key into the lock, shoved the door open, and stepped inside.

Landes ground the cigarette butt into the car ashtray and checked the dashboard clock. "Less than ten minutes since our call, and the roads are slick hell. Black ice everywhere.

"This mountain scenario is baffling," he continued thoughtfully. "Unless—"

Conrad looked up. "Unless what?" he repeated, his voice rising. "Unless what?"

"Well, we've been stumped on the motive so far."

Conrad gave an impatient nod.

"Assume these crimes are related." Landes ran his tongue across his lips. "Let's try another path. Number one, a clever extortion plan is thwarted at Bentleys Royale, and a buyer disappears. Number two, the perpetrator has a vendetta against his father, and Ashleigh is the bait to lure him to the cabin before they flee. Wainwright could very well be the real target."

"How do the attempts on Ashleigh's life fit in?"

Landes sighed. "And that infamous note. Those are the chinks in the logic of my theory."

"Maybe they're not even leaving from LAX."

"So this location may not so far-fetched?" Landes reached in his pocket for the package of Kents. "Thought of that—a definite possibility. Yet with new identities, and probably disguises to go along with them, our boys are probably feeling pretty safe."

Conrad checked his watch again. Less than five minutes had passed. Even that was too long. *God, I've never felt so impotent.*

Wainwright burst into the living room. The door banged into the adjoining wall with a force that rattled all the nutcrackers on the ledge above the fireplace mantel. His eyes locked with Ashleigh's. He was about to cross the room toward her but stopped short when he saw his son with an arm around a thin, pale man. *He has to be more than ten years Anthony's senior,* thought Wainwright. His heart thudded to the pit of his stomach. *Or . . . could it be AIDS?* All the supportive words he'd mentally prepared for his only son died on his tongue.

"Mitchell!" Ashleigh cried out, and she leaped to her feet.

"Sit down," Tony commanded. Then he turned to his father with clenched fists. "What are you doing here?" His voice was strong and he held his ground, but Ashleigh noted a flicker of fear in his stone-cold eyes. Her breath caught as she witnessed the silent contempt on the faces of both the father and the son.

The muscles in Mitchell's jaw tightened when his steely glare settled on Bradley. "You have exactly five minutes to get your things together and haul your ass out of here."

Bradley blanched but stood his ground.

Tony glanced around fleetingly, his eyes falling to the gun on the mantel. An instant later it was in his hand, pointed directly at his father. "You're through giving orders." He steadied the barrel with the awkward attachment. "You're not in control! Not anymore."

With a look of incredulity, Mitchell stared back at his son. Then he stepped forward, his hand extended. "Don't be an ass. Give me that thing before you hurt someone."

There were now less than three yards between them. "Take one more step and I'll shoot." Tony released the safety catch.

"Mitchell, stop. He means it," Ashleigh warned.

Mitchell continued his forward movement, his hand still outstretched. "Relax. Mama's boy isn't going to shoot."

Bradley froze, but his eyes darted from the gun in Tony's hand to Mitchell and back again to his lover. "Tony, don't. For God's sake, put that thing down."

As he reached for Tony's arm, a muffled crack pierced the air, like the cork popping from a bottle of champagne.

Ashleigh felt as though she were watching a scene played in slow motion. Mitchell was still on his feet, his hand extended. Slowly, he moved the outstretched hand to his shoulder. Blood seeped between his fingers.

"Didn't think . . . you . . . had the guts." Mitchell wove unsteadily, and Ashleigh went to him.

Tony made no move. Bradley lowered himself into the armchair.

"I'm okay," Mitchell said, half walking and half staggering the few steps to the couch. Ashleigh held on to his arm, and he sank down on the heavily padded cushions.

When she turned back to Tony, he was perched on the arm of the overstuffed chair beside Bradley, whispering something in his ear.

"Tony," she said, "your father needs a doctor."

A deafening crash from below snapped Danielle from her drowsy half sleep. With her hands now tied behind her back, she struggled to ease herself off the bed, wanting desperately to see what was going on, wishing she didn't have the cloth in her mouth that prevented her from calling out.

Awkwardly picking up the loose rope across the hardwood floor, she tiptoed to the door in her stocking feet, eased it open, and stepped onto the threshold—but could go no farther. The banister overlooking the living room was a good six yards from her doorway. The rope, which was tied securely around the pedestal of the sink in the master bath, kept her from gaining a view beyond the long hallway between the master and guest bedrooms. An army of angry voices floated down the corridor, but she was unable to make out the words.

She softly closed the door with her shoulder and retreated to the bedside armchair, where she tried to figure out what she would say to Ashleigh when they came face-to-face. If *we come face-to-face.* Now that Jeff Bradley was under Tony's spell, she could not count on him to protect her. And how about Ashleigh? Danielle traveled the entire gamut of emotions: relief . . . fear . . . embarrassment . . . shame. Unmitigated shame. *Oh my God.*

Question after question tumbled through her aching head. *What have I done? How can I explain that I didn't know what Jeff and that horrible Tony were up to?* She was still having trouble believing that Jeff had deceived her. *How could he be involved with someone like Tony Lane? How could this plan to save my job have gone so wrong? When did the scheme to manipulate the figures turn into a scheme to steal money— to actually* steal money *from Bentleys Royale?* She tried to stretch her memory, to remember what had happened after she told Jeff and his rogue partner that she could not go through with their plan. She had no memory of leaving the rooftop that night. This afternoon when Jeff had talked about that night and what had happened, he'd called it an accident. But she felt sure that wasn't the case, and she had wanted to press him then. But as her thoughts turned to Ashleigh, her mind shut down.

In the middle of Danielle's attempt to pull her thoughts together, a shot rang out. Her heart leaped, and for a moment she nearly forgot to breathe.

CHAPTER
121

Tony stared at his father—the target of his anger, his unrelenting vengeance. "You'll live," he said. "Wouldn't have it any other way." Far from worrying about his father's injury, he only wondered what else he might have done to bring him down. *If only I'd had more time, I could have bankrupted the egotistical prick . . . But at least I've managed to tarnish the sacred name of Wainwright. Jeff and I will be out of reach, and he'll have a lot of explaining to do.*

Wainwright, his head cupped in his hands, elbows on his knees, looked up at him. "Why do you hate me so much?" he croaked.

"I could write a list from here to kingdom come and still not cover it all." There was a tremor in his petulant voice. "You demanded I play football, then didn't even come to my games."

"What?" Wainwright struggled to get to his feet, blood seeping down the front of his shirt onto the carpet.

Ashleigh put her hand on his uninjured shoulder and pushed gently. He shrugged away but remained seated, staring at Tony.

"Are you telling me that because I missed a few lousy games when you were a kid, you turn into a fag and try to ruin me?"

"Shit, how fucking stupid can you be?" Tony glared at his father. "Forget it. Chalk that one up to your goddamned ignorance. You may be hot shit when it comes to stealing corporations, but you're just a miserable SOB. Nothing I think or say or do has ever meant a damn to you."

Trying to stand, Wainwright shoved his hand in the pocket of his trousers. "You were given every opportunity, but your ever-loving mother turned you into nothing but a spoiled, pampered wimp. While I was out busting my butt to provide for you . . ." He was almost on his feet now, his face contorted with pain, and he clutched his wound, struggling to catch his breath. From his pocket he pulled out Tony's discarded Rolex.

Ashleigh, her cheeks hot with anger, could take no more. "Stop, both of you! Just stop!" The blood had now soaked through Mitchell's shirt, somewhere between his shoulder and his heart. She couldn't tell how close Tony had come to fatally shooting his father.

She bent over Mitchell, whose breathing was ragged. Grabbing a loose pillow from the corner of the couch, she said, "Lie down. We have to try to stop this bleeding." When nobody moved, she repeated more firmly, "Please lie down."

Mitchell leaned back on the pillow she had fluffed up.

She struggled to lift his legs up onto the couch, but he resisted, saying, "Stop fussing. Just get me some water."

"I'll get it." Bradley headed to the kitchen, away from the crackling tension.

Mitchell did not lie down, but his expression changed visibly as he looked at his son. "I've heard your ingenious computer scam has thrown Bentleys Royale in a tailspin."

"Nothing like it could have been," Tony scoffed. "Would've been a whopper of a payday if that buyer hadn't gotten cold feet." Bitterness peppered his tone.

"Where have you got Danielle Norman?" Wainwright asked.

Tony just gave a thin, insincere smile.

Ashleigh wanted to wipe that smug look off his face, but she held herself in check. Danielle was here somewhere—she just knew it.

"How did you expect to be paid?" he asked.

He eyed her with uncertainty, but ego prevailed. "If we'd made it to the CRTs that night, La Scalla purchase orders would have gone straight into our offshore account and the legit purchases would have been erased before hard copies were generated. By wiping out those purchases, we would've made sure the bell didn't go off so soon."

"You mean to say there'd have been no record of purchase from the legitimate vendors, just those of your phony one?" Settling into the couch, Mitchell grimaced, but he went on. "What would happen when the merchandise hit the warehouse?"

Tony grinned. "Initially the paperwork would be issued, and then I'd wipe out the computer input at the DC."

"Initially?"

"Shit, you don't think this plan could have a long run, do you? A month at most, before Medley and the other resources would start screaming for their money. By then, we'd have hit the road with at least two and a half mil in our Swiss account. We've got to take care of these two and split." Tony shouted to Bradley. "Forget those damned books!"

Bradley looked up from the pile of magazines he was straightening into a diagonal line—about a three-inch overlap, so the title of each was in view. "What?" He glanced first at his wristwatch, then at the mantel clock. "What's the rush?"

Tony raised his finger to his lips and said, "There's a change in plans." Before his partner could object, he added, "Trust me. I'll explain later."

Ashleigh slowly rose to her feet. "Please, Tony, call a doctor. Look . . . he's losing blood." She looked across to Mitchell, who was just beginning to stir.

Ignoring her, Tony picked up the rope beside the table and said to Bradley, "This will have to suffice for the two of them."

Ashleigh glanced at the gun in Tony's hand. Tony followed her gaze. "Don't even think about it," he said, and leveled the barrel directly at her head. "Wake up the old man."

"Why?" She saw the color rise from Tony's neck into his face. Through clenched teeth, he replied, "You're going upstairs. Both of you."

The peril of their situation—the prospect of being bound and left in this remote location—hit a nerve. Facing Tony, she said, "Your father can't be moved."

It was Bradley who answered. "The heaters are upstairs. It'll be too cold down here when that fire dies."

Tony waved the gun, gesturing again for her to get Mitchell to his feet. With a derisive grin, he said, "You speak softer than my father, lady, but your bent for control comes through loud and clear." He paused. "Well, this is one situation where *you're not in charge.*"

With Bradley at one elbow and Ashleigh at the other, Mitchell came to his feet, slowly gaining his balance. A moment later, with an unexpected show of strength, he jerked his arm from Bradley's grasp.

CHAPTER
122

"You win, Taylor. We have no choice. I'll make the call to the local police."
Landes pulled the Honda to a stop at the side of the road, snapped on the overhead light, and began fingering through his pocket notebook.

Conrad nodded. They must have passed the private road to Wainwright's before making the U-turn. *They hadn't a prayer of finding it in the dark. Not with their sketchy directions.*

Midway through punching in the number for police assistance, Landes hesitated. "Listen," he said, as he leaned down to adjust a small black instrument that was crackling with static. "That's it . . . That's what we've been waiting for."

Perplexed, Conrad stared at the squawking instrument and flashing red buttons as Landes cupped his hand to his ear and leaned toward the speaker. Then he heard a steady bleep.

The transmitter? Thank God!

"There's a light-emitting diode here," Landes said, pointing down to the panel of glowing lights."The more lights, the nearer we are." More lights blinked on.

Just inside the bedroom door, Bradley flipped on the heater.

They're going to leave us here, Ashleigh thought. *Without food, water . . . Without knowing where Danielle is . . .* Agitation overcoming fear, she cried out, "Where is Danielle? I need to see her."

"She's asleep in the master bedroom."

"Danielle!" Ashleigh hollered at the top of her lungs, without a second thought for her own safety. "Danielle! Are you here? Are you alright?"

Tony slammed the palm of his hand down on the dresser. "Enough! That double-crossing bitch is alive and well—relatively. If you want to keep it that way, stop with the demands and do what you're told. You—on the bed!" He gestured to Wainwright with the gun.

"Cut . . . the . . . theatrics." Wainwright sat on the edge of the bed, his hands together in front of him. His breathing was labored. "If this . . . is what it . . . takes to . . . make you . . . feel like . . . a man . . . be my . . . guest."

"Mitchell, don't," Ashleigh said, her voice just above a whisper. But it was too late. Tony smacked Wainwright across the face with the back of his hand—the one holding the gun.

As Wainwright wiped the blood from his lip, Tony thrust the gun out toward Bradley, whose eyes were riveted on Tony's father.

"Oh, sweet Jesus," Bradley said. "Was that necessary?" Tony's look silenced his protest, and Bradley took the gun.

Wainwright wiped the corner of his mouth again and slowly began to rise. Tony pushed him back down, and with little effort lifted his father's legs up onto the bed.

Ashleigh watched in horror as Tony bound Wainwright spread-eagled to the outer bars of the brass bed. "Please stop. The wound . . . It's bleeding . . . You're hurting him."

"Isn't that just too bad?" Tony gazed up at Ashleigh and then back at his father. "He's tough. The indestructible Wainwright." He paused a beat. "Isn't that right?" Then, turning to Ashleigh, he said, "You're next," and gestured to the straight-backed chair in the corner.

"No," Bradley said. "Not her. Just lock the bedroom door."

"No way," Tony replied. Their eyes locked in a challenge.

Ashleigh stood frozen in place. She was no longer merely afraid. She was terrified.

Finally Tony continued, "It's too risky. We'll call the police before takeoff and tell them about the cabin."

Bradley handed Tony the gun. "Fine. I'll take care of it." He approached her with the rope in his hand.

"Make damn sure you tie that tight, or I'll take over."

Bradley asked her to put her arms around the back of the chair, and Ashleigh did not hesitate. But he did not pull the rope tight enough to cut into her skin as Tony had earlier. Though Bradley stuffed something in her mouth, the strip that went around her head was loose compared to the one Tony had stretched around Mitchell's head.

Finally the two kidnappers left, locking the bedroom door behind them. In the utter silence that surrounded her, Ashleigh perceived every sound as if it were magnified. She heard the garage door open and the roar of a motor, followed by uninterrupted stillness for what seemed like hours. Within moments, however, she heard the muffled sound of a steady tapping on the wall.

"Have I got a surprise for you!" Tony's voice was filled with boyish ela-tion as he slipped behind the wheel of the Volvo.

While uneasy about what had transpired, Bradley wasn't bothered that much about leaving Wainwright tied up in the locked bedroom. The gunshot wound wasn't fatal, and besides, Mitchell Wainwright was a judgmental pain in the ass. But Ashleigh McDowell was different. He was deeply ashamed of his part in the vengeful kidnapping.

"Hey, where are you?" Tony said as he gently patted Bradley's knee.

"Sorry, just thinking."

Impatiently, Tony said, "Stop worrying. You can call the police from—" He slammed on the brakes. "Shit. Chalk one more up for the old man."

They had just backed out of the driveway and turned to descend the narrow road when they saw a white Mercedes, caught in the reflec-tion of their headlights, glaring back at them. The car was completely blocking the road.

Tony took his foot off the brake and guided the station wagon to within a few feet of the Mercedes. Then he hopped out of the car, opened the driver-side door of the luxury car, and put it in neutral.

In less than ten minutes, they had slid the car far enough to clear the way, pushing it toward the steep side of the mountain road, where it got caught up in the scattered, snow-covered shrubbery just a few feet down. "We're on our way!" shouted Tony, again sounding like a gleeful schoolboy.

Bradley turned up the car heater and asked, "Okay, so what's your surprise?"

Tony smiled broadly, the strain of the past weeks behind him. "Number one, we're not going to LAX. And number two, we're not flying to Switzerland."

Landes made a second U-turn on the main road. There was no traffic heading in their direction, and coming toward them was only one vehicle—a Volvo station wagon.

The steady beep from the transmitter grew louder. Landes slowed the car. Conrad pointed to a partially concealed pathway just beyond a stop sign. "Turn here." He remembered that they had passed this spot less than ten minutes before.

As they neared the top of the steep private road, Landes switched off the headlights. In the pitch-black darkness, however, he flipped on the parking lights. After a few more yards, he killed the engine and stuffed the car keys into his shirt pocket. "Let's get out here," he said, pulling on his suit jacket before stepping onto the slick, snowy pathway.

Conrad put his windbreaker on and walked around the car to join Landes. He was wearing a pair of loafers and lightweight wool pants, and he stepped gingerly to avoid slipping. His feet were already frozen.

Landes pointed out a series of tire tracks on the road. He and Conrad began to hike carefully toward the cabin, along the crest of the hill. Smoke rose from the chimney, but the cabin was dark except for a dim illumination from the second floor.

Conrad was the first to notice the Mercedes balancing precariously on the side of the mountain, just a few feet away. "That's the car Ashleigh's been driving."

"Right, but it was Wainwright behind the wheel today," Landes whispered. He stepped closer and shined his flashlight through the rear window of the car. "No one's inside. Let's check the cabin."

Landes stopped in front of the garage. "It's too quiet." He drew his gun and pointed out the tracks to the front door. "Keep your head low and follow me."

"Deadly quiet," Conrad said as they crept up the steps. His mind shot back to the Volvo station wagon they'd seen on the main road.

Landes turned the handle on the door. It was locked.

Before Conrad had a chance to think, Landes pushed him back and broke the windowpane beside the door with the butt of his gun, then reached in and turned the knob. The crash echoed through the still night. There was no other sound until Landes threw open the door, banging it against the wall.

Stunned, Conrad glared at the agent.

"Place looks deserted. No point in tiptoeing around."

Landes slid through the open doorway, staying close to the wall. His gun was in his right hand, supported at the wrist by his left. Conrad followed.

Warm red embers glowed in the fireplace.

Landes moved quickly through the first room and on to the next, pointing his gun this way and that as he went.

Behind him, Conrad moved forward cautiously and flipped on a table lamp. Scanning the room, he spotted a dark stain on the floor and leading to the couch. He drew closer to the couch.

One cushion was soaked with blood.

"Landes," he called. His heart thumped loudly within his chest.

Landes appeared from a doorway beyond the dining area, his gun still drawn. He followed Conrad's gaze to the couch. "Don't jump to conclusions. If they wanted to kill Ashleigh, they wouldn't have taken the time to drive up here." He cleared what sounded like a very dry throat. "Checked the garage. No car, but there's water from melted snow on the floor." He shook his head. "They've gone. Probably taken Miss McDowell with them."

"Why would they take her with them?"

Landes frowned. "Maybe as insurance for a clear getaway. But I still can't figure this trip to the mountains, even if my theory about the son's revenge is on the mark. If they actually have a flight from LAX and plan to make it, they're cutting it pretty damn close."

"And Wainwright?" Conrad asked as he checked the cushions from the couch and ran his fingers down into the crevices.

"No time to ponder." Gesturing to his gun, Landes said, "Know how to handle one of these?"

Conrad shrugged. "Never aimed at anything but a target."

Landes turned the handle toward him. "Take it. Check things out upstairs. I'll check the basement."

Conrad nodded and headed toward the staircase. As he got closer, he noticed large splotches of blood leading up. He hesitated for just a moment, then took the stairs two at a time.

In the cold, dark room, Ashleigh heard a loud crack, followed by silence. She grew still. *Have Bradley and Tony returned? Or could it be some-one else?* No matter how far a stretch, she prayed it was Landes or the police. She went back to work, trying to squeeze her hand through the tight bracelets of rope, the bindings biting into her wrists.

Mitchell's breathing was becoming more erratic. Even before they'd been bound and gagged, his strength had been waning. She feared for his life if medical help did not come soon. *And what about Danielle?* she wondered anxiously. *Is she tied up in the next room? She must be here—probably just on the other side of that wall. But in what condition?*

Now someone was bounding up the stairs. Ashleigh listened as doors opened and closed. *That isn't Bradley or Tony!* She tried to push the cloth out of her dry mouth with her tongue and tugged fiercely on the wrist bindings. She stared at the door, willing it to open. Finally, she saw the knob twist in the sliver of moonlight that bounced off the brass. Someone rattled the door. Then, to her horror, she heard the footsteps retreat.

Ashleigh forced herself to think rationally. If only she could free a hand, she could pull the gag from her mouth. She attempted to clear her dry throat, to give a muffled scream. Maybe she could knock her chair over. If only she could move to the hardwood floor so the sound wouldn't be absorbed by the large throw rug upon which the chair sat. *If only . . .*

Conrad took off down the stairs. "Landes!" he hollered. "Need you upstairs!" He grabbed an iron poker from the fireplace.

Landes scrambled up the stairs ahead of Conrad. He saw irregular splotches of blood on the hardwood floor leading to one of the doors. He put his shoulder to it. It didn't budge.

"Wait," Conrad said, grabbing hold of Landes's wrist. "Listen."

Landes stood frozen in place, hearing nothing but the sound of their own breathing. He gave Conrad an inquisitive glance. Then he, too, heard something. A faint but steady rhythm. A repetitious three taps followed by a pause.

The two men looked at each other, then wordlessly rammed their shoulders against the door. It gave a little but didn't open.

Conrad forced the poker into the gap between the door and the frame. Slowly the wood began to splinter, and Landes gestured toward the poker. "Keep the pressure here." Conrad took hold of it with both hands and threw his body into the effort. Still nothing. Finally, Landes stepped back and put all his force into one strategic kick.

The door flew open. The room was pitch-black. As Conrad's eyes began to adjust, he heard labored breathing and a throaty murmur. He headed toward the sound.

Landes flipped the light on. "Jesus," he muttered.

Conrad blinked, and his eyes darted from Wainwright to Ashleigh, who was tied to a chair jammed against the brass footboard of the bed, her arms behind her back. He lunged forward, straight to her, and untied the cloth knotted at the back of her head. Her hair fell loosely around her shoulders as he removed the gag in her mouth.

"Thank God," was all he said.

Ashleigh ran her tongue around the roof of her parched mouth and over her lips as her eyes adjusted to the bright light. Conrad worked gently, untying her hands and ankles. She looked from Conrad to Dick Landes and back again. The first thing that came out of her mouth was, stupidly, "What are you two doing here?"

Conrad smiled, and Ashleigh instantly refocused. "Danielle. She's here. I have to go to her."

Conrad's smile faded. "Danielle? Here? Where? Have you seen her?"

"I don't know for sure. I think she's in the next room."

Landes took off down the hallway. "Danielle Norman?" his baritone called out.

Ashleigh continued, "And Mitchell. We must get him to a doctor quickly. He's been shot."

Conrad's gaze shifted to Wainwright and then back to Ashleigh. He winced at the sight of her wrists—especially the right one. They were raw and sticky with blood from her attempts to free herself. His jaw clenched as he worked on freeing her hands without hurting her further.

Once she was free, he cut the ropes from the brass frame of the bed with his pocketknife and began to remove the ends from Wainwright's wrists and ankles.

Ashleigh rose slowly, stiff and sore. She desperately wanted to go to Danielle, but first she must check on Mitchell.

125

Danielle cautiously pushed open the door of the master bedroom and stood at the threshold. It was not Tony. It was not the police. The man who had spoken her name was clad in a dark suit and dress boots, not a uniform.

His eyes darted around the room as he untied the scarf from her head. Danielle's mind reeled. Her tongue pushed against the cloth as he dislodged it from her mouth and then untied her hands.

"Yes," she said. "I'm Danielle."

Then someone stepped in front of him. *Ashleigh.* She pulled Danielle into her arms and smoothed her hair, examining her from head to toe, asking over and over again if she was alright. Danielle could no longer hold her tears in check.

When Ashleigh finally released Danielle from her embrace and stepped back, she introduced her to Dick Landes. But when Conrad Taylor stepped into the room, Danielle's tears transformed into audible sobs. Her relief turned to despair.

How can I ever explain my duplicity? I wish Jeff Bradley and his partner had killed me.

Ashleigh's eyes took in the room and the rope tied to Danielle's ankle. Her fingertips were red and raw, and blood seeped through the cloth wrapped around her ankle. Ashleigh's mind was spinning. Though Danielle had been held captive for much longer than she had, at least the men—most likely Jeff Bradley—had taken care of her basic needs. Hundreds of questions shot through Ashleigh's head, but they could wait.

Danielle's skin is so pale it's almost translucent. Although she'd seen Danielle only a couple of weeks ago and noticed her tremendous weight loss, she seemed even frailer now. *What did those monsters do to her?* But as her eyes took in the room she noted that they seemed to have provided food, bathroom access . . .

"Did you get my note?" Danielle asked.

So there really had been a note. "No. Tony told me you had written one to me, but I didn't receive it."

"Oh, Ashleigh! I've made such a mess of things. There's no excuse for what I did, but at least that note would have told you—"

"Did you mail it? Leave it in my office?"

"No. I was going to leave it in your in-box before I left for New York." Tears rolled down Danielle's pallid cheeks. "When I realized that I'd been lied to, I wrote the note to explain everything to you. Later that night, though, during the State of the Business address, I made up my mind that no matter what happened to my career, I couldn't be a part of Jeff's plan. I was heading up to meet Jeff and his friend as we'd planned, but I'd decided that I couldn't go through with it. I planned to drop off the note in your office afterward, but then everything went wrong. Jeff says it was an accident, but I really don't know. They told me I fell and hit my head, but I don't remember anything about that. I don't know where the note ended up. All I remember is Tony's angry face. Then I guess I was unconscious for quite a while. When I woke up, I was on the rooftop, inside the tower."

Ashleigh had heard Tony's version of the story, and now she wanted to hear Danielle's. But between her current frailty and her faulty memory it was clear that Danielle would be unable to fill in the missing links. *Will we ever find out the truth?*

CHAPTER
126

Pocino rushed up the stairs to his studio apartment and hastily rummaged for the key. From inside he heard the phone's persistent jangle. He jammed the key into the lock and heard his answering machine switch on.

Lumbering across the shag carpet toward the phone, he heard the slow, measured tone that was unmistakable. "This is David Jerome," said the voice. Pocino snatched up the receiver.

"Sorry, sir. Just walked through the door."

Jerome said, "I'm returning your call."

"Yes sir. I called to inform you that it was not Danielle Norman's body that was found this morning. But there's more." There was no response, so Pocino went on. "Ashleigh McDowell was kidnapped early this morning. She was—"

"Hold it, Ross. Did you say that Ashleigh has been kidnapped?"

"Yes, sir. She was taken to the Wainwright cabin in Big Bear. It seems Danielle Norman had been held there for the past two weeks."

"The Wainwright cabin?" the president repeated.

"Right. This is a long story, but Miss McDowell is okay and on her way back to Long Beach."

"And Danielle?" Jerome asked.

"I don't have all the details, but there is no longer any doubt that Jeff Bradley and Anthony Wainwright are the ones behind the extortion in your Fine Apparel division."

"Wainwright?" he parroted.

"Mitchell Wainwright's son."

Rocking back and forth on his heels, and in as few words as he could muster, Pocino told Jerome about Landes and Taylor following the trail to the Wainwright cabin and what had transpired there. "As I understand it, Wainwright refused to be taken to the hospital in San Bernardino. Insisted they go to Long Beach Memorial, so the five of them are on their way now." Then he added, "A couple of LBPD officers are waiting at the hospital as we speak."

"Where are Jeff Bradley and the Wainwright boy?"

"They're booked with Swiss Air on tomorrow's 6:05 AM flight to Zurich. But they won't get away. We know their new IDs. The airport police have LAX covered from now till takeoff, and LAPD has issued a U.S. Customs stop. Even in disguise, they won't slip away." And to make sure of that, Pocino planned to be there himself—three hours before the flight.

Before hanging up, Jerome asked about Ashleigh's condition. Satisfied with the answer, he thanked Pocino for calling and said, "I appreciate it. Please keep me informed. Don't hesitate to call me at any time—night or day. And if you speak to Ashleigh, ask her to call me immediately—regardless of the hour." He said nothing about Danielle. He could not share his pain over her betrayal, and certainly not with the security chief.

Jerome sank back into his desk chair. He'd planned to spend the entire weekend working on the long-range plans for Bentleys Royale, going through the mountainous piles of computer printouts strewn across the top of his massive desk. Now he had a lot more to deal with than he had bargained for.

He thought about all the seemingly unrelated facts that Ross Pocino had thrown at him. Kidnapping? Embezzling? Wainwright's son? The most baffling thought was, why had Ashleigh been kidnapped? *It is impossible that she would be involved in the Fine Apparel fiasco. Or is it?* He clamped his eyes shut. *Not a chance.*

CHAPTER
127

"The Cayman Islands?" Bradley repeated. *What is this crazy kid talking about? Has he gone over the edge?*

Tony slowed for a hairpin turn, a smile tugging at the corners of his mouth. "Don't worry. Everything's under control." His voice rose in excitement. "You're going to love it. Instead of cold and snow, we'll have sun, surf, and sand. Soon you'll be rid of that blasted cold you can't seem to shake. You'll be good as new!"

"Tony, you're scaring the holy hell out of me. Did you switch our destination from Zurich to the Cayman Islands? How? Why?"

Tony clucked his tongue. "Don't worry, Jeff. This was no spur-of-the-moment decision."

"But it's one you made unilaterally. I had no input." Bradley tensed. "I thought we were partners."

"We are. Give me a chance to explain." He snuck a glance at Bradley. "I'm not sure why we decided on Zurich in the first place. Neither of us is into skiing. 'Why not the Cayman Islands?' I thought. The Caymans and Luxembourg are the big, new monetary 'havens.' All transactions are held in secret—not even the IRS is given the time of day. We'll be free and clear, with plenty of time to enjoy the sun and fun."

Grinning, he went on. "My pal Jimmy has made all the arrangements. We've got a cozy cottage on the coast of Cayman Brac. Inexpensive and real private. We walk out our front door right onto the smooth white sands and into the clear blue water."

"Never heard of it." Bradley shook his head quickly. "But that's not the issue. Tony . . ."

"Hold on. Leaving from LAX is too risky. I didn't want to worry you, so here's what I did." He gestured to his parka in the backseat. "Look in the inside pocket."

Bradley pulled out a blue plastic envelope and quickly unzipped it. Inside was an American Airlines folder and two passports. He leafed through a stack of tickets—Ontario International to Dallas, Dallas to Miami, Miami to Grand Cayman, and in a separate folder, two inter-island tickets on Cayman Airways from Grand Cayman to Cayman Brac for the following week. "How long ago did you make these plans?"

"The day my shithead father dropped in on us. I figured that our original plans could easily cave in." Tony reached over and squeezed Bradley's shoulder, massaging the tight muscles. "I've worked out all the details. You haven't felt right lately, and I figured the less you knew, the less you'd worry."

"How much did all this cost?"

"Don't worry. The tickets to Zurich are on the old man's American Express. I left the airline folder for those tickets in the apartment."

Fear hit Bradley like an earthquake, ripping the ground from underneath his feet. When he could speak, he said with an unsteady voice, "Our names are on that folder."

Tony smiled. "Yeah, I know."

Bradley was incredulous. Did Tony understand? "I mean our new IDs! They're written on the outside of that jacket!"

"Exactly." A smug expression flashed across Tony's face as he pointed to the passports in Bradley's lap. "The Anderson and Kimble IDs are history. Take a look at our new ones." He cocked his head toward the passports. "We'll pull off at the first rest area and change for our new roles. All the stuff is in the duffel—your wig, my four-inch lifts. Same scenario as before. We keep our distance at customs and while boarding at each leg of the trip." Still grinning, he said, "It's gonna be a piece of cake!"

"What a night," Conrad said when Ashleigh finally emerged from the emergency room at Memorial Hospital. She walked briskly and held her head high, but he knew she must be ready to drop. His eyes fell inadvertently to her bandaged wrists.

"It's not as bad as it looks," she said, following his gaze, then asked, "Is Danielle still with the police officers?" She gestured toward the closed door beside the emergency room cubicles, where she'd seen the officers take Danielle after her ankle had been bandaged and she'd been thoroughly checked by the medical staff.

Conrad nodded, a pained expression crossing his brow. "I tried to buy you some time. Asked if they could talk with you in the morning, but they wouldn't budge. Said they needed to talk with you about the kidnapping tonight, while it was still fresh in your mind—before time dulled your memory."

Fat chance, Ashleigh thought, but with a barely audible sigh, she said, "I'd just as soon get this behind me." She turned in the direction of the closed office door, just as it opened and banged against the wall.

A uniformed police officer dashed out. "Doctor!" he hollered at the top of his voice. "Need a doctor, stat!"

Ashleigh froze momentarily, and then she ran past the officer and through the open door, oblivious to the rapid footfalls behind her.

Danielle lay prone on the floor, her skin a chalky white. Kneeling down beside her, Ashleigh took her wrist and felt a faint pulse as she watched the gentle rise and fall of her thin chest.

Before she could form a single sentence to ask about Danielle's condition, she felt a strong hand on her arm, and looked into the eyes of a young female doctor in green scrubs. Ashleigh backed away immediately as the doctor began tending to Danielle. She looked up at the police officers. "Did she faint?"

Shaking his head, the officer who had called for the doctor helped Ashleigh to her feet. He introduced himself as Officer Mark Ur. "She said she felt dizzy. Since there was no couch, Steve and I figured it was best to get her to the floor so she—"

The clattering wheels of a gurney interrupted him. It was being propelled by a couple of men in scrubs, down the tiled corridor and across the threshold of the small office.

Will this night ever end? Ashleigh thought.

While the police officers couldn't have been more polite or considerate, having to give them a blow-by-blow account of everything she knew, or thought she knew, was exhausting, especially when she was so distracted. She needed to know Danielle's condition, but no one could tell her. All that the doctor was able to tell her was that Danielle was dehydrated and most likely in shock after her ordeal. That she would know more after running some tests.

When the officers finally told Ashleigh and Conrad they could be on their way, she said, "I'd like to check on Danielle."

Wordlessly, Conrad met her eyes, then took her coat from the back of the chair and draped it over his arm as they walked toward the elevator.

"I know they won't allow visitors in ICU. But if I say I'm Danielle's sister—"

"It's too soon to find out much, but . . ."

Conrad's words blended with the background music of the elevator. Ashleigh's thoughts drifted back to the last time she had ridden this elevator, the night that Dan had been taken from her. The opening of the doors brought her abruptly back to the present, however, and her thoughts turned back to Danielle.

As they expected, no one in the ICU had any information to give them.

Waiting for the elevator once more, Ashleigh turned to Conrad with a troubled expression on her face. "Do you know what will happen to Danielle?" She looked up, meeting his eyes, and he knew she wasn't talking about her physical condition.

Oh God, thought Conrad. *Ashleigh has been through so much. And now this . . .* Obviously, Danielle would be charged with theft and embezzlement. He could think of nothing to reassure her. *What can I say?*

Interpreting his hesitancy to answer as a sure sign that Danielle's future was bleak, Ashleigh's voice broke and so did she. Like air gushing out of a balloon, her bravado dissipated. She shook with silent sobs. It seemed that once she let go, she couldn't stop—not for a long, long time.

Conrad held his arms around her, letting her weep till the shock abated and the first shivers of a deadened calm engulfed her.

"We'll check back first thing in the morning," Conrad said. Glancing at the clock, he corrected himself. "I mean, later this morning."

He was about to help Ashleigh into her coat when she said, "I can't leave until I talk to Mitchell. He's not being released tonight."

He frowned.

"It's not the gunshot wound. Apparently that's minor. It's his blood pressure. When the officers finished questioning me, they said they were going up to Mitchell's room to talk to him. But I've lost all concept of time."

Moments later, they stepped out onto the fourth floor. Not wanting to be a third wheel, Conrad said, "I have a couple questions for Officer Ur, so I'll meet you back here in a little while." He knew Ashleigh was not in love with Mitchell Wainwright. But still, he didn't like the idea of leaving her alone with him for too long. She was vulnerable right now. Would Wainwright try to take advantage of that? Conrad wouldn't put it past the man.

The piped-in lyrics of the Beatles' "Yesterday" filled the hospital waiting room. Alone in the stillness, Ashleigh thought, *How true—just days ago, my troubles did seem to be so far away.*

"Gran," said Ashleigh, "just wanted to remind you that tonight's the night of the black-tie dinner dance honoring Princess Anne."

"Yes, I remember," came her grandmother's reply through the phone line. "Have a lovely time, dear. Lawrence Welk will soon be on, and I'm quite content. You know that I always love to see you, but you must have a life of your own. I want so much more for you than work and taking care of a silly old woman."

"I love my work, and I don't know any silly old woman," Ashleigh laughed. "Take care of yourself. I'll see you in the morning." And she hung up the phone.

Waiting until the last possible moment, she locked her office doors and slipped the gold, full-skirted Victoria Royal gown over her head. If there had been any gracious way to get out of this gala affair, she would have taken it, but as a member of the management team . . .

Ashleigh pulled her shoes on, then picked up her gold minaudière and dropped her lipstick inside. She took a deep breath and gave a final glance in the mirror. *If all goes well, I can slip out around ten o'clock.*

When she stepped off the elevator to strains of music that soared above the din of the crowd, she saw that the second floor of Bentleys Royale had been transformed. The cathedral of merchandise had become a party palace for the rich and famous. In the Designer

Sportswear area, where the dance floor had been set up, she searched for a familiar face. The only ones she recognized were those of actor Michael Caine and his lovely wife, Shakira, who had just launched her own line of exotic dresses.

Rounding the corner into the Salon, she saw that this room was just as crowded. Dozens of small, round tables draped with white cloths and overlaid with alternating purple and lavender toppers were scattered throughout the room. The color scheme was part of the theme—Passion—in honor of Princess Anne, who was a fan of Elizabeth Taylor. The favors were small bottles of the actress's Passion perfume, which had been placed in the velvet drawstring bags to the right of each lady's place setting.

Ashleigh walked over to join Susan Thomas, the sales promotion director, who wore a worried frown as she tugged at one of the long white tablecloths.

"Need some help?" Ashleigh smiled. The fact that no one could see whether the tablecloth was exactly the same distance from the floor all the way around didn't matter to Susan. She took her job seriously and wanted everything to be perfect.

Susan straightened up and returned the smile. Her black-and-white Oscar de la Renta gown was in the season's fashionable midcalf length. "Thanks, but this is the last table." She leaned forward, surrounding Ashleigh in her cloud of fragrance: her usual Joy perfume, Ashleigh noted—not Elizabeth Taylor's Passion. Susan pointed toward the small cluster of beautiful people around Mr. Jerome, near the Chanel Room. One man stood nearly a head above the others. Noticing Ashleigh's gaze, Susan said, "Have you met Mitchell Wainwright . . . the Third?" Her voice dragged out the last words.

"No," Ashleigh answered. "Wainwright Enterprises?"

"Wainwright Enterprises was founded by his father," Susan said. "But I understand that Mitchell now runs the show."

"He does indeed," said Viviana De Mornay as she glided up to join them, clad in a simple yet elegant black Valentino gown. With a devilish glimmer in her eye, the fashion merchandising director said, "He can hang his tux in my closet anytime."

"Is his wife involved with the charity group sponsoring this event?" Ashleigh asked.

"No wife." Susan grinned.

Viviana added, "Pictures in the View section of the L.A. *Times* testify to the fact that there is no shortage of ravishing women available to hang on his arm, or to run their dainty little fingers through that gorgeous mass of thick silver hair." She fluttered her slim fingers as if she'd like to be one of those women.

Ashleigh was curious. "Why is he here?"

"He recently acquired Medley Originals," Susan explained.

"Not heralded as a friendly takeover," Viviana added. "I just hope he won't make any drastic changes."

Susan and Ashleigh exchanged glances as they watched Viviana float through the crowd to join Mr. Jerome and his small entourage. Following a fanfare in the next room, the crowd fell silent as the president of Bentleys Royale stepped up to the lectern to announce Princess Anne's arrival.

For the next forty-five minutes, Princess Anne stood in the reception line and graciously greeted the guests. Remembering the British consulate's request, Ashleigh kept her comments brief. She was glad she'd learned that a curtsy was not expected.

Afterward, as she worked her way through the crowd, she felt a hand on her elbow and turned to find Mr. Jerome. The good-looking corporate raider stood beside him. Following the introductions, Mr. Jerome disappeared into the throng. Mitchell Wainwright, however, offered his arm.

"Shall we go in to dinner?"

She slipped her hand under his arm. "Thank you," she said. "I'm at table six."

"You *were* at table six. You are now at table two, beside me." He smiled down at her. "Viviana De Mornay said that she would be happy to change places."

I'll bet, Ashleigh thought. But the tinge of discomfort faded as Mitchell Wainwright introduced her to the three couples sitting at their table.

"And Liz Taylor . . . ?" asked the woman to Ashleigh's left.

"She has pneumonia."

A bearded man from the other side of the table joined in. "Doesn't she always?"

Everyone smiled.

Mitchell Wainwright was a charming dinner companion, and Ashleigh was relieved to find that he was the first man she'd met since Dan's death who didn't seem intent on impressing her. In spite of herself, she was impressed.

When the orchestra began to play "I'll Take Romance," Wainwright took her hand and led her to the dance floor. "Tell me about yourself," he said. "Who are you? How did you get started in this business? Where are you from?" He guided Ashleigh smoothly and effortlessly across the floor.

"I'm actually a native. I was born in Long Beach . . ."

As she spoke, she felt herself drawn to him, alive in his arms. She was shocked to feel her body responding to his touch.

"Mitchell, we keep talking about me," Ashleigh finally said, trying to break the spell. "Tell me about you. What's it like to take over a corporation?"

Wainwright was silent for a moment. "It's difficult to describe. It's the mental challenge, I'd say. Negotiation is my strength. I don't physically run every business. But I target those that have potential and make it possible for them to become profitable and survive. I am able to create jobs for hundreds of people."

The strains of "Some Enchanted Evening" filled the air, and as they floated across the dance floor, her partner was greeted by a half dozen friends or acquaintances. He merely smiled and nodded to each one. Time seemed to evaporate. He made her feel as though he had eyes only for her.

When the orchestra took a break, they returned to their table, to cold coffee and melted baked Alaska.

From her spot at table six Viviana gave Ashleigh an unsettling glare. Susan Thomas also caught Ashleigh's eye, and gave her a warm smile and a thumbs-up sign rolling her eyes in Viviana's direction.

Ashleigh excused herself, picked up her minaudière, and headed for the ladies' room.

When she returned, Viviana was just leaving table two. She looked anything but pleased. Mitchell Wainwright was sitting alone, looking as content as Viviana was ruffled. If he were the cause of her leaving in a huff, he was oblivious or he simply didn't care.

"I thought I'd find you out on the dance floor." Ashleigh smiled, realizing suddenly that she was now happy that she'd come to this affair without a date.

"Not interested," he said, and pushing back his chair, he rose. "I've found the woman I intend to make my dance partner—and my wife." Then, as if he'd merely asked her for the next dance, he slipped his hand in hers and led her through the dwindling crowd and onto the parquet dance floor once more.

The door to Mitchell 's hospital room swung open, and memories of that first night faded as the nurse emerged. Mitchell stretched out his hand toward Ashleigh and said, "Please, come and sit down."

She pulled the chair closer to his bed, but did not take his extended hand in hers.

"Ashleigh, I don't know what to say. You've been through hell tonight and I didn't make it any easier. And as for Anthony—"

"Mitchell, don't. You must get some rest."

"What did I ever do to produce such an abomination? He's no son of mine. He despises me as much as I . . ."

Her anger began to swell. "You're living in another century, Mitchell. What about Tony? Didn't you hear a word he said? Did you ever consider how he might feel, having you as a father and watching as your marriage to his mother fell apart? Or are you too tied up in yourself and your homophobia?"

Pushing himself up against the pillows, he said, "My God, Ashleigh. You can't actually be shifting the onus onto me! To defend someone who's terrorized you for the last two weeks—even tried to kill you?"

"But you must care about him—at least a little. He's your son! You told the police that the shooting was an accident!" All at once, she realized that Mitchell had only done so to protect his own ego—not his son. She stopped abruptly. Bearing in mind Mitchell's blood pressure, Ashleigh resolved to remain calm. "There's nothing to be gained by listing Tony's crimes. This is no time to—"

Mitchell struggled to sit up straight in his bed. "Is it so important to make me the villain?" The hateful glint in his eye reminded her of the same look she'd seen in his son's.

Tears sprang to her eyes. "Please, lie back down." She was not up to more conflict. She rose from the chair and said, "Try to get some rest, Mitchell. I'll talk to you tomorrow." She didn't look back as she closed the door behind her.

At dawn on Monday morning, unable to sleep, Conrad rolled out of bed and took a quick shower. He was in his office at corporate headquarters by five twenty-five, ready to settle down with the past six months' summaries of Bentleys Royale transactions in Fine Apparel.

When he reached his desk, he found a pile of neatly stacked file folders; on top was a legal-size sheet of lined yellow paper. It had been roughly torn from one of the ubiquitous pads that permeated the organization. The signature at the bottom of the sheet was unmistakable—the security honcho's familiar scrawl—as was the characteristic straight-to-the-point message and smeared ink from his erasable ballpoint pen.

> *Sunday 1/26/86*
>
> *Please accept my two weeks' notice. No hard feelings. Found a job that suits me better.*
>
> *Ross Pocino*
>
> *PS. Can stay a little longer if you need me. New boss is flexible.*

The last line brought a smile to Conrad's lips. He would miss Pocino. He'd grown to respect his expertise. He had a replacement in mind—a bright young man whom he'd promoted to a similar position at Buffum's—but perhaps he could call Pocino in on a freelance basis . . . ? Conrad considered this intriguing option as he dove into his paperwork.

As the hour neared ten o'clock, there was a heavy knock on his office door.

"Come in."

The door swung open and banged against the oak file cabinet. Ross Pocino stepped into the room, his hands shoved deep in his pockets. Without so much as a *good morning*, Pocino said, "Bradley and the Wainwright kid never showed up at LAX. The police have jurisdiction. They're canvassing airports within a two-hundred-mile radius of Los Angeles and Big Bear. They've also put out an APB and faxed the men's pictures to all international airports, but the Customs stop didn't snag anyone." He sighed. "It seems we're back to square one. We know they have phony passports, but chances are the new IDs won't be for Anderson and Kimble. And if they were smart enough to buy domestic air tickets and pay cash, we're dead in the water."

"Have you spoken to Ashleigh?" was Conrad's reply.

"A few minutes ago." He smiled. "Guess that ticket folder was a deliberate red herring. But hindsight is twenty-twenty."

Conrad shook his head. "You're telling me they knew that Landes and I would be fingering through the trash in their abandoned apartment?"

Pocino absently scratched his head. "Sure. Remember, this is the guy who thought up the copycat Escort that showed up in Palm Desert and the underground parking. That Wainwright kid is damn smart. He knew, alright!"

"The brains behind this whole extortion was Wainwright, not Bradley?"

Pocino nodded. "I'd bet my bottom dollar it wasn't Bradley."

Conrad's attention fell on a different comment. "Did I understand you to say that the police have taken over?" He frowned and looked down at the transaction summary he'd been working on. "How about the FBI?"

"So far, neither the crimes nor the victims crossed the state line." The hefty man perched awkwardly on the arm of Conrad's sofa. "So no federal offense."

Conrad rose and walked to the window. "Are the police working with you, or are you out of the loop?"

"If the Norman dame isn't blowing smock up our—" Pocino stopped short, reining in his profanity. "Until we filled them in last night, we knew a hell of a lot more than law enforcement did."

Conrad nodded. "Well, I know you'll keep doing the best you can." He paused, lifting the yellow sheet of paper. "And about this . . . The organization is . . . I'm sorry to see you go."

"Yeah, well, no offense meant by it. Just found something that'll suit me better."

"Landes?"

"You got it."

Conrad smiled and held out his hand. Pocino shook it with his usual gusto.

CHAPTER
131

As threads of morning light filtered through the sheers in her bedroom, Ashleigh awoke with a start. She had been so relieved to get back home early this morning that she hadn't even bothered to pull the drapes before falling into bed. Totally exhausted, she'd dropped off the moment her head had hit the pillow.

Automatically reaching for the clock on her bedside table, she winced at the pain in her right wrist and clumsily knocked the clock to the floor. She retrieved it with her other hand, she was surprised to find it was nine forty-five.

Mr. Jerome had suggested she come in a bit later today, but the longer she waited to bring him up to date, the more difficult it would be. Slipping out from beneath the warmth of the comforter, she traipsed across the room, plucked up her slippers, and headed for the coffeemaker while slipping into her robe. The sleep had done wonders for her worrying mind. She had no idea how the law might deal with Danielle's naïveté in the elaborate embezzlement scheme, so she must stay focused on what she actually knew. Otherwise her mind would shut down completely, and right now she needed a clear head.

The light on the answering machine showed four messages. Ashleigh sat down in a chair and set her coffee on the table. First, she called Long Beach Memorial to check on Danielle. All she could get from the receptionist was that her friend was in stable condition. For now, she'd have to be satisfied with no bad news.

When she pressed PLAY on the answering machine, the voice on the first message was unfamiliar. "This is Richard Lowe, Long Beach Police Department. We spoke last night." Ashleigh reached for the pencil and paper she kept by the phone, but the policeman rattled off the number so rapidly that she had to run the tape back twice before she could write down every digit. It had come in at six ten that morning.

The second message had come in at six thirty. It was from Ross Pocino. "Sorry to call so early," he began, "but it appears that Bradley and the Wainwright kid were no-shows on the Swiss Air flight here at LAX. They—" The message cut off.

The third had been recorded immediately after the second and was also from Pocino. "Your tape ran out on me. Anyway, I'd like to talk to you ASAP." He left the number to his pager as well as his office.

The fourth message was from Mitchell—a command that she was to call him the moment she woke up. The call had come in at twelve minutes after eight.

She picked up the receiver and dialed. But her call was not to Mitchell's hospital room. It was to Ross Pocino.

An hour later, Ashleigh arrived at the store. Betty met her halfway down the corridor. "Mr. Jerome called twice, and you have a mountain of other calls," she said breathlessly, waving a stack of phone messages in front of her.

"Good morning, Betty." Taking the messages, Ashleigh said, "First I'll grab a cup of coffee, then I'll return Mr. Jerome's call."

Betty gasped. "What happened?"

Glancing down at her bandaged wrist, Ashleigh answered, "Oh, that. A failed suicide attempt," she said with a wry smile, knowing that Betty would take her flip response as a sign that there was no time to fill her in. Disappearing into her office, she closed the door behind her with the heel of her shoe.

Ashleigh shuffled through the messages. How many times was she going to have to repeat her story? If only she could call a press conference and answer everyone's questions at once. She smiled at the thought of it. *Well, I'd better get started.* She spread the phone memos on the table, arranging them in order of priority, and made mental notes on how information might be relayed through others to those with a need to know.

She heard a firm knock on the office's back door—not the one adjoining her reception area—and looked up. A young man from the maintenance staff stood in the doorway. He held out a crumpled envelope, dirty and stained with oil. "One of the men who was here working on the elevators found this."

She frowned as he thrust the filthy envelope toward her.

When she did not immediately take it, he explained in more detail. "We found it at the bottom of the elevator shaft. Next to number three. The one that goes to the rooftop. It has your name on it."

Ashleigh thanked him. When he left, she smoothed out the envelope. Danielle's familiar script popped out at her. Ashleigh's name had been written in burgundy ink, and there was a hand-drawn butterfly in the corner.

Ashleigh smoothed the crumpled note again and again as she read it. *At last,* she kept thinking. Perhaps this note would give her some of the answers she needed. But the bright fluorescent lights stabbed at her eyes as she read, and she felt the floor tip as though she were on board a banking airplane.

> *Dear Ashleigh,*
>
> *I wish I had time to speak to you, but the State of the Business meeting is in less than an hour, and I have to be on a red-eye to New York afterward. If I fail to make the best buy of my career while I'm there, it's all over.*
>
> *I just found out that I've been a pawn in a terrible extortion scheme that could affect not only Bentleys Royale but the entire Bentley's organization. I'm so ashamed. I should have come to you before things got out of hand. Until today, I didn't realize how bad it was, or how much damage I might do. If we were face to face right now, I'm sure you would ask me to start at the beginning. So here goes.*
>
> *I've become friendly with one of my resources, a former buyer for Bentleys Royale. His name is Jeff Bradley, and he represents Lady Adrianna. He knows plenty about Adele Watson and how she works. By cutting Fine Apparel's open-to-buy to the bare bones right*

before the holidays our entire division is fighting an uphill battle. Anyway, Jeff said he knew how to salvage my career. He could get merchandise on loan from Lady Adrianna and Medley Originals, and then input purchase orders for more merchandise from other vendors with no one being the wiser. As long as the merchandise sold. He called it a "foolproof plan." I should've known not to fall for it. But, being the eternal optimist, I gave him Adele Watson's authorization code for inputting the orders.

I was so stupid and naïve. I just kept thinking that without my career, I'm nothing.

Jeff went with me to pick up the shipment of Medley Originals at the DC today. A friend of his works there—he's a computer whiz with access to the Bentley's CRTs. He's erasing records of checked-in merchandise! Purchase orders for Medley Originals will be on hold, so I won't show up as overbought. Then he'll do the input for payment after we have enough sales to cover the POs. How could I be so gullible!

We hand-carried that merchandise to La Jolla and Palm Springs this morning. On the way back, it hit me—the enormity of what I'd done. I tried to back out, but Jeff confessed to me that he and his friend had worked out a plan to steal two million dollars from Bentley's. And I had already given them access to Adele's code! Jeff's friend, whoever he is, has access to a group of duns numbers from resources that are no longer in business, and he's set up phony accounts.

I told Jeff that I wouldn't be a part of it, but he pointed out that I was in too deep. I would lose not only my job but any chance of being hired anywhere. I could even go to jail! Plus, Jeff told me he loved me like a sister and that he would help me. I know he does care for me. He's been the rock that held me together since

Ted . . . well, you know. So he called his friend. He said that they had worked out a way to make all my unauthorized purchases disappear from the system—but I had to get the two of them into the store tonight, after closing. He promised he would ask his friend to put a stop to the embezzlement plan, but I'm not sure whether to believe him. And I don't know if the friend will listen anyway.

I probably have no hope of keeping my job. After what I've done, I don't deserve it anyway. I've been a fool. I'm most likely just putting off the inevitable, but I can't take the chance of hard copies of my sales and stock appearing before New York. I know exactly how to approach Anne Klein for advertising and markdown money. At least I can make a final contribution to good taste and quality, and I can prove to Adele Watson that quality sells and will bring profit to the bottom line.

I am meeting Jeff and his friend on the sixth floor, where we'll wait until after lockup. When everyone is gone, we'll go down to accounting so he can doctor the records in my department. Then we'll leave by taking the fire escape outside the Bridal office window, and Jeff and I are catching the red-eye.

I would have waited to tell you all this next week, when I come home, but I no longer trust Jeff. I plan to keep my eye on him and his friend—but they may have a plan of their own. If so, I don't know how to stop them. I don't know how far they will go . . . And I want you to know, just in case, that I am sorry for my part in this. After all you and Gran have done for me, the ideals and morals you both tried to drum into me, I feel like such a fool. Please, please, please forgive me.

I'll see you when I return. Don't say anything to Mr. Jerome unless you absolutely have to. I must tell him myself.

The note was signed in Danielle's flamboyant hand. Ashleigh read it through twice and still the full meaning did not sink in. When it did, she found herself trembling. Danielle had known she was in danger, and yet she fought for Bentleys Royale right up to the very end.

There was another wrinkled sheet of paper inside the envelope. It was dated January 12, 1986, in the upper right-hand corner, and it began: "I, Danielle McIntyre Norman, being of sound mind . . ." Ashleigh squeezed her eyes shut tight. What lay ahead for Danielle? She would soon be facing multiple counts of embezzlement and theft. If Mitchell made good on his offer of reimbursement, perhaps she could avoid jail time—maybe not. No matter what, her job could not be saved.

In moments, her head began to clear, and a positive thought hit her; Danielle was alive, and Ted Norman would not benefit from her disaster in any way. There was some justice after all.

When Ashleigh entered Mr. Jerome's office, with the envelope containing Danielle's note clutched in her hand, she saw that the president was not at his desk—nor was he alone. He was seated in his customary spot at the head of the long table where the management group assembled for their periodic meetings. On the far side of the table was Conrad Taylor, who gave her a supportive glance. Next to him she noticed Mr. O'Brien.

Not having anticipated such a formidable gathering, she wondered, *What do they already know?*

As coffee was served, she tried to think where she should begin. When the door shut behind the tearoom waiter, she felt all eyes on her. To her relief, Mr. Jerome said, "Conrad has filled me in on as much as he knows of your abduction."

Ashleigh nodded, thankful that she did not have to start from the beginning.

Mr. Jerome took a sip of his hot water and lemon. "And now we'd like you to fill us in on the rest—especially how this relates to Danielle Norman and to Bentley's."

Mr. O'Brien interjected, "Yes, and as you know, everything goes into writing in the Personnel file to prevent possible lawsuits. For the record, then, could you begin at the point where you were pushed into the limousine?"

"Is this really necessary?" Jerome looked pointedly at his watch.

For a moment O'Brien said nothing. Then, addressing Ashleigh, he said, "I'd like to jot down the relevant facts."

Ashleigh understood. Although she'd gone through it all the night before with the police, she knew he would want to have everything in writing, directly from her. She told him about the abduction as rapidly and succinctly as she could, careful not to skip pertinent details. Finally, she reached the point where Bradley told her what had happened to Danielle. But she could not begin by telling them what happened on the rooftop—she had to go back further, to explain how she'd become involved in the extortion scheme.

She reached to the middle of the table and poured herself a glass of ice water. "Before I came up here, I was given this note." She held out the crumpled, dirt-stained envelope. "One of the maintenance men said it had been found at the bottom of the elevator shaft."

Mr. Jerome shifted in his chair, his impatience evident.

James O'Brien looked from the president to Ashleigh before he said, "Let's see if we can simplify this." He cleared his throat, rotated his shoulders, and in his typical matter-of-fact manner, began to relate all the facts that had been gathered.

Ashleigh smoothed the note yet again, imagining O'Brien, who had a law degree but had gone straight from law school into Personnel, presenting evidence to a jury. He was leading her into the tight spot she'd hoped to avoid. And she predicted his next words.

". . . so from the hair and blood left behind, we can safely assume that Miss Norman was at the very least injured on or near the tower." He gestured toward the ceiling.   "Now," O'Brien asked, "do you know exactly what happened on the rooftop?"

"Only what I was told." Ashleigh felt a burning sensation rise from her neck to her cheeks. *How could she articulate what she did not fully understand?* "I don't know what to believe. Jeff claims that Danielle's injury was an accident."

"An accident?" Jerome and O'Brien echoed, their tones skeptical.

Conrad stepped in. "Please, let Ashleigh relate what she was told. We can deal with our opinions later."

The other men nodded and shifted their full attention to Ashleigh.

"I'll make this as brief as possible, but for it to make any sense without a lot of backtracking, I need to begin with how Danielle became involved with Bradley and the extortion plan." Since there were no objections, she told them what she knew.

"Were Bradley and Norman lovers?" O'Brien asked.

"No. Some of our buyers thought there was a personal relationship between Jeff and Danielle," Ashleigh said. "Others knew Jeff was gay, but since he was once married and has two children—"

Conrad interjected, "Bradley and Mitchell Wainwright's son are lovers."

Mr. Jerome's face reddened. "Let's not waste time on his sexual orientation. It's irrelevant. Let's move on."

"Danielle's fear of losing her job made her an easy target, and I think it was Tony, not Bradley, who took advantage of her naïveté." Realizing that she'd stated an opinion, she hurried on. "Initially, I don't believe the extortion plan was premeditated—at least not on Jeff's part. I think he wanted to help Danielle."

All eyes were now directed at her. "I don't have all the details, but Jeff told Danielle he had a friend who worked at Bentley's Distribution Center: Anthony Wainwright. Mitchell's son goes by the name Tony Lane. I believe it was he who turned Jeff's foolish plan to fudge Danielle's numbers into the criminal extortion plan."

"Hold it." O'Brien broke in. "Are you saying that the Wainwright kid worked at the DC?"

Ashleigh nodded. "This is a complicated story. If you will allow me to read Danielle's note, I think we can save a lot of time." She felt her heart beat faster. There was no one who wanted this to be over more quickly than she did. Even Conrad's presence failed to ease the strain.

She read the note without interruption, then commented, "The fact that Medley Originals was the company used for a large number of unauthorized purchases was no coincidence—Tony took full advantage of access to their computer systems."

O'Brien spoke up, "I don't follow. How—"

Conrad held up his hand. "Okay, I'll make this short and to the point. Wainwright's son, this Tony Lane, was the mastermind behind this elaborate extortion plan. Without his father's knowledge, and under his assumed name, he landed a part-time computer tech job at Medley. He had the inside access, the know-how, and the motive to put the plan in motion. That motive was not only money but revenge on his father, whom he hated."

"But how does this relate to Ashleigh?" O'Brien asked. "Ashleigh, do you know why these two men attempted to kill you? Do you know why you were kidnapped?"

"Danielle told Tony and Jeff about the note she'd written to me—the one I just read—exposing their scheme. But that's just part of it. I . . . I . . ." Her voice faltered. "I believe my kidnapping was Tony's way of getting back at his father, while the attempts on my life were his efforts to protect Jeff Bradley." She paused to collect her thoughts. "The more I think about it, the less I'm convinced that the bomb in my car was a miscalculation. It wasn't just meant to scare me. I think Tony Lane meant to kill me."

"Did the Wainwright kid admit to being the one behind those acts?" O'Brien said, still scribbling notes on his pad.

"No," came Ashleigh's reply. "But he was definitely the aggressor yesterday. Bradley seemed uneasy about the whole thing."

"You said you thought Wainwright—the son—tried to kill you to protect Bradley. How about himself—how would he be protected?"

Those frightening words—*tried to kill you*—played over in her head. "Until the night Danielle disappeared . . ." She stopped, her nails digging into her palm, then took a breath and forced herself to go on. "Danielle only knew that Jeff had a friend who was a computer hacker. She hadn't met Tony—didn't even know his name. I had no way of tracking this back to him—only to Bradley." She took another deep breath.

Conrad sprang to his feet. "This has gone far enough!" His voice rose, and all eyes turned toward him. "What do you want from her? She has no business even being here today!" He glared at Jerome and O'Brien. "It's been less than twenty-four hours since she was kidnapped, threatened with a gun, and left tied up in a locked bedroom with a man she feared could be dying from a gunshot wound." His eyes rested on her bandaged wrist. "Then she's asked to relive everything that happened. Can't you see she's not up to this?"

Jerome nodded his head. "Conrad, you're absolutely right. In my haste I have indeed been insensitive." Turning to Ashleigh, he said with a warm, sympathetic smile, "Please forgive me."

Ashleigh felt the tears well in her eyes, his sympathy breaking through her defenses. "It's okay. I want to help."

"Good. We don't want to cause you any harm, but there are things we need to know."

"But first let's take a five-minute break," suggested O'Brien. "Perhaps you could use a few moments of privacy, Ashleigh. Then we can wrap this up as quickly as possible." He left the room, and Mr. Jerome followed suit.

Ashleigh was relieved when Conrad made an excuse to stay.

Conrad walked around the table and slid into the chair next to her. "How's the wrist?" he asked, placing his hand gently on her forearm. There was so much he wanted to tell her.

"Not too bad."

"You must be totally drained," he whispered as he touched her cheek. The moment of intimacy was short-lived, however. He pulled his hand away when Mr. Jerome's secretary walked in.

Méchie apologized for the interruption. Then she said to Ashleigh, "Mitchell Wainwright is on line two."

Ashleigh looked up. "Tell him that I'm in a meeting."

"He says it's extremely important," Méchie said, not without a touch of sympathy.

Ashleigh sighed. She had no choice but to excuse herself.

When Ashleigh returned to the management table, the three others had already reassembled. Palpable tension filled the room. In an effort to diffuse it, she began again.

"I realize that Danielle Norman's failure to understand that she was being used has put her in an impossible position." She paused. "Danielle was extremely gullible, as she stated in her note to me. It wasn't until the day she was scheduled to leave for New York that she finally caught on—that she realized the motive for getting Tony access to the CRTs in the headquarters store was not to save her job. That it was in fact an elaborate plan to extort millions of dollars. Danielle confronted Jeff Bradley about this, but he convinced her not to call off their meeting. He told her that they would put a stop to the extortion plan, and she wanted to believe him. She hoped that they would just meet so Bradley's friend could reverse the falsification of her numbers, but she couldn't be sure that's how it would end up.

"So Danielle hurriedly scribbled the note I just read to you. She got to the meeting just as everyone was filing in, and took a seat in the back row, close to the tearoom entry. She planned to slip out a few minutes early to meet the two men in the display storage area on the rooftop, where they would wait until the store was vacated."

Resting her eyes on Jerome, Ashleigh continued, "But yesterday Danielle told me that something you said during your address, Mr. Jerome, touched her soul. She knew she couldn't go through with it anymore. She couldn't be involved in the manipulation of Bentley Royale's numbers, for any reason.

"She crept out of the meeting and went up to the sixth floor. When she stepped off the elevator, she met Tony for the first time. Though scared out of her mind, she told them that she wanted out. Tony grabbed her by the arm and yanked her. She hit her head on the corner of the fuse cabinet. Jeff said it knocked her out cold. He said it was an accident."

"Did Jeff tell you how they got out of the building?"

She nodded and turned to Conrad. She knew he would have helped her if he could, but she was the only one who could tell this story. She was the only one who had heard the story directly from the two men.

Finally she spoke, her voice barely above a whisper. "Jeff said they panicked. He knew they needed to get something to stop the bleeding, but before they could collect their wits, they heard the roar of the elevator. They didn't know who it could be. Jeff said Tony picked Danielle up and they hurried out onto the rooftop.

"Tony said that the moment they stepped outside, the door slammed shut like a vault. They had no way of reentering the store. That ruined their whole plan, so they decided to cut their losses and run—but Danielle was still out cold. They couldn't afford to leave her there—maintenance would find her right away the next morning, not giving them enough time to escape. So once they were sure no one was left in the building, Tony hoisted Danielle over his shoulder and followed Jeff toward the old fire escape ladder. But when they got to the edge of the roof, they found that the section from the roof to the fifth floor was out. They were stuck on the rooftop until the next morning."

Taking a deep breath, she continued. "After maintenance arrived early the next day to make sure the roof area was in order for the Salute to Hollywood preparations, they left the door unlocked. However, Jeff said they couldn't leave Danielle behind or take the chance that she might alert someone in the store, so since their original plan had been to covertly give Danielle a powerful dose of sleeping pills, drive her car to the LAX airport parking lot, and leave her there while they made their escape, Tony had sleeping pills with him." She sighed, trying her best to get to the end. "As soon as it was safe, Tony kept Danielle captive in the tower while Jeff went for water. They gave Danielle four Halcion sleeping tablets, telling her it was aspirin for her splitting headache."

"Halcion," O'Brien repeated. "Thought they'd been taken off the market."

Not wanting to digress, Ashleigh went on. "Jeff said that when they were sure Danielle was out cold, they made her as comfortable as possible, then went home to clean up. That must have been when I saw him at the elevators, though I didn't realize it until later." She paused to take a much-needed breath. "Later that same day he and Tony hid in the stockroom of Better Sportswear till after lockup. Jeff then retrieved the steel-lined trunk that he had brought in earlier from Lady Adrianna, and Tony reactivated the elevator. They took the trunk to the tower and put Danielle inside."

Mr. Jerome, who was familiar with the rolling six-foot-long vendor trunks, asked, "How were they able to get the out of the store without setting off alarms?"

"They took the trunk down to the Men's Clothing buyer's office on the first level and went out that window. No alarm went off."

Mr. Jerome and O'Brien exchanged a quick glance. This came as no great surprise, since the equipment in the fifty-seven-year-old building was often unreliable.

"Then they transferred Danielle to Tony's car," Ashleigh continued, "and Jeff drove Danielle's VW to her house. Jeff was the one at her house—he hid in the bushes when Ross Pocino and I were there that night —before he was picked up in the blue Karmann Ghia."

"And after that?" O'Brien was the first to break the silence.

"They took her to the Wainwright cabin."

Ashleigh adjusted her position again, and with a flood of relief, she said, "That's all I know."

CHAPTER
136

Ashleigh wearily mounted the wide concrete stairs to Memorial Hospital, wishing she hadn't agreed to stop by before returning home that afternoon. Now that Mitchell was out of danger, he was proving to be increasingly difficult.

She passed the reception desk and continued straight to the bank of elevators on her right. The elevator door directly in front of her opened, and she found herself face-to-face with Naomi and Mitchell Wainwright the Second.

Naomi's eyes were red and moist, but she attempted a smile as Ashleigh greeted them. The cold gray eyes of the older man held hers briefly. Had Mitchell told them that their engagement was broken? Did they know the real story about their grandson?

Naomi stepped forward and embraced Ashleigh, but there was no sign of warmth from her ailing husband. He stood beside his wife as straight as his infirmities allowed.

Naomi stepped back and slipped her arm through her husband's. "I'm so glad you're here, my dear. I just hope you can get through to my—to our thickheaded son." Her eyes returned to her husband. It was clear they shared a special warmth and affection. It was also clear that they were at odds regarding Ashleigh.

Naomi held her chin high and asked, "Ashleigh, would you please stop by the house tonight?" Her voice was steady, her eyes pleading. In her own way, Naomi Wainwright was as controlling as her son, but less self-absorbed.

"Yes, of course," Ashleigh said, concealing her reluctance as best she could.

A well-groomed woman with short salt-and-pepper hair walked briskly out of Mitchell's room. Ashleigh couldn't help but notice the woman's erect posture and white uniform—the type that had been regulation when Gran was a nurse. Inadvertently, she glanced down at the woman's rapidly moving shoes, remembering how Gran stood at the kitchen sink five nights a week, cleaning, polishing, and buffing her own snow-white shoes.

The nurse headed down an adjacent corridor, moving with such haste that her rubber heels emitted a squeak on the linoleum.

Ashleigh hurried on to Mitchell's room, pausing just inside the doorway. Despite his left arm being in a sling, Mitchell had emptied the contents of the narrow closet onto his bed and was awkwardly pulling at the knot of his blue dressing gown with his right hand.

Looking up, he said, "Well, it's about time."

She stared at him and then strode to the foot of the bed. "Isn't it too soon to be checking out?"

Feeling far weaker than he had anticipated, Wainwright slowly lowered himself onto the wide wooden arm of a visitor's chair that stood a few feet from the closet. He nodded toward the other chair.

Ashleigh did not move.

"Alright, Miss McDowell," he said. "You win!"

"I wasn't aware there was a contest," she replied, and she pulled the other chair a distance from his, the metal legs scraping across the floor.

"Sorry." He smiled with all the sincerity he could muster. "Didn't mean to snap. I had no right to take my frustration out on you." Wainwright saw there was no warmth in Ashleigh's eyes—only indifference. For the first time he realized the strain she'd been under these past weeks.

"I came as soon as I could."

"Any further news about Anthony and . . . ?"

"Jeff Bradley." She shook her head.

"Nothing?" he pursued.

"I don't think I can go through the scenario one more time," she said impatiently. "No one knows what has happened to either of them."

Although she'd told him she couldn't go over all of it again, she sat down and did just that.

When she got into the interactions between his son and the older man, Wainwright no longer listened. He heaved himself out of the chair and began to pace the length of the window, then turned to face her. "I hoped Anthony would get himself sorted out before bringing disgrace to the family."

Ashleigh blinked, but did not respond.

"Can't you see the position that he's put me in? What he and that pathetic queer—"

"Mitchell, there is no point in trying to discuss this," Ashleigh said. "You have a closed mind."

"You dare to pass judgment—you, who cocoons yourself within the crumbling walls of Bentleys Royale." With a look of derision he said, "Well, Miss Holier-Than-Thou as far as the rest of the world is concerned, Anthony is my son. Whatever he has done is bound to taint the Wainwright name."

Supporting his wounded arm with his right hand, he leaned back against the narrow strip of wall between the two windows and held Ashleigh with a confrontational glare. "I suppose you'd like to remind me again that the ultimate survival of the retail trade depends on the unique sensitivity and creativity of that greatly misunderstood population. Spare me."

Ashleigh rose and strode toward the partially opened door without a backward glance.

"What does it take to convince you?" Mitchell challenged, "Does it take more than witnessing the demise of Bentleys Royale? I'd think by now you could see what little effort it took a clever computer hacker to send that fine old store and all its tradition right down the tubes."

The door clicked shut.

Ashleigh pulled into the Wainwright property, on a private, beautifully landscaped cul-de-sac. After bolting out of the hospital, she had headed for Park Estates. Uncharacteristically, she had no plan of action. In fact, she hadn't a clue as to what Mitchell's parents already knew or suspected about the weekend's events. How should she handle this conversation?

Nearing the tall electronic gates of the Georgian-style mansion, bathed in a blaze of light, she realized she had no choice. She knew exactly what she must do.

Naomi Wainwright stood in the open doorway waiting for Ashleigh to park her car.

"I'm so happy you made time to come tonight, and I feel terrible asking you to do so after your ordeal, but—"

"I understand. It's alright."

While ushering Ashleigh into the home, Naomi quickly explained that her husband, who was still recovering from his recent stroke, had gone up to bed.

Ashleigh waited until Mitchell's mother hung her coat in the closet below the circular staircase and turned back to face her, before asking, "Has Mitchell told you we are no longer engaged?"

Nodding, Naomi said, "Let's go into the library."

The heels of Ashleigh's pumps echoed on the marble floor as she followed Naomi across the entry and through the carved mahogany doors. Her eyes wandered over the floor-to-ceiling bookcases surrounding her. She had not been in this room before. It was impressive. She studied the unusual wallpaper. The muted intensity of the dark colors would have been grotesque on an entire wall, but used sparingly, the choice was tasteful and captured a precise touch of quality. The ambience of under-stated elegance was the hallmark of the Wainwright home.

Ashleigh chose the high-backed armchair directly across from the leather sofa where Naomi had seated herself. She leaned forward, intent on confronting what she knew she must.

Naomi began. "I must know what is going on. You just don't know what it's been like."

"Excuse me," Ashleigh broke in. Unaccustomed to interruption, the older woman showed a clear note of surprise in her expression, but Ashleigh forged ahead. "Before we begin, I'd like to know what Mitchell has told you."

An elderly woman in a black uniform and white apron entered the room.

"Thank you, Mrs. Clark," Naomi said, and nodded toward the mahogany coffee table between them.

Surrounded in silence, Ashleigh was aware of the faint tread of the woman's rubber-soled shoes as she made her way across the hardwood floor to the edge of the Oriental carpet. No one spoke until the silver tray was neatly arranged beside the Steuben bowl on the low table. Mrs. Clark placed a Limoges cup and saucer and a demitasse spoon in front of each of them, then looked at Ashleigh and asked, "Tea or coffee?"

When at last the door clicked shut behind her, Naomi leaned forward. "Mitchell has told me next to nothing." When Ashleigh did not respond, she went on. "He told us only that Anthony is in trouble again. That our grandson had taken you to the cabin against your will. But he said nothing about the gunshot wound—only that Anthony had a gun and that it had gone off accidentally." Maintaining her erect posture, she adjusted her position on the leather couch. "He said that Anthony had chosen to turn his computer talents to stealing money rather than making it, and that these latest shenanigans involved Bentleys Royale as well as Medley Originals and some other vendor."

"And that is all that Mitchell told you?" She wondered if he had told his mother about Danielle's "accident," but it was unlikely that he had revealed the attempts on Ashleigh's own life—or his feelings about

Tony's homosexuality. Her teeth clenched. Did he want them to hear about it from the media?

Naomi sighed and said, "Ashleigh, I don't know where to turn. My husband's physical condition is, of course, my greatest concern. But I am also terribly troubled about Mitchell. He keeps everything bottled up inside, and one of these days I'm afraid he will have a nervous breakdown." She blinked, and then her eyes sought Ashleigh's. "I had prayed that you might somehow shed some light on this."

Ashleigh could not let her go on. "Please, listen. What I have to tell you is not going to be easy for either of us."

CHAPTER
138

Slowing the rental car in front of the door to her underground garage, Ashleigh reached for the remote control, then froze. In the dimly lit area just off to her right, she saw the tall figure of a man.

The man stepped from the shadows into the glow of the streetlamp. She saw him clearly, his hands shoved deep in the pockets of a brightly colored parka. A wave of relief washed over her.

Conrad Taylor strode purposefully to the side of the car. Ashleigh opened the window and he ducked down, popping his head into the opening. "I know you're absolutely exhausted, Ashleigh, but I had to talk to you tonight, before tomorrow's meeting."

"Let me park the car," she said. Things were moving too rapidly for her to trust her own feelings.

After she had pulled into the parking space, he held her door open and helped her out of the car.

When they reached the garden area in front of the condos, Conrad gently placed his hands on her shoulders and turned her to face him. "There is so much I want to say to you. I'd like to just pull you into my arms and forget all about Bentley's and Bentleys Royale."

Ashleigh stepped back and smiled. "You said you needed to talk to me about tomorrow's meeting?" To her own ears her voice had a strange, overly bright ring to it.

"Right. First things first." He stared at her cautiously. "The timing is lousy, but I must tell you about several recommendations I've been forced to make." His expression was one of deep consternation. "No point in skirting the issue. My job is to make Bentley's profitable—both divisions. Unfortunately, I've had to recommend some harsh budget cuts."

Ashleigh brushed off the concrete bench beside them and sat down.

"Mainly within Bentleys Royale, I assume," she said.

Conrad nodded. "I've had no choice but to suggest eliminating unnecessary duplications in the department store and specialty store divisions. I was forced to recommend specific cuts in executive personnel."

"Conrad, you said you weren't going to skirt the issue." She paused. "I assume that one of the positions you are recommending for elimination is mine." It wasn't a question.

"It's nothing personal, Ashleigh. If it were, yours would be the last job I'd touch. After all you've been through, I feel like a complete cad showing up at this hour to tell you, but I had no choice. My job is to set this organization in the black." He grasped her hand. "But you needn't worry about your career. No matter what happens, you'll have a top-level job—a much bigger and better one than you have now—working with the department stores as well as the Royale division. My recommendations are just that—recommendations. None has been set in concrete, and not all of them will be adopted, but I had to let you know."

Ashleigh tensed. *There it is again—bigger is better. Well, not for me.* She didn't buy that philosophy. She would always opt for quality over quantity. Numb, she remained silent as Conrad filled her in on all the grisly nuances of his plan.

His words swam disconnectedly through her head. What he was proposing was not only unsound, it was dangerous. It would destroy the very essence of Bentleys Royale.

"I understand that you must make your mark," she said.

"Ashleigh, it's my job. I can't let personal feelings stand in the way of what I feel is right for the total organization."

She shook her head. "You can't just nibble away at the structure of an organization without tearing out the heart, Conrad."

Suddenly, Ashleigh realized that the man sitting before her was not the man she'd begun to think she could be falling in love with. He had become an adversary.

CHAPTER
139

Ashleigh switched on the bedside lamp and glanced at the clock. A few minutes before five. Three hours earlier, bone-tired and unable to keep her eyes open, she'd stripped off her clothes and fallen into bed. But sleep had eluded her. She was wide-awake.

Throwing back the covers, she slid out of bed and donned a robe. On her way to the kitchen, she heard the familiar thud of the *Los Angeles Times* against her front door. When she opened the door and knelt to pick it up, her eyes fell on bold black type atop the article in the lower left-hand column of the front page.

ATTEMPTED MURDER—KIDNAPPING—GRAND THEFT

Crime Deals a Paralyzing Blow to Bentleys Royale

The austere atmosphere inside the Bentley's corporate office building did little to settle David Jerome's nerves.

"Merging buying responsibilities could cover some of the short-fall," Conrad Taylor said. Cosmetics, Furs, and Fine Jewelry were the target areas. Though reluctant to give up any portion of Bentleys Royale's autonomy, Jerome realized that unless Wainwright's bail-out came through, he would have to make concessions. However, he would hold fast when it came to Fine Jewelry—he'd be damned if he would leave the selection of that merchandise in the hands of a department store buyer.

As Taylor stated the obvious, and O'Brien nodded in agreement, Jerome curbed his temper. He surveyed the faces around the ninth-floor conference room table. Mark Toddman leaned back in the leather arm-chair at the head of the table, his arms behind his head. Notably, the CEO assumed an unusual role—that of an observer. His inherent calm was infuriating.

"With all due respect," Jerome said slowly, with an air of confidence that he did not feel, "while I appreciate your research, we have gone through this scenario before."

He turned his focus toward Toddman. "You know my position. However, I am aware of the bottom-line commitment and of our profit obligations to Consolidated. When the year-end figures are compiled, I will present a solid plan to recoup losses and set Bentleys Royale in line for a profitable year." The end of the fiscal year was only five short weeks away, and while no one mentioned the blow dealt by the computer fraud, without the bailout, drastic reorganization was inescapable.

Toddman lowered his arms and leaned forward, resting his elbows on the table. "David, while the ultimate decision is yours, I believe that it's in our mutual interests to explore all options now." His tone conveyed a determination to probe the possibilities.

Jerome nodded. "Of course." He glanced down at his Rolex. His own management meeting was scheduled for nine o'clock—just twenty minutes from now. He excused himself and called Méchie to tell her that the management meeting was to begin without him.

When he returned, the unavoidable—and in his opinion, the least viable—options had been put on the table. The consensus of the meeting participants was that he should consider eliminating at least one of the Bentleys Royale management positions. Their assurances that the specialty stores division's needs would be met and would be given a high priority were preposterous. The thought of leaving either Sales Promotion or Personnel in the hands of the corporate organization was repugnant. While he was unwilling to lose either of these executives, if it had to be, he would take his chances with Personnel. He could not afford to relinquish control of Bentleys Royale's advertising. If they lost the coveted back-page location in the Metro section of the *Los Angeles Times*, it would be lost forever. The effect would be devastating. He could not take that risk.

In Mr. Jerome's fifth-floor office, there was a buzz of excitement around the management table. The conversation centered on Ashleigh. The management group wanted to know why she'd been kidnapped and what it was like to be held captive.

There was no point in wishing this entire affair was behind her; it had to be faced head-on. It was clear from her peers' comments and questions that they already knew how Danielle, along with Jeff Bradley and Anthony Wainwright, who were still at large, had jeopardized the autonomy of Bentleys Royale.

Ashleigh quickly summarized her day of terror and what she knew about the computer fraud. Then she suggested that they compile an agenda before Mr. Jerome returned from downtown. Speculation about the consequences of the fraud took priority, however, and neither Laura nor Ashleigh was able to pull the group back on course.

They were finally settling down to the business at hand when Mr. Jerome arrived.

Viviana De Mornay waited impatiently in the empty corridor just outside Ashleigh's office. Surreptitiously glancing down at Ashleigh's left hand as she rounded the corner, she felt a surge of pleasure at the sight of her bare ring finger. "I realize this isn't the best time, Ashleigh, but I must talk to you."

"Could you give me a couple hours—"

"This won't take long," Viviana interjected as she followed Ashleigh into the reception room.

Ashleigh paused to pick up her messages and ask Betty to hold her calls. Then she gestured Viviana into her office.

Viviana's attention was drawn to the flesh-colored bandages on Ashleigh's wrists. *My God, maybe this really isn't such a good time.* But, fingering her pearls, she thought, *My time is far too precious to waste. I must find out how much Ashleigh knows.*

Viviana intended to cover all the bases. The final draft of her masterpiece, entitled *Quality Never Goes Out of Fashion*, was now with the typist, ready to be printed as the buyers' in-house guide. As much as she longed to have her latest fashion bible actually published and in wide distribution, it wouldn't be smart to ask Philip about the Updike acquisition again. When it came to Philip, romance was her priority.

"If it's about this weekend—" Ashleigh began.

"No, it has nothing to do with that," Viviana broke in. "I'm sorry to hear about your engagement, by the way. But what I need to know is whether Wainwright was successful in his bid to take over Updike's publishing house." *A little too blunt, perhaps, but at least it's out in the open.*

Ashleigh stared at her blankly and then repeated, "What do you need to know?" There was a note of incredulity in her tone.

"Well, I guess I should say, what I'd like to know."

Ashleigh still didn't understand. "You probably know more about it than I do. Why a small publishing house in Atlanta is such a big deal to either Mitchell or Sloane is a mystery to me."

Viviana eyed her skeptically and raised a brow. "He hasn't told you about the writer who has signed with Updike to publish an exposé— a downright nasty one—on hostile corporate takeovers? And the men behind them?"

"Philip Sloane and Mitchell Wainwright are at the top of his hit list, I presume?" Ashleigh frowned. "That's nothing new. They've been targets for months. But I'm not sure why that would make this acquisition so important for either of them. They've been featured plenty of times, in the *Los Angeles Times, Forbes, Newsweek, People, Business Week, Women's Wear Daily*, and scores of other pieces—not always pleasant."

"Ah, yes. But those articles are focused strictly on their business tactics. Philip tells me that this author has uncovered certain skeletons in his closet—and he's sure that the man has dug up plenty on the Wainwrights too."

Ashleigh paled. "Well, Mitchell's so-called dirty linen has already been aired publicly."

Viviana felt heat rush to her cheeks and raised the palm of her hand in protest, but Ashleigh took no notice.

Ashleigh rose. "Are you saying that the motive for this takeover is to silence an author?"

"Not necessarily," Viviana said, with a knowing lift of her well-shaped brow.

Silence filled the room. Viviana was the first to break it.

"What if, instead of silencing the author, the goal is to influence the editing of the material—to the victor's advantage?"

When Ashleigh walked Viviana into the reception area, Betty was not at her desk. She poured another cup of coffee and returned to her office, closing the door.

Leafing through her messages, she saw that Conrad had called at ten fifteen and Mitchell had called again. The rest of the messages were in-house, and while she had no heart for more questions, they must be faced. Sinking into her desk chair, she punched in Conrad's extension.

The second he came on the line she said, "I'm returning your call, but I also want to apologize about last night. I was—less than friendly."

"No need," Conrad said.

"For me there is," she insisted. "You were only doing your job. I should not have acted as if it was personal."

"Ashleigh, I respect your loyalty to Bentleys Royale, but I didn't call to talk about business. There's a new band playing this weekend over at the Windrose."

A band? That sounded fun. Ashleigh was ready to forget about all the recent upheaval and just unwind, block out the past two weeks. They quickly agreed on the time and managed to conclude their brief conversation with no mention of business—or of Danielle.

Next she rang Mitchell's office number.

"Wainwright Enterprises." Ashleigh did not recognize the voice on the other end of the line.

"Is he in?"

"May I ask who's calling?"

She gave the secretary her name and was quickly told that he was not in.

"Please tell him I returned his call." Ashleigh wondered what was on Mitchell's mind, what issue he thought he needed to dredge up now. She would have to wait to find out.

CHAPTER
141

Tony felt the 747 bank. He leaned forward and looked out the window as they descended through a haze of cumulus clouds. Catching his first glimpse of the island, he felt himself relax, and he glanced down at the travel brochure.

"Listen, Jeff: 'From your first moment in the Cayman Islands, welcome is how you'll feel,'" he read aloud. "'Located just 480 miles south of Miami, Grand Cayman, Cayman Brac, and Little Cayman form our relaxing island trio, where the weather is warm and the people are even warmer.' The Garden of Eden couldn't be any better than this. Sweeping white sand . . . clear blue water . . ." Turning in his seat, he gently squeezed Jeff's shoulder. "We're here. Be landing in a few minutes."

Jeff stretched and yawned. "Just resting my eyes." He smiled and craned his neck around Tony to look out the window.

Tony unbuckled his belt and gestured to trade places. He didn't have to ask twice. As the plane circled to land, Tony studied his companion. If anything, the lighter hair color should have made Jeff's complexion appear less pale, but it hadn't. Even with dark glasses partially hiding his eyes, Tony noticed the dark circles.

Minutes after a bumpy landing, they stepped down onto the tarmac into blinding sunlight and moved on to passport control. Tony blinked his eyes, adjusting to the brightness. *Thank God we made it. With a good dose of sun and relaxation, Jeff will be healthy in no time.*

If Jeff was nervous, it didn't show. He handed the false passport to the woman in the booth and smiled as she flipped though his documents. She nodded him through and reached for Tony's documents. They moved on to collect their luggage. Anyone watching would have deemed them complete strangers.

Dick Landes eyed Wainwright coldly. This was the second phone call Wainwright had accepted within the few minutes since he'd ushered Landes into the lavish office on the top floor of the impressive Ocean Boulevard high-rise.

Pushing his chair back, Landes moved as if to stand and said, "Call me when your calendar is clear." His voice was controlled, but he'd had it with this egotistical bastard. After all, Wainwright had asked for this meeting.

Wainwright covered the receiver as Landes rose from the armchair in front of his desk. "I'll be right with you." He gestured for Landes to sit back down while saying into the phone, "I'll call you back within the hour." In one swift movement, Wainwright hung up the phone and pressed the intercom. "Hold all calls for the next"—he glanced at his watch and then looked at Landes—"twenty minutes?"

Landes nodded.

"First of all, Dick, you've been with Wainwright Enterprises for more than ten years. I'd like you back on retainer," Wainwright began, pacing in front of the tall windows overlooking the harbor.

"As I said the other day, I'll follow this case through to conclusion, but you will need to contract with another agency for the future." Wainwright nodded that he understood, though he didn't look happy about it. Landes continued, "Has Anthony been in contact with you?"

Wainwright stopped abruptly and faced him. "What do you think?"

"Given your obvious lack of support, I'd be surprised if he had."

"You are correct. I haven't heard a peep from him."

"Well, we have nothing significant to report at this point, in spite of the wide net that was immediately cast over all international airports.

However, if your son and Jeff Bradley made it out of the country, it appears they must have dropped the Kimble and Anderson identities. Probably adopted new ones. Maybe even used disguises. And they must have been smart enough to initially take domestic flights." He grimaced in grudging respect. "Pretty smart young guy you've got there."

From the look on Wainwright's face, Landes didn't think he appreciated that last comment.

At ten o'clock Friday morning, Conrad returned from a task force meeting feeling good about the current state of the business and the turnaround in the Bentleys Royale figures. They just might avoid some, or perhaps all, of his recommended executive cuts.

"Mr. Taylor," the secretary said, "Mr. Toddman would like to see you. He's in the executive conference room with—"

"Now?" Conrad asked, not even pausing at her desk.

The moment he opened the door to the conference room, he saw Ralph Lerner, the CEO of Consolidated, seated at the head of the table beside Mark Toddman.

Conrad knew there could be only one reason for this visit from Lerner: the presidency of Bentley's. This was it. Had Lerner flown in from Cincinnati to offer Conrad the job, or to tell him why he wasn't yet ready for this monumental career move?

Lerner, a heavyset man with a receding hairline, rose and shook Conrad's hand, and said, "Please sit down." He gestured to a chair near the head of the table and walked to the other side, taking a seat directly across from Conrad. After a brief discussion regarding the present retail climate, Toddman excused himself.

Conrad had met with Lerner once before in the Bentley's corporate offices, and again two and a half weeks ago in Cincinnati, in a formal, in-depth interview. If he hadn't made an impression at that time, it was too late now. The decision had already been made. This was no interview.

"I read your long-range plan this week," Lerner stated.

The silence was heavy, but Conrad let the sentence hang in the air.

"Very impressive." Lerner's gaze was penetrating. "Particularly in view of the fact that you've been on board less than six months."

Conrad returned his direct eye contact, attempting to read between the lines.

"And I understand," Lerner added, "that you were the one who discovered the computer fraud in the Royale division."

"We don't have the exact dollar amount at this time," Conrad admitted. "However, we caught it early and have put procedures in place to avoid further damage. We have an excellent chance of full restitution. For the next few weeks, extra hours have been added to Central Purchasing to sift through the paperwork, and no resource checks are being cut without backup documentation."

As Lerner discussed the situation at Royale and his prediction for the fourth-quarter and year-end results, Conrad felt a dryness in his throat. Involuntarily, his jaw muscles tightened. *The CEO is biding his time. Setting me up for being turned down on the presidency. Well, damn it, I'm not going to be put on hold.*

The next time the CEO paused, Conrad asked, "Have you made your decision on the presidency of Bentley's?"

The older man's expression did not change, and he took his time before answering. "Yes, as a matter of fact we have." He pushed back his chair and stood.

With aggravating slowness, the CEO ambled to Conrad's side of the table and extended his hand. "May I be the first to congratulate you, Conrad?" His palm was cool, his handshake firm.

Reaching inside his jacket, Lerner withdrew a folded piece of paper and handed it to Conrad. It read:

Effective 3-1-86, Conrad Taylor, Vice President of Finance and Operations, is appointed President of Bentley's, reporting to Ralph Lerner.

"Your appointment will be announced two weeks from Monday morning at the management meeting. Happy to have you aboard," Lerner concluded. Then he promptly outlined an agenda for Conrad's week of orientation that was to begin Monday morning in Cincinnati.

Back in his own office, Conrad leaned back in his chair, his arms behind his head and his fingers interlaced. The words from an old Peggy Lee tune—"Is That All There Is?"—filled his head. *What's wrong with me?* His big moment of victory seemed hollow somehow.

His climb to the top had not been unexpected—it was the opportunity that had lured him from Buffum's, which had been sliding down a slippery slope since being bought out by an Australia-based conglomerate. Bentley's was the place to be. *So where is my elation?* What he felt now was like discovering a slow leak in a gigantic hot-air balloon after pumping in that final ounce of helium.

He leaned forward and mentally pounded his balled fists on the edge of his desk. *Who am I trying to kid? Ashleigh is the key.* Only she can make it all worthwhile.

The sense of betrayal that had flickered in her eyes earlier that week when he'd told her of his proposed budget cuts haunted him still. *Hell, how can I compete with her blind devotion to Bentleys Royale?* This was one area where he found her closed and immovable. It was as if Bentleys Royale represented her identity.

And yet . . . The image of their night together in his condo replayed vividly in his head. When he'd held her in his arms and they'd made love throughout the night, he'd been sure that nothing could come between them. She had wanted him as much as he wanted her. He couldn't have been wrong about that. But how did she feel now? The woman he shared that evening with in Palm Springs and the one he'd seen Monday night were two different people—worlds apart. He felt as if he were losing something precious, even though he knew he'd never actually possessed it in the first place.

In less than a month, she'd grown roots in his heart.

It's not over yet, he thought. *Not by a long shot.*

Exactly one week later, David Jerome stood at the head of the management table. In the tense atmosphere all eyes glanced toward Ferrari—the last member of the management team to arrive, rushing through the doorway with a sizable stack of computer printouts.

Jerome's eyes connected with those of each executive around the table, as was his style. Although doubt, pride, and hope battled fiercely within him, he knew his message must be strong and clear. He felt the weight of ten pairs of eyes focused on him. "The future of Bentleys Royale is in your hands," he began.

Lowering himself into his chair, he continued, "On the one hand, I am tremendously proud of what this group has accomplished in a tough retail climate. On the other hand, we have failed to reach our profit commitment."

No one spoke. Jerome was conscious of the shifting of positions around the table, breaking the stillness of the room.

"We must make significant budget cuts for the first quarter." He paused in order to let that sink in. "Fortunately, the radical cuts that we considered earlier are not necessary. We will not merge any buying jobs with the department stores, nor will we turn any management functions over to the Bentley's corporate staff."

There were murmurs around the table. Jerome raised the palm of his hand toward the group, then slowly lowered it. Silence again permeated the room. "This would not have been possible without the reimbursement from Wainwright Enterprises, which covers our damages resulting from the computer fraud. And more importantly, it would not have happened without each of you. However, we cannot . . ." He cleared his throat. "We *must not* fail to deliver our sales and profit commitment this year."

Tension swiftly turned to jubilation and then even more swiftly shifted to concrete proposals.

After Ashleigh vocalized her personnel strategy for combating the impact of Nordstrom's on their share-of-market and the merchants began discussing their plans, her mind slipped back to the short meeting she'd had with Mr. Jerome prior to this one.

She had insisted that she was not in any way responsible for Mitchell's decision to assume the financial obligation of Bentleys Royale. In fact, when they'd last spoken, Mitchell had been preoccupied with his role as victim.

She and Jerome had also discussed Danielle. Ironically, the young buyer had not lost her touch. While it had not been enough to turn the tide, her final selections of unauthorized purchases had made a significant contribution toward recouping a portion of their 1985 profit lost.

Ashleigh felt a pulse jump in her temple as her thoughts flew back to Danielle. She was being moved into hospice care today. The fact that she would not be facing charges for embezzlement was of little consolation since Ashleigh had learned of her terminal lung cancer.

Mr. Jerome's announcement brought Ashleigh back to the issues at hand. Tomorrow was the formal review challenge, where he would present the performance evaluations for the entire management team. She had gone over each review with him, in preparation for their nine o'clock meeting with Toddman and O'Brien. Two members of the team were to be officially placed on probation: Don Horowitz and Adele Watson.

At the elevator doors, Laura Cameron caught up to Ashleigh and pulled her aside. "How about lunch?"

"Sorry, Laura. I've got to make the final revisions to the long-range plan. Maybe tomorrow?"

As she crossed back to the elevator and punched the button, Laura caught hold of her arm. "What is it?" Ashleigh asked as she turned back.

Laura's brows pinched together in a frown. "Has anyone told you that Walt died?"

"Walt?"

"Walt Adams. The troubled sales associate—Jeff Bradley's former roommate. Officially, he died of pneumonia," Laura said. "He went into the hospital just last week, and he seemed to be recovering. Apparently he had a relapse and died in his sleep." She paused. "What most of the buyers believe, though, is that he had AIDS."

CHAPTER
146

In spite of having returned to LAX in the wee hours, Conrad was up early for a Sunday morning. For a solid week in Cincinnati he had kept his mind focused on business. He became a sponge, picked Ralph Lerner's brain at every opportunity, and soaked up the subtle nuances of the corporate world of Consolidated. He had been too busy to think about Ashleigh twenty-four hours a day. But images of her had drifted through his mind at consistent intervals and totally possessed him when his days came to an end.

Taking his portable phone out onto the terrace, he swung his foot up to the seat of one of the iron patio chairs and leaned forward. With his eye on Ashleigh's condo, he imagined that he could see her there, and dialed her number. He knew what he wanted and what he had to do. If Ashleigh was unable to commit to a relationship, somehow he would have to get her out of his system. He would not compete with her blind loyalty to the specialty store division.

A drowsy voice answered on the third ring.

"Sorry," he said, and glanced down at his watch. "Did I wake you?"

"Conrad? I can't believe it . . . It's nearly nine," she answered, her tone much brighter. "I'm glad you called."

"I've got a lot to tell you. When can I see you?" He watched the steady stream of marathon runners rounding the corner from Bayshore to Second Street, and waited.

"I'm spending the day with Charles," Ashleigh said, "but I should be home around five or six." She paused. "On second thought, why don't you join us?"

A family outing was not at all what he had in mind, and he was on the verge of turning down her offer, when he thought of the day stretching endlessly before him. "You're sure he won't mind?"

Ashleigh ran her hands through her hair, then picked up a brush and hurried into the bathroom. Her hand shook as she splashed water on her face. *Yes, Conrad is the kind of man I could fall in love with. Perhaps I have already.*

But there is a more important question, her mind insisted. She knew that Conrad wanted her, but like Mitchell, he'd never said he loved her. Not yet. If she let herself fall for him, what would happen if it ended? What would life be like afterward? For a moment she stood motionless. Then she said aloud, "I don't think I could go through that again."

She was still mulling it over when the buzzer sounded. At Conrad's greeting, she called into the intercom, "Be right down."

The deep tone of his voice caused her to grow light-headed, as if she'd drunk champagne on an empty stomach. How could she have forgotten the effect his voice had on her?

When she stepped off the elevator, he rose from the lobby sofa. His gaze caught hers, and she felt herself being pulled toward him, as if the walls were being drawn together and suddenly he was close enough to touch. She wanted to reach out and embrace him, but instead she just stood there, an unbearable awkwardness restraining her.

"You look gorgeous," he said, taking her hands in his and kissing her lightly on the cheek.

They fell into light, nonthreatening conversation as they walked into the sunny coolness of the morning. Ashleigh shed a degree of her unease. *Relax,* she commanded herself. *Stop turning this into something that it's not.*

A few minutes later they were in front of the twelve-foot-high front door of Charles's home, where Mary greeted them. After brief introductions, Ashleigh led Conrad into the living room. Charles bustled in through the library door, struggling with the top button of his white oxford-cloth shirt.

Ashleigh smiled and said, "Here, let me help you."

Charles returned her smile. "Thank you. But first I believe you should introduce me to your young man."

Ashleigh, amused by his stilted choice of words, made the introduction.

"Charles Stuart," Conrad repeated. "As in C.G. Stuart?"

Charles chuckled. "No one has called me C.G. for a very long time."

Ashleigh felt the blaze of Conrad's eyes. She had seen his mouth move, had heard the words, but there was an infinite lapse before she made the connection. Then it hit her. *How could I have brought Conrad here today before telling him about Charles?*

At first she intentionally had not told him. She'd never told anyone in the Bentley's organization that her "Grandpa Charles" was the man with the dream—the dream that had materialized into Bentleys Royale. But she'd had every intention of telling Conrad. The opportunity just never presented itself. And this morning, when she'd invited him to join them, her mind was on Conrad. Bentleys Royale had not even crossed it.

Conrad couldn't believe his fate. To meet the man behind Bentleys Royale like this! "How much of the concept for Bentleys Royale actually came from your visit to the 1925 Paris Art Deco Expo?" he asked.

"It was quite a strong influence," Charles said. "Art Deco was a total departure from the symmetrical Beaux Arts architecture of the times. And I had always had a fascination for color and form . . ."

Even as he listened with fascination, a voice inside Conrad's head asked, *Why didn't Ashleigh tell me?* He felt something snap inside, a drop-dead kick to the future he'd planned.

Around five o'clock, Mary joined them in the living room. Charles glanced up at her and good-naturedly said, "Please, my dear, do stop hovering."

He picked up the water glass and swallowed the two pills she'd placed in his hand. Then he rose and turned to Conrad. "I've enjoyed our visit immensely." He smiled with a touch of chagrin. "Please do come back. Next time I promise not to monopolize the conversation."

Ashleigh and Mary followed Charles upstairs.

The old man's mind is still razor-sharp, Conrad thought as he waited alone in the living room. Charles was a charming host, and it was clear to see that he adored Ashleigh. At Conrad's prodding, he had told stories of the beginnings of Bentleys Royale. Conrad was surprised to find himself enthralled by Charles's sense of detail—his ability to eliminate the mundane as he captured the bewitching aspects.

He'd told of early uphill battles for the store's survival. "Black Tuesday, the most catastrophic day in the market's history, and forerunner of the Great Depression, hit at the same time as our opening." Charles had smiled and continued, "Bentleys Royale became known as 'Stuart's Folly.' But we managed to weather the storm." Ashleigh had delightfully embellished his tales. If he skipped over some of the details that appealed to her, she filled in, as if she herself had been there. Her eyes had glowed as she told of the stars and celebrities who were part of the grand store's early days. She had fondly boasted of how Charles had managed to coddle the carriage trade through the Depression. "He actually flagged key accounts and sent out bills when the patrons were best able to pay," she'd said with a glow of pride.

Those days were gone, but for Ashleigh and C. G. Stuart, they would never die. Conrad was intrigued, but a sad thought settled in his mind. *How can I compete?*

CHAPTER
147

Conrad eased the Jaguar from behind the silver Lincoln parked in front of Charles's stately home.

"I should have told you about Charles," Ashleigh said.

Conrad felt the heat rise from around his collar. "Yes, you should have." He didn't trust himself to say more.

"I'm sorry. I'd intended to tell you for some time now, but when you called, I . . . I just didn't think about it."

"Afraid I don't buy that."

He felt her stiffen. She hesitated and then said in the same frigid tone as his, "Well, it's true."

Conrad felt himself unraveling. A silence fell between them as his Jaguar pulled up to the curb across from her condo.

"I am sorry, Conrad. You knew I was brought up by Charles and my grandmother. Few people at Bentley's or Bentleys Royale know that. I never wanted special treatment because of who he was, so I got used to keeping that to myself. But I'm sorry that you were blindsided. That was not fair."

"No, it wasn't." His tone was a bit lighter. He thought he understood now, and he realized that he was overreacting. He turned to Ashleigh, took her hands in his, and said, "Truce?" He leaned over and kissed her lightly on the lips, but felt her pull away slightly.

"Truce," she repeated, her voice a little guarded. "Now, earlier today you said that you had a lot to tell me . . ."

All of Conrad's carefully prepared words had vanished with his introduction to C. G. Stuart. "How about a walk along the bay?"

She eyed him skeptically, but reached for her coat. Coming around to open her door, he noticed the faint mist and a nip in the air and was glad to help Ashleigh into her coat. As they walked along together, she stuffed her hands deep in her pockets.

No point in beating around the bush. "Ashleigh," he began, "you know I've just returned from Cincinnati, but I didn't tell you why I had gone."

She smiled at him. "You've been appointed president of Bentley's."

It had been inevitable. But the fact that it had actually happened hadn't occurred to Ashleigh until she heard herself say the words. And yet the instant those words slipped through her lips, she knew with a certainty that they were true. Her stomach did a lazy somersault.

"How did you know?" He had a stricken expression. "It's not to be announced for another week."

She forced herself to ignore the topsy-turvy feeling inside and tried to sound lighthearted. "Just an educated guess. But on target, I see. Congratulations." Ashleigh smiled and kissed him lightly on the cheek, then quickly withdrew, her gaze drifting across the bay.

It was too cold to walk along the waterfront for long, so he took her hand and led her across Bayshore toward her condo, hoping to continue their conversation upstairs. They hurried inside, and Ashleigh shrugged out of her coat as Conrad pushed the door open. Folding the coat over the back of a dining room chair, she walked directly to the wet bar. If only she could forget about Conrad's recent appointment and the untenable gulf it created.

"Well, what did you think of Charles?" she asked.

"A remarkable man. And now I think I have a better understanding of your devotion to Bentleys Royale."

She poured them some Chardonnay and sat down on the couch beside him. "Between Gran and Charles, I grew up thinking there was nothing more grand. It was a sad day when it was sold to Consolidated."

"I understand Charles wasn't in favor of the buyout."

"No. After his cousin John Bentley died, Charles took over as chairman of Bentley's and appointed Morris Sandler, his son-in-law, as president. Unfortunately the son-in-law, with the full support of Charles's daughter, started his own stockpile. Caroline has been diagnosed as a paranoid schizophrenic, so she's not the most stable individual." She took a sip of her wine and continued. "There was an acrimonious war between them when Consolidated Department Stores proposed the buyout. Sandler wanted it, while Charles was opposed. In 1964 there was an extremely tense stockholders' meeting, and Charles lost the battle . . ."

Ashleigh looked over the rim of her glass. "But I'm sure you've heard enough about this."

Conrad did not take his eyes from hers. "I'm fascinated by the personal aspects of the takeover." Then he put his glass on the coffee table. "But not as much as I am by you." He tilted her chin up. His voice was no louder than the water lapping on the bay below when he said, "Ashleigh, I don't want to waste another day of my life without you. I want you by my side always."

He didn't say he loved me. Say it, she willed. *Say you love me.* But the words didn't come. Could Conrad share Mitchell's belief of love being solely the fabric of fairy tales?

Suddenly she felt lost and alone, as if she were stranded on a small raft in the middle of a vast ocean. She couldn't believe her ears. "Are you asking me to give up my career?"

Conrad shook his head. "I would never ask that of you." *The problem is, she doesn't need me. She doesn't need anyone.* And now that he thought about it, that independence was partially why he'd fallen in love with her. "But I won't lie to you. Inherently, two high-profile careers in the same organization could be a problem." He was sure she would have no difficulty in landing a position in any number of major organizations, as vice president of Personnel, Human Resources, or whatever they chose to call it. But he'd hoped that she might let him into her life, might let him to take over some of that love she had reserved for her work. That was before he met Charles and discovered how deeply ingrained Bentleys Royale was for Ashleigh. Far more than a career, it was her life.

Ashleigh rose, and when she looked down at him, her eyes were filled with pain. "From the beginning, my position at Bentleys Royale has made our relationship awkward."

"Awkward, but not impossible." Still, if she couldn't commit to loving him . . . *Perhaps it's better to have nothing than to have a piece of something that's bound to bring me pain.* He smiled sadly and heaved himself up from the couch. "Thank you for taking me to meet Charles."

A strained silence settled between them like a slowly sinking ship.

As she walked Conrad to the door of her condo, Ashleigh struggled against the tears welling at the back of her throat. *I thought he was different. I thought I was important to him—not just someone to dangle on his arm.* He had said he wouldn't want her to give up her career, but she felt sure that wasn't true. She should have cleared the air once and for all—found out where she fit in his life. But she'd held back, as if her mouth had been sealed tight. The words would not come.

Was it her pride? Was it fate that allowed her to come so close to love and then lose it again? She didn't know. All she knew at this moment was that she hated him—hated him and loved him with all her heart. As Conrad kissed her softly on the lips and headed toward the elevator, Ashleigh's heart ached for him, and for herself. She quickly closed the door behind her, knowing that she'd reached a point where even if she tried to cry, no tears would come. They were frozen inside her. She'd felt this way just twice before, first at Dan's bedside and again at Gran's grave. Except this time, part of her had died.

CHAPTER
148

Tony impatiently thumbed through a U.S. edition of *Business Week* in the deadly still waiting room at Grand Cayman's Faith Hospital. He flipped from page to page but hadn't registered a single image. Outside, the streets overflowed with Mardi Gras–type crowds—the celebration was in honor of Queen Elizabeth's birthday. Within the hospital walls, the only interruptions in the absolute silence were the occasional clearing of a dry throat and the barely perceptible whisper of turning magazine pages.

He checked his watch for the second time in less than five minutes, already a half hour later than his scheduled appointment. Though tempted to return to the check-in counter, he knew it was pointless. The receptionist had told him that Dr. Sergeant should arrive any minute. His was the first appointment.

Tony was prepared for the worst. Jeff had been in and out of the hospital since they'd arrived in the Caymans, nearly five months ago now. Today they would have the results from Miami General, where Jeff had been airlifted for extensive testing.

"Mr. Turner," the nurse announced. She stood in the doorway of the corridor leading to the doctor's office.

Tony, wired into his new identity, automatically tossed the magazine back onto the chrome-framed table and followed her. The image in his mind of Jeff's dull, sunken eyes and distended abdomen tainted his hope with fear. He prayed for his partner, and he prayed for himself.

After the perfunctory greetings, Dr. Sergeant gestured him into the chair facing him. Tony stated bluntly, "Please, give it to me straight."

The doctor nodded. "I intend to do just that. Mr. Dixon's test results are conclusive and consistent with the symptoms. The excessive weight loss, the jaundiced skin tone . . ."

As the doctor's voice droned on, Tony's mind temporarily screeched to a halt. He tried to force his brain to perform, to think positively, but it was little use. "What are his chances? Can he get a transplant?" he asked. He knew there was a waiting list for liver transplants. But patients often died during that wait.

Before Dr. Sergeant responded, a frightening probability hit him. It wasn't just the cost of such an operation that concerned him.

"Where would we have to go for this kind of operation?"

CHAPTER
149

The dinner party at the Wainwrights' was in full swing. Naomi had seated Mitchell next to Christine Yates, his secretary—or "administrative assistant," as she preferred to be called.

Christine has never looked lovelier, Wainwright thought. Her short blond hair, winged back from her face, set off her eyes. They were light blue, he noticed for the first time. Looking at her with a fresh view tonight, he wondered why he had never before taken notice of her as a woman. Until tonight, their conversations had been limited to business—his business.

He appraised her clinically now. Christine was quite attractive when she slipped out of her officious business persona. And she was intelligent. Observing the gleam in her eye, her unwavering attention to his every word, and that ready smile, he realized that her focus was on him alone. She was clearly a woman who was not dependent—she had a demanding job that she was good at—and yet he could tell that she was one who did not have her own mountains to climb. One whom he imagined would devote herself totally to the man she loved.

God, how practical I've become, he thought. *As well I should! I'm forty-nine years old and fed up with the dating game.*

In the midst of relating his latest coup to Christine, Wainwright felt a pair of eyes at the back of his head and turned. His mother stood at his left shoulder. He stopped midsentence when he saw her colorless face.

She leaned down and whispered in his ear. "There is a call for you, Mitchell. You can take it in the library."

He frowned, knowing how unusual it was for Naomi Wainwright to allow calls to interfere with her formal dinner parties.

She must have noticed his expression. "It's Anthony," she explained.

Wainwright excused himself and hurried to the library, closing the door behind him. When he picked up the phone, he felt the blood rush to his head, pressing like hot fingers against the inside of his skull. The line was dead.

He clicked the receiver button quickly, to revive the connection, and heard only the dial tone. Replacing the receiver, he turned to go, but the phone rang once more.

He picked it up. "Hello." A familiar voice greeted him.

Chapter

150

Ross Pocino poked his head around Ashleigh's open office door and grinned. "Have a minute?"

Ashleigh motioned him in. He wore a sport shirt and slacks and appeared at ease. Life outside the corporate structure apparently suited him.

"What brings you here?" she asked. She'd seen little of him since he'd joined the Landes Agency.

"Just in the neighborhood and thought I'd drop by."

Ashleigh smiled knowingly. "Come on, Ross. What's up?" she asked as he plunked himself down on the other side of the table.

"Well, it's like this." He paused dramatically.

Ashleigh wasn't sure whether he was impersonating Humphrey Bogart or James Cagney. *Same old Pocino.*

"I know the romance is dead in the water, but do you ever see Wainwright?"

"Mitchell?"

He appeared on the edge of making some smart retort, then thought better of it and merely nodded.

"Occasionally. Why?"

"Just curious."

But Ross Pocino wasn't the idly curious type—she knew that for a fact. *He has something on his mind—why else would he come to see me?* "Any word on Mitchell's son or that Jeff Bradley?" she asked.

"Nothing official," he replied. "We're no longer on LAPD's need-to-know list. The ball's in their court now, and they've made it damn clear that they want us out. But as I'm sure you know, Landes will be following this case through to the bitter end."

Ashleigh thought for a moment. "Tony left a paper trail of charges on his father's credit cards for a dozen or so airline tickets, going to all parts of the world. Mitchell was not pleased."

"That's right. It appears that you've been kept well informed. But they were all dead ends. Probably paid cash for the tickets to their actual destination." Pocino leaned forward, balancing his weight between his hands, which were planted firmly on the table. "We need your help. Landes and me, that is." He paused. "Wainwright's up to something, and we're out of the loop."

"Meaning . . . ?"

"He's received at least two calls from his son—one at the office and one at home."

"You're monitoring his calls." It wasn't a question.

"Sure. But our friend the computer wizard is too damn smart to stay on the line long enough for a trace." He stood up slowly. "Wainwright doesn't deny that he's heard from Tony. He says he assumed they were out of the country, but he doesn't know that for sure."

Mitchell would be dropping by later, but Ashleigh didn't mention it. "How do you like the new job?" she said, clumsily changing the subject.

"I'm on to you, Miss McDowell." Pocino smiled. "If you happen to see Mr. Wainwright and find out anything we should know, just tell me, will you?" With a wide grin, he said, "Job's terrific. Beats the hell out of racking up shoplifting stats. And Landes is a hell of a guy." And he turned to go.

Ashleigh was left to draw her own conclusions.

Later that evening, Mitchell arrived at Ashleigh's condo with an iced bottle of champagne.

Ashleigh opened the door. "Right on time."

He followed her in.

"How's Christine?" Pictures of Mitchell Wainwright's engagement to his former assistant, Miss Christine Yates, had been splashed across the second page of the View section of Sunday's *Los Angeles Times*. A photo and an article had also made the society column in the *Long Beach Press-Telegram* that same Sunday.

Mitchell gave a shrug of his broad shoulders and arched a thick, dark brow. "Don't be so damn smug," he said and walked over to the wet bar. Then he gave her a boyish smile. "Okay. You were right. I would never have been satisfied with being less than number one. Christine admitted that she'd been carrying a torch for me for years, and yes, I do indeed find that most appealing." He poured the champagne into two fluted glasses. "I hate like hell having to compete for a woman's time, as you well know. Satisfied?"

Ashleigh was struck by his candor. "Congratulations, Mitchell!" She tapped her glass against his. "Speaking of acquisitions," she asked, "are you now in the publishing game?"

"No, I let it go. No point in trying to edit family history at this point. Decided to throw this one to Sloane—I've got bigger fish to fry. Besides, with the new power of the leveraged buyout, there's no point in going after a small company worth mere millions when for even less effort, I can control a conglomerate worth billions."

Ashleigh sank down on the sofa and leaned back into the soft cushions. Mitchell sat in the armchair across from her.

"I've been following the Allied Stores deal, and I find the whole philosophy behind the LBOs mind-boggling," she said. "If I wanted to buy a business worth a hundred thousand dollars, I'd need a hundred thousand dollars, but for a billion . . ." She dropped her musings to ask, "What conglomerate are you targeting?"

"I've got a couple in mind."

"Amalgamated? The rumors are rampant."

"Could be." Mitchell was noncommittal. "But let's not get into that now. What's happening between you and Taylor?"

Ashleigh blinked. She wanted to snap back that it was none of his business, but somehow she managed to convey an indifference that she did not feel. "Nothing more than friendship, and I suppose, a mutual respect."

"Come off it," he scoffed. "There's no reason to deny it now. You are absolutely free."

"That I am. But Conrad Taylor had nothing to do with anything that happened between you and me."

"I don't exactly buy that. Well, it's none of my concern. But that Taylor is a shrewd one. Not the type you usually find in a corporation."

Ashleigh did not comment.

"I'd considered clearing the Wainwright name by compensating Bentleys Royale for Anthony's shenanigans." He tilted his glass and emptied the contents. "Taylor came to see me the day after you and I had our shouting match. He presented, in black and white, the advantages of my potential contribution in terms of tax dollars. But as you pointed out, I'm a businessman, not prone to altruism."

Ashleigh was silent. She had no idea Conrad had been involved. *Why didn't he tell me?* She had no time to consider this, however, as Mitchell launched into the real purpose of his visit.

"Anthony has called."

"Yes?" Ashleigh stretched out her glass.

Wainwright calmly poured more champagne. When he spoke again, he seemed to fumble for words. "Ashleigh, I'd like us to be friends. In some ways you seem to know me better than I know myself. And that's damn unsettling, since I don't care to be dissected or psychoanalyzed. But right now . . . I'll take all the help I can get."

"Tell me about the call," Ashleigh said.

"Calls," he corrected. "The first call came at my folks' house in the middle of a formal dinner party. The line was dead by the time I got to the library, but when I replaced the receiver, it began ringing again before I got to the door. It was Anthony." Wainwright hesitated. Then, with a firm set to his shoulders, he continued. "That call didn't go at all well. Like a damn fool, I demanded to know where he was, and he hung up."

That came as no surprise, but Mitchell's openness did. Ashleigh remained silent as he pulled an envelope from his shirt pocket.

"Received this a week ago," he said, handing it to her.

It was postmarked New York. When she pulled the two sheets of paper from the envelope, she saw bold block printing on the page, as if a stencil had been used. Her mind shot back to the manila envelope she'd found in Bev's foyer. The same block letters were used in the misspelling of her own name.

Looking straight into Mitchell's unreadable eyes, she asked, "Do you still have my key?"

He gave a dry, mirthless laugh. "Obviously Anthony helped himself to my keys. Guess you already figured that out. Read his letter?"

Father,

You claim I am no longer your son. Well, I figure that's not your decision to make.

Save yourself a heap of trouble, the postmark on this envelope will lead you nowhere. There's no way that you or the authorities will find us unless we choose to be found.

Recently, I've had plenty of time on my hands, and my portable computer has been a constant companion. Writing has become my therapy and my salvation. You might expect me to apologize, but I can't. Through this self-imposed catharsis, I've made some amazing discoveries and some important decisions.

I'm through with lies and manipulation. I have plenty of regrets, but reliving your regrets is like driving only in reverse. By not accepting who I am, you humiliated me, and I was angry. I could never measure up to the Wainwright image you wanted for me. But what I did was wrong.

I won't try to justify my actions. However, I want you know what happened and what was going on in my head at the time.

I swear that what happened to Danielle Norman was an accident. I know you don't believe in coincidence or fate, but I swear I know nothing about that body found in the Medley delivery truck.

Danielle's accident presented a multitude of problems, and I was paranoid. It now seems that this all happened to someone else—someone I no longer know or care to know. If not for Jeff, Danielle might have died. Going back to Big Bear was risky, but Jeff insisted on seeing to it that Danielle was taken care of. If she hadn't changed her mind . . . If she hadn't hit her head . . . If someone hadn't come along . . . If all this hadn't happened, we would have committed the perfect crime and gotten away with millions. Then I wouldn't be so worried about the immediate future. The fact that we were trapped out on the rooftop until the next morning—it ruined everything.

The crime against Bentley's was for money, but the crime against Wainwright Enterprises was personal. The car explosion was something entirely different. I was sick with fear that we'd be caught, and filled with hatred. I wanted to protect us from being found out. I had nothing against Ashleigh McDowell. Didn't even know her, though I knew she was your fiancée, which I guess was part of the equation. My intention was not murder, at least not on a conscious level. But I was inexperienced and careless with the explosives, and I'll admit that I had revenge on my mind—childish revenge. I can't argue that.

If she had died, I would have deserved to hang. Like I said, I had nothing personal against the woman, other than the fact that she was a treasured possession of yours. I couldn't stand the idea that you had given her the love you had denied me.

Kidnapping Ashleigh was the last manifestation of my madness. Jeff fought me all the way on this, but finally went along after I agreed to check on Danielle before we left. I don't even know why I decided to do it. Maybe her kidnapping was pure and simple revenge aimed against you. Maybe I always knew that you'd follow us. Maybe I imagined that by hurting her, I would hurt you.

Revenge, I've learned, is most destructive to the avenger. Luckily my most vicious and depraved acts failed. I have no further wish to harm you and am sorry for the damage I've done.

Wow. What do you know? I began this letter saying

I could not apologize, and now I have. If this doesn't prove the power of purging your soul on paper, I don't know what does. But my apology does not excuse you.

When I needed a father, you made me feel like trash. Maybe you couldn't help it, and maybe things might have been different if I'd tried harder to talk to you, but I doubt it. I rehearsed what I'd say, but I never got up the nerve.

Why am I writing? What do I want? I'm sure that's what you're asking yourself, so I'll get to the point. Jeff has been very ill. He's been in and out of the hospital since we arrived here. We just got word that he needs to have a highly specialized operation. I can't tell you more, but I have a proposal. I will call your office eight o'clock Monday morning, June 16. At that time I will tell you where to go to receive my next call.

I know I don't have to tell you my rationale. I learned from a pro.

Tony

Mildly curious as to why the letter was handwritten if a portable computer was Tony's constant companion, Ashleigh handed it back to Mitchell.

"Did he call?" she asked.

"He called, alright." Wainwright tugged at his bottom lip and a thoughtful expression crossed his face. "You know what he wanted?"

Ashleigh shook her head, but instantly and intuitively said, "Money?"

"Exactly. What do you think I should do?" Mitchell's expression gave nothing away.

"I thought you said you had no idea where he was."

"That's right. He's calling again tomorrow morning at eight for my decision. Same routine as before, but I know that he has no intention of telling me where he is." With a benign smile, he said, "No trust, I'm afraid. By the way did you notice the letter was handwritten on my letterhead?" She frowned. If there was some significance to handwriting the note, she didn't get it.

"Printer was most likely a local product that might be traced. Leave it to Anthony!"

"Mitchell, please, what is it you want from me? Reassurance? Answers? I have neither."

"Sit down, Ashleigh. Please. This isn't easy for me. I think you know that."

Without sentiment or censure, she said, "If you want me to tell you that you are blameless, I cannot. On the other hand, there is no point in trying to lay blame. The only question is, what are you going to do about it?" She paused, looking into his eyes. "Do you care for Tony?" Even in his moment of crisis, she couldn't bring herself to use the word *love* with him. "Do you really care what happens to him—not just how his behavior reflects on you and the Wainwright name?"

Mitchell heaved himself out of the armchair and walked over to the wet bar, then turned to face her. He let a silence settle about them. "I don't know. I know that's not a good answer, and it's one I seldom accept. But it's God's honest truth."

Wainwright stared at the silent phone and checked his watch yet again.

He sank back against the soft Italian leather headrest of his desk chair and studied his surroundings with a critical eye. He had created the most lavish office in the most enviable high-rise building in downtown Long Beach. He'd driven the architects mad, but the capacious offices drew the most prestigious attorneys and business executives in the area—men like himself who were willing to pay the price for the ambiance of success. The irony hit him squarely, and he shook his head sadly.

The shrill ring from the telephone snapped him back to the present, and he sprang forward in his chair and grasped the receiver. Answering with an air of forced casualness, he noticed that the hand that held the receiver shook.

A half hour later Wainwright waited for Anthony's call as instructed: in the second phone booth from the entry of the courthouse on Ocean Boulevard. He tried to suppress his irritation. Ashleigh had labeled him a control freak, and though he'd never come right out and admitted it, he knew it was true. Allowing his son to call the shots was unnatural and unsettling. But what choice did he have? He was not in control, and while Anthony and his friend continued to evade the law, the balance of power was not in his favor—especially since he had no way of locating him.

Wainwright knew he had only one way of exerting his control.

He answered the phone on the first ring. "Yes, I've thought it over. I can't agree to your terms."

A light laugh came through the phone lines, sad and tired "No surprise there, *Father*. In that case, I need to get back to the hospital."

"Hold it, Anth . . . Tony. I didn't say I wouldn't help you. The fact is, I will. And I promise I won't inform anyone of your whereabouts."

"That won't be difficult." His son's voice was heavy with sarcasm. "You'll never know."

"Hear me out . . . please. I will not send the money by the circuitous routing you outlined, nor will I hand it over to anyone but you. However," he added, "I will bring the money myself."

There was a long silence.

Then Tony spoke firmly. "No, we can't take that chance. I told you, I'm willing to return after we find a donor and Jeff is out of the woods. We'll turn ourselves over to the authorities and stand trial. But not until we find a donor and get him this operation."

"And if you don't find a donor?"

"We'll find one. But I need the money now."

"In that case, listen to my plan." Wainwright took a deep breath. "You'll have to trust me."

Ashleigh glanced down at the unwatered plants on her veranda. *With my brown thumb,* she thought wryly, *I might as well give up.* Picking off the dead leaves, she glanced across to Conrad's penthouse. He was so close, and yet he might as well have been in a different country.

She heard the phone and stepped inside, turning down the volume on the stereo.

It was Mitchell. "Slow down," she said. "I haven't understood a single word."

"Sorry," he said, slipping into a more normal cadence. "I have a plane to catch, but I have to ask a favor."

"So ask," she said, amused at the uncharacteristic excitement in Mitchell's voice—like a kid going off to camp, not one of the most notorious corporate raiders in the country.

"I'm on my way to meet Tony."

To meet . . . Tony? His choice of words gave her pause; he'd used the name his son preferred. "Where?"

"I'll find out en route. Don't have time to explain. Landes has the details."

"You're going alone?"

"That's the way it's got to be. I may be gone for a while, so what I'd like you to do is convince Landes that I'm not holding out. For now, you and he will know almost as much as I do."

"About what?" she asked impatiently, thinking he was talking in circles.

"Everything." He paused, then said indulgently, "Tony hasn't told me where he is—"

"My God, Mitchell!" Her voice rose sharply. "You can't be an accomplice to their crimes—attempted murder, kidnapping, fraud—"

"Hold it. I have no intention of becoming an accomplice. Hear me out. All I know is my first stop, but I'm not free to disclose that. I will contact Landes before I return—with Tony *and* Bradley. And I guarantee they will stand trial. That's all anyone need know."

When Ashleigh replaced the receiver, she felt as though she'd come down too fast in an elevator. Mitchell had made a complete flip-flop, and it amazed her. How had he managed to cool that self-righteous indignation of his and focus his finely honed negotiating skills on his son? It was a mystery to her.

He had taken the first step. Still, his motivation was unclear. Was it paternal instinct or concern for his reputation?

CHAPTER
153

Ashleigh parked her car and headed straight to the front patio, where she knew she'd find Charles. Approaching the white gazebo, she quickened her steps. Charles was kneeling down, plucking an odd weed from his bed of pansies—the peculiar little flowers that had come to mean so much to him and Gran.

"When did you creep in?" Charles asked as he rose and returned her smile.

"Good morning," Mary said as she walked toward them with a white wicker tray of coffee, tea, and all the paraphernalia.

When they were alone and seated at the patio table, Charles said, "If I asked you to have dinner with me tonight, would you be available?"

Strange wording. He had something on his mind—Ashleigh was sure of that—but she simply answered, "Yes."

"And last night?"

She nodded, amused at how much he and Gran had in common. "Grandpa Charles, please don't worry about me. I am not sitting home alone every night."

Charles radiated with delight. "Oh, how I've missed having you call me that."

"You have?"

He nodded. "You know, I've seen quite a lot of that young man you brought here several months back."

"Conrad?"

"I certainly don't mean Mitchell Wainwright." His voice was gruff and his tone dismissive. "Never could see the two of you together."

"Conrad Taylor has been here?"

"Now don't get your knickers in a twist," said Charles, his British upbringing surfacing as it so often did. "In case you didn't know, he jogs along here every morning." He gestured to the walkway along the open bay frontage, and then he gave her a roguish grin. "He stopped by for the first time a couple of weeks ago, when our timing just happened to coincide. The fact is, the man is totally smitten with you."

Smitten? What a strange, old-fashioned word. Ashleigh knew exactly what he meant. *But Charles doesn't understand. How could he?*

He moved his chair so that it touched hers. Reaching out, he gently tilted her chin so that her eyes met his. "I've tried not to interfere, but I can't stand by without comment while you wall yourself off from something rare and precious."

"Grandpa Charles," Ashleigh began, but stopped when she saw the simple shake of his head and his troubled expression.

"Please indulge this old man. You've heard this story scores of times before, but I promise to keep my meandering to the absolute minimum and tell just what I think is relevant. Bear with me."

He reached out and squeezed her hand, then began, "As a very young man, I had a dream. And before my thirtieth birthday, I saw that dream unfold. Bentleys Royale became my heart and soul. My identity. It was the only thing with substance and meaning . . . until your grandmother came into my life."

As Charles spoke of those early days with Gran, Ashleigh saw the parallels that he was trying to form. But there was no parallel. Charles had loved her grandmother. There was never any doubt about that. She could not say the same about Conrad Taylor.

His voice drifted back. "Conrad doesn't want to let you slip through his fingers, but he says he can't compete." He paused. "Darling girl, please don't let anything come between you and true love. Bentleys Royale will not keep you warm at night. I realize what it has represented to you since you were a toddler, but it is, in fact, only brick and mortar."

"Grandpa Charles, Conrad may want me, but he's never once said he loves me."

"And you've told him that you love him?"

"No, of course not."

"But you do. Don't you?"

She nodded. "I think so." Somehow she couldn't lie to Grandpa Charles as she had to herself.

"You've often said that your grandmother and I were victims of our generation, and that may be true. But we were mostly victims of our own making. Don't let that happen to you. And for God's sake, don't let the passion that your grandmother and I shared for Bentleys Royale put a burden on you. Times have changed. That era has ended. Choose your own fate, darling girl."

"I don't believe that elegance and fine quality will ever be out of date. Nor do you," Ashleigh challenged.

Charles laughed out loud. "Touché! But there's room in your life for more than elegance. Don't create artificial impediments. I see no reason why you and Conrad can't be effective in the same corporation. If the two of you are as bright and competent as I believe you are, you can work it out. And no one will challenge you."

Could that be true? Have my fears been real or just an excuse, something to hide behind? Have I just been looking for a way to avoid the risk of being hurt once more?

"If you love this man, don't let anything stand in your way." He paused. "Or has your career become more important than love and a family of your own?"

Ashleigh blinked, then looked him directly in the eye and answered, "No."

That night when she returned home, she sat on her veranda looking across to Conrad's condo. His lights were on.

Charles's words swam in her head like the unrelenting sea. She turned each phrase over in her mind, like a diver scrutinizing a pearl for flaws. Then she hit on a truth of her own: Her major regrets in life so far had stemmed from the things she hadn't had the courage to do or say, not the other way around. Well, she had to make a start here—had to stop treading water and get on with her life. Without risk, she'd have nothing—nothing that really mattered.

Pushing away her fear, she stepped inside and reached for the phone. That was when she noticed the blinking red light on her answering machine. She pressed PLAY.

Above the echo of her heart pounding in her ears, she heard the faint strains of Shirley Bassey's rendition of "Feelings." Next came Conrad's deep voice. "I must talk with you tonight, Ashleigh. From my veranda I saw your car pull into your garage, and I'm praying you won't toss me out when I arrive at your door in approximately three minutes!"

Ashleigh sank down onto the sofa and for a moment forgot to breathe. In a hazy blur she heard the intercom, pushed the button to open the downstairs door, and opened her own door. She heard the elevator doors in the hallway open, and at long last felt herself being gently drawn into Conrad's strong arms.

In a voice not much louder than a whisper, Conrad said, "Ashleigh, I love you. I want us spend the rest of our lives together." His tone left her with no doubts. "Whatever challenges may lie before us, together we can overcome them."

With tears spilling down her cheeks, she threw her arms around his neck—and felt the emotional roller coaster she'd been riding for months roll to a stop.

Ashleigh looked up at the overcast sky. June gloom. Tears pooled in her eyes. No matter how many visits, no matter how many pep talks, it wasn't becoming any easier. It just didn't seem fair that Danielle couldn't be given another chance. Ashleigh's prayers, and those of many others, had not been answered.

Conrad gripped her hand as they climbed the stairs to Evercare, and he tried once again to reassure her that Danielle was getting the best care possible. The concept of hospice care was a relatively new phenomenon, just approved in the United States. And just this year, the Medicare benefit was being made permanent. That was something to be thankful for.

But Danielle's life should not be coming to an end. It wasn't fair.

"About six months," Dr. Wigod had predicted, after informing them that Danielle had terminal lung cancer and had refused treatment. And four of those months were already behind them.

When Conrad pushed open the heavy door, they saw Danielle in the lobby. She was sitting in her wheelchair. Her pale skin was nearly translucent, and she appeared to have lost still more weight.

Ashleigh turned her head for a second to blot away the tears, then planted a smile on her face and moved forward to greet Danielle.

Danielle spotted them, and her eyes lit up. She was wearing a big smile when she asked, "Can you give me a push? I'd like to go out to the patio."

"Sure thing," Conrad replied. "But first I think we'd better pick up more than that thin sweater. It's a little chilly out today."

"Good idea. I'm always cold, even inside. There is a royal blue shawl at the foot of my bed, " Danielle said with a wide grin that lit up her ashen face. "You just missed Viviana. She sailed in here about an hour ago. She brought me this gorgeous cashmere shawl."

In an instant, Conrad appeared with the shawl. "It's beautiful," Ashleigh commented, not at all surprised at either the fashion maven's exquisite taste or the fact that she'd come to visit Danielle. She knew how much Viviana cared about Danielle and of all the tears she'd shed over the young buyer's fate. "I thought she was in New York."

"She's something else," Danielle said. "She arranged to fly from the Long Beach airport so she could stop by here. She said she wanted me to see her fashion book, which is just hot off the presses." Danielle giggled. "She said she couldn't stay long because she was off to spend the weekend with Phillip Sloane."

The man she thinks is destined to make all her dreams come true. Ashleigh exchanged a glance with Conrad.

"But I'd like to go outside for a while."

Outside it was cool, but not too cold. Ashleigh and Conrad had discussed whether or not they should tell Danielle about Jeff Bradley, and in the end they decided they must. They couldn't take the chance of her finding out on her own. Though very weak, she still had good days, and she was not yet so full of pain medication that her mind ceased to function. She still read the newspapers and loved having visitors—all those friends who had loved her. And she was relieved to find that her friends at Bentleys Royale did not blame her for the Fine Apparel debacle. They blamed Jeff Bradley and Tony Wainwright.

So Conrad and Ashleigh had done their best to keep Danielle informed about life outside the walls of Evercare. She seemed pleased to find out that neither Bradley nor Tony had anything to do with the body in the Medley Originals delivery truck that had necessitated Pocino's trip to the morgue. It had, indeed, turned out to be one of those rare coincidences— the result of a domestic quarrel. She saw no need to go into the details

"Danielle," Ashleigh said, once they were seated at the patio table outside the reception area. Her voice was soft, and she was afraid it must sound somewhat reticent, but she'd so wanted to spare Danielle. "I'm afraid I have some sad news."

"Jeff's dead." Tears spilled down Danielle's pale skin.

Stunned, Ashleigh took a moment before she was able to speak again. "You knew?"

Danielle shook her head. "I knew he was ill, and when you told me about the liver transplant—" Her voice broke.

"I'm so sorry. The transplant came too late. He just wasn't strong enough." Ashleigh's heart was about to break for Danielle. She knelt down beside her and took hold of both of her thin, ivory-colored hands.

In gulping sobs, Danielle sputtered, "He wasn't a bad person. He was kind and always there for me. That's why it hurt so much when I found out he'd lied . . ." When Danielle's eyes met Ashleigh's, there was no sparkle.

"What about Tony? Has Mitchell gone to see him in jail?" Danielle asked.

Ashleigh shook her head. "He took care of the expenses for Jeff's liver transplant, paid for Tony's attorneys as well as yours, and reimbursed Bentleys Royale. However, he made it clear that he wanted nothing more to do with his son until Tony got himself straightened out."

"Did he honestly—? Oh, never mind. I hate that narrow-minded . . ." She didn't finish. Shifting her focus, Danielle said, in a barely audible voice, "I love you both so much. You two, along with Gran and Charles, have given me so much, and I'm so ashamed for what I've done. And I know this terrible disease is my retribution."

Then shaking her head, she reached up to cover her own mouth, an unspoken plea that they let her continue. "Please pray for me. I pray for forgiveness every night, and I feel closer and closer to Gran every hour. Even when I couldn't forgive myself, I'd always known that Gran would forgive me." She swallowed hard, and ran her tongue around the roof of her mouth, then gulped in some air.

"Grandpa Charles and Mary came to see me. I was so glad I had a chance to tell him how much I loved him." She hesitated. "He is so kind and so wise. I felt so much better after his visit. He helped me to let go of so much of my self-loathing. He made me see that, like Gran always told me, God can see into my heart. I told him that I'm hoping to see Gran real soon." Her eyes lifted skyward. "He told me we would all be together one day."

Ashleigh could not speak.

Danielle reached out and took her hand. Looking from Ashleigh to Conrad, she said, "Please don't be sad. I am ready to go to a better place. When the pain gets worse, they will give me morphine and let me sleep." She squeezed their hands. "I really do believe that one day we will all be together again. I'm not afraid." Then she grinned. "I just get to be the first."

Conrad brushed his hand lightly across Danielle's cheek. "You are in our prayers, and I believe that you have nothing to fear. Your Gran will welcome you into her arms." He smiled. "Now, let me tell you some news that I think will make you very happy."

Danielle dried her eyes with the back of her hand and smiled back at him. "I was wondering when you two were going to tell me." Her eyes danced, glistening with tears as Ashleigh held out her left hand, revealing the tasteful solitaire diamond that announced her love for Conrad, and his for her.

AUTHOR'S NOTE

The shopping landscape portrayed in *Webs of Fate* seems light-years away from that of today. Indeed, much has changed in the world around us over the past decades.

This novel is set in the mid-1980s, a time when most of our favorite department stores still flourished. The majority of these were regional organizations—they did not span the entire nation—and many of us were fiercely loyal to our favorite stores. We were confident that they housed our kind of merchandise, that their sales associates knew our tastes, and that we would receive wonderful service.

It was a delight to call a friend for a day of shopping and lunch in a favorite department store tearoom. Perhaps you still remember those unique menus and your treasured choices. In the past, although we loved to find true bargains, we did not expect it day in and day out. "Guess how much I saved" had not yet become a status symbol. Value was not based on price alone.

Many of us would like to turn back the clock to those "good old days." Or would we?

In the mid-'80s, before our beloved department stores began to vanish, we lived in a far different world. There was far less technology, and it seems now that our lifestyles were far less hectic. Yet if we study those "good old days," we will discover that we also enjoyed far fewer conveniences.

Let's flash back to the past.

Computers did not come into wide popularity for home use until about 1997. Before that time, we depended far more on letter writing and "snail mail." E-mail was a foreign concept to most of us. The majority of computers were huge machines operating in large businesses. Early printers produced substandard text, in dot matrix rather than solid type. Documents were printed on rolls of paper with sprocket holes on each side. The standard font was Courier—these first-generation computers and printers lacked the sophisticated font styles we have come to expect.

Remember electric typewriters? Most small businesses, along with the majority of the population, still used them. While a huge step up from manual typewriters, which required herculean strength in each of our fingers and thumbs, they were a far cry from the word processing of today. They printed each letter directly onto the paper. Corrections were made not on the screen but on the paper itself. Products like Wite-out (1966) were a major revelation for typists, who no longer had to retype the entire page because of those inevitable mistakes.

Word processing was first introduced in 1981 but did not gain momentum until the late '80s; due to the lack of home computers, it was confined mostly to business use. The first computers that made their way into our homes were Apples, which at first did not have a hard drive—just one floppy disk drive. Before a second floppy drive was added, we could not add words to our spell check such as our own name, street address, etc. The hard drive was a gigantic advance but initially came with only 20 megabits of storage space (the equivalent of a single file drawer) and very little memory, causing the machine to operate at a glacial speed. Now that we use Windows rather than MS-DOS, we need several gigabytes of storage and we are able to access information at lightning speed.

Before the 1990s, carbon paper (which left purple residue on hands and clothing) was used if more than one copy was needed. Photocopy machines were used widely in corporations, but were not yet cost-effective for most small businesses and households. Typewriter ribbons, which commonly ran out of ink in the middle of a long project, had to be changed and invariably turned hands black, blue, or whatever color ribbon was used.

Fax machines became popular in businesses in the '80s but were not in wide use in our homes. I recall our department store buyers being in absolute awe of those early fax machines. They found it hard to imagine that they could send their correspondence to Europe, Asia, etc., in less time than it took to place a phone call. Finally, unaltered information that was far more reliable than word of mouth! The major drawback of those early faxed documents was the limited lifetime of the text. Because they were printed on rolls of slick paper, the print tended to rub off or fade over time.

The most life-altering advance in the past few decades, however, has been wireless technology. No longer are we tethered by twisted cords to a landline that allows us the mobility of only a few feet. The beginning of cell phones can be traced to the 1940s. At that time they were not a huge step up from the two-way radios used in taxicabs, police cars, and other service vehicles. By 1967 mobile phone technology was available; however, the user had to stay within one cell area. In 1971 AT&T submitted a request to the FCC for cellular service, but it took more than ten years for the company to gain approval.

From 1983 to the end of the 1980s cell phones grew in popularity. But due to their size, most cell phones weren't made to be carried in your hand. Car phones became extremely popular. A few models came in briefcases with an extremely large battery. Motorola came out with what was considered a lightweight for its time; it weighed about 28 ounces, was 13 inches x 1.75 inches x 3.5 inches, and was known as "the Brick." Those were the days when seeing someone walking down the street or in a public place alone and in animated conversation might have caused us to doubt their sanity rather than jumping to the conclusion that the person was on a Bluetooth. This improved in the early 1990s with second-generation cellular phones, which ranged from 100 to 200 grams; they were handheld devices that were truly portable, without the need for a large battery.

Today, making a phone call is far from the only use of a cellular phone. Your phone may contain your contacts, your calendar, and your lists of tasks and priorities. For some, the mobile phone has become their own personal GPS and has opened the highway to online information. Even if you don't use or even desire to take advantage of all these conveniences, they are available if ever you should want them.

We often complain that today's technology has made it nearly impossible to make the world go away long enough to catch our breath. But how many would give up what that technology has brought us? We are no longer required to stick close to home when expecting a phone call; we can easily adjust our time and location when meeting a friend or loved one; we no longer have to sit for hours wondering why our family members or friends have not arrived safely at an agreed-upon time. We merely pick up our cell phones and expect that the party we want to reach picks up. So do we really want to turn back the hands of time? Probably not?

Now, what does all that have to do with the world of retail? Actually, quite a lot. As life changes, so does the world of department stores. However, when the pendulum of change swings, it often swings too far one way or the other, and corrections must be made. We are currently observing major changes and corrections in the world of upscale department stores.

Since the introduction of department stores in the 1850s, change has been inevitable and, well, constant. Department stores have evolved as they faced one major form of competition after another; first there were the "dime stores," followed by discount warehouses, specialty store retailers (such as a TV store, the yard goods store, etc.), mail order catalogs, and the Internet. Their relevancy in the world we now live in has even been challenged. Savvy department-store merchants have generally met the competition head-on. After evaluating the shopping arena, retail management has made the necessary adjustments, and these stores have survived and continue to prevail.

If we look back far enough, we can remember a time when department stores carried almost everything we could imagine. They met nearly all our actual or perceived needs and most of our wants, too.

After careful evaluation, however, upscale department stores dropped the areas of merchandise in which they could not adequately compete with those who specialized in specific commodities. That was when we saw TVs, furniture, appliances, yard goods, notions (buttons, thread, zippers), etc., disappear from many of our department stores.

Being on the management team of the West Coast division of Federated Department Stores (now Macy's, Inc.), I was privy to some of the rationale for evaluating the viability of selling areas in terms of the dollars per square foot that they generated. While reasonable and rational criteria were applied in most cases—department stores could not hope to be competitive with each and every specialty store, after all. However, in my opinion, it was a huge blunder to evaluate store tearooms and restaurants in terms of sales per square foot. Out of necessity, these areas are spacious and could not be expected to compete with merchandising areas on a sales-per-square-foot basis. Many tearooms closed, and new stores were built without them. What wise merchants failed to factor in was that when their patrons left their stores to get something to eat or drink, they did not return. Today, corrections have been made in many exciting new stores, and more changes are planned for new stores and the remodeling of others.

As this novel goes to print, we are emerging from what is considered the worst financial crisis since the Great Depression of the 1930s. The fallout from this recession, which began in the final quarter of 2007, dealt a devastating blow to the retail community and therefore to the national economy, since retail sales account for at least seventy percent of our economy. We witnessed the liquidation of national chains Circuit City, Mervyns, and Linens 'n Things, to name a few. Hundreds more stores were downsized or closed. Even the large conglomerates such as Macy's, Saks Fifth Avenue, Kmart, and Old Navy were forced to close less-productive locations.

Fortunately, the fourth quarter of 2010 brought the ray of hope economists were looking for. While still cautious, shoppers are returning to the stores and beginning to make purchases beyond their immediate needs. While this upturn in the economy is a positive sign, it is no promise of a quick fix. Since the number of people employed far outnumbers those unemployed, we customarily notice economic recovery more rapidly than recovery from unemployment (which rose to double digits in some areas of our nation during this period). For significant growth in our economy to occur, however, unemployment must continue to be reduced, and there must be a greater shift from part-time to full-time employment.

On top of it all, retailers faced this difficult recession on the heels of their recovery from the takeovers and mergers of the '80s. The drastic expense cuts they were forced to make in order to survive had a negative effect on their customer service and, in turn, sales. Most retailers, including our largest department store groups, are dedicated to bringing excellent customer service back into their stores. In the author's note to my last novel, *Twisted Webs*, I mentioned that by giving individual store managers entrepreneurial power along with absolute accountability, Macy's has made significant strides in its customer service—but as many of you point out, the company still has a long way to go in many of its less-trafficked locations.

Having grown weary of a sales climate where the true value of an item is perpetually unknown, many consumers are now demanding, and are willing to pay for, the return of quality and service in their department stores. Retailers face a serious conundrum. They must maintain the perception of value and savings while regaining consumer confidence.

The major change we will see going forward is the shift to large promotions. Since we are hardwired now to expect extra value—and we have been programmed to relate that value to the percentage we save on our purchases during a given period—upscale department stores have become more and more creative. Insider programs that offer special saving and incentives are a step toward regaining customer loyalty.

With a desire to emerge from the "cookie cutter" image and shelves full of identical merchandise, intelligent retailers with stores spanning the nation are dividing their stores into smaller and smaller regional groups. By studying those smaller regions, their buyers are better able to select merchandise appropriate for the area. After all, a best seller in Minneapolis is unlikely to enjoy the same status in Palm Springs.

While online sales continue to grow at a rapid rate, they currently amount to a small percentage of total retail sales. Major retailers have remained competitive, however, by forming their own online catalogs. They offer the added advantage of allowing customers to return their online purchases to one of their brick-and-mortar stores. Many consumers still want to see and feel the merchandise they buy, and some former online consumers have switched to nearby retail locations, where they can walk in to rectify a problem without delay.

Department stores are here to stay. While Walmart and other warehouse discounters will continue to flourish and to suit the needs of certain price-conscious consumers, they fall short of satisfying the majority. America lost quite a few department stores during this past recession. Some might have been closed even without the recession, since intelligent retailers continually evaluate their locations and close those that are least productive. Department store retailers are optimistic about the future, however, and many new locations have sprung up or are on the drawing board. To name just a few . . . Nordstrom's, with its charming restaurants, is experiencing multiple store openings from coast to coast, with many more on the drawing board through at least 2012. On a more moderate level, Kohl's stores are popping up everywhere, and Forever 21, with its inexpensive, trendy clothing, is growing rapidly. These retailers have discovered that remodeling is more cost-effective than building from the ground up and began filling some of the fallen "big box" store locations long before we emerged from the most recent recession.

What do you predict for the future of department stores? Please visit www.darlenequinn.net. I'd love to hear your views.